THE PLATINUM
REUNION

T V HARTWELL

The Platinum Reunion

ISBN 978-0-9962825-4-3

Copyright © 2017 by T V Hartwell

First Edition

*The following story contains mature themes, strong language, and sexual situations and is intended for adult readers.

www.tvhartwell.com

Printed in the United States of America

The Platinum Series

Book One
The Platinum Triangle

Book Two
The Platinum Rebound

Book Three
The Platinum Reunion

THE PLATINUM REUNION

Book Three
The Platinum Series

Chapter One

"Jake, I don't know what you're talking about," Tom said, sounding perplexed and taken aback by his son's hysteria.

Jake was trembling. Filled with rage, confusion, and disbelief, he could barely keep his voice calm and even. "Reverend O said that Mom told him before I called off my wedding that Amanda was my sister. It's as if he knew the wedding would be canceled. What the fuck, man. What's going on?"

There was silence on the other end of the line. Tom didn't answer back at first.

"Dad! Are you there? What's going on?"

"Jake, calm down. As I said, I don't know what you're talking about. Amanda…your sister? Where'd he get this ridiculous story?"

"Mom! He said Mom came to him and told him right before my wedding. He was surprised that I didn't know. When he said it, I gave him this look like, 'What the fuck?' And then he got all nervous and uncomfortable and said that he thought I knew. When I told him that I didn't know what he was talking about, he said, 'You should speak with your parents' and refused to say anything more."

"I don't know what to tell you, son. I'm as stupefied as you are right now as to why he'd tell you this wacky story. Amanda's not your sister. What? Did he suggest that she was some love child of mine or something?"

"He didn't say."

"Well, who does he think is the parent of whom? Amanda's certainly not related to me or Jamie. You and Harry are the only two kids we had." Tom chuckled, seeming more amused than disturbed by this story. "I think our well-meaning priest may be growing a little senile," Tom continued jokingly, trying to make light of the situation. "Seriously, he probably counsels so many people and families from the parish that he's getting his stories and the people involved crossed. I'm sure this is all a big misunderstanding. Your mother will be amused, no doubt. How bizarre."

"But why would he say something like that if he wasn't sure about it? He's around the same age as you and Mom, so he hasn't exactly reached the point in his life when senility is commonplace."

"Jake, I can assure you, he's mistaken. Amanda's not your sister or any other kind of relative of ours. We're not blood relatives to the Climents in any way whatsoever. If we were, we would've found out about it way before now and staked our claim to our share of the family fortune. This is so ridiculous. I can't believe this, and I can't believe he accused your mother of telling him this story. There's no way in hell she told him that. I mean, can you imagine?"

"You're probably right," Jake slowly conceded, feeling relieved and a little embarrassed by his seeming gullibility. "But he sounded so sure of what he was saying. It was weird. But then, I agree that I can't imagine Mom going to talk to him…about anything personal. They're not exactly close friends, are they?"

"No. Not at all. I mean, we've known Tim for years and consider him a dear friend of the family, but he's not someone your mother or I would naturally turn to or confide in about anything. At least, that's to the best of my knowledge. I guess I shouldn't speak for Mom. Maybe she secretly complains to him whenever I drive her nuts about God knows what."

"Yeah, for constantly leaving the toilet seat up and leaving your stinky socks on the floor all around the house."

"Yeah, exactly right," Tom said with a chuckle. "Seriously, though, what a bizarre story. Can't wait to tell Mom about this. You caused my heart to stop there for a minute. Not because of the story but because you sounded like you were having a nervous breakdown. I haven't heard you sound that upset since you were carjacked in high school."

Jake laughed at himself, feeling foolish. "I know. Sorry, Dad. I guess I overreacted."

"What made you go and see Tim in the first place?"

"Oh…it's a long story. I'll tell you later," Jake said, still sitting in his car outside Revered O'Mahoney's house. Jake became uncomfortable sitting there because he sensed that someone was near his car, watching him. That carjacking he'd experienced years before as a teenager still spooked him. Jake switched on the ignition so that he could pull away. "Anyway, I'm sitting here in my car, Dad. I need to get your advice on a client issue I'm dealing with at the moment, so I'll call you back later tonight or sometime tomorrow."

Jake hurriedly ended the call with his father, but just as he was about to drive off, there was a knock on the passenger side window. Jake jumped at the sound and turned his head quickly to see a figure looking through the window at him. It was dark and Jake couldn't make out who it was at first. He initially thought it was a homeless man motioning at him to roll down the window, but then Jake realized it was Reverend O'Mahoney. At that point, he went ahead and let the window down.

"Jake, you left your wallet," the reverend said as he stuck his arm through the open window to hand it to him. "You must've dropped it on your way out."

Jake took it from him. "Oh…jeez. I didn't even realize I'd pulled it out of my pocket. Thank you."

"Well, you left in a panic. I'm so sorry to have upset you," the reverend said with sympathy in his voice.

"No worries. I just got off the phone with my dad, and he's pretty sure you've got things a little mixed up. Think you're confusing our family with another one at the parish, perhaps?" Jake spoke with a hint of irritation in his voice.

The reverend bit his tongue and did his best to remain diplomatic. "Although we didn't get to finish our conversation about all that's been troubling you lately, I have one parting word for you." The reverend paused and then gravely said, "The truth will set you free."

CHAPTER TWO

After finding out that Jake had had not one but two sexual liaisons with another guy since they'd ended their friendship, Kirby's hurt progressed to anger and then rage. When he'd returned home from the gym, Kirby entered the house, closed the door behind him, and stood there in the living room, fuming. He tossed his keys to the wall so hard that they deeply chipped the plaster. He walked into his bedroom and sat on the edge of the bed. He rubbed his hands against his shaved head and then covered his face, sighing hard and deep. "You fucking son of a bitch." Kirby got back up and ripped the sheets off the bed. He began beating the pillows and slamming them to the mattress before tossing them aside to the floor. "I hate your ass. I could choke you right now. Son of a bitch." Kirby went for his phone. He needed to talk someone.

Kirby didn't even offer a greeting when his cousin answered his call. He just yelled into the phone. "I'm done with Jake. I hate his faggot ass so much right now."

"Oh my God! What happened?" Myla asked, sounding alarmed but eager to get the scoop.

Since Kirby had come out to Myla more than a month before on Christmas Eve, she had become his go-to person for discussing relationship issues and his ill-fated love for Jake in particular.

"You're not going to believe this."

"What? What happened, Kirby?"

"I finally ran into Jake at the gym today."

"Okay. How is he?"

"Still sucking dick. He's already moved on to another dude. And another black dude, at that."

"What?" Myla yelled in shock.

"You heard me."

"Who's the guy?"

"This knucklehead dude from the gym named Reggie. He's a fitness model with half a brain. He can't get a real job so he models and pretends to be a trainer, mostly to lonely old women and gay men who like to ogle him."

"So Jake told you this? He admitted to hooking up with him?"

"No. Reggie told me. I saw them talking to each other at first. And then, as Jake started to leave, I walked up to him to say hello. It was my first time seeing him since October, when he moved out. So I say hi and ask him how he's been, and he acted like a complete jackass. I mean ice cold."

"What did he say?"

"Not much, really. He asked how my parents were and about the TV show—"

"Okay. That was nice—"

"Oh, please. It was all fake. He really didn't give a shit. Just making small talk. That's all. So anyway, I asked him if he'd gotten my messages, and he was like, 'Yeah, but I don't have time to talk to you because I'm on my way to an appointment.'"

"And then what happened?"

"Nothing. He just left."

Myla gasped. "Mannnn…I can't believe he just blew you off like that and after not seeing you for so long. Did you confront him about Reggie? I thought you said he wasn't into other guys. That he'd only been with you."

"I spoke to Reggie after Jake left. I was doing my workout and Reggie came up to me, and we started talking. So I asked him how he knew Jake, and—get this—he said Jake had reached out to him on this gay hookup app called Alpha Beta—"

"Alpha Beta?"

"Yeah, the guys on there who are tops are listed as alphas and the bottoms are betas. So you know up front before contacting someone who does what."

"Oh Lord," Myla said, sounding as if she were giving a verbal roll of the eyes.

Kirby chuckled at her, piling on with more details. "Yeah, tops show off their dicks and bottoms show off some ass and then they pick and choose which they'd like to try out."

"Okay, Kirby. You can spare me the gory details. I get it," she said as Kirby laughed. "I can't believe Jake would do something like that. I mean, it's not like I know him all that well, but based on the little I do know and what you've told me, this doesn't sound like him."

"I can't believe it. I'm so upset right now. It makes me wonder if he's done this before. He came down so hard on me when I admitted to fooling around with other guys, and now it looks like he may have been doing the exact same thing. It's like…dude, really? What a hypocrite."

"So what are you going to do?"

"I don't know. Maybe this was the wake-up call I needed. I should just forget about his weak, sorry ass and move on."

"Hmmm," Myla uttered contemplatively while Kirby remained silent for a moment on the other end of the line.

"Maybe I should just go back to dating girls, period. That way I could make my mom happy. Live a normal life, have kids. I'm not sure I'm really cut out for this gay thing anyway. I'm tired of the bullshit. I can't take it anymore."

"But do you really want to date girls again, Kirby?"

"Yeah, I still like girls," he said unconvincingly.

"But are you prepared to be faithful and commit yourself to a serious relationship with a girl without fooling around on the side with a guy like you were doing when you were with Laren?"

Kirby didn't answer her at first.

"Well?"

"I don't know. I think I could be with a woman and do what I need to do to keep her happy, but I can't sit here say that I might not stray every now and again."

Myla sighed, sounding disappointed. "See—"

"I'm just being honest with you," Kirby said defensively. "I like women, but I like being with guys too. What am I supposed to do?"

Well, you can't have your cake and eat it too, Kirby. You need to make up your mind and decide what you want, because no woman is going to want a man who's disloyal and cheats on her, especially with another man. It's bad enough when a man cheats with another woman, but with another man? That's too much—"

"I know, I know…," Kirby trailed off.

"You need to follow your heart and leave Aunt Joyce out of this. Making her happy is not a good enough a reason to marry a woman, let alone bring kids into the situation. You need to know deep down that a woman is right for you and what you truly want. Do you feel you can fall in love with a woman, Kirby? I mean, really in love, deep in love? Did you ever feel that for Laren?"

"No," Kirby said flatly. "I liked Laren a lot when we first started dating, but I can't say that we were ever in love. At least, I wasn't."

"So have you ever really been in love with a woman?" Myla asked, sounding curious but doubtful.

Kirby paused a few moments before finally answering her. "To be completely honest, the only person I feel I've ever really been in love with is Jake."

"Do you still love him?"

Kirby winced and snickered to himself, struggling to come up with an answer that guarded his heart. "I don't know… I guess… I don't know what I feel right now, really."

"From your tone, it seems like you do. It's okay. That's why you're so angry right now…because you love him, and he hurt you. You should confront him and tell him how you feel."

"But I've already done that. What more can I say? At this point, it's pretty clear that he doesn't feel the same way about me. Jake cares more about his image. He wants to have a wife and kids to keep up appearances because that's what's expected of him. He doesn't want to be in a relationship with me or with any guy, it seems. He just wants someone who will stay on the down-low with him. Someone he can keep in check and get to go along with what he wants, on his terms."

"You two sound very much alike. Just a minute ago you were saying that you should marry a woman and have kids too…because that's what's expected of you. If you're not willing to be faithful and only want to be married just for show, to keep up appearances, and to make other people happy, then you're both fucked up."

Kirby didn't have a comeback.

"You should stay away from women, Kirby, because you know almost any woman who gets with you is going to want to keep you to herself. You're a hot commodity. You have so much going for you. On paper and in the flesh, you're exactly what a lot of women want and dream of having. But you can't keep stringing them along like you did Laren, knowing that you like guys and hooking up with guys on the side. That's not right."

CHAPTER THREE

Leading up to his meeting with Reverend O'Mahoney, Jake had battled with himself over whether to pursue Amanda again. He increasingly felt that their chance at reconciliation was slipping away. Amanda seemed so radiant and happy beside Adam. When they'd broken up before, while Jake was still attending law school, Jake and Amanda had remained in contact with one another and secretly rendezvoused several times, unbeknownst to Adam. This time around, however, Jake and Amanda's communication had ceased entirely. There were no more text messages, late-night phone calls, or secret hookups. It felt over. Done. But after his meeting with Reverend O'Mahoney, Jake became more determined to seek a reunion with Amanda against the odds. With the claim of Amanda being his sister emphatically dismissed by his father, he'd put the thought behind him. It seemed too far-fetched and improbable to him anyway. The following day, his mother, Jamie, sent him a text that further assuaged any lingering doubt. Her tactic was at once direct and cunning.

I heard you found out about your secret sister yesterday. Now you know why I didn't want you to marry her all this time. :)

Jake reckoned his mother's nonchalant reaction was nothing more than playful sarcasm. He replied, *Lol. That would be quite the well-kept secret. But you've never been good at keeping secrets.*

This is true, Jamie wrote back.

As the week progressed, Jake couldn't get Amanda out of his mind. Despite Reverend O'Mahoney's parting admonition to him, "The truth will set you free," Jake took those words to mean something else entirely. The truth to him was that he regretted walking away from Amanda. It was a mistake—a mistake that he needed to correct. Jake felt that if he didn't try to reconnect with Amanda and reclaim their love, he would regret it for the rest of his life, and he'd never be free of the agony of thinking about what could've been.

***

"Hey, buddy," Jake said, greeting Will at one of their favorite craft beer watering holes near the beach in Santa Monica.

"Hey, man. Happy Friday!" Will said as he and Jake did the slap-and-grab handshake.

"Happy Friday, indeed. It couldn't get here soon enough. What a week. I see you've already started without me, bro."

"Well, you were running late. Thought I'd get a head start on things," Will said with a grin.

"I'll have what he's having," Jake said to the waitress who showed up to their table in short order.

She gave Will that *remind me again* look before saying, "Pliny, right?"

"You got it."

"Niiiice," Jake said. "Definitely on my top five list of favorite craft beers."

"Mine too," Will agreed before ordering a second.

"Well, don't get too carried away there," Jake said playfully, clearing his throat demonstrably to feign alarm. "I'm going to get drunk tonight, and I'll need you to take me home, or maybe I can crash with you and Kerry at your pad."

"Whaaat? How'd you get here?"

"I drove, but I need to get drunk, dude. Seriously. I can't wait until my birthday next weekend. I want to get inebriated now," Jake said with a somewhat uncomfortable chuckle and then sighed heavily, shaking his head.

"Are you okay, bro? What's going on?"

"Just a lot of crazy shit." Jake looked down and stared blankly before admitting what he'd been feeling but had yet to share with anyone. "I miss Amanda, Will."

Will sat quietly for a moment. "To be honest, that's not what I expected to hear you say."

Jake looked up at Will with eyes that were soft and slightly red. "It's the truth."

"Here you go," the waitress said, placing Jake's beer in front of him. "Can I get you guys something to eat?"

Jake and Will looked at each other as if they barely understood the question. Both seemed too tongued-tied to offer a response quickly enough. The waitress eyed them side to side before lifting the menu card at their table out of its holder and placing it down in front of them. "Well, take your time and have a look at the menu. I'll come back."

"So do you want to get back with her?" Will asked, picking up the conversation.

Jake didn't answer him at first. He took a sip of his beer and then stared down at the table.

"It kind of looks like that train has already left the station, bro."

Jake peered up at him. "Whattaya mean?"

"She's still with Adam Weinstock. She's become, like, this big celebrity now. They seem pretty serious, from what I can tell."

Jake snickered and looked away as he said something under his breath.

"I mean, I don't really know, but Kerry talks to Brook pretty regularly," Will said, referring to a classmate and mutual friend of theirs from Stanford who was to be one of Amanda's bridesmaids. "In fact, we saw her not that long ago, and she says that Amanda's doing really well and that she and Adam are, for all intents and purposes, officially a couple now."

"Well, they were officially a couple the last time too, and she promptly dumped him the minute I asked her to marry me," Jake sneered before taking another sip of beer.

Will was slightly taken aback. "Wow. So you really are serious about getting back with her."

"I am," Jake said flatly. "Letting her go was a big mistake."

"Then why'd you do it? You said that you'd fallen out of love with her. Are you in love with her again now, or are you just jealous about her having a new boyfriend?"

"I never really stopped loving her. I made that all up."

Will looked at Jake with befuddlement on his face. "You made it up?"

"I broke up with Amanda for a completely different reason. Based on something that I'd found out, or rather, that was told to me by a very credible source."

"Who? What'd they tell you? Did she cheat on you? Was she still seeing this dude Adam the whole time behind the scenes?"

"No, no. Nothing like that. I really can't tell you right now. I've been sworn to secrecy, and I can't reveal the source. And please don't say anything about this to anyone, including Kerry. You tell her everything. I swear."

"I won't—"

"I'm serious, man. I really don't want more rumors and gossip flying around."

"I won't. I promise. I won't say anything to Kerry. You and I both know how big her mouth is."

Jake gazed at Will for a moment in a suggestive fashion before saying with a chuckle, "Yeah, I know how big her mouth is, all right. I banged her before you did, remember?"

Will chuckled along uneasily. "You dirty son of a bitch. Get your mind out of the gutter, dude."

"Just sayin'."

Will shook his head and rolled his eyes. "Anyway—"

"Anyway," Jake continued, quickly turning serious again, "what I was told about Amanda doesn't make any sense to me now."

"Why?"

"Because she's back with Adam. If what I was told were true, I don't get how she could be dating this guy again…so openly and so soon after our breakup."

"You know, I recall at Lyle's New Year's Eve bash, when Kerry and I first told you that Amanda was back with Adam, you seemed shell-shocked, like you were completely taken by surprise."

"That's because I was," Jake admitted. "If I could tell you why, you'd understand."

"Why not tell me now? Come on, dude. Don't you trust me?"

Jake hesitated for a moment. "It's not that I don't trust you. It's just that I gave my word not to repeat to anybody what I was told. At this point, I don't care anymore about what was said. I just need to get to Amanda and convince her that I still love her and that we should be together."

"But what about the gay rumors?"

"What about them?"

"You think she'd be willing to take you back after all that?"

"Is Brook still spreading that shit around?"

"I don't know. Not to us. I mean, we never believed it when she told us. Did you confront her about it?"

"No. I haven't spoken to Brook since before the wedding was canceled. Has anyone else brought this up? Like, any of our other friends?"

"No. At least not to me."

The month before, shortly after New Year's, Will had told Jake that Brook told him and Kerry that Jake was in a gay relationship with Kirby, and that was the real reason for his breakup with Amanda. Jake vehemently denied the accusation, rationalizing to himself that he was being truthful since the reason for the breakup, in his mind, had nothing to do with Kirby and everything to do with the imminent danger he'd been told Amanda was in. Jake had emailed Amanda right away, begging her not to reveal what he'd disclosed to her about his relationship with Kirby. Although he'd never heard back from her, the rumor seemed to fade and, to his relief, hadn't picked up much steam.

"You know, I've never asked you this before, but I'm curious. Did that rumor have anything to do with you and Kirby no longer being friends?"

"In part, but there's more to it," Jake acknowledged. He hesitated for a moment before disclosing more information. "You know, a friend of his is the one who started the gay rumor."

"Really? Who is it?" Will asked with a wide-eyed look of surprise at this revelation.

Jake smirked. "This dude who's in love with him."

"What? How do they know each other?"

"They use to work together for—guess who?"

"Who?"

"Adam Weinstock."

"No way."

"Yeah, he and Kirby worked on the filming of *Hell-bent*, which Adam produced, of course. This guy apparently still works for him."

"He does? What's his name?"

"Antonio. Antonio Villar. Don't repeat any of this. Please," Jake said.

"Okay, I won't. But he's the one who started the rumor that you and Kirby are gay? Are you serious? Why would he say that?"

"Because he's jealous," Jake blurted, appearing irritated and defeated.

Will was incredulous. "Jealous of what?"

"My relationship with Kirby."

"But why?"

Jake just shook his head and sipped his beer. He became emotional, suddenly appearing sad and teary-eyed.

"Dude, are you okay?"

"Yeah, I'm fine. I'm fine," Jake repeated as he rubbed his eyes with his hands. The conversation paused for a moment, but not before Will took notice of Jake's body language, sensing that his breakdown with Kirby had taken a toll.

"You and Kirby have been friends for so long. Since middle school. I can barely remember any of my friends from middle school. You shouldn't let anything or anyone come between you two. You guys have such a close bond and so much history. Don't you miss him at all?"

"I do miss him," Jake admitted.

"You think you two will ever patch things up?"

"I don't know. I saw him earlier this week at the gym."

"How is he?"

"He seems to be doing fine. He's getting ready to shoot his TV pilot."

"Oh yeah, that's right. That's so cool. I'm really happy for him. I know he co-wrote the script, but is he directing it too?"

"I don't know. But anyway, I've got to figure out a way to get Amanda to talk to me. Any ideas?"

"What about Julie?"

"I'm going to have to break things off with her. I can't keep her hanging on any longer. It's not fair to her, especially knowing that she wants more. I just don't see a future with her."

After their blowup a month before, when Jake saw Amanda on TV at the Golden Globes with Adam, he and Julie had made up. Jake apologized to Julie for treating her so coldly, and they'd resumed their casual dating relationship. Although Jake had agreed not to hook up with other girls from work, it was now mutually understood that they weren't in an exclusive relationship and both were free to date other people outside the office. However, Jake sensed that Julie really wasn't all that interested in seeing other people and that she likely agreed to keep their relationship casual and open-ended to appease him. He knew she was compromising her principles and bending her exclusivity-before-sex rule in the hope that he'd come around and choose her as his one and only.

Jake and Will spent the rest of the evening barhopping and downing numerous drinks. Will eventually had to pull back so that at least one of them was still relatively sober and able to get them home. Meanwhile, Jake drank himself into oblivion as he said he would. The night ended with Kerry opening the door to find Will struggling to carry Jake into their apartment. She helped Will lay Jake down on the sofa to crash. Then the two of them watched and giggled as Jake rambled in a drunken stupor before he finally settled down and quickly fell asleep.

CHAPTER FOUR

As it was Oscar weekend, Amanda was the object of attention not only of Jake but also of many others, but for a completely different reason. After her big splash in the custom-designed Alana Dupree frock she'd worn the month before to the Golden Globes, Amanda and Adam had made a few more high-profile red carpet appearances. Since Adam's film was a Best Picture nominee, that meant making the rounds to numerous awards shows, industry events, and charity balls leading up to the main event, the Academy Awards. With each red carpet appearance and event, Amanda's style was noted by the press, along with her relationship status as the girlfriend of Oscar and Golden Globe–nominated producer Adam Weinstock. The fact that she was a billionaire heiress, socialite, and budding fashion designer with a Stanford degree to boot made her all the more captivating a subject. Amanda was more than happy to take advantage of the attention and increased visibility to drum up interest in her soon-to-be-revealed high-end handbag line. She and Lucy had hired a public relations firm to coordinate their launch strategy and to create buzz. Not all that hard to accomplish given who Amanda and Lucy were, combined with the fact that they both were dating well-known Hollywood A-listers.

The day before the Oscars, they had a photo shoot scheduled with *Town & Country*, which planned to do a feature on the pair in anticipation of the launch of their new bag line. They were to appear on the cover for the magazine's upcoming issue, "The Forty Under Forty List of Movers and Shakers from American Dynasties."

Alana Dupree had been invited to participate in the shoot as well. "It was so nice of Rod to let us use the house for the photo shoot," Alana said, referring to her former husband and Lucy's father, British rock star Rod Simon. After going back and forth over a location shoot in Los Angeles, the photographer and magazine finally settled on using the lush grounds and palatial home Rod still owned, right next door to Amanda's parents' house in Holmby Hills.

"They hardly ever use it, but now that he's doing shows in Vegas, they've been coming here more often. However, as you can see, they barely keep any clothes here. If it weren't for me and Theo, this big ol' house would sit empty most of the year," Lucy said, referring to her younger brother who, following in his father's footsteps, was in a fledging music band of his own, mostly traveling and doing gigs in clubs and small venues around the country.

"I want to go see Rod's show," Amanda said. "I'm so sorry I missed opening night. If it weren't for the London premier of Adam's movie, I definitely would've gone."

"Don't worry," Lucy said. "We'll make a plan to go. There's plenty of time. He'll be performing at Caesars for the next three years. We'll plan a weekend. We're overdue for a Vegas excursion anyway. We'll get some of the girls together and rent one of the penthouses at Caesars or the Wynn."

"Now, that would be fun," Amanda said with an eager smile, liking the sound of that.

"It's a great show. I tell ya, after all these years, Rod is still at his best when he performs live on stage," Alana said.

"You went?" Amanda asked.

"Of course I did. Wouldn't have missed it. I support Rod just like he's always supported me. We're still great friends. After all, he was initially my biggest investor when I launched my label."

"Really?" Amanda asked. "I didn't know that."

Alana smirked. "I guess he's still my biggest investor, technically."

"He is? I didn't know Rod co-owned the Dupree label with you."

"He doesn't," Alana said with mirth on her lips as she and Lucy looked at each other knowingly. "I'll take his money, but he's not entitled to any return on his investment."

"Wait, how'd you work that deal?"

"It's called a divorce settlement, honey" Alana said like a punchline.

Amanda laughed at herself. "Oh. Duh."

"You all look absolutely fabulous," the photographer said as he walked up and surveyed the three of them, each sitting in a high director's chair as the makeup artists and hairstylists applied finishing touches.

"I know scheduling us was nearly impossible," Lucy said. "I'm surprised *Town & Country* still wants us for the cover. It shouldn't have gotten so difficult, having to reschedule and everything. Honestly, we're not the divas we seem to be."

"Oh, no worries. You each have a lot going on right now. I'm just so glad we could get you three together at the same time here in LA and so soon after we had to cancel shooting in New York."

"Well, you can thank Oscar for that," Alana said. "When Oscar throws the biggest party of the year to dole out golden statuettes, everyone descends here en masse for the festivities."

"So will Mom be on the cover with us? It seems unclear at this point," Lucy said.

"I don't know. It's up to editorial," the photographer said. "I think they'll make a decision once they've seen all of the proofs and after the cover article is finished."

"I hope so. You're our inspiration," Amanda said, leaning over to hug Alana, who was sitting in the middle between her and Lucy.

"I think that's the idea. To show one generation passing the baton on to the next," the photographer said.

"A fashion icon and her two favorite girls ruling the world. How's that for a headline?" Alana said buoyantly, grabbing Lucy's and Amanda's hands on either side of her and raising them up in the air, beaming and proud.

They eventually moved to the twelve-hundred-square-foot dressing room that Alana once claimed as her own and had custom-designed when she and Rod were still married years before. It looked like a small luxury boutique and provided a nice backdrop for a few interior shots. They then moved outdoors by the Olympic-size pool surrounded by lush green landscaping for some additional shots in the bright California sunshine. The photographer directed and guided them through a set of different poses—first just Amanda and Lucy together and then Alana joining them, looking very much like the fashion diva she was known to be with her two protégées at her side.

"Okay, ladies. It's a wrap!" the photographer said as his small crew applauded and complimented the women and the success of the shoot. "These all look so great. It's going to be hard to choose which ones to use," he added. Amanda, Lucy, and Alana came over to him and hovered around as he swiped through a few of the shots on his digital camera to show them. "Too bad they will end up only using one or two of these."

"Amazing. All those photos to get the one perfect shot," Amanda said.

"But they're all so perfect," the photographer said flatteringly.

"No, Amanda's so perfect…in every single shot," Alana said. "Look at her."

"I know," Lucy added in mock irritation. "God, I hate you. Why does the camera like you so much more than me?"

Amanda grinned bashfully. "Oh, come on. You guys look just as great. Look at these shots. You're both beautiful."

"I know what it is," Alana continued over her. "She's still in the afterglow. New boyfriend, a new bag line, magazine covers, all the great press. You're on top of the world right now. Watch, she's going to steal the show again tomorrow night at the Oscars. You wait and see. Tom Ford's lucky you chose to wear him."

"I know," Lucy agreed and carried on, sounding happy for her friend, albeit begrudgingly.

Amanda tried to brush the talk aside by reaching to hug and thank the photographer for his work and time. Alana and Lucy followed suit before the three women made their way back inside the house. They headed to the kitchen for some wine and munchies, where their conversation took a turn.

"I don't mean to sound jealous. You know that I love you and that I'm really happy for you and Adam," Lucy said. "Cass and I look forward to hanging out with you guys after the show. The Elton John party should be a blast, like it is every year. You know it'll be extra special for us since that's where Cass and I met a year ago."

"Oh yeah! That's right! What a great way to celebrate your one-year anniversary. I'm so happy for you two. I hope this one lasts. I really do. You guys are perfect together," Amanda said, placing her hands to her heart, feeling warm and fuzzy for her BFF.

"Well, you and Adam are perfect together, too," Alana chimed in. "Aren't you completely in love?"

Amanda hemmed and hawed her way through her feelings. "Well... yes...but—"

"But what? You're not completely taken with him by now? What's wrong with you?" Alana asked, sounding incredulous, curious, and playful all at once.

"Jake's gotten into her head. I bet that's what it is. Is he still hounding you? Sending you emails and texts?" Lucy said, annoyed.

"What?" Alana exclaimed.

"Didn't I tell you?" Lucy said to her mother.

"No, I don't think you did."

"He's been emailing and texting her, begging that she not tell anyone about his homo ways." Lucy rolled her eyes and shook her head.

Alana gasped before Amanda spoke up defensively. "He only emailed me once."

"When?" Alana asked.

"Last month. I guess word was getting around about him and Kirby."

"Well, what'd he expect you to do?" Alana asked. "Not tell anyone about him cheating on you?"

"And that he's gay!" Lucy declared.

"I don't know what he expected," Amanda said. "I really wasn't thinking about it, to be honest. I just naturally told my close friends and family after he admitted to cheating. I wasn't trying to out him or anything. I think that's what he thought I was doing, but I wasn't."

"Did you speak to him?" Alana said.

"No. I didn't email or call him back. Adam was so mad when I showed him Jake's email," Amanda said with a snicker. "He wanted to use his media connections to expose Jake's quote 'alleged' gay relationship as the reason for our breakup since there's been a lot of speculation but no real explanation or official statement given about why our wedding was canceled."

"Can you believe that?" Lucy said looking at her mother and grinning devilishly at the idea.

"And? Did he do it?" Alana asked as if the idea sounded perfectly acceptable to her.

"No! Of course not. Are you kidding? I don't want that kind of attention. 'Jake leaves Amanda for his gay lover.' Can you imagine? And what does that say about me? Some of my closest friends still can't believe I didn't know, considering how long this gay affair lasted."

"Show Mom the email," Lucy said. "Do you still have it?"

"Yeah, I do." Amanda reached for her purse to retrieve her cell phone. She began scrolling through her messages as Alana and Lucy looked on in anticipation. "Okay, here it is." Amanda handed her phone to Alana.

"Mandi. How cute. He still calls you by your nickname," Alana said sarcastically before continuing to read silently.

Mandi,

I'm hearing from friends, Will and Kerry in particular, that Brook and perhaps Lucy and others are spreading rumors that I'm gay and repeating what I told you about me and Kirby. Even my family's hearing things. I know how much you must hate me right now, and I regret hurting you, but please stop telling people that I'm gay and that I left you for Kirby. That's not true. I swear to God that's not the reason why I left. I admit that I cheated on you and I'm sorry. I regret what I did and know I don't deserve you. I'm trying to work on myself, to become a better person, and getting rid of people I don't need in my life. I'm not even friends with Kirby anymore. I should've ended my relationship with him long ago. I don't want to be associated with him. I'm not gay, and I'm not in love with him. So please, please, please don't tell people that, and tell your friends to stop saying it too. Please.

Jake

Alana rolled her eyes and sighed as she handed the phone back to Amanda. "So what'd you do?"

"I just called and emailed everybody I confided in and asked them not to repeat what I'd told them. Jake's a lawyer. His dad's a lawyer. His whole family's full of lawyers. I don't want to get sued for slander."

Alana balked. "Sued! For what? He can't sue for slander if it's true. He admitted to you that he's gay."

"Well, he didn't exactly admit to being gay. Actually, he doesn't feel he's gay. He said Kirby's the only guy he'd ever been with and that he might be bisexual."

Lucy snickered and shook her head in annoyance.

"Amanda, are you over him? I mean, really over him? Because he's right when he says he doesn't deserve you," Alana said, eyeing Amanda intently.

"Yeah, I'm over him," Amanda said, sounding dubious.

"It doesn't sound like you are," Alana said as Lucy looked on with exasperation in her face.

"I mean, I still care for him and have compassion. You've got to have a little compassion, right? I'm not saying I want to get back with him. Not at all. It's just that as the months have passed by and I've had more time to think things through, I actually pity him in a way and feel sorry that he's been carrying this secret about himself around for so long and couldn't talk about it. Look at how he's trying to cover it up in his email. For obvious reasons, he doesn't want this to impact his career and reputation. How many people in Jake's positon openly admit to being bisexual?"

Alana smirked. "Definitely wouldn't be the best career move. Society's just beginning to embrace the gays. Bisexual? Hmmm," she said in mock contemplation, "I think that group needs its own PR campaign."

"I just wish he would've told me. I mean, I would've been crushed, but at least it wouldn't have seemed so deceitful had he just admitted to me that he was bisexual from the get-go."

"But would you have still dated him had he admitted that to you in the beginning? In the very beginning, when you first started dating?" Lucy asked.

"No, probably not. But I would've been supportive as he tried to figure out who he was and what he wanted. I mean, we have tons of gay friends," she said, looking at Lucy.

"And so do I. I work in the fashion industry, for God's sake," Alana interjected whimsically.

"I have nothing against people who are gay or bisexual or whatever," Amanda said. "I'm more angry and upset with Jake for cheating. Regardless of whether you're bisexual, when you're in a relationship, you should stick with the one you're with. It doesn't matter what your sexual orientation is. It's wrong to cheat. Period."

"Well, you hold on to that thought, because regardless of whether he has sexual identity issues or not, the fact is that he lied, deceived, and cheated on you for a very long time. You deserve better. Much better. And the nerve. That he'd expect you to cover his ass for him after all of that." Alana stopped herself to sigh and huff. "Don't get me started."

"I know. Seriously," Lucy said, agreeing with her mother's sentiments.

Amanda just stared at Alana solemnly, contemplating her words. Despite what Jake had done, she still had a soft place in heart for him. In fact, she still loved him despite her best efforts to suppress such feelings. Although she viewed a reunion as implausible, Amanda nevertheless wanted to replace her bitterness with sympathy, especially if Jake did in fact have a stronger desire to be with a man than a woman but perhaps was too afraid to admit to it. After all, Amanda knew of men, including a first cousin of her mother's, who had lived as straight while secretly gay and then proceeded to marry and have children because that's what was expected, only to come out of the closest later in life to the shock and dismay of family and friends.

Although Amanda trusted Alana and Lucy like family, she nevertheless felt compelled to protect Jake's privacy by making the issue about her own privacy. Something she knew they'd want to protect. "Don't worry. We're not getting back together. And thank you for being so supportive and understanding. But I don't want to be identified as the source of any gossip, especially in the press, so thank you both for helping me to squash the gay rumors. I just want to put this whole thing behind me and move on."

Chapter Five

After the Academy Awards show ended at the Kodak Theatre in Hollywood, Adam maintained a gracious, sportsmanlike demeanor as he and Amanda began to make the rounds to the various after-parties, taking photos and answering questions from the press. He and his film had come away empty-handed. *The King's Speech, The Social Network,* and *Black Swan* captured most of the top awards between them.

Adam introduced Amanda to some of the big winners of the evening, such as Natalie Portman, who'd won the Best Actress Oscar for *Black Swan*, and Colin Firth, who'd won Best Actor for *The King's Speech*. They'd posed for photos with the show's hosts, Anne Hathaway and James Franco, at the Governors Ball. Amanda and Anne hugged and chatted amiably, discussing their mutual connection to different fashion designers like Alana Dupree, Tom Ford, and Zac Posen.

After a quick nibble on the dinner served at the Governors Ball, the official Oscar after-party, Amanda and Adam headed out on their way to the two biggest and most highly coveted after-parties of the night—*Vanity Fair*'s soiree and then Elton John's annual fundraising bash benefiting AIDS research.

After they got into the limo and drove off, Amanda leaned in to Adam and kissed him on the cheek while holding his hand. She could tell that he was disappointed despite his cheerful outward appearance at the ball. "Adam, you are being such a good sport. That was so classy of you. The way you congratulated Colin Firth even though I know how strongly you felt Tom deserved to win Best Actor."

"No, he deserved it," Adam said with resignation and a hint of dejection in his voice.

"I know you were hoping to win something tonight—"

"If anything, I was hoping to get Tom the Best Actor award. I really didn't expect to win Best Picture, but I honestly thought Tom would win. I guess the Academy doesn't like the two Toms. Tom Cruise and Tom Field are now both zero for three. The Academy just doesn't seem to like them, I guess."

"Gee, I wonder why," Amanda said with mild sarcasm, knowing that Tom Field's perceived eccentricities made him fodder for unfavorable press just as much as Tom Cruise's had.

After the short ride down Sunset Boulevard to the Sunset Tower Hotel in West Hollywood, the *Vanity Fair* party was already in full swing with a room full of invite-only, high-wattage A-listers from film, television, music, fashion, and sports—Jane Fonda, Tom Hanks and Rita Wilson, Justin Timberlake and Jessica Biel, Quentin Tarantino, Jamie Foxx, Jennifer Hudson, Cameron Diaz, Jude Law, Taylor Swift, Serena Williams, Mick Jagger, Madonna, Oprah—the list was endless. Basically everybody who was anybody was there. Intermingled among them were the glittery socialites and billionaires who likewise were often celebrated and feted on the pages of *Vanity Fair*, including Camilla and Rick Climent. Noticing her mother huddled in a corner with Anna Wintour, Alana Dupree, and Naomi Campbell, Amanda wanted to make a beeline over to them to say hello, but Adam was engaged in animated conversation with Aaron Sorkin, who had just won the Oscar for Best Adapted Screenplay for *The Social Network*. She thought to herself, *It's Aaron freakin' Sorkin for God's sake.* She wasn't about to leave Adam's side. Not at that moment. Amanda reminded herself that she was *his* date and this was *his* night even though his film didn't win anything.

About ten minutes later Amanda felt a tap on her shoulder just as Adam and Aaron were wrapping up. She turned, and there stood her mother with Alana at her side.

"Hi, darling," Camilla said as she reached to hug her daughter.

"Oh! Hi, Mom," Amanda said as she hugged back. "Where's Dad?"

"He's around here somewhere. He was chatting up Bob Iger last I saw him," Camilla said, referring to the chairman of The Walt Disney Company.

Alana greeted and hugged Amanda, too.

"You look so beautiful. Tom dressed you well," Alana said, admiring Amanda's frock .

"You look beautiful too," Amanda said to Alana just as her mother grabbed her by the wrists and pulled her in close to command her full attention.

In a low voice, Camilla asked, "So how's he doing?" slightly nodding her head in Adam's direction. But before Amanda could answer her, Adam finished talking to Mr. Sorkin.

"Alana! How are you? Long time no see," Adam said as he and Alana embraced. Given the high-powered circles in which they both traveled, they already were acquainted with each other. Plus, Alana knew that Adam and Lucy had been friends for a while and that Lucy was the one who'd originally introduced Amanda and Adam way back when.

"Indeed it has. So good to see you. You're looking as dapper as ever," Alana said to Adam flirtatiously with a twinkle in her eye. "You remember Camilla, don't you?" she said, directing his attention to the mother of his girlfriend.

"Of course I do," he said, turning to greet Camilla. Ever the charmer, Adam reached to shake Camilla's hand, but when she offered it to him, he lifted it up and kissed it instead. "Camilla, it's such a pleasure to see you again."

Camilla couldn't help but be anything other than flattered by the gesture. Adam's engaging manner and good looks, punctuated by his piercing blue eyes framed by his dark features, would make any woman swoon. Clearly taken, Camilla caught her breath and cleared her throat before she managed to return the greeting. "Well…Adam…the pleasure's all mine."

"You look great, Camilla. There's no doubt about where Amanda gets her beauty from."

"Oh, stop. That's very nice of you to say. I think the last time we saw each other was at the fundraiser we hosted at our home for the LA Opera two years ago."

"That's right. I remember it well and meeting Plácido Domingo. That was a very nice event." Adam looked at Amanda and smiled. She smiled back at him. That was the first and only time she'd introduced Adam to her parents when they'd previously dated.

"We'll have you back," Camilla said.

"Thank you. I would enjoy that."

"This is such a big night for you, Adam, and for your career as a filmmaker," Camilla said. "Congratulations! Your parents must be so proud of what you've accomplished."

"Oh, thank you, thank you," Adam said bashfully. "But I didn't win anything, so—"

"Oh come on," Alana interjected. "This is the second time you've received Oscar nominations in multiple categories for one of your films."

"And Golden Globe nominations too," Camilla added.

"I know. That's what I tell him all the time. Just being nominated is such a big deal, and this is your second time," Amanda said, trying to butter him up.

As the four of them continued to chat among themselves about the winners and losers of the night, sharing opinions about who was most deserving of an Oscar and who wasn't, Lucy and Cass eventually found and made their way over to them.

"I was wondering where you two were," Amanda said to them before introducing Cass to her mother since they hadn't met before.

Camilla seemed to take a liking to the young actor immediately—chatting him up about his career and his life growing up in Australia.

As a descendant of French nobility, Camilla knew that Cass's surname, Bettencourt, was of French origin. When Cass confirmed his French heritage and identified the village in Northern France from whence his ancestors came, it struck a chord, and he and Camilla hit it off. Suddenly seeming more impressed with Cass than with Adam, Camilla turned her attention and praise to Lucy and her Oscar-nominated French-Australian beau.

"I think he's a keeper, Lucy," Camilla said with a smile and a wink. "You two make such a lovely pair. Don't they?" Camilla continued, looking for agreement from Alana.

Alana beamed, appearing proud of Lucy and satisfied with her choice of mate. "Yes, they do. But Amanda and Adam do too."

Amanda searched her mother's face, hoping to hear similar approval of her Oscar-nominated boyfriend, but Camilla just glanced at them with a forced smile before changing the subject.

I guess not, Amanda thought.

Camilla seemed to like not only Lucy's boyfriend more than her daughter's but also Lucy's attire. "Lucy, you look so lovely. You always pick the perfect dress to complement your figure."

"Oh, thank you," Lucy said somewhat awkwardly, seeming surprised at the compliment. Lucy looked over at Amanda, appearing uncomfortable at having her best friend's mother gushing over her instead of her own daughter. Lucy shrugged her shoulders as if to say, *Why me?* After all, Amanda was the one getting all the good press and accolades for her style by tastemakers and fashion aficionados.

"And that style is very age-appropriate," Camilla continued.

What, mine isn't? Amanda nearly said before stopping herself, it having not been lost on her that her mother had yet to offer a compliment or even acknowledge the design she was wearing from Tom Ford. She took the compliment to Lucy as a dig at her choice.

As Camilla continued to shower praise on Lucy, followed up with questions about the upcoming launch of the Novel bag line, Amanda fell silent and fought to keep her eyes from welling with tears. Amanda had managed to make it this far in her young life without much praise or approval from her mother, but she yearned for it nonetheless. In that moment, standing there, she felt angry and hurt. In Amanda's mind, her mother hated her dress, appeared to think her new boyfriend wasn't up to snuff despite his accomplishments, and viewed Lucy as the more knowledgeable one to speak to about their shared business venture. *You hardly ever ask me anything about the bag line. I didn't know you were so interested*, Amanda thought as she glared at her mother conversing with Lucy and Alana.

After mingling and hobnobbing at the *Vanity Fair* party for a while longer, Adam and Amanda hopped back in the limo to head over to Elton John's party next. Camilla was on both their minds.

"I think Camilla has a crush on Cass," Adam said.

Amanda snickered and shook her head as she stared out the window of the limo, still annoyed at her mother.

"Seriously. Did you see the way she was fawning over him? I mean, I don't know your mother that well, but I think she wishes you were with him instead of me. I got the impression she doesn't like me all that much. Maybe I shouldn't have kissed her hand. Was I too forward?"

"No, it's not about you. It's about me. She can't bring herself to say anything positive about me or anything I do, unless she's giving a speech in a room full of people like she did at my bridal shower. But then, that's only meant to draw attention to herself and how great a mother she wants the world to perceive her to be. Did you hear how she complimented Lucy on her dress? Telling her that it was more age-appropriate than mine?"

"She said that?"

"That's what she meant."

"Your dress looks way hotter than Lucy's. And it was designed by Tom Ford. Are you kidding me?"

"And then she starts asking Lucy and Alana about the bag launch as if I wouldn't know anything about such things. She never asks me a fucking thing about the business, and all of a sudden she wants to know what's going on."

Adam smirked. "You're basically the face of the brand now."

"That doesn't matter to her. In fact, she's probably jealous about all of the attention I'm getting."

Adam looked at Amanda, dumbfounded. "I guess I didn't realize you and your mother butt heads."

Amanda sighed. "You don't know the half of it."

***

Upon arriving to the Elton John bash, Adam and Amanda made the rounds, mingling with more celebrities and posing for more photos. They eventually met up with Lucy and Cass there, and together they all huddled in a corner on lounge sofas, sipping fancy cocktails. They toasted Cass and Lucy's one-year anniversary, commemorating the fact that they'd met at the very same event a year before.

"You two have already surpassed my expectations. Given the survival rate of Hollywood courtships, I honestly didn't think you'd last this long," Adam said to them.

"We had a bet going about this," Cass said.

"Oh my God," Amanda said, knowing of the bet but never saying anything to her friend about it.

"What? What was the bet?" Lucy demanded.

"He thought that we would've broken up before the end of last year," Cass said.

Lucy gasped, incredulous.

Adam grinned sheepishly as he sipped his cocktail. Then he tried to defend his presumption. "Well, given both your track records—"

Lucy screeched, cutting Adam off. "Excuse me!"

Adam busted up laughing at her, as did Cass and Amanda.

Lucy got in Adam's face. "My track record? I don't know what you're talking about. And considering we were all in Sydney together on New Year's, you clearly lost the bet, Adam." Lucy gritted her teeth and poked the side of Adam's forehead with her index finger playfully. "You lost, buddy. Lost, lost, lost. So there."

Adam continued to laugh at her before pulling her hand away from his face. "I know Cass just wanted to prove me wrong so he could win the bet. Now that that's out of the way, we'll see if his player instincts resurface. So don't be surprised, Lucy."

Cass was incredulous. "Whaaat? Wait a minute, mate, the same thing could be said about you. You have the reputation for being an even bigger player than me in this town. I think Amanda's the one who should be on the lookout. Look out for this man, Mandi. Seriously," Cass said, turning to her.

"Dude, no way. You're a much bigger player than me," Adam said grinning. "Look at who you've dated, bro."

"Oh my God, what a prick—" Cass retorted before Lucy interrupted them.

"Okay, okay. While you two act like douche bags and argue over who's the bigger player in Hollywood, Amanda and I are going to go freshen up, and then we're hitting the dance floor."

"I know. You guys are acting so lame," Amanda added as she and Lucy got up to step away.

Minutes later, Amanda and Lucy stepped out of the ladies' room raving over Heidi Klum, whom they'd just run into and exchanged a few words with. They had met her several times before, mostly at Fashion Week events in New York.

"Oh my God. I love her. She's so gorgeous," Lucy gushed.

"I know. I do too. She's flawless. Can't believe she's had four children. That's how I want to be after having four kids. I swear…," Amanda said as she and Lucy continued walking directly toward a tall, dark, handsome man neither of them noticed at first. They were so engrossed in conversation that they nearly crashed into the man before his greeting startled them to attention and stopped them in their tracks.

"Hello, ladies," Kirby said.

CHAPTER SIX

"Kirby! Oh my God," Amanda said before she instinctively reached to hug him without even thinking about it at first. That's how she normally would've greeted him, especially if she hadn't seen him in a while. Kirby hugged back, but the minute their bodies connected, they both recognized the awkwardness and didn't linger, pulling away quickly.

"Hi, Lucy. How are you?" Kirby said, turning to look at her.

"Hi, Kirby," Lucy said, smiling awkwardly, appearing giddy, intrigued, and stunned all at once. "I'm fine. How are you?"

"I'm good. Everything's good," he said, revealing his trademark beautiful smile.

"I didn't expect I'd see you here," Amanda said.

"Yeah, a producer friend of mine bought a couple of tables and gave me and another friend tickets."

"Oh. Nice. That sure does beat spending three thousand of your own money for a single ticket."

Kirby grinned. "Sure does. How about you?"

"I'm here with Adam. Adam Weinstock. I believe you know him," Amanda said, her mood quickly shifting from surprise to vexation.

"Of course. How is Adam? This was a big night for him."

"He's fine," Amanda said curtly while staring Kirby straight in the eye with a look that read, *So what the fuck, man?*

Kirby broke her gaze. He looked down, rubbing his chin and appearing uncomfortable.

Silence fell between them momentarily. Amanda turned to Lucy, who looked back at her as if trying to tell her friend with her eyes, *Let's go*, but Amanda wasn't budging. She had wanted to confront Kirby for a while, and now was her opportunity.

Amanda looked back at him. "I think we need to talk."

Kirby didn't say anything. Still rubbing his chin curiously, he just looked at her, then over at Lucy, and then back at Amanda.

Lucy touched Amanda on the arm. "Are you okay?"

"Yeah, I'm fine. Just give me a few minutes," Amanda said softly to her.

"Okay. I'm going back over to Cass and Adam."

Once Lucy stepped away, Amanda looked at Kirby with deep resentment on her face. "Gee, where do I begin?"

"Uh...," Kirby uttered, still contemplating his choice of words, looking to the ceiling, then back at her. Just when he appeared on the verge of saying something intelligible, he went from rubbing his chin to covering his mouth with his hand as if to keep himself from delivering whatever was on the tip of his tongue in the wrong way. He then jammed both hands in his pants pockets sheepishly before finally saying, "I'm sure you must have a lot of questions."

Amanda sighed heavily. "Well...basically...Jake told me everything...I guess. How you two had been sleeping together and whatnot." She looked away and shook her head as she spoke. Feelings of disbelief and anger began to rise within her again after lying dormant for a while. "I don't understand, Kirby," she continued. "Were you two in love? And then it's my understanding that you had a thing going with Adam's assistant, Antonio Villar, too, all while you were dating Laren. I don't get it."

Kirby spoke haltingly. "It's...complicated. And I'm not sure there's anything I could possibly say that would make it sound palatable to you."

"You were cheating. You and Jake were both cheating. Fucking each other and God knows who else, while you had girlfriends. I mean, seriously? How could you deceive Laren like that and deceive me? How shitty."

Kirby sighed, closed his eyes, and shook his head in embarrassment before he spoke. "Amanda, I honestly don't know what to say other than I'm sorry, sorry for the pain you've been put through."

"So is it true...that you and Jake were in love with each other?"

Kirby didn't answer her directly. "Jake and I really aren't talking anymore. We had a falling out."

"Did he know about you and Antonio?"

"No, he didn't. And by the way, Jake never had a threesome with me and Antonio."

"Yes, I know. I spoke to Antonio about that, and he admitted that he mistook Jake for someone else. So is that why you and Jake aren't talking to each other...because of Antonio?"

"Pretty much."

"So Jake thought you were with him, but you were fooling around with Antonio behind his back and Jake got jealous."

"I guess you could say that. I mean...I think there's a little more to it, but that's about right."

"What? Is there something else?"

"Well, I told Antonio about my relationship with Jake—"

"And Jake was trying to keep it a secret, right?"

"Right."

"So you and Jake were together then. You were lovers. That's why he broke up with me, because he wanted to maintain his relationship with you, secretly, and then you outed him to Antonio. He'd chosen you over—"

Just before Amanda could complete her train of thought, she was interrupted. "Everything all right here?" Adam said after walking up on them.

"Oh, hi. Sorry. We ran into each other and started talking. Everything's fine. We're just having a little chat here," Amanda said as Adam studied her face, seeming concerned.

"Kirby, how are you? Long time no see," Adam said, turning his attention to Kirby.

"Hey, Adam. I'm doing well. Thanks. Congratulations on your Oscar nominations. You've had a good year."

"Thank you. I appreciate that, and congratulations to you, too. I heard about your TV pilot."

"Oh, yeah. Thank you. We start taping in a week."

"Excellent. I'm happy for you. You're coproducing it with Jeff Hoefflin, right?"

"Right."

"Excellent. Jeff's a talented guy. I hope everything works out for you guys and that your show gets picked up for a full season."

"Yes, I do too," Kirby said with a forced smile.

Although the exchange between them was polite, it felt icy. Kirby figured he knew all he needed to know about Adam and Adam figured he knew all he needed to know about Kirby due to their mutual connection, Antonio. With nothing more to say to each other, there was an awkward silence before Adam cleared his throat and looked at Amanda, then back at Kirby. "Well, it was nice seeing you," he said to Kirby as he wrapped his arm around Amanda's waist, applying a little pressure to escort her away.

"Wait," Amanda said, stopping Adam. "Can you give us just a few more minutes?"

"Sure," he said hesitantly.

Amanda sensed Adam's alarm and annoyance. "I'm sorry. I'll be over there in a minute. Promise."

When Amanda turned to look back at Kirby, he proceeded to pick up where she'd left off. "I know what you were about to say, but Jake didn't choose me over you. He didn't leave you to be with me. His intentions were to marry you and to end his relationship with me, at least physically speaking."

"Then why did he leave?"

Although irked with Jake after learning of his liaisons with their mutual pal from the gym, Kirby nevertheless felt obligated to keep his promise to his former longtime friend and not reveal what he knew about the payment Jake had been offered by Amanda's own father to break things off with her. Kirby sighed and again contemplated his choice of words before he spoke. "Jake is the one who needs to explain that to you."

"Explain what? What more is there to know?"

Kirby shook his head as he struggled to come up with something else to say to her other than the truth, which he'd sworn never to reveal.

Seeing that Kirby was remaining tight-lipped, Amanda threw up her hands in frustration. "So what about you?"

"What about me?"

"I mean…are you exclusively dating guys now? Are you trying to get back with Jake? What's going on with you?"

Kirby glared at her. He wanted to say, "Who I'm fucking isn't any of your business, bitch," but he took the high road, skipped over answering her first question, and instead answered the second. "No. I'm not trying to get with Jake. In fact, I hadn't seen or spoken to him in months until recently, when I ran into him at the gym. Things are pretty much over between us. There's something I still need to confront him about, but we're done as friends." Kirby paused for a moment before asking, "So what about you? Are you trying to get back with Jake?"

Amanda balked. "Does it look like I'm trying to get back with Jake?"

"Well, you asked me. I thought I'd ask you too. Are you still in love with him?"

"Are you?"

"I asked you first."

Amanda sighed in annoyance, sounding defensive. "No. I'm not. I've moved on, in case you haven't noticed."

"I'm not sure I'm one hundred percent convinced."

"Convinced of what? That I've moved on?"

"That you're not still in love with Jake."

"I'm not one hundred percent convinced that you're not still in love with him. You didn't even answer if you were or not, but I can tell that you are. It's written all over your face."

Kirby didn't have a comeback. He just stared at her, unprepared and unwilling to pour out his feelings to her about the range of emotions raging inside him—love, anger, sadness, and betrayal. After all, he was complicit in causing her to have the exact same feelings about Jake he presently felt.

Keeping her own feelings close to the vest and not wanting to send any mixed messages, Amanda made sure to underscore the point about having moved on. "Anyway, I'm dating Adam now. Are you dating anyone?" she asked in a tone that sounded doubtful.

When Kirby didn't answer her, she seized on the opportunity and let him have it.

"Hmmm," she uttered with a smirk. "Kirby, if you want Jake, he's all yours. Go ahead and claim him. You're both lying, deceitful cheats anyway. You only care about yourselves and don't give a shit about who you hurt. You deserve each other as far as I'm concerned. Good-bye!"

Amanda turned to step away from him, but then she turned back around to say one more thing. "Oh, when you see Jake again, you can tell him not to worry. I'll keep your little secret to myself."

"What secret?"

"That you're both gay even though you go around fucking girls to appear straight."

Chapter Seven

Jake had avoided Julie all weekend long. He'd deliberately decided not to stay the night or hang out with her in any way. Jake liked Julie, even admired her, but he couldn't keep their office fling going any longer with his heart and mind set on reclaiming Amanda.

"Hey, stranger," Julie said as she peeked her head inside Jake's office door the Monday morning following Oscar weekend.

Jake was rapidly typing a memo on his computer but stopped to acknowledge her. "Hey!"

Julie walked toward him and folded her arms as Jake returned to typing, seeming occupied. "So did you have a hot date over the weekend?" she asked.

"Nooo. Why would you think that?" Jake said, incredulous.

"Don't get all defensive."

"I'm not. I just don't know why you'd think that."

"Well, last week when I asked you about your plans for the weekend, you seemed less than enthusiastic—"

"Whattaya mean less than enthusiastic?" Jake said as he continued to type.

"Like…you were being vague…as if you had other plans or something that you didn't want to tell me about. I just assumed you had a date," Julie said with a shrug of the shoulders.

"Nope," Jake said as he kept typing.

"Oh well, I see you're busy. I'll let you get back to work. Sorry to interrupt."

Just as Julie turned around to step out of Jake's office, he asked, "You want to grab lunch later?"

She looked back at him. "Sure."

Fifteen minutes past noon, Jake swung by Julie's office. They headed out together to walk across the street from their office building to a favorite Mexican spot.

As they gabbed about office politics and personalities on their walk over to eat, they passed by the Jonathan Club. Feeling a little nostalgic, Julie grabbed Jake by the arm with both her hands and leaned in to him. "There's our old spot. We haven't been there in a while. Want to take a little detour?" she said playfully in his ear.

Jake smirked and tried to appear amused at the recollection of their past hookups there, but he hoped Julie wasn't being serious. As they walked past the club's entrance, Jake stared straight ahead and quickly changed the subject. "I think I'm going order the carnitas tacos this time. I've been craving those all morning."

Julie took the bait. "Mmmm…sounds delish."

After they'd ordered and found a place to sit, Julie had their earlier conversation still on her mind. "So are you going to tell me what you did this weekend?"

Jake had just taken a bite of his taco. He held up his index finger. He chewed his food longer than he typically would've and even took another bite, contemplating his choice of words.

Julie silently and patiently waited as she continued to eat her food too.

He didn't want admit to getting wasted so badly on Friday night that he didn't realize he'd crashed at Will and Kerry's pad until he awoke the next morning on their sofa. And he was too embarrassed to say that he'd watched the Oscars Sunday night just so that he could ogle Amanda in private at home alone.

"It was a pretty chill weekend—just errands and stuff. I actually spent a lot of time thinking about things."

"Like what?"

Jake sighed and then stared blankly as he spoke. "About me. My life. I'm really not happy, Julie," he admitted.

Julie stared at Jake quietly for a moment. Then she put her taco down and wiped her hands with her napkin. She looked down contemplatively and then back up at Jake, who didn't meet her gaze. "What's wrong? Why aren't you happy?"

Jake didn't initially answer her. Struggling to find the right words to say, he remained silent, still staring blankly.

"This is about Amanda, isn't it? You miss her."

Jake took a drink of his soda before he answered, speaking in a slow, reflective manner. "It's just…this is not where I expected to be right now. You know?"

Julie sounded frustrated. "Jake, I don't understand. Why'd you break up with her in the first place?"

Jake sighed. "I received some information that I never expected to hear, and I reacted to it by breaking up with her because I thought that was the best thing to do at the time."

"What information?"

"It's complicated, and I really can't go into any detail."

"Was she cheating on you or something?"

"No, nothing like that. Really, I can't talk about it."

Julie stared at Jake, perplexed, while he continued to stare blankly ahead, not meeting her gaze. They sat in silence for a moment before Jake continued.

"What's done is done. It is what it is," Jake said with defeat and resignation in his voice.

"And she's dating Adam Weinstock, which you obviously know by now. They were on TV at the Oscars together last night."

"I know."

"They seem pretty happy to me."

Julie's assertion was the same as Will's, but Jake turned and looked away in irritation. Although he'd seen with his own eyes that Amanda appeared happy, deep down Jake felt that she probably still loved him more than Adam and that he could convince her to take him back despite his infidelity. Amanda had loved him too much, too hard, and he hadn't deserved it. He sat there temporarily transfixed by the memory of making love to Amanda as she cried and told him how much she loved him and that she'd do anything for him. It was a scene they'd repeated many times. The intensity of her love and adoration for him, the surrendering of herself and of her own ambition—having left her career in New York to move back to LA to be his wife and mother to his children—often made him sick with guilt for his disloyalty. In that moment, guilt began to seep in again. Guilt for walking away from her and lying about his reasons for doing so instead of telling her the truth and confronting her about her alleged illness. However, Julie's peskiness and growing impatience snapped Jake's attention back to her.

"So what are you going to do? You've made your choice. At some point you've got to accept it and move on with your life…unless you intend on trying to get back with her. Is that what you want?"

"I don't know," he lied, wanting to be more circumspect instead of revealing his intentions to her flat-out.

Julie shook her head in annoyance and sighed. "If you're still this conflicted about Amanda after having broken up with her six months ago, then I think we should cool things off a bit and not continue to sleep together. You need to figure out what you want."

Jake didn't protest. He just nodded his head but felt relieved Julie was the one to suggest they end their ongoing fling.

"It's very obvious that things between us aren't going anywhere fast. Let's face it—we were both curious for a long time, and wanted a taste. I've had my fill. You've had yours. We've had our fun. Now it's time for us to move on and get our relationship back on track. Back to the way it was. This whole friends-with-benefits thing has been very distracting, to say the least. It's really not me, but I made an exception. I'm getting too old for this kind of bullshit."

Jake grinned as he watched Julie quickly evolve before his very eyes from the love-struck wannabe girlfriend she'd morphed into back to her normal self—dispassionate, rational, and in control. "Thanks for letting me off easy, Jules. I'm sorry if I've seemed flakey about things. I still have a lot of shit to work through in my personal life, and you've been very patient with me."

"Oh, don't mention it. We were friends and colleagues first, and friends and colleagues we shall remain. Now I'm going to get me some more salsa," Julie said nonchalantly as she stood. "Want anything?"

CHAPTER EIGHT

Jake couldn't have hoped for a better outcome in his breakup with Julie. He had initially feared that she would be bitter and that their relationship would be strained, making it difficult to work together. However, as the week progressed, they easily settled back into a strictly platonic relationship marked by collegiality and mutual respect for one another as legal professionals. It was as if the torrid love affair in which they'd been engaged over the last four months had never taken place. Jake suspected that perhaps deep down Julie was more upset than she'd let on, but he concluded that she was too self-possessed and full of pride to show any emotional attachment. Whatever the case might've been, it was over. Now he could turn his attention in earnest to winning back Amanda.

Jake had decided that first and foremost he needed to phone Rick Climent. Out of a sense of professional integrity, he wanted to let him know personally that he'd had a change of heart and intended ask Amanda to take him back. Jake also wanted Rick to know that he intended to keep his promise and not reveal what Rick had told him in confidence about the state of Amanda's mental health despite his growing skepticism. At the same time, however, Jake wanted Rick to understand that he was prepared to face the consequences of Amanda's supposed illness head-on, and if there were any relapses of her psychotic episodes as "Maggie," he would be committed to making sure that Amanda received the help and medical attention she needed. Jake knew that Rick had objected to his intervention before, but he didn't care anymore at this point. He owed Rick nothing.

He hadn't taken Rick's money, and he hadn't signed any agreement. Jake's mind was made up. If Amanda became his wife, as originally planned, he and she, together as a couple, would be in charge of her medical needs, not her parents. *That's the way it should be*, Jake concluded, the thought was more clear and obvious to him now than six months before.

By the end of the week, Jake was ready to make the call. He had rehearsed what he wanted to say to Rick over and over again in his head. Although he suspected what he had to say wouldn't be received very well. Jake knew that he was no longer considered a part of the Climent fold. He'd been effectively banished from the family, and he knew the revelation about his secret relationship with Kirby made him persona non grata and a social outcast to them. The audacity of him to call Rick now and so randomly to explain his intentions to reunite with his daughter and seek her hand in marriage yet again would most likely be met with derision, if not outrage. Nevertheless, Jake held firm to his plan, convincing himself that Amanda had been stolen from him and that he'd been taken advantage of. In his mind, his intentions were good and pure. At the time, it seemed like the morally correct choice to support the Climent family's efforts to save their daughter from her self-destructive, suicidal alter ego. However, he now had doubts about the severity of her alleged illness. How could she be doing so well after what he'd been told? Seeing Amanda appear more healthy and radiant than ever before and with a new boyfriend at her side made Jake angry—so angry that he continued to brush aside thoughts about what else might've motivated him to break up with her so willingly, without a fight.

Jake decided to call Rick's office. Perhaps an appointment could be arranged for them to speak in person.

"Climent Partners," Rick's assistant said upon answering the phone.

"Hi. This is Jake Doyle. Is Rick available?"

"Oh…hi," the assistant said, sounding a bit surprised, as if she recognized Jake's name. She continued to speak cautiously. "And what is this regarding?"

Jake nearly blurted "Amanda" but quickly thought that sounded too forward and suspicious. He didn't want to cause alarm. "It's a personal matter."

"Uh…okay. Let me see if I can get him for you. One moment, please."

Jake surmised that she did recognize his name. Otherwise she wouldn't have been willing to place him on hold to find Rick. While he waited, Jake wondered if Rick was even at the office. After nearly sixty seconds had passed, the assistant came back on the line.

"Mr. Doyle?"

"Yes."

"I'm sorry, but I wasn't able to get a hold of him. Can I pass along a message for you?"

"I'd prefer to speak with him directly. Maybe I could arrange to come by the office to meet with him."

"I can see if that could be arranged. I'll have to run it by Rick and get back to you."

"Do you still have my numbers?"

"I'm sure we do. Let me check here," she said.

Jake could hear her typing.

"Yes. Here you are."

"It's pretty urgent. The sooner a meeting or phone call could be arranged, the better. Whatever's most convenient for Rick."

"I'll see what I can do."

After confirming Jake's contact information with him to make sure what she had in her database was still current, they hung up. *He probably doesn't want to talk with me*, Jake thought, believing that the assistant had likely reached Rick but that he'd refused to take Jake's call.

Chapter Nine

Amanda and her sister Alexandra lay next to each in Amanda's bed. Alex stretched up her arms and yawned as she looked over at her older sister, already awake.

"Good morning," Alex said.

"Good morning," Amanda said before she yawned, too, and giggled at herself. "Why does that always happen?"

"Yawning's contagious. Didn't you know? It's like a virus, except it doesn't make you sick."

Amanda leaned over to hug Alex and kissed her on the cheek. "I'm so glad to see you. Thanks for spending the weekend with me."

"Awww…I'm happy to see you too." Alex hugged Amanda back. "Better than being at home in that big empty house. Even with Mom and Dad there it still feels so empty, doesn't it? I need to get my own place in LA to come home to when I'm not training in Santa Barbara."

"Well, until you do, you're always welcome to stay here with me when you come down." Amanda broke their embrace to lie flat on her back again.

"So what do you want to do today?"

Amanda groaned. "Oh…I don't know."

"What's wrong? You sound a little down."

"Nothing," Amanda said unconvincingly as she turned her head away to stare out the window. She paused for a few seconds. "It's Jake's birthday today."

Alex balked. "So do you plan on sending him a bouquet and wishing him a happy birthday or something?"

Amanda chuckled half-heartedly. "No. But I am a little curious to know what he's doing to celebrate."

"Why?"

Amanda lifted her shoulders to mimic her words. "I don't know. I just am."

Alex sighed. "I'm worried about you."

"Why? Just because I'm curious to know what he's doing for his birthday?" Amanda said defensively.

"No. Because you have a tendency to bring him up without any prodding."

Amanda snickered. "No I don't."

"Yes you do."

"Anyway, did I ever tell you that Jake apparently has a new girlfriend?"

"See what I mean?" Alex said smartly.

"Oh, hush," Amanda retorted.

"No. I don't believe you told me. Who is she?"

"Someone he works with at the office."

"Really? How'd you find out he was dating someone at his work?"

"Nana told me."

"Nana? How would she know?"

"She and Jake's grandmother have mutual friends, and they gossip among themselves like typical rich old ladies do because they have nothing else better to do."

Alex snickered.

"So anyway, Jake's grandmother told one of Nana's friends that Jake brought this girl over for Thanksgiving and that she's older than him."

"Older? How much older?"

"Nana said in her thirties."

"That's interesting."

"I think I know who it is."

"Who?"

"Her name is Julie, if I'm recalling correctly. She and Jake work closely together. I met her a couple of times, once at the firm's Christmas party and then again at their summer picnic. I always suspected she had a crush on Jake. I bet she's the one."

"So what about Kirby? Do you really believe they've parted ways as Jake claimed in that email he sent you last month?"

"Oh! I've been meaning to tell you. I've been so crazy busy lately that I forget that I haven't brought you up to speed on certain things. So I ran into Kirby last weekend after the Oscars. He was at the Elton John party."

"He was? Oh my God. No, you didn't tell me that," Alex said as she sat up in bed in rapt attention.

"Lucy and I had just come out of the bathroom, where we ran into Heidi Klum—I'll tell you about that too—and there he was. We literally walked right into him."

"Did you speak to him?"

"Of course I did. It was the first time I'd seen him in months."

"When's the last time you saw each other?"

"Before the wedding was canceled. Sometime in August. Anyway, I confronted him about everything. How he was fucking Jake, fucking Adam's assistant Antonio, and fucking his girlfriend Laren all at the same time."

Alex smirked. "Did he try to deny any of it?"

"No. He didn't."

"Did he say anything about why he did what he did? Try to offer up some sort of explanation for his whorish behavior?"

"No, not really. He said it was complicated, which is the same thing Jake said." Amanda slapped her hands to her cheeks and shook her head in bewilderment. "Ugh. Don't get me started. It makes me angry every time I think about it. He and Jake fucking the whole time we were together. Six years, Alex. Six fucking years!"

"So are he and Jake still friends? Are they still lovers? What's going on with them?"

"He told me they're not friends anymore, which is the same thing Jake said in that email."

"The email where he begged you not to tell people that he's gay even though he basically admitted to you that he was," Alex said with a roll of the eyes.

"Well, he actually didn't admit to being gay. He said that he's probably bisexual and that Kirby was the only guy he'd ever been with."

"Which I don't believe. Do you?"

Amanda sighed. "Who knows? But he's clearly bisexual if he's dating girls again."

"Unless this chick Julie is just his beard."

"Funny you should say that. Charlie and Lucy think the same thing."

Alex huffed in exasperation. "Enough about Jake, Kirby, and their madness. How's Mr. Weinstock?"

"Adam's fine. He said to tell you hello, by the way. I miss him already."

"Where is he?"

"He's in Toronto working on another film. He's directing it himself this time. It'll be his directorial debut."

"Oh, wow. How exciting. That's amazing. He was just nominated for a Best Picture Oscar and you guys were flying all over the place for these premiers promoting it and he's already out working on his next film? Does that guy ever rest?"

"No," Amanda said with a giggle. "He has, like, three or four film projects in development at any given time. I'm so bummed though."

"Why?"

"Because I probably won't see him again until we have the launch party for the bag line in New York."

"Why don't you go visit him in Toronto?"

"We talked about it. But my schedule between now and the launch event is crazy. I can't take any more time off. Lucy and I have a lot of work to do leading up to it. We have tons of appointments scheduled next week. She's been so patient about me traveling around with Adam for his premiers, award shows, and pre-Oscar events. It's been fun, but I'm glad it's over. I'm exhausted. That's why I'm here at home this weekend. So I can just relax and get some rest before I fly to New York on Monday. Besides, he's busy working with his crew, even on the weekends. I would just be a distraction. Seriously. They work morning, noon, and night. All we would have time for is a quickie, and then he'd leave me at the hotel or I'd just be standing around the set watching them work. Even though I miss him dearly, I'll just wait until I see him in New York for my launch party. It'll make the reunion all the more sweet."

"You guys have spent a lot of time together over the last couple of months. And all the press you've been getting. It's crazy. They're even saying that you two are headed down the aisle and that you were caught scouting wedding venues in Paris together. What's up with that?"

"I know. How ridiculous."

"Where did that story come from?"

"Who knows? People like to make shit up."

"But you guys did go to Paris."

"Yes. We went after the London premier for less than forty-eight hours. All we did was go out to eat, go out to drink, and visit a handful of private art galleries because, as you know, Adams's a collector. Someone must've seen us, and then the rags decided to manufacture this story to make it sound as if we were doing something more interesting than simply hanging out and lying low, but that's all we were doing."

"Well, whatever you do, please don't elope. I still want to be the maid of honor in your wedding."

"Don't be silly. Of course you'll be. Besides, I don't think eloping is Adam's style. He's the type of guy who'd probably enjoy a big fancy wedding—a big fat Jewish wedding."

Alex laughed. Amanda giggled along.

"Seriously, Adam loves a party, and a wedding would provide a good excuse to throw a big party. Plus, he has a big family and they're all very close. His mother would probably kill him if we eloped and didn't include the family. You know he took me to have Shabbat dinner with his family right before he left for Toronto. It was the first time he'd ever invited me to do that with him."

"Awww…how sweet is that?"

"I know."

"Look at you. You're glowing."

Amanda turned red and laughed. "Shut up. No I'm not."

"Yes, you are," Alex said, reaching over to pinch Amanda's cheeks.

Amanda continued to laugh while grabbing Alex's wrists to pull her hands away.

"Are you in love? Mandi, are you in love?" Alex repeated, poking at her sister.

"I love him," Amanda said, sounding more contemplative than affirmative in her answer.

"Hmmm. As much as you loved Jake?"

"Well…no. I mean…you can't really compare my relationship with Adam to my relationship with Jake. Jake and I were together for a long time. It felt more organic. We grew together. He's the first guy who ever made me feel loved… truly loved. There's a passion, a sense of abandon, a complete surrendering of yourself that's kind of uniquely experienced only with a first love, I believe. It's different."

"Okay. I can go along with that, but do you see yourself marrying Adam one day?"

"Yeah…maybe…I don't know," Amanda said with a change in her body language—folding her arms across her chest and appearing uncomfortable with the question.

"What? Why are you being so pensive? One minute you seem like you're on cloud nine about Adam and the next minute you seem tentative and doubtful about a future with him."

"I *am* on cloud nine about my relationship with Adam, and I do love him, but that doesn't mean I have to be ready to marry him right this instant."

"So let me go back to something you just said. You said that Jake made you feel truly loved. Now that you know that he'd been cheating on you the whole time, do you still believe he truly loved you?"

"I know that what Jake and I experienced together was real, especially in the beginning. There was a love there. It might've been flawed and imperfect in the end, but it felt genuine and real at the time." Amanda hopped out of bed and began to walk toward the bathroom, wanting to disengage from this uncomfortable conversation. However, before she could close the door behind her, Alex had one final question.

"Mandi, do you still have feelings for Jake? Be honest."

"I don't even know what that's supposed to mean. Do I still have feelings for him," Amanda repeated with sarcasm. She began to pull off her pajamas in an attempt to appear preoccupied and unconcerned with Alex's line of questioning.

"Mandi, you know what I mean. Do you still have feelings for him? Do you still care for Jake?"

"Oh, Alex, please. I'm going to take a shower now," Amanda said before quickly closing the bathroom door.

CHAPTER TEN

Kirby along with Jeff Hoefflin, his writing partner and co-producer, had all of the actors come in on Saturday for a final table read for their TV pilot. The table read, Hollywood-speak for a line-by-line read-through of the script by the actors cast for each role, allowed Kirby, Jeff, and the director they'd hired to identify any last-minute problem areas with the script before they started shooting the following Monday.

After the table read had concluded at seven in the evening, everyone, especially the actors, seemed anxious to head home for the remainder of the weekend. The show could be a big break for Kirby, Jeff, and the actors too, and they knew that it would be game time come Monday morning when they all had to show up to the studio bright and early for hair, makeup, and wardrobe. Once most everyone had hurried out, Kirby and Jeff remained behind to exchange notes.

"That's a wrap," Jeff said in exhilaration, lifting his hand to high-five Kirby

Kirby smiled broadly and chuckled while high-fiving Jeff back. "Not quite yet, homes. We haven't filmed anything yet."

"I know, but after spending the last couple of months having guys in suits at the network nitpicking at our script and doing my best not to fart in their faces at their stupid suggestions for changes, getting to this point feels like a small victory. I swear...I've never dealt with a bigger group of wusses in my life. They like the concept for the show and give us the green light to shoot the pilot and then want us to make all sorts of changes at the last minute."

"I think they're just a little nervous. That's all. They want to make sure we don't offend anyone in the Jewish or black community. An Orthodox Jewish man falling in love with and marrying a single black mother will be groundbreaking TV. In hindsight, having her serve him her smothered pork chops recipe and then having him not protest but admit that he liked them and asking for more probably wouldn't have gone over too well with the purists in the Orthodox community."

"Oh please. I'm Jewish. Trust me, some Jews, in fact many, secretly crave and eat pork, too. The fact that he was willing to admit that he was violating a dietary law to win her over and not insult her showed that he was human. At least we included the scene of him at the temple repenting during Yom Kippur. At first they all liked that scene and thought it was funny. Remember?"

"Oh well. They changed their minds. What's done is done. I still like the script overall. Don't you?"

"Yes, I agree, it's still a good script, and I feel pretty confident that we'll get picked up as a full series. It's just been a frustrating process getting to this point. Luckily we have good agents. They have far better negotiating skills than I do. If it weren't for them holding this deal together and running interference, it would've fallen apart."

"Yeah…you are sort of a hothead," Kirby said, tongue in cheek.

Jeff smirked. "My hothead's getting us a TV series."

"Word," Kirby said with a chuckle. "I can't wait to start shooting on Monday. After making all of these last-minute revisions to get the script right and spending the last two months going through nearly a thousand head shots to cast six roles, it's a relief to finally see everything coming together. We have the right cast and a great script. I'm excited, man. This is all a dream come true."

"Well, we've got a lot more work to do beginning Monday, so don't go out and get slammed this weekend and show up to the studio late and hungover."

"Oh, no. Absolutely not. I'm going to be fresh and ready to roll come Monday morning."

"Yeah…we'll see," Adam said teasingly as he gathered his things, preparing to leave.

Kirby chuckled. "No, seriously, man. I'm not planning on doing any partying this weekend. Although I do plan on crashing a party."

"Crash a party?"

"Yeah. I wasn't invited, but I'm going to go and make my presence known anyway, just for the hell of it."

"Whose party?"

"Jake's. It's his birthday."

"What happened to you guys? Haven't you two been friends, like, since you were in diapers?"

Kirby chuckled. "Not quite that long, but he's been avoiding me, and I need to confront him about something. I can't wait to see the expression on his face when I show up. It'll be priceless."

Chapter Eleven

Jake smiled broadly and chuckled a few times at the long list of birthday messages on his Facebook page. So far there were more than two hundred posts and counting, mostly from prep school classmates, Stanford classmates—undergraduate and law school—fraternity brothers, random friends and colleagues from work and elsewhere, and a few from various cousins and other relatives. Although Jake mostly traveled with a tight-knit circle of close friends, he'd managed to accumulate and maintain a network of relationships that was deep and wide. His charm, friendly demeanor, and outgoing personality were traits that made him disarming to many people who otherwise might've been intimidated by his striking good looks and rich, frat boy, country club image, an image that had been amplified by his long courtship of a billionaire heiress. That he could be so attractive, rich, and smart yet so affable and down-to-earth had won him many admirers and fans over the course of his young life. Moreover, the fact he had actively volunteered for Amnesty International throughout college and law school and developed a keen interest and passion for assisting refugees and activists fleeing political persecution in countries ruled by oppressive regimes allowed people to see a different side of him, a side that was more substantive, humane, and empathetic. Everyone wanted to be Jake's friend, and he was good at making people feel like they were, even if they weren't part of his inner circle. It was that inner circle, mostly consisting of a select mix of prep school friends and Stanford classmates and fraternity brothers—about twenty guys, some bringing girlfriends—that would be joining Jake for a low-key get-together to celebrate his twenty-seventh birthday that Saturday night.

After reading through the messages and responding to a few of them, Jake tossed the phone down on the bed and hopped in the shower to get ready for the birthday party. In a good mood and feeling uplifted by all of the doting birthday messages, Jake dried off and walked into the bedroom to crank up the music pumping through his computer's stereo speakers. "Sexy and I Know It" from LMFAO was playing. Jake blasted it while he sang along and danced around in his birthday suit—gyrating his hips, pumping his pelvis back and forth, and rubbing his hands up and down his chest and abdomen sensually. "'I'm sexy and I know it…Girl look at that body…Girl look at that body…,'" Jake crooned as he imagined doing a striptease for Amanda as he'd often done in the past during foreplay. With his body hard and buff from a workout earlier that day, Jake liked how he looked and felt, enjoying his private moment.

Jake combed his hair and put on his clothes. Shortly thereafter, Pax, one of Jake's oldest friends from prep school, picked him up. Together they drove to The Cottage, a bar and nightclub in Santa Monica, where they were to meet up with everyone.

"Thanks for picking me up, bro," Jake said.

"No problem. Since I'm sobering up and cutting back on my alcohol consumption, I don't mind being your designated driver this evening. It's your birthday, dude. You can drink and party all you want tonight. I'll get you home safe. Don't worry about it."

"I appreciate it. It was so embarrassing passing out at Will and Kerry's place last weekend. Don't want that to happen again. I think I must've of blurted something incriminating about myself during my drunken stupor."

"Why do you say that?"

"Because they were looking at me all weird when I woke up and told me that I had said some pretty strange things—"

"Like what?"

"I don't know. They wouldn't tell me. They just laughed it off. Kerry's was like, 'Oh, Jake. You poor, tortured soul. You really open up and bare your heart when you're in an inebriated state. We're going to have to get you drunk more often…to see what other golden nuggets of information slip from your tongue.'" Jake spoke in a mocking, girly tone before rolling his eyes and shaking his head in annoyance.

Pax laughed. "That's hilarious. I've got to find out what you said. Now I'm curious. They might've been pulling your leg, though. You know Will's such a prankster."

"Maybe. Maybe not. If I did say something revealing, I trust Will. It's Kerry I don't trust."

Jake and Pax arrived at The Cottage. The place was packed, as was typical for a Saturday night, but a space had been reserved for Jake's party.

Greeted like a hero when he arrived, Jake made the rounds, receiving warm smiles and bear hugs. Jake and his pals spent the time reminiscing, laughing, and telling stories about each other as they sipped beers and cocktails and munched on charcuterie, cheese, dips, and toast from the small plates menu.

"Thanks for putting this together," Jake said when he reached Will and Kerry, who had reserved the space and set everything up with the bar.

"Of course. It didn't require us to do much," Will said.

"Where's Julie?" Kerry blurted. "I thought you would bring her."

"We're not dating anymore."

Will gave Jake a knowing look while Kerry gasped. "Why? What happened?"

"I told you it was never serious. Why act so surprised?" Jake said, sounding a little defensive.

Kerry huffed. "I wanted to meet her."

Pax, who was standing in earshot of this exchange, butted in. "Are you guys talking about Jake's playmate from the office?"

"Yeah. Did you ever meet her?" Kerry asked.

"No. None of us got to meet her, but I sure did hear a lot about her," Pax said with a devious smirk.

Jake started to blush as he sipped his beer.

Kerry turned to Jake and piled on. "I thought I was going to finally get to meet her tonight. She sounded like a really interesting person, and the perfect match for you. I can't believe you broke up with her."

"Oh well," Jake said with a grin, looking at Will.

"Oh well," Will said back to him with a grin of his own. Other than Jake's boss, Mike Wallace, Will was the only person who knew of Jake's intentions to get back with Amanda. Will leaned towards Jake and said in a low voice, "I see you've put your recovery plans in motion."

"Yes I have," Jake said discreetly with a chuckle.

"What?" Kerry said, trying to get in on the secret exchange.

"Nothing," Jake and Will said in near-perfect unison.

"Well…like you said, I guess I shouldn't be so surprised after hearing you dribble on about hoping Amanda and Kirby would take you back—"

"What!" Pax exclaimed, cutting her off.

Jake froze. His face turned white and his eyes widened as he glared at Kerry.

Kerry continued, "You didn't hear?"

"Kerry," Will said, trying to stop her, but she kept going.

"Jake passed out on our sofa last Friday—"

"Oh yeah, Jake told me on the way over here—"

"He was completely slammed. I don't think I've seen him that slammed since we were in college. Anyway, he was saying to Will when they got back to our place, 'Do you think Amanda will take me back? Maybe Kirby will take me back.' The way he was slurring his words, it was so cute and so sad at the same time."

"Oh my God." Pax smirked, covering his mouth and turning to look at Jake.

"I did not," Jake said, incredulous.

"Yes, you did. Didn't he, Will. Tell him."

Will shook his head, seemingly not wanting any part of this, but he spoke up in his friend's defense nonetheless. "He was drunk, Kerry. We all say crazy shit when we're drunk."

"So that's what you said? So you want to get back with Amanda?" Pax asked Jake.

Embarrassed, Jake tried to blow it off. "I don't know what you guys are talking about. I don't recall any of this."

"That's because you were drunk, bro," Pax said.

"You know what they say. The truth comes out when you're drunk. Damn it! I should've videotaped you. You should've seen him. He looked so hurt and sad. He was practically in tears talking about getting back with Amanda and Kirby," Kerry said, seeming to enjoy watching Jake squirm.

"So you *do* miss Kirby after all, huh?" Pax said. "You've been so hard-nosed about not wanting to see him or do anything with him anymore."

"Maybe the rumors really are true about their secret little bromance," Kerry said devilishly.

Jake and Will both gasped.

"Secret bromance?" Pax asked. He hadn't heard the rumor. Pax and the other prep school friends Jake and Kirby shared were still in the dark. Will and Kerry knew only because Brook Sterling, a Stanford classmate and one of Amanda's bridesmaids and close friends, had told them.

"Kerry, would you shut the fuck up?" Will said to her. "Seriously... cut it out."

Kerry gasped and huffed. "Don't talk to me like that, Will. Don't tell me to shut up."

Will stepped close to her, face-to-face, and spoke in a low, firm voice. "I told you not to say...."

Jake couldn't exactly hear what Will said to her, but he had an idea. The gay rumors were false and must not be repeated. Ever! Jake could count on his good buddy to help him get that message across.

Jake and Pax quickly scurried away, neither interested in sticking around to watch Will and Kerry go at it. Jake felt agitated. *I can't believe I said all that. Fuck!*

Just before they integrated themselves with the rest of the group, Pax offered Jake reassuring words. "Don't worry about it, bro. I'm sure I say stupid stuff too when I'm drunk. No big deal."

Chapter Twelve

When Kirby arrived at The Cottage, a long line had already formed to get inside. The usual Saturday evening crowd of young, mostly good-looking twentysomethings had arrived early to secure a spot inside the ever-popular venue known for its laid-back attitude and cool, chic California vibe.

Kirby walked straight up to the front of the line. "Hi. I'm here for my friend's birthday party. I believe there's a space reserved."

"What's the party's name?"

"The party's for Jake Doyle."

The attendant looked down at her clipboard and then back up at him. "Yep. You're at the right place. They have the billiard room and part of the back patio. Have you been here before?"

"Yes, I have. I know my way around. Thanks," Kirby said, proceeding to go inside.

Kirby surveyed the room, checking out the scene as he squeezed past people to make his way to the billiard room. As he did so, a couple of girls tried to make eye contact with him and hold his attention when his hard, muscular flesh pressed up against theirs. Kirby toyed with them by glancing back and grinning, but he kept moving. As he approached the open doorway of the billiard room, he could see a group standing around with their backs to him, singing "Happy Birthday."

They were just finishing the song when Kirby stepped into the room. He stood at the back, looked over shoulders, and watched Jake blow out the candles on his cake. After he did so, everyone cheered and applauded. Kirby discreetly applauded, too, not quite ready to draw attention to himself.

"Speech, speech," different people shouted at Jake as he glanced up at them with a broad smile across his face.

Looking bashful, Jake blushed and laughed. "Speech? Oh, come on. Just have another drink and get smashed. The next round's on me."

The room cheered and people chattered loudly in response to the gesture, seeming pleased, but then Jake continued to talk.

Kirby kept his head bowed and stood behind a couple of guys tall enough to shield him from Jake's view.

"No, seriously—"

"Whaaa… You weren't being serious about the drinks?" one of Jake's friends shouted playfully.

Jake chuckled. "I wasn't being serious only about you. Everyone else's drink I'm paying for," Jake said to roars of "Ohhh!" and then laughter at the guy, a fraternity brother of Jake's.

Jake continued, "Anyway, as I was saying, thank you all for coming. It means a lot to me that you all came. As you know, this past year ended on somewhat of a sour note for me personally. Although it was my decision to end my engagement, it was still a very difficult thing to do, and I feel bad that friendships on both sides have been broken as a result. But you guys have stuck with me, supported me, and tried to encourage me, each in your own way, through a difficult time, and I want you to know how much I appreciate the messages, the phone calls, the late night conversations over a beer or two—"

"Or three…or four…or five," Will interjected comically to laughs around the room.

Jake giggled at himself and continued. "Yes, and getting wasted with me and allowing me to crash on your sofa as I self-medicated myself back to recovery and some degree of sanity. I've known most of you since college and some of you since middle school, even. I can't think of anyone not already in this room who has been a better friend to me than each of you."

At that remark, Kirby lifted his head. "Really?" he said under his breath, and then he stepped away from the two guys he was standing behind and moved over to his right so that he and Jake were in each other's direct line of sight.

"I couldn't have asked for a better group of—" Jake's heart skipped, and he paused midsentence when he spotted Kirby standing at the back of the room.

Kirby folded his arms and glared hard when Jake's eyes met his.

Everyone in the room turned around to see who or what Jake was staring at.

"Oh. It's Kirby," a voice from the group said.

"Oh shit," Pax said in a low voice.

"Hey, Kirby," someone else said cheerily.

Kirby nodded his head and sported a restrained grin in reply.

But before Jake lost control of the room, he squared his eyes back on Kirby, tightened his jaw, and quickly regained his composure. He raised the level of his voice to redirect everyone's attention back to him. "As I was saying, I couldn't have asked for a better group of friends, and I wanted to make sure that all of you whom I actually invited here tonight knew how much your friendship means to me."

"Ahhh," some of the girls and guys both sang in a sentimental but playful fashion before applause broke out around the room.

Immediately afterward, Pax beelined over to Kirby and slap-grabbed hands with him. "What's up, man? What are you doing here?

"What does it look like I'm doing? I'm crashing the party. And thanks for the tip, homey."

Panic crossed Pax's face. "Don't tell Jake I told you about the party. He'll kill me."

"Don't worry about it," Kirby said nonchalantly as another friend approached to greet him.

Although annoyed that Kirby showed up unannounced and uninvited, Jake tried to play it cool. He proceeded to cut his cake and hand slices out to his guests.

Kirby approached Jake from behind and lifted his index finger to his mouth, signaling to those standing around that he wanted to sneak up on him.

Jake bent over slightly to cut another slice of cake. When he rose to hand it to the next person waiting for a piece, he bumped into Kirby, who was standing directly behind him.

Those standing around giggled uncomfortably when they witnessed Jake's response to the collision—tense and cold. Jake didn't even say hello. He ignored Kirby as he acknowledged and handed the slice of cake to another person standing nearby.

"Oh, so you're still not going to talk to me?" Kirby said in a firm voice.

Jake took a deep breath and then turned around to face Kirby. He spoke in a low voice. "Why are you here?"

"Because you won't return any of my calls and messages, and I need to talk to you."

"There's nothing more for us to talk about, Kirby. Now, will you please leave and not cause a scene?" Jake turned to cut another slice of cake.

"Jake," Kirby said, firmly grabbing Jake by the arm, "I need to have a word with you."

Growing visibly angry, Jake flinched and then turned to look at Kirby. "Speak to me about what?"

"About Reggie, that's what," Kirby deadpanned. He needed to say no more. The confident, cold-blooded expression on his face said it all.

Jake glared at Kirby in silence for a moment. Kirby glared back.

"Are you guys all right?" Will came up to them and said, but neither answered.

"Do you want to have this conversation right here, right now...in front of all these people? Because if you do, I'm down with that," Kirby said, not caring that those standing around could hear him loud and clear.

Jake sighed hard and shook his head in annoyance before turning to place the cake knife down on the table. Without saying anything, he calmly walked out of the room, toward the bathroom. Kirby followed behind him.

Jake shoved the restroom door open hard and, upon seeing that the room appeared empty, he turned to face Kirby and unleashed. "How dare you fucking come here, to my fucking birthday party, uninvited, and make a scene. What the fuck are you doing?"

Kirby scratched his head and furrowed his brow for emphasis. "You know, it's funny. That's the exact same question I wanted to ask you. What the fuck are you doing…with Reggie?"

Jake didn't answer at first. "I don't want to talk about this," he finally said.

"Well, I do," Kirby said, but right at the moment a couple of bar patrons entered the restroom.

"Will you just leave?"

"No. We need to talk."

"Not right now," Jake said as he walked out of the restroom.

Kirby followed behind and then grabbed Jake by the arm to turn him around to face him. "Then when?"

"Not here."

"Okay, then where? I'll meet you. When will you be leaving the party?"

"I don't know. We might go someplace else afterward. Just leave, Kirby. Okay?"

"I'm not leaving until you agree to meet with me. Later tonight, tomorrow, I don't care. But I'm not going to let you off the hook about this."

Jake sighed hard. "Okay, fine. I can meet you tomorrow around eleven, but then I have to leave to go meet up with my family. They're taking me to brunch for my birthday."

"That's fine. I'll meet you at your place."

"Do you even know where I live now?"

"I have a way of finding things out. I'll show up at your door tomorrow morning at eleven a.m. sharp." Just before Kirby stepped away to go, he pointed his finger in Jake's face. "Don't stand me up, Jake, because if you do, I'm going to start telling people the real reason why we're not friends anymore. Tell them the truth. I'm not protecting you anymore.

Not after this. Not after what you've done while passing judgment on me and treating me like shit."

CHAPTER THIRTEEN

Jake lay in bed the following morning, anticipating the confrontation that would ensue with Kirby within a couple of hours. He contemplated what he'd say to Kirby about his liaisons with Reggie. Although he'd hooked up with Reggie a couple of times, Jake had since blown him off. Jake reckoned that his withdrawal from Kirby—which had engendered a sense of longing, reminiscence, and sadness about their lost friendship—drove him to Reggie. However, he felt that slowly but surely he was overcoming his urge for connection and intimacy with Kirby the longer he kept him away. Besides, despite hooking up with Reggie, Jake had had far more hookups with different girls since his breakup with Amanda combined with his extended casual dating relationship Julie. Therefore, Jake convinced himself to believe that as far as his sexuality was concerned, he was straight—or at least, straight enough. He now just needed to convince Kirby of the same thing and push him away for good.

Jake eventually got out of bed, showered, and dressed. However, as the hour of Kirby's arrival drew near, Jake grew increasingly anxious and agitated. The more he thought about what had transpired the night before at The Cottage, the angrier Jake became, especially about the threat Kirby made about outing him to their friends. Jake started talking aloud to himself as if Kirby were in the room with him. "This is my fucking life, Kirby. I don't have to answer to you or explain myself to you. I can do whatever the fuck I please. Lay off me, okay? I don't want you in life my life anymore. I hate you," Jake shouted as if he was looking at Kirby directly in the face but then his voice broke, and tears formed in his eyes. The uttering of such words even in an imaginary conversation was too painful. In that moment, Jake felt hate. He felt anger. But he also felt hurt because deep down he felt love, love that he couldn't fully suppress for his friend.

Jake plopped himself down on the sofa and buried his face in his hands. He tried to settle himself down and clear his mind of the conflicting thoughts and feelings that ran through it, but time was up. The moment of truth had arrived when, at eleven a.m. sharp, his phone rang and Kirby's name appeared across his caller ID.

"Hello."

"Hey. It's me. I'm outside your building."

"I'm on the fourth floor. Number four-zero-eight," Jake said before buzzing Kirby in.

Jake took a few deep breaths and paced back and forth in his apartment until he heard Kirby's knock at the door. When Jake opened the door to let Kirby in, he didn't say anything at first. Neither did Kirby. They just glared at each as if picking up exactly where they had left off the night before.

While Jake held the door open, Kirby walked in and lightly brushed him with his shoulder. Jake took it as provocation. He quickly slammed the door shut and got in Kirby's face. *I'm not afraid of you*, Jake thought but said with his body language.

Kirby stepped in closer so that he and Jake were nose to nose and eye to eye. His adrenaline racing, Kirby was so intense and filled with anger that his nostrils flared with each breath. "So now you're ready to give up your booty, huh? What…I wasn't good enough for you? Are you a size queen now? Was I too small for you? Huh? You like being Reggie's BITCH?" Kirby yelled and then pressed the tip of his nose to Jake's to underscore his ire.

Feeling challenged by Kirby's aggressive stance, Jake wasn't about to back down. He rode with it and decided to take a shot at Kirby's pride and ego. "Yeah, I liked it," Jake sneered. "He could teach you a thing or two. I didn't realize what I'd been missing. And yeah, he's bigger than you. Better than that limp-ass ding-a-ling of yours."

"Is that right?" Kirby smirked. Just as Jake attempted to turn away from him, Kirby used both his hands to grab Jake at the collar of his T-shirt and yanked him hard so that they were face-to-face again. "You sucked on my cock like a champ for more than ten years. Never heard you complain before."

"Well, I'm not sucking on it anymore. Now get your motherfucking hands off me," Jake said as he struggled to pull himself loose from Kirby's grip. "Get off me. Get off me," Jake yelled as Kirby swung Jake around to push him against the front door.

"So you like being a bitch, huh?" Kirby said and then licked the tip of Jake's nose to taunt him. "See. I knew it. I always knew you wanted dick. That's the real motherfuckin' reason you broke up with Amanda—because you wanted more dick but didn't have the guts to admit to it. I bet you were fooling around, sucking dick behind my back, the whole time."

"Fuck you," Jake said while still trying to push Kirby off him, but he was overpowered.

Kirby slammed Jake back up against the door. "No. Fuck you, bitch. Dogging me out for messing with other guys while you were doing the same damn thing."

Jake hadn't been, but this was not the time for a sensible, rational conversation. This was a fight, and Jake didn't feel the need to prove Kirby wrong or provide him an explanation for his hookups with Reggie. In fact, Jake reveled in telling Kirby that Reggie was a better lover than him because he knew that would hurt him. And in that moment, Jake wanted Kirby to feel the same hurt he felt when he'd first learned that Kirby had secretly maintained a sexual relationship with Antonio. Jake had never admitted to Kirby his hurt and jealousy over Antonio, but the sense of payback felt good nonetheless.

"Think whatever you want to think, man. I don't give a fuck. Now get off me and get the fuck out of my house. Meeting with you is pointless," Jake said, still wrestling to break free.

"I know you don't give a fuck. You're a cock-sucking bitch and proud of it. Aren't you?" Kirby said before taunting Jake again, licking the tip of his nose and then kissing it. Kirby went to kiss Jake on the lips next, but Jake turned his face away. Kirby used his right hand to hold Jake's face at the jaw and then he kissed Jake hard, pressing his thick tongue to Jake's lips to push through his mouth.

At first Jake grabbed Kirby's wrist to pry loose his hand from his jaw and managed to turn his face away again, momentarily stopping the kiss. However, Kirby turned Jake's face back and pressed his lips hard to Jake's, attempting to push his tongue through Jake's lips again.

Jake wanted to resist Kirby. He wanted to hurt him, physically and emotionally, but Kirby's touch, although aggressive and taunting, triggered a lustful urge in him. He allowed himself to succumb to it, if just for a fleeting moment. Jake kissed Kirby back, opening his mouth to welcome Kirby's tongue. Savoring its taste once again, Jake licked back wildly. The connection brought about a stiff hard-on immediately. However, as he found himself slipping under Kirby's spell, Jake abruptly stopped and pulled his head back as if coming to his senses again. "Get off me. Get off me," he yelled, resuming his attempt to push Kirby away.

"You know you want this. Admit it. Why are you still fighting it?" Kirby said before pressing his lips to Jake's again.

With his defenses weakening against the sensual forces rising up from within and overtaking his body and mind, Jake kissed Kirby back. Their tongues collided and tangled hungrily with a sense of longing and desperation but also with a hint of aggression and combat. They weren't making or showing love but instead channeling their rage and anger toward one another through the release of pent-up sexual frustration and energy.

Kirby reached down to grab Jake's ass, hard, pulling him forward so that their bodies were pressed together. Although Jake continued to kiss back, he didn't want to wrap his arms around Kirby. That seemed too affectionate and conciliatory, and this wasn't about reconciliation. So he grabbed Kirby's arms in a futile attempt to pull his hands away from his ass. Even though his boner was throbbing and eager to burst from his shorts, Jake still wanted to put up a fight and show resistance. However, the longer Kirby had his thick, juicy, delicious pink tongue buried deep in his mouth, the more overwhelmed Jake became by the sensations of lust and desire permeating his body.

Within moments, Jake stopped trying to pull Kirby's arms away and simply held on while Kirby slipped his hands underneath Jake's shorts and underwear to feel the hard, round, muscular flesh of his buttocks. Kirby grabbed and squeezed Jake's butt-cheeks tightly before using the middle finger of his left hand to tease Jake's hole.

Jake pulled his head back to break their lip lock. "You still want that, don't you?" he said in a taunting, provocative way.

Kirby looked at Jake squarely in the eye and answered back in an equally taunting and provocative way, "I own you. You're always gonna be my bitch."

Not liking the sound of that, Jake slapped his open hand to Kirby's face to push it away in disgust. "Fuck you. I'm not your bitch and never will be."

Kirby stumbled backward slightly as Jake moved to step away from him.

Kirby swung his left arm to slap Jake back, but Jake ducked fast enough so that Kirby barely swiped his chin. "You motherfucker," Kirby yelled as he leaped to tackle Jake. Jake held out his arms to prevent Kirby from pulling him down. They tussled momentarily, using their arms to push and pull each other around. Kirby tried to swing Jake down to the floor while Jake tried to break loose from Kirby's grip. After a few moments, Jake broke free and then began swinging violently at Kirby with his fists.

"Oh, you want a piece of this? You want a piece of this, bro?" Kirby yelled as he ducked back to keep Jake from connecting.

"I'm gonna fuck you up," Jake said. In that moment Jake felt so angry and threatened that he wasn't thinking or seeing things clearly. He didn't care that Kirby was bigger, stronger, and more muscular than him. Jake just wanted to land a punch right on the chin or nose. He just wanted to hurt Kirby.

Kirby, feeling not at all afraid or threatened, started to laugh at Jake, taunting him. "Look at you, man. You swing like a girl. What a bitch," he said as he ducked and dodged.

They were like two fighters in a boxing ring—Jake on offense, stepping forward, swinging and throwing jabs and Kirby on defense, dancing around, moving backward and dodging. Kirby escalated his verbal taunts and insults. "You swing like a girl, man. Seriously…that's the best you've got? What a faggot."

The utterance of that word *faggot* lit a fuse in Jake. It was the word every guy dreaded being called, the word that insulted a guy's sense of identity and pride as a man and challenged his masculinity. The word sent a message to Jake that there was a dent in his armor as a man that made him appear not masculine enough. Despite having had two sexual encounters with Reggie and years of liaisons with Kirby, Jake still viewed himself as straight. And for a guy who had worked so hard to mask and conceal his same-sex attraction for so long—continuing to date and hook up with women—being called *faggot* was jarring. The insult was enough to muster in Jake the footwork and dexterity to land a punch to the right side of Kirby's jaw.

Caught off guard, Kirby didn't even see it coming. His head popped back when the bones in Jake's knuckles met the bone of his jawline. Initially it felt as if it had been dislocated. Kirby shuffled his jaw back and forth a couple of times and realized that he could at least still move it and open his mouth. However, on defense and needing to protect himself, he couldn't worry about the extent of his injury now. Intent on taking Jake down and gaining the upper hand, Kirby lunged at Jake, barreling his head into his chest like a bull, so fast and with such bodily force that Jake fell back on the sofa.

With Kirby on top of him, Jake began swinging for dear life, anticipating that Kirby would return the blow. But Kirby grabbed Jake's wrists to stop him from swinging and pinned them back behind Jake's head.

"Why are you doing this to us? I fucking love you. I love you," Kirby said.

Jake, struggling to break free, yelled back, "I hate you."

Kirby held down Jake's wrists more tightly and repeated, "I love you. I don't want to fight. I don't want to hurt you, bro. Stop this. Why are you doing this to us? I want to be with you."

"You should've thought about that before you started fucking Antonio," Jake said bitterly.

"You know Antonio means nothing to me. It's you that I want. What more do I need to say or do to prove that to you?" Kirby released Jake's wrists and held his head in the palms of his hands. "I love you. I love you," Kirby said again, his voice breaking and tears filling his eyes. He bent down and attempted to kiss Jake, but Jake wasn't having it.

His hands now free, Jake swung and landed another punch to Kirby's right cheek. Because he was pinned down on his back, Jake didn't deliver this punch as hard as the first one, but it was enough to prompt Kirby to retaliate this time. Kirby didn't waste any time or hold back. Like a reflex, he slapped Jake's face, hard.

It was so hard that Jake saw sparks fly, the kind of sparks that occur when the brain is trying to process and interpret the electrical impulses triggered by blunt force trauma. Jake attempted to land another punch, swinging wildly, but was quickly disabled when Kirby grabbed him by the neck and began choking him.

Jake looked up at Kirby and saw the rage in his face, seething and gritting his teeth while applying pressure to Jake's trachea, cutting off oxygen. Jake immediately started struggling to breathe, gasping for air and flushing in the face. He reached for Kirby's wrists to try pulling his hands from his neck, but Jake knew that Kirby had him and that there was little he could do at that point. Jake's vision started to blur as his eyes reddened and filled with tears from the stress and pressure that was preventing him from breathing freely. When he felt himself losing strength and slipping out of consciousness, Jake gave in and stopped pulling on Kirby's wrists. All he could do was ask for a reprieve. "Kirby...please," Jake pleaded, barely able to get the words out.

Kirby promptly stopped. He pulled up off Jake and stood to his feet, appearing in shock.

Jake sat up and massaged his neck. He gave a deep-throated cough a few times before he was able to speak. "What are you trying to do… kill me?"

Kirby just stared at him in a daze for a moment before he responded. "I'm sorry, man. I lost control. I never wanted to hurt you. I never wanted to hurt you," Kirby said before he broke down in tears and raised his hands to cover his face.

Incredulous and startled by what had just happened, Jake was unforgiving. "I couldn't breathe. I nearly passed out, asshole. I hate you. I fucking hate you so much right now. Get out. I never want to see you ever again," Jake yelled, rising to his feet.

Kirby picked up his phone and wallet from the floor, which had somehow fallen out of his pockets in the melee. With tears streaming down his face, he said one more time, "I'm sorry, man."

"Get out!" Jake screamed as he watched Kirby, with head bowed, turn to walk out quietly and close the door behind him.

CHAPTER FOURTEEN

Kirby drove back home feeling regret and remorse for what had just transpired. He hadn't meant to hurt Jake, but after taking two punches to the face, his temper boiled over and he instinctively reacted to defend himself. He knew things with Jake would get testy, but he hadn't anticipated a physical altercation. He had hoped a hot-blooded argument with Jake would have concluded with a hot-blooded make-out session followed by sex, finally leading to the resolving of the differences between them, when all would be forgiven. However, it now seemed that his relationship with Jake was irrevocably broken. All chances for a reconciliation now gone. It shook him, and he needed to talk to someone. When Kirby got home, he called his cousin Myla.

"Hey, cousin," Myla said cheerfully when she answered her phone.

"It's over, Myla. Me and Jake are now officially over."

"Why? Did you finally talk to him?"

"We got into a fight."

"A fight? What do you mean, a fight?"

"We got into a fight."

"As in a physical fight?"

"Yeah. He punched me in the face. Twice."

"Whaaat!" Myla yelled. "Oh my God. Are you all right?"

"I think my jaw might be slightly dislocated. I'm not entirely sure. At least I can talk, but it feels funny," Kirby said, stretching his mouth open and shut while rubbing his jaw.

"Where were you?"

"At his house. I crashed his birthday party last night to confront him but, of course, he didn't want to speak to me there, so we agreed to meet at his house this morning."

"Where was his birthday party?"

"At The Cottage in Santa Monica."

"I bet he wasn't happy about that. Why'd you crash his party?"

"Because he wouldn't return any of my calls or messages," Kirby retorted defensively.

"So what happened? Why did he punch you?"

"As soon as I walked in the door he got in my face, and we started jawing at each other. From there, things got heated pretty fast, and we started tussling. Then I kissed him."

"You kissed him?"

"Yeah. And he kissed me back at first. But then we started tussling and jawing at each other again."

"Wait. I don't get it. He kissed you but then you started arguing again?"

"You know. It was all in the heat of the moment. You've never been in a fight with a boyfriend or lover where you fuss and fight and make out at the same time?"

"No. But my love life or lack thereof is a whole other story. Anyway, continue."

"So, we were kissing and tussling at the same time at one point. And then he said something, and then I said something, and then he pushed me in the face."

"He pushed you in the face? What did you say?"

"It was in the heat the moment. I don't remember," Kirby lied, not wanting to go into all of the detail about the sexual taunts and innuendo he and Jake had thrown at each other. "I slapped back at him and then we started wrestling. I was trying to tackle him, to hold him down, but then he went crazy on me and started throwing fists. I didn't want to fight him like that. I kept ducking and pulling back to keep him from hitting me but then he landed one on my jaw. It all happened so fast. I barely remember everything."

"Did you hit back?"

"I didn't at first. I managed to tackle him down and held his arms back. I tried to tell him that I didn't want to fight, that I didn't want to hurt him, that I loved him and wanted to be with him."

"But—"

"But he wouldn't listen to me. I let go of his arms so that he could see that I wasn't going to try to hit him back, so he could see that I wasn't trying to hurt him, but when I let go, he started swinging at me again, and he nailed me in the face, near the same spot as before."

Myla huffed and sounded incredulous now. "And you didn't hit back? What did you do?"

"I started choking him."

"You choked him?"

Overcome with emotion and disappointment, Kirby broke down and started to cry, not able to speak for a moment.

There was a pause on the other end of the line at first. Then Myla began to speak again, her voice filled with concern and alarm. "Kirby? Are you okay?"

"No, but I'll survive. I didn't mean to hurt him. Despite everything, I still loved Jake. I tried to tell him—"

"Oh my God, Kirby. You're scaring me. You choked Jake? Where is he?"

"I guess he's still at home. I don't know. Oh…he probably left to meet his family by now. They were taking him to brunch for his birthday."

"So Jake's okay?"

"Yeah. I think he's fine."

Myla sighed heavily on the other end of the line. "Oh, thank God. For a second there I thought you were telling me that you had killed him or something. Seriously…you nearly gave me a heart attack, Kirby."

"No, I didn't kill him, but I nearly killed him."

There was another pause on the line between them momentarily. Kirby sniffled a few times and then got up to grab some tissue.

"So where do you go from here?" Myla asked softly.

"I don't know. I feel like killing myself right now."

"Kirby, don't say that. Why would you say that?"

"Because I do. I just want to roll over and die right now. I hate myself. I just feel so low right now, like I'm not good enough…for anything or anyone."

"What are you talking about? You have a deal with GTV right now to produce your first TV pilot. You have so much going for you—"

"But even with the pilot, I feel like it's Jeff who's getting all of the attention and the credit. They treat me like I'm just a fucking understudy even though the show's mostly my idea, and I wrote most of the script."

"That's probably because they know him better. He's already produced a couple of pilots before, hasn't he? I'm sure everything will change once—"

"You know what Jake said?" Kirby asked, interrupting Myla and not really paying attention to what she was telling him. "He said that Reggie's a better lover than me and that he could teach me a thing or two in the bedroom. I mean, seriously? I still can't believe he hooked up with that dude. I can't get over that."

"Kirby, listen. Hear me out. You've got to get past that. Get that out of your mind and move on. You're smart. You're attractive. You have a family that loves and supports you. You have great friends. You have a great network of contacts in the industry. You're twenty-seven and you're producing a freakin' TV show. I mean, come on. That's amazing! You've got so much going for you. You're going places. You can't allow this setback with Jake to take you down, to keep you from moving forward. Some relationships last and some don't. That's life. Some people come into our lives for a reason, for a specific purpose—to help us grow, to challenge us, to struggle with us, to teach us something about ourselves we didn't know before."

"I'm not sure I know right now what this experience with Jake has taught me, though."

"Well, I guess, for one, that you're capable of loving a man and loving him hard. I've known you since we were in diapers. Jake is the first person you've ever admitted to being in love with. After all of the girls you've dated over the years, I would have never in my wildest dreams thought that the person you'd love and want to be with the most would be another guy."

"Well, now I really know. He doesn't love me back. Not anymore."

"Do you think Jake ever really loved you?"

"I thought so."

"Hmmm," Myla uttered, sounding doubtful. "I know its cliché to say, but there are plenty of fish in the sea. While Jake's trying to figure out who he is and what he wants, it's time for you to find a man who's worthy of you and of everything that you have to offer. You deserve that, Kirby. You deserve to have someone who will love you back openly and completely and not try to keep you tucked away and hidden in a closet like you're some kind of secret sex toy with no feelings or emotions. I think Jake was objectifying you. Using you for sexual exploitation when it was convenient for him while maintaining this straight, frat boy façade because that's what he thinks he needs to do to get ahead and maintain his status and position. Now it looks like he's found someone else to objectify. And clearly he has a type. He goes from you to this guy Reggie? I don't know. It seems like Jake has a particular craving for chocolate, if you ask me."

A craving? An object for sexual exploitation? That's not what Kirby wanted to hear. He knew his cousin was trying to cheer him up and provide a booster shot to his self-esteem, but he was too upset and distracted to talk with her any further.

"Hey, listen. I have another call coming through," Kirby lied. "It's Jeff. We're taping the pilot tomorrow, and I'm sure he wants to go over a few last-minute things. I'll call you back later. Love you. Bye."

Kirby ended the call feeling even more distressed. Deep down, he had truly believed that Jake loved him once, but now he had doubts. Jake had put up such resistance to the idea of them being together romantically as a real couple, and then he brazenly admitted to hooking up with Reggie with such braggadocio. Kirby wondered if perhaps he had been objectified by Jake—used by him to fulfill a secret sexual fantasy, to satisfy a fetish. Myla had a point. Jake had moved on to another guy, another black guy who worked out and had a nice physique just like Kirby. Maybe it simply was only about the sex, his body, and the size of his endowment all along, Kirby thought. The expression of love during the act was, perhaps, just pretend, merely a part of the fantasy Jake had used him for.

It was an extreme view for Kirby to take on his long relationship with Jake, but the view was now more uncertain and unclear than ever before. It made Kirby question everything he thought he knew. The idea that he was nothing more than a sex object to Jake made him feel like shit and less than human. The feeling of rejection was made worse by the belief that Jake had perhaps lied to Kirby about him being the only guy he'd ever been with before Reggie. Memories of Jake and Will together, horsing around in a suggestive, homoerotic way at the bachelor party in Las Vegas, resurfaced in Kirby's thoughts. It made him angry, sad, and confused. Maybe he didn't know Jake as well as he'd thought. And the idea that someone else had touched Jake and loved on him the way Kirby had, for so long, was too much to take. Even worse, the thought that Reggie had entered Jake, fucked him at Jake's invitation, felt like a dagger straight to the heart. Kirby had always believed that intercourse would be an experience reserved for him and him alone if Jake had ever decided he wanted to go that far with another man. Now Kirby felt robbed. He felt cheated out of what he thought was his to have. He knew he didn't own and control Jake, but his sense of possessiveness over him and his body could be intoxicating. The idea of Jake and Reggie together sexually crippled Kirby with such intense jealousy that he felt rejected; he felt weak; he felt played; he felt betrayed; he felt like a bitch. And he hated himself for having those feelings, for allowing himself to be turned out like that by a man. It wounded his pride, but he couldn't help it. He loved Jake too much.

Disconsolate and overcome with so many conflicting emotions, Kirby lay on his bed, flat on his back, and then took the pillow, pressed it to his face, and screamed. It muffled his loud cry. He wanted to smother himself and tried to do so, but it required more energy and effort than he was exerting. He came close but ultimately didn't have the will. He threw the pillow aside, then curled into a fetal position and wept until he fell asleep.

Chapter Fifteen

After he'd cooled off, Jake felt terrible about the way things went down with Kirby. The fight was not what he had expected or wanted but, already on edge before their clash occurred, Jake felt that he had gotten sucked into it. That Kirby had provoked him. When he awoke and prepared himself to leave for work Monday morning, he nearly called Kirby to express regret for his part in their altercation and apologize for punching him. He also wanted to set the record straight and inform Kirby that things were not as they'd seemed between him and Reggie. However, Jake decided to let it go, at least for now. *Save it for another time*, Jake concluded. He wanted to stay focused on the task at hand—taking the necessary steps to reunite with Amanda.

Jake had checked his voice messages and emails throughout the weekend to see if Rick had responded to his call, but he hadn't heard back from him. After he'd arrived to work, Jake waited until noon to phone Rick again.

"Good afternoon, Climent Partners," a female voice answered on the other end of the line.

"Hi. Good afternoon. This is Jake Doyle. I believe I might've spoken to you last week—"

"Oh, yes. Hi, Jake. How are you?"

"I'm fine, and you?"

"I'm doing great. Thanks for asking."

"I haven't heard back from Rick, and thought I'd try reaching him again. I don't mean to come across as pushy, but it's kind of urgent, and I was hoping to speak with him as soon as possible."

"Well, I did pass along your message. He's not in the office right now, but I'll be sure to let him know that you called again and that it's urgent."

"Uh…okay. I really appreciate it. Thank you. Bye for now."

"Bye, Jake."

Jake felt tempted to ask her if he should try calling Rick on his cell phone. However, he didn't ask the question, thinking that the assistant likely would've given Rick the heads-up. Jake's suspicion had grown over the weekend that Rick might be avoiding him and likely wouldn't return his call. Without any further hesitation or thought about it, Jake began to dial Rick's cell number, hoping to catch him off guard, without his gatekeeper. The phone rang three times before an automated voice answered and requested the name of the caller.

"Jake Doyle," he said back robotically.

"One moment, please, as I try to locate the person you are calling," the automated voice said. A symphonic melody played in the background as Jake sat and waited apprehensively.

After nearly sixty seconds, the automated voice returned. "I'm sorry, but the subscriber you are trying to reach is not available. Please leave a message after the tone."

Now annoyed, Jake sighed and shook his head. "Hello, Rick. This is Jake Doyle. I've left a couple of messages with your office recently but decided to call you directly on your cell in case you didn't receive them. I know a lot of time has passed since we last spoke, but I've had second thoughts about my decision to break off my engagement to Amanda. I wanted to talk with you about it. I know how busy you are, but I'd be most appreciative if you could call me back at your earliest convenience."

After he left his message, Jake walked down the hall to the break room to grab a bottle of water from the refrigerator.

"There you are. I think this is the first time I've seen you all day," Julie said as she too stepped into the breakroom and retrieved a bottle of water from the fridge.

"Oh. Hey. How are you?"

"I'm fine. So how was your party, birthday boy? It was at The Cottage in Santa Monica, right?"

"Yeah. It was great. We had a lot of fun. There were about thirty-five, thirty-six of us altogether. We had the pool room all to ourselves and the outdoor patio adjacent to it."

"Nice. That's such a great spot, right there on Ocean Avenue with the view and everything."

"Yeah. It is."

"Well, sorry I didn't make it. I just thought it might be a little awkward now in light of our changed circumstances. I can only imagine how eager your friends must've been to meet the person with whom you were having an office fling."

"It wouldn't have been awkward. I think you would've been perfectly comfortable around my friends. They're nice people."

"Oh well, perhaps another time. Moving on to a different topic, I'm surprised you weren't on the conference call with Rick Climent this morning."

"Conference call with Rick Climent?"

"Yeah."

"Wait…you spoke with Rick Climent…this morning?"

"Yes."

"I didn't know anything about it. Who else was on the call with him?"

"Mike, Teddy, and me. He's going to be setting up an employee stock ownership plan at a couple of closely held companies, and he wants us to draw up the documents. It looks like he wants to use the ESOP to create an internal market so that he can cash out and sell his ownership stake in each company. I guess he's decided that's the best way to recoup his investment."

"And Mike asked Teddy to participate on the call?"

"I guess so. Why else would he have been there? I mean…I know that you and Teddy as second-year associates work with all of the partners in our practice group, but I would've assumed that Mike would've asked you to work with us on this since you already know Rick and have a relationship with him. I must admit I was a little surprised."

"I'm not," Jake said, dejected.

"Why? Because you broke off your engagement to his daughter?"

No, because I'm trying to get back with her, Jake thought to himself before he hurriedly walked out of there without answering her. He went back into his office and closed the door behind him. He paced back and forth for a few moments as he thought about what his next move should be. Yes, it was true. Teddy, like Jake, worked with most of the partners in the practice group on client matters. However, more often than not, Mike used only Jake. Did Mike not ask him to assist this time because he knew that it would be awkward for Rick, or did Rick tell Mike that he didn't want Jake working on his business matters any longer? Should he confront Mike head-on and ask him if he'd spoken to Rick about his intentions to reconnect with Amanda? Should he wait another day, hoping that Rick returned his call, or should he just forget about talking to Rick altogether? After all, Jake wasn't seeking Rick's permission to reach out to Amanda. He and Amanda had already been in contact with one another and had met since their breakup. On top of that, Jake knew that Rick wouldn't approve of any effort to reignite a romance with his daughter and that Rick's financial offer to stay away from her was still on the table. "What's the point?" Jake asked himself.

However, as the day progressed to evening, Jake came to conclude that it would be better to notify the Climents of his intentions in case Mike had not spoken to Rick after all. If Amanda was indeed as mentally ill as they'd claimed, he wanted to demonstrate a degree of sensitivity to their concern and worry as her parents. Therefore, Jake thought, at a minimum, he should at least send Rick and Camilla a note informing them of his change of heart. He decided he would send them a handwritten note by courier to their residence explaining the reason for his decision to reverse course. That way he could show them a degree of courtesy and assure them of his commitment to Amanda's safety and well-being without appearing to be seeking their approval or blessing to pursue her again.

Just as Jake started to pen his note, he thought, *Wait! Why not call Camilla?* It suddenly dawned on him that he could call and tell her of his change of heart. Although Rick had been the one to tell him of Amanda's alleged illness and persuaded him to cancel the wedding, he was speaking on both his and Camilla's behalf, Jake presumed. "Rick's avoiding me, so I'll just call Camilla and get this over and done with quickly. I'll call her right now," Jake said aloud to himself as he lifted his cell phone from his desk and speed-dialed her number from his contact list.

CHAPTER SIXTEEN

One of the Climents' housekeepers answered the phone when Jake called.

"Hi. Good evening. Is Camilla home?"

"Who's calling?"

"This is Jake Doyle."

"Jake Doyle?" the housekeeper repeated, sounding surprised and as if she wanted to make sure she heard him correctly.

"Yes."

Then she said delicately, "Amanda's ex?"

"That's me," Jake said as he rolled his eyes.

"Oh, oh, okay, okay. One moment please."

Jake sighed and shook his head in annoyance, thinking that Camilla would likely be just as disinclined to take his call as her husband. After a brief hold, the housekeeper returned to the line.

"Mrs. Climent not available now. What this regarding?" the woman asked sternly in a strong accent that sounded as if she were from a southeast Asian country like Thailand, Cambodia, or the Philippines.

"Is she home?" Jake asked in frustration. "Can you just put her on the phone?"

"She not available now. What this regarding, please?"

"It's about Amanda."

"Amanda? What about her? What do you want?"

Jake grew impatient. "Would you please just put Camilla on the phone? This is a private, personal matter that I'm not going to sit here and discuss with you."

"Okay, okay. Wait…one moment please."

Jake could hear a shuffling sound on the other end of the line. It seemed as if the woman was trying to mute the phone with her hand, but Jake could faintly hear her speaking to someone before her voice trailed off into silence. "He says it's private matter…."

The shuffling sound continued and Jake could hear voices again, but he couldn't quite make out what was being said until finally, he heard a voice he recognized.

"Give me the phone…just give me phone," Jake heard Camilla say.

"Hellooo," Camila sang in her characteristically polite, aristocratic manner.

"Hello, Camilla. It's Jake."

"Well…hello, Jake. How unexpected it is to hear from you."

"Indeed, it's been a while, but I appreciate you taking my call. I hope that you've been well."

"Why, thank you. That's very kind of you to say. So…to what do I owe, shall I say, the surprise of this call?"

"Well, I don't want to take much of your time, but I have something important to tell you. I've been trying to reach Rick but haven't been successful, so I thought I'd try you instead."

"What is it?"

"When I decided to call off the wedding and break off my engagement to Amanda, I did so hastily because it felt like the situation was urgent and called for immediate action. However, with the passage of time and deeper introspection, I now feel that what I did was a mistake."

"A mistake?"

"Yes, a mistake. I love Amanda, Camilla. At the time I thought I was doing what was best for her…to keep her safe…to keep her from harm. But after seeing her appear so happy and her normal self these past six months, I now feel that we could've weathered any storm she faced together as a married couple."

"Wait a minute. I don't understand. What are you saying? You broke up with Amanda willingly—"

"Yes, I did. But to be perfectly honest with you, I feel like I was a little misled."

"Misled?"

"Yes. I do. I know that you and Rick have your concerns and only want to protect Amanda, but if she can live a happy and normal life with Adam, why can't she do that with me?"

Camilla snickered. "I think you should ask yourself that question. You dumped my daughter and then ran off with another man."

"Camilla, despite what you may have heard, I did not run off with another man. I made mistakes during my relationship with Amanda, big mistakes, but I'm still in love with her, and I intend to win her back. That's what I wanted you and Rick to know. I know you're worried about her mental health, but so am I, and I will do whatever it takes to help her stay happy and well, so that she can continue to lead a normal life."

Camilla balked. "Jake, you're the last thing Amanda needs for her mental health. You're a liar and a cheat. Sleeping with your best friend the whole time you were with my daughter. Are you kidding me? You have a lot of nerve...calling here to tell me you love my daughter and want her back after you left her to be with another man."

"Camilla, that's not why I left Amanda and you know it. I did what you and Rick wanted."

"What Rick and I wanted? What are you talking about?"

"What do you mean, what am I talking about?"

"You're speaking nonsense. Your deceitfulness has nothing to do with Rick and me. You were cheating on my daughter, for God's sake. With another man. And then you dumped her right before the wedding."

"Why are you acting like you're so surprised that happened? That the wedding was canceled? You had a hand in that."

"What?" Camilla yelled. "Jake, I don't know what the hell you're talking about, but I think you're completely nuts, to be honest…."

"Camilla, you and Rick told me to break up with Amanda because she's supposedly sick," Jake yelled back in an attempt to interrupt Camilla, but she didn't appear to catch what he said as she continued to yell over him furiously.

"You're nuts! Amanda doesn't want you back, Jake. How dare you, to think you can just waltz your way back into her life and into our family after what you did. Amanda's much better off without you. Haven't you noticed? She's been all over the press. You're wasting your time. Leave her alone and move on with your life already. And please don't call here again. Neither of us, Rick nor I, is interested in speaking with you or having anything to do with you ever again, so back off," Camilla said before slamming the phone down.

Jake sat there at his desk, dumbfounded. He didn't expect Camilla to welcome him back with open arms. In fact, he anticipated her scorn and disapproval. In his mind, he was only trying to do the right thing by informing the Climents that he was breaking what he'd thought was a mutual agreement between them that he not marry Amanda. Camilla's refusal to acknowledge that point during their call, however, raised questions in his mind. Had Rick acted alone? The person who likely knew the answer to that question worked right down the hall. Jake impulsively walked out of his office to find Mike Wallace without recognizing the fact that the hour had grown late and most people had already left the office for the day. Jake could see that Mike's door was closed, but he proceeded to knock on it anyway. There was no answer.

Jake decided to head home himself. Just as he was about to take the elevator down to the garage, his phone rang. Seeing who it was on his caller ID, Jake answered it.

"Hey, Dad."

"Jake, where are you?" Tom's tone was solemn and serious.

"I'm leaving the office now to head home."

"Uh…there's something…we need to talk…right away."

"Is everything okay?"

Tom sighed heavily before he answered—the stress in his voice apparent from the very start. "Actually…no, things are not okay. Can you drop by the house on your way home?"

"Okay. What's going on?"

"It's something I'd rather not discuss over the phone. We'll tell you when you get here."

Chapter Seventeen

Jake drove toward his parents' house in Windsor Square. He wondered what was so urgent and foreboding that it made his father unwilling to offer even a clue over the phone. *Did someone die? Maybe it's Harry. He's been in an accident*, Jake thought as his mind raced with one dark thought after another. Jake issued a voice command to his phone.

"Call Harry Doyle."

The phone rang several times before going to Harry's voicemail. "Harry, it's Jake. Call me back right away. Got an awkward call from Dad. Something's wrong, and he wants me to come to the house. I just left the office. He wouldn't tell me what it was. Thought you might know something. Anyway, call me back. Okay? Bye."

A few seconds later, Jake tried again. "Call Harry Doyle."

Still no answer. Only voicemail. Jake began to panic. "Oh my God. It's Harry. Something's happened," he said aloud to himself. Jake was tempted to call Harry's girlfriend but decided against it out of an abundance of caution. He didn't want to cause any undue alarm based on nothing more than wild imaginings.

Jake pulled up to his parents' house, which looked unusually dark. The lights that led up the brick steps of the sloping lawn to the front door were off, as were the exterior lamps that graced each side of the large wood-framed door of the English Tudor home.

Distracted with ominous thoughts, Jake rang the doorbell before remembering he had a key. He opened the door to let himself in. The lights in the entry hall and front rooms were off, but there was enough light coming from the kitchen in the back to see. Tom emerged just as Jake started to make his way in that direction. Tom didn't say anything at first as he walked toward Jake.

"Why are all the lights off?" Jake asked.

Tom flipped the switch to the entry hall lights but didn't answer him.

"For a second there I thought nobody was home."

"We're here," Tom said, sounding melancholy.

Tom's demeanor combined with the dark, quiet energy of the house spelled gloom in Jake's mind.

"Where's Mom?" Jake asked as he followed Tom into the living room.

"She's here…in the study."

"Is she coming out? You said you both needed to speak with me."

Tom sighed as he blinked rapidly a couple of times, appearing to fight back tears. "I don't think she wants to face you."

"Why, Dad? What's going on? You're scaring me."

"I don't even know where to begin," Tom said.

Jake stared at Tom for a moment before asking, "Is it Harry?"

"No, Harry's fine."

Growing impatient with Tom's hesitation and lack of forthrightness, Jake raised his palms with an expression on his face that said, *WTF!*

"So…you know when you told me about that meeting you had with Reverend O'Mahoney?"

"Yes."

"Well…there appears to be something to his story."

"What are you talking about?"

"He called and wanted to speak with Mom last week. She wasn't home, so I took the message and told her that he'd called. A couple days later I asked her if she had called him back and she didn't give me a straight answer. She was being kind of vague about whether she had or not. At first, I didn't think anything of it, but then I thought about what you'd told me concerning the conversation you'd had with him, so I decided to call him back. I wanted to know if everything was all right and see if there was something I needed to know. I couldn't figure out why he and Mom were talking and why she was being so evasive about it."

"Dad, I'm sorry, but can you get to the point?"

"I am. I'm getting there," Tom said with nervous energy. He cleared his throat and looked off to the side before returning his gaze to Jake. "So I called him and asked him if everything was okay and...I don't even know why I'm going into this level of detail, but long story short is..." Tom paused again as he sighed and ran his hands through his perfectly trimmed and neat blond hair with its streaks of gray throughout.

"What, Dad? Just tell me."

"...your mother had an affair...years ago, before you were born, and there's a possibility, ever so slight in my view, that I'm not your biological father."

Jake's mouth fell open and his face immediately flushed as he stared at Tom in stunned silence. Tom stared back at him and waited, allowing Jake to absorb the weight of his words.

After a few passing seconds, Jake managed to speak. He was beyond incredulous. "You might not be my father? That can't be possible," he said with a hint of anger and disbelief in his tone.

"I'm not even convinced myself that it's true. I am your father...no matter what. But I felt you needed know and that you should hear about this from us and not somebody else. We'll do DNA testing and resolve this once and for all. Put it to rest."

"This is crazy. I can't believe what I'm hearing right how. So what does Reverend O have to do with this?"

"That's where the story gets a little murky and all the more unbelievable. Your mother did meet with him before your wedding...to admit to having the affair."

"Did you know about the affair?"

"No. I didn't. She went to Reverend O to admit to having the affair but also to reveal the name of the person she'd had the affair with."

"And this is the guy who might be my real father?"

Tom didn't answer Jake. He just looked at him grimly with his thin lips locked tightly together. His mouth trembled slightly and small beads of sweat began to appear across his forehead.

"Who is it? Do you know him?"

Tom sighed. "Yes…I do, and so do you."

"I know him?"

"Yes."

"Who?"

"Rick. Rick Climent."

"Rick…Climent?" Jake slowly repeated. "Am I in the *Twilight Zone* right now?"

"Frankly, it feels like that for me, too, but you know that your mother and Rick have a history. Little did I know that they had rekindled things shortly after we had gotten married."

"This is fucking crazy. You have got to be shitting me right now. You're telling me that all this time I'd been dating my freakin'…half-sister?"

"This will all likely turn out to be entirely spurious—"

"But how could this happen? How come nothing was ever said before now?"

"Your mother was too afraid to tell you…to tell me, even."

"This is insane. Where is she? Where the fuck is she?" Jake demanded as he started to walk out of the living room to find Jamie. However, just as he stepped into the entry hall, there she stood. She had been leaning up against the wall, quietly listening.

"Jake," she said softly, sorrowfully, as tears streamed down her face.

"How could you?" Jake yelled. "How could you allow this to happen… to let this go on for so long and not tell me?"

"I wanted to protect you."

"Protect me, or were you trying to protect yourself?" Jake said, looking at her with a cutting glare, feeling contempt.

Jamie reached and grabbed Jake by the arm to plead with him. "I never thought you'd meet Amanda. I never thought your paths would ever cross. I tried to break you up numerous times. You know that. I did everything I could to persuade you not to see her—"

"Give me a fucking break. You did everything you could except tell the truth," Jake said as he yanked his arm from his mother's grip. Jake placed both hands to his face and turned away from her before he continued to speak with agony and disbelief in his voice. "Oh my God, I feel sick to my stomach right now. I can't believe this is happening."

When he turned back around, Jamie walked up to him, her face wet with tears. She placed her hands softly to his chest. "Jake…I'm so sorry—"

Jake pushed her hands away. "Mom…seriously…get off me."

Jamie persisted in her attempt to demonstrate remorse and regret. "Jake, you know how much I love you. I made a bad choice. I know there are no words to justify what I did. I just wanted to keep our family together…to keep everyone happy."

Tom stood and watched quietly. He folded his arms and shook his head in disappointment as Jamie continued to talk.

"I felt so ashamed of what I'd done. I just thought that it would be best to put it behind me and never speak of it again. I kept this secret—the affair, the possibility of Rick being your father—to myself because I never wanted you to feel tainted or scarred in any way by my mistake. I didn't want Tom to think that you belonged to anyone other than him, to think that you weren't his son fully and completely. Please forgive me…I'm so sorry—"

As Jamie reached to touch Jake again, he stepped away from her. "Mom, please! Sorry isn't good enough. Not right now. So all this time, during college and law school and during our engagement, you would say all this shit about Amanda, how she wasn't good enough for me, that she was too superficial, too spoiled, that she lacked talent—none of which was true—but you said all that to get me to stop seeing her instead of simply coming clean and admitting the truth? I mean…don't you think it's borderline sociopathic to have allowed your son to date a girl who might very well be his half-sister? First of all, I can't even believe that it's true, but if it is…for God's sake, we could've ended up having a child together. Do you realize how fucking crazy that is?"

Tears continued to stream down Jamie's face as she struggled to come up with the right words to say, but she had little to offer up. "Jake…I know I owe you more than an apology. No words could ever explain away or justify what I've done. I was just trying to keep our family together, to keep you all from being damaged by my poor judgment. I know I've failed you as a mother. I don't know what else to do. I'm so sorry…."

As Jamie's tears morphed into a full-blown sob, Jake felt numb to his mother's humiliation. He was so full of bewilderment and disbelief that there was no space left for compassion in that moment. Instead, he started piecing things together in his head, namely the ostensible circumstances under which he was asked to leave Amanda.

Jake looked at Jamie intensely with a furrowed brow as he quickly connected the dots. "Does Rick know that I might be his son?"

As Jamie wiped her face with her hands, she muffled her response through sniffles.

However, Jake couldn't quite make out if that was a yes, so he asked again in a firmer tone. The irritation in his voice was apparent. "Does Rick know?"

"Yes, yes…Rick knows," Jamie said as if the words were being pushed out of her mouth involuntarily.

"How long has he known? Since I was a kid?"

"No. I didn't tell him until shortly before you were about to get married. He knew nothing before then."

Jake's eyes widened with amazement. "Holy shit! Then you must know that he was behind my breakup with Amanda. The story he told me, that's a lie, isn't it?"

Jamie frowned. "I don't know what you're talking about."

"Don't lie to me. For God's sake, you've told enough lies already. You were in on this. You knew—"

"Yes, I knew…I mean, I had told Rick that you might be his son and that we needed to do something to stop you and Amanda from marrying, but I don't know what he said to you or what he did. He said that he would handle it, so I let him. I assumed he paid you off—"

"Oh, so you just assumed that he paid me off?" Jake said sarcastically. "You really think I'm shallow like that?"

"No, no. That's not what I meant. He called and told me that you had agreed to call off the wedding. He didn't tell me what he had offered you or how he'd convinced you do it. To be perfectly honest, I didn't dwell on it much. I was just relieved that it worked, but then—"

Jake trembled with anger. "Do you want to know what he told me? What he and Mike Wallace told me?"

"What does Mike have to do with this?" Tom interjected upon hearing his best friend's name.

"Mike was involved, Dad. I guess you wouldn't have known. Everything was kept strictly confidential, but he's Rick lawyer, or at least one of his lawyers. Mike was the first person to approach me about breaking up with Amanda. Rick asked him to do it."

"Really?" Jamie said with surprise at this news.

"So what did he tell you?" Tom asked.

"They said that Amanda suffers from multiple personality disorder."

Jamie balked, appearing completely stunned.

"Yeah…exactly," Jake retorted in response to the expression of befuddlement on both Tom's and Jamie's faces.

"So Rick told you nothing about this?" Jake said, looking at Jamie.

Jamie didn't verbally respond. The perplexity in her face said it all.

"First Mike told me. Well…he didn't exactly tell me what she allegedly had. He just said that it was a very serious, life-threatening illness and told me that the Climents thought it was in Amanda's best interest for me to call everything off and break up with her. Of course, I refused at first, so then Mike, Rick, and I met at The California Club, and that's when they said Amanda had an alter ego named Maggie who was threatening to harm her if she got married. Supposedly, Maggie is a twin sister Amanda had and that I never knew anything about—who died when they were still kids from some rare blood cancer. They said Amanda was so traumatized by her twin's death that she started acting as if she were Maggie while she was still a child and has continued to do so off and on throughout her life, but in a detrimental way."

"Did you ever see any signs of this...split personality?"

"That's the thing, Dad. Not at all. They said she only acts out this way around her family, mostly Rick and Camilla. I couldn't believe it when they told me, but then they said that when Amanda becomes Maggie, she harms herself, and that Maggie was threatening to harm Amanda, to kill her if she married me, because she was jealous of me and felt like I was taking Amanda away from her."

"That's the most outlandish story I think I've ever heard," Tom said.

"I know it is, but then they pointed out that when Amanda was in boarding school at Cate, she became anorexic after she'd gotten involved with this dude she'd started dating. She became so severely sick that she had to be admitted to a treatment facility."

"And you know that to be a fact?" Tom said.

"Yes. That is true. Amanda told me that she had suffered from anorexia during boarding school and received treatment for it. The surprise to me was hearing from Rick and Mike that the reason she became that way was because Maggie was, quote, 'starving' Amanda because she didn't like that she was this guy Raoul. They told me that Maggie was now threatening to harm Amanda again if she proceeded to marry me. I know it sounds really crazy, but they were so convincing and the situation seemed so dire and grave. That's how they made it sound, that it was urgent, and time was of the essence to act quickly."

"Oh my God. How bizarre," Jamie finally managed to say, sounding and looking genuinely astonished.

Tom looked to her to clarify what she knew. "So Rick told you that he'd handle getting Jake to call off the wedding but didn't give you any indication of how he planned to do it?"

"No. Absolutely not. I mean...I trusted him to a certain extent, but he said nothing of getting Mike involved. I thought he'd offer you money," she said, looking at Jake.

"Well, he did. He told me this story and offered me money to walk away and keep quiet about everything. That would be my compensation, so to speak, for taking the fall and looking like a jerk for dumping Amanda at the last minute."

Tom widened his eyes, his curiosity obvious. "How much did he offer?"

"Five million."

"Oh," Jamie said as she raised her eyebrows in amazement. However, it was unclear if she was amazed because she thought it was a good offer or a lowball offer. Tom, on the other hand, was more clear and unambiguous in expressing his opinion.

"That cheap son of a bitch. He should've offered you fifty million," he said, gritting his teeth. "I can't believe Mike was in on this."

"I must admit, that was clever to get Mike involved," Jamie said.

Tom turned to look at her with scorn. "So this whole thing has to be a lie. That's what they told Jake to get him to call off the wedding. Rick, like you, didn't want to have to tell the truth and admit to the affair he'd had with you, so you conspired with him to concoct this ridiculous scheme, which, at the end of the day made Jake look like the biggest prick on the planet for dumping his bride at the last minute. How could you have let our son suffer like this?"

"Tom, I swear, I had no knowledge of this. I knew that Rick would speak with Jake and try to get him to end his relationship with Amanda, but I didn't know anything about this story and about Mike's involvement."

"It really doesn't matter that you didn't know. What matters is that you deliberately conspired to deceive Jake and you let him take the fall for your indiscretion. You say you wanted to spare him any harm from your mistake and yet you laid the burden of it squarely on his shoulders so you wouldn't have to suffer any consequences for your actions—so you could maintain your squeaky-clean, morally upright image, which we now know for certain is a complete fraud. I can't believe that you could be so heartless and so…utterly bankrupt of any sense of moral culpability in all of this."

"I do feel morally culpable. I do, I do," Jamie cried.

"But it's too damn late. Don't you see? The damage is done. Our son was made to look bad after breaking up with a girl he probably shouldn't have been engaged to in the first place. Had you told him, told all of us, the truth from the very beginning, this whole fiasco could have been avoided. We could have at least determined paternity years ago, but you allowed this to go on for so long without saying anything. As I've said, I have my doubts, but what if Jake and Amanda turn out to be half siblings after all? What if they'd had a child together?"

Jamie's face turned white. She covered it with her hands in shame and sighed hard before she spoke. "They did."

"What do you mean, 'They did'?"

Jamie burst into sobs again. "Amanda was pregnant."

"Amanda was pregnant?" Jake said with alarm.

"She miscarried. Oh God, I'm so sorry. Please forgive me."

Jake's anger quickly turned to heartbreak and disbelief. He became overcome with emotion. "She miscarried? When? How do you know this?"

"Rick told me right after you broke up with her. She was already pregnant and dealing with morning sickness a few days leading up to the wedding."

"Oh my God," Jake said as he slapped his hands to his forehead in disbelief, recalling that indeed, Amanda, had not been feeling well just days before their scheduled nuptials.

"Rick said that she miscarried after about five weeks. It was in October."

"Jamie," Tom said with resignation. He needed to say no more. It was as if his profound disappointment in his wife and her secrets was beyond the utterance of any additional words.

"Oh, no…no…no…no…." Jake moaned, turning to walk away as he rubbed his hands through his hair and held his head in anguish and despair.

CHAPTER EIGHTEEN

Amanda was on the hunt for an apartment to lease while she was in New York. She was leaning toward a place in the East Village where her best pal Lucy lived. Amanda loved her condo in LA, but the more time she spent in New York, the more she contemplated moving there permanently. After all, that's where her business was based, and as the fashion capital, New York was where she hoped to make her mark. In the aftermath of her breakup with Jake and her lost pregnancy, Amanda's focus had shifted from being a wife and mother to being a full-time entrepreneur and business woman. Her Novel handbag line had quickly become her number-one priority. Adam had a place in New York, too, and traveled all the time anyway, so she figured a potential relocation wouldn't hamper their budding relationship.

It was just before noon, and Amanda had a handful of apartment viewings that had been lined up by her real estate agent. Amanda had arrived right on time for her first viewing—a newly renovated walkup just steps from Union Square. On the way over, the agent had called to inform Amanda that he was running a few minutes late. However, he'd arranged to have the building's super let her into the unit so she wouldn't be delayed.

Amanda walked through the bright, airy space alone. She liked what she saw and began to imagine herself living there. She'd had gotten so caught up in her thoughts about how she'd decorate the place that she almost didn't notice her ringing phone. She decided to answer it when she saw who it was on the caller ID.

"Hey, Mom."

Camilla got straight to the point. "Guess who called me yesterday?"

"Who?" Amanda asked curious and eager to know.

"Jake!"

"Jake?"

"You won't believe. I am so beside myself. I almost didn't tell you but I couldn't help it. I figured you needed to be warned."

"What did he want?"

Camilla huffed in her demonstrative, haughty way before she answered. "To tell me that he regretted his decision to break up with you and that it was the wrong choice to make and that he wants to get back together with you. Can you believe that? The nerve of him to call here after what he did…"

Taken aback and completely caught by surprise, Amanda didn't say anything initially. She just listened in stunned silence as her mother ranted.

"…sleeping with his friend Kirby while carrying on a relationship with you. He tried to say that had nothing to do with his decision, and then he said something about doing what Rick and I wanted him to do."

That caught Amanda's attention. "What you and Dad wanted? What's that supposed to mean?"

"I have no idea. I told him he was out of his mind. He might've even been a little drunk or stoned for all I know."

Jake…stoned? Amanda frowned at the notion. Jake drank, but he hadn't done drugs for as long as she had known him. However, this wasn't the time to challenge her mother over such triviality as Camilla continued her train of thought on the other end of the line.

"I mean, think about it. Why would he call me? Why does he need to tell me this? Did he think I would help him out or be sympathetic? That I would try to help facilitate a reunion between you two or something? How stupid could he be?"

"But why would he think that you and Dad wanted him to break up with me? How weird," Amanda said aloud contemplatively.

"I literally have no idea what he's talking about. We always treated him with warmth, kindness, and generosity, unlike how that goody-two-shoes mother of his treated you. We were supportive of you two getting married from the start…the whole time. We nearly spent more than two million dollars on your wedding, for Christ's sake."

"This is so weird. I don't understand why he called you. What did he expect you to say or do?"

"Exactly! That's my point."

"So did he say anything about why he regretted breaking up with me?"

"Oh! Yes! He's jealous of you and Adam. That's basically what it boils down to. He sees how happy you are and how well you're doing and wants back in on the action. I guess he misses the limelight. Who knows? He sees that he had a good thing in the palm of his hands and then tossed it aside. Now he wants it back. No way. I don't think so, pal."

Amanda sighed in frustration. She had moved on and was now fully engaged in her business partnership with Lucy and excited for their soon-to-be-launched handbag line. On top of that, her romance with Adam was intensifying. She was slowly but surely beginning to see herself with him long-term, no longer viewing Adam as simply the Hollywood playboy with whom she was having a sordid affair. She now saw herself as his girlfriend and had begun to reimagine their relationship as that of husband and wife potentially and a Hollywood power couple in the making. But she found Jake's overture to her mother confusing, frustrating, and intriguing all at once. She had worked so hard to suppress any remnants of feeling or attachment to Jake, but this news made her feel a certain level of glee.

"So he misses me, huh? Good. He should," Amanda said.

"So he hasn't tried calling you yet?"

"No. Not at all."

"If he does—"

"If he does," Amanda quickly said over her mother, "I'll tell him the same thing I've told him before. We're over. Done. End of story."

"You never told him about the baby, did you?"

"No. Of course not," Amanda said as if that were obvious.

"Okay, just asking."

"And I never intend to. There's absolutely no reason for him to know about that at this point. How would I tell him that? Can you imagine the conversation? 'No, Jake I don't want to get back together with you. And…oh…by the way, I was pregnant with your baby but I miscarried. Sorry. Just thought you'd want to know that. Now fuck off.'"

On the verge of tears, Amanda's voice cracked when she said the last few sentences. She was surprised at her emotion. Imagining telling Jake that the baby they'd so frequently talked about and dreamed of having together died before birth caused the pain of it all to resurface. Amanda didn't want her mother to detect her momentary sadness, so she acted interrupted.

"Oh…Mom, my agent's here. He just walked in the door." He hadn't.

"Agent?"

"I'm looking at an apartment in the East Village right now."

"Oh. Have you found something you like?"

"I think so. Okay, gotta go, Mom. I'll call you back later to fill you in. Bye now," Amanda said hurriedly before Camilla could get in another word edgewise.

After she ended the call, Amanda's eyes watered as she stood there alone in the empty space. She walked over to the large windows that overlooked a picturesque park across the street and noticed children playing as their mothers stood around watching and chatting among themselves. For a moment, Amanda felt the urge to be there with the other young mothers. That's what she had pictured herself doing after marrying Jake. Having his babies and being a doting mother to their children. But then she had to look away to force herself to disengage from that fantasy.

"It's too late, Jake. It's too late," Amanda said as she wiped away tears from her eyes and resumed her inspection of the apartment.

Chapter Nineteen

"Law offices, this is Patti."

"Hey, Patti. Jake."

"Hey, how are you this morning?"

"To be perfectly honest, not well. I feel shitty, actually."

"Uh-oh. What's up?"

Jake's voice was heavy and distressed. "It's a long, sordid story. I really can't go into any details, but it's kind of a personal family matter."

"Oh no. Is everything okay?"

"No, not really. I won't be coming into the office today."

"Oh my goodness, Jake. Is there anything I can do?"

"No, but thanks for asking."

"What do you want me to tell people?"

"I need to accompany my dad somewhere today, so if anyone really needs to know, just tell them that I needed to take the day off due to an urgent family matter."

"Okay. I'm so sorry. If there's anything I can do, please let me know."

"Thanks, Patti. I'll be all right. I should be back in the office tomorrow."

Jake actually wanted to head into the office that morning and confront Mike right away about the story he'd sold him about Amanda's alleged mental illness. However, Tom had convinced Jake to hold off until they'd taken the paternity test later that day. Jake was now certain that the mental illness story was nothing more than a tall tale devised to cover up the truth. It had worked, but Jake couldn't help but to feel a bit foolish and gullible. At the same time, however, he felt deep resentment and anger toward Mike. He had known Mike since he was a child, and other than his own father, Mike was his closest mentor and professional advisor. How Mike could participate in a scheme to cover up the truth and lie to Jake's face was something neither Jake nor Tom could comprehend.

A few hours later, Tom arrived to pick up Jake. He called Jake on his cell to let him know that he was waiting downstairs in the car. Tom had secured a time for them to do DNA testing at a private lab.

Jake made it outside and hopped into the waiting car without saying anything at first. Although he had spoken to Tom earlier that morning on the phone, it felt awkward—an awkwardness Jake had never felt before around the only man he had ever called Dad. He had a hard time believing that anyone other than Tom could be his father, but in light of his mother's admission, Jake couldn't ignore the possibility that might be the case. Given the extreme measures Jamie had taken to keep the affair a secret for so long, Jake tried to mentally prepare himself for the worst.

"How are you feeling?" Tom finally asked as he drove them toward the freeway.

Deep in thought, Jake hesitated at first. "All right…I guess. I didn't get any sleep last night."

There was a momentary silence between them. Jake looked over at Tom but quickly looked away when it appeared that Tom was about to look back at him. Jake felt sad and embarrassed for his dad. He almost asked him how he was feeling, but Jake already knew and thought it would be stupid to ask. How would any husband feel after suddenly learning that his wife had had an affair and that his firstborn might belong to another man?

Jake decided to ask a more casual question. "So where's this lab?"

"Santa Monica."

"How'd you find it?"

"Google. It's the first one I found that could take us today and provide lab results within twenty-four to forty-eight hours."

"Really? That quick? I thought it would take longer than that."

"Yeah, they're pretty quick."

Jake was relieved it wouldn't be any quicker. God forbid he'd be told right then and there, shortly after taking the tests, that Tom wasn't his biological father. What would he say to Tom? What would Tom say to him? How would he feel in that moment? Was he truly prepared to hear that Tom wasn't his father? Jake looked over at Tom again. Tears filled his eyes as he viewed Tom's profile. He looked battered and broken. A handsome man, Tom normally appeared relatively youthful, spry, and athletic for his age while maintaining a distinctively patrician bearing that was understated, subtle, and dignified. Jake took pride in being Tom Doyle's son. He not only had learned to model Tom's behavior and way of being but also idolized him—playing football at the same prep school, attending Stanford for college and law school, beginning his career at a white-shoe law firm, becoming engaged at a relatively early age, all things Tom had done before him.

Jake became overcome with emotion. He felt pain for Tom. He felt pain about the whole situation. Although Jake fought to keep the tears from falling, the heaviness of his voice revealed the depth of his emotion and feeling.

"Dad, I'm so sorry this has happened."

"Sorry? You don't need to apologize. This is not your fault, Jake."

"But you don't deserve this, and I feel really bad."

Tom reached over and patted Jake on the knee with his right hand to comfort him. "You don't need to worry about me. I'll be all right, Jake."

"I want you to know, no matter what the test results say, in my mind, you will always be my father. You are my father, dammit! And I will never see it any other way. Period. I couldn't have asked for a better dad. You taught me everything I know. Everything! Starting with the basics like how to tie my shoes, how to ride a bike, how to throw a ball and how to play every other sport, how to make friends, and then, as I got older, how to be a lawyer, how to manage relationships. You taught me the importance of building trust and loyalty in relationships. I'm probably not as good at it as you are—in fact, I know I'm not—but I wouldn't be where I am or who I am without your guidance. Whatever goodness and decency I have in me is because of you. You can never be replaced. I really don't give a damn what the lab results might say. I don't even think we need to do the paternity test, because in my mind it won't change anything about our relationship."

Tom appeared emotional and waited a few moments, seemingly to hold himself together. "Thank you, son. It means a lot to me to hear you say that. I think when I suggested last night that we do this as soon as possible, it was more to rule out that anyone else was your father other than me. I wanted you to have peace of mind. But for what it's worth, it's not important for me to do the paternity test either. You're my son. End of story."

"I'm just so angry at Mom and angry at myself for not seeing right through this…this whole lie about Amanda being sick and all. It makes sense now. Things never really added up. There were never any signs that she had a split personality, but Rick and Mike came across so sincere and made the situation seem so dire and urgent."

"You can't blame yourself for this. You did what you thought was right."

"But then I started questioning things after I noticed Amanda dating Adam."

"That's the producer you told me about?"

"Right. Rick was even willing to pay me more than five million to make sure I stayed away from her after I'd started to question why they hadn't intervened to stop her from dating Adam."

"Well, now you know why. He didn't want you snooping around for information."

"I can't believe that Amanda and I might be siblings, Dad. I can't get over that. I mean… how fucking crazy is that? We'd been sleeping together throughout most of our relationship. And then to find out that she was pregnant. Jesus Christ."

"So you didn't know anything about that before you broke up with her?"

"Not at all. I had no idea. All I remember is that right after I had gotten back from Vegas for my bachelor party, she had become a little sick and was throwing up. We thought it might be the flu, but I guess that must've been the early onset of morning sickness instead."

"That's probably right."

"You know, I hadn't yet gotten around to telling you this, but I'd been thinking about trying to get back together with her."

"With Amanda?" Tom asked skeptically.

"Yeah. That's why I'd been trying to get ahold of Rick here recently—to tell him that I had a change of heart about the whole situation."

"How do you feel about getting back together with her now?"

"Well…obviously conflicted. I can't marry my sister. Shit!" Jake said as he ran his fingers through his hair and shook his head in bewilderment. "The thought of Amanda as my sister makes me nauseated. I really can't believe that it's true. And I can't fucking believe Mom allowed this to happen and for so long. How could she do this to me? Do this to you?"

Tom's jaw tightened as he looked straight ahead, his eyes focused on the road. He didn't seem to want to discuss his wife and her behavior. He remained silent as Jake continued to talk.

"I can't even fathom what Amanda's reaction would be if she knew we might be half siblings."

"Well, finding out whether she is or not is probably a good enough reason to proceed with the DNA test."

"Yeah, I guess that's right. I'm actually more interested in knowing that than I am in knowing whether or not I'm Rick Climent's son."

"Jake, you're my son," Tom said as he reached to grab and hold Jake by the hand as he continued to drive down the freeway toward Santa Monica.

"And you're my dad," Jake said, looking back at him while squeezing Tom's hand tightly in a show of solidarity.

Chapter Twenty

Jake headed to the gym after Tom had dropped him off following their appointment. Working out would be a good stress reliever, he concluded, and it was something he did religiously anyway. Since he wasn't returning to the office until the following day, he could get to the gym earlier than he normally would and beat the after-work crowd.

"Damn," Jake said to himself when he walked through the gym doors and saw all of the people. It was fuller than he'd anticipated.

The girl working the front desk recognized Jake and greeted him cheerily. "Hey, Jake!"

"Hey, Monica," Jake said, returning her smile.

"You're awfully early, aren't you? We don't typically see you here until, like…seven or after seven, right?"

"Yeah, I took the day off, so I thought I'd get my workout done a little early today, but I can't believe how many frickin' people are here. Don't these people have jobs? Jeez."

Monica chuckled. "It's always busy here. This is actually pretty light. So are you meeting up with Kirby?"

Jake looked at her, puzzled. "Meeting up with Kirby?"

"Yeah, to work out. He just arrived, too, like, five minutes before you did. You guys still work out together, don't you?"

"No. Actually we don't anymore. I didn't know he was here, but thanks for the heads-up," Jake said as he proceeded through the turnstile with a forced smile to conceal the sudden unease and awkwardness he felt. He hadn't expected to see Kirby so soon after their big brawl. At some point, Jake had intended to apologize and express his regret to Kirby for the way things had gone down, but in that moment, that's not what he'd come prepared to do. He almost turned around to walk back outdoors but felt self-conscious about doing so, especially in front of Monica. He didn't want to seem rattled by the news that Kirby was in the building.

As he discreetly scanned the gym for a Kirby sighting, Jake made his way upstairs to the cardio area for a quick ten-minute warm-up on the treadmill. He put his earphones in and selected a song from his playlist. He then set the treadmill to manual mode and began a light run to get his heart rate up. Jake's mind raced with a myriad of thoughts—a sense of estrangement from his mother, the newfound bond and closeness he felt to his father, especially after the time they'd spent together that afternoon, his phone conversation with Camilla and her seeming lack of awareness about the plot that had unfolded to separate him from her daughter, conflicting emotions about Amanda, and now, added to the mix, apprehension about seeing Kirby. Jake took a deep breath to settle down and allowed himself to get caught up in the melody and lyrics of the song that blared in his ears.

Jake had planned to spend ten minutes doing cardio before heading downstairs to the weight area to begin lifting. He stared blankly up ahead at the TV screen hanging from the ceiling before he looked down and noticed that he had only fifty seconds left. He stopped running and began to walk briskly as he slowed the speed down on the treadmill. He looked back up at the TV screen and then scanned the room, barely turning his head to look left or right. However, from his peripheral vision, he noticed that the treadmill to his immediate right was now being used. It had been empty before. The second Jake turned his head for a quick glance, he felt as though his heart had stopped. It was Kirby, right there next to him.

Kirby turned to look back at Jake, meeting his gaze as he walked briskly on the treadmill. "Hi."

Jake pressed the stop button on his treadmill and pulled off his earphones. "Hi. I didn't even realize you were there."

"I literally just stepped on the treadmill a few seconds ago. I said hello to you but you were like in outer space or something."

"Sorry, bro. I didn't hear you. I had my music on blast. How are you?"

"I'm doing great. We shot the pilot yesterday."

"Oh, yeah? How'd it go?"

"Very well, but I'm tired, man. We worked all day yesterday and much of the weekend too. I needed to come to the gym to decompress a little."

"So what's next?"

"We're in postproduction now, editing and getting it ready to submit to the network."

"When will you know their decision whether to turn it into a series?"

"If not by next month, early May for sure."

"Wow. That's exciting, man. Congratulations again. Seriously, I really mean that. I hope it gets picked up and becomes a huge hit."

"Thanks. Appreciate it."

Jake couldn't help but notice that Kirby seemed confident and relaxed as he strutted on the treadmill with an even, steady rhythm. It was as if he and Jake hadn't gotten into a physical altercation forty-eight hours before. Jake wondered if Kirby had moved on already. Although Jake had an apology on the tip of his tongue, he felt too bruised and bowed to utter it. Kirby wasn't even looking at him anymore as he continued to walk purposefully on the treadmill, staring straight ahead as if Jake and whoever Jake might be sleeping with were trivial matters that he now could care less about. Jake felt so overcome with shame and embarrassment about his family's secret that he even felt inferior to Kirby in that moment. The guy whose heart he'd broken now appeared unaffected by him. To Jake, Kirby looked proud and accomplished—as someone on the brink of producing his first comedy show for a major TV network should feel. A total stud. In stark contrast, Jake had just visited a private lab to learn whether or not the man he'd called Dad his whole life was truly his father. The whole sordid affair was humiliating. Jake had never felt lower.

Jake stepped off his treadmill, intending not to say anything further to Kirby. "What more is there to say? I suck," Jake said to himself under his breath.

Just as Jake began to walk away, Kirby called out to him. "Jake." Kirby hit the stop button on his treadmill and stepped off it. Jake turned to face him.

"Listen, man, I just wanted to tell you that I'm sorry for choking you. I really felt bad about it afterward…bad about the whole confrontation. It shouldn't have gone down like that. I honestly just wanted to talk to you and clear the air, but my emotions got the best of me and I acted out in a way that wasn't constructive or useful in any way whatsoever. I mean… you shouldn't have punched me either, but I know that I instigated the fight. I came into your house already turned up, and I regret that. I'm sorry, man."

"I apologize, too, bro. I was planning to call you, to tell you how bad I felt. We've never fought like that before."

"I know, man. I can't recall us ever hitting, punching, or choking one another. Ever. I felt sick to my stomach afterward."

"I felt sick about it too. I'm so sorry, bro," Jake said in earnest.

Kirby scratched his chin and grinned. "You know, I must say, you've got a pretty mean right jab. Didn't know you could hit like that, bro. You nearly broke my jaw."

Jake grinned half-heartedly, feeling a little embarrassed. He looked away for a moment as he contemplated what to say next. He wanted to open up and tell Kirby what was going on with him, but he didn't know where to begin.

"Are you all right, man?" Kirby asked with a look of concern.

Jake sighed as he continued to glance away momentarily. Then he looked Kirby straight in the eye. "There's so much I need to say to you."

Kirby stared back at him but remained silent.

Jake started to vacillate as his heart raced with apprehension. "I don't want to hold you up. I know you've got a lot going on right now. We can talk later," Jake said as he started to pull away.

Kirby grabbed him by the arm and spoke softly. "Jake. Talk to me now. I've always got time for you. You know that, bro."

Jake looked around the gym, which seemed to be growing ever more crowded by the minute. "Why don't we go outside," he said.

Jake and Kirby walked downstairs to the first floor and out the front door of the gym. Jake led the way and kept walking until he reached his car, which was parked nearby on the street. "You want to sit inside?"

"Okay. Sure," Kirby replied as he walked over to the front passenger door and hopped in.

Now sitting in the driver's seat, Jake took a deep breath and sighed again before speaking. "I guess I should start with what you came to talk to me about this past weekend. Yes, it's true, I did hook up with Reggie. I hooked up with him twice. The first time was on New Year's Eve, or in the early morning hours after, to be more precise. The second time was a week later. I haven't been with him since."

Kirby looked over at him skeptically with a raised eyebrow.

"Kirby, I swear to God, I'm telling you the truth. Those were the only two times I hooked up with him."

"But why? I don't understand. You told me that you really didn't want to be with a guy, and then you go and let him fuck you?"

"Kirby, you don't understand—"

"No, you don't understand," Kirby said in a raised voice dripping with emotion. "That hurt me, man. And what you said back at your apartment about Reggie being better in the sack and shit—"

"Kirby," Jake repeated to interrupt hm. "He didn't fuck me. I never let him fuck me. Okay? I just said that to make you mad. I was bullshitting you. He never touched me like that, at least not with his dick. With his finger but not his dick."

Kirby stared at Jake hard for a moment. "Did you want to?"

"I thought I did at first, but I couldn't do it. I regret meeting Reggie now. I acted on impulse. I was horny and craving a hookup with a guy. That's all it was. Pure and simple. You and I weren't talking anymore—"

"No, you weren't talking to me," Kirby replied defensively.

"True. I wasn't talking to you, and so I looked for somebody else to get off with."

"So where do things stand with you and Reggie now?"

"I'm done. It's over. We hooked up twice and that's it."

"And who else?"

"Who else?"

"Yeah, who else have you been hooking up with?"

"No one. Not any guys, if that's what you mean."

"Hmmm." Kirby didn't sound convinced as he folded his arms across his chest.

"Kirby, I swear to God, there haven't been any other guys. I've mostly been dating this chick I work with."

"Yeah, I heard about that, but I know you, Jake, and I'm having a hard time believing that you have given up on hooking up with guys completely."

Jake turned to look at Kirby, incredulous. "What? Why? You know that you are the only guy I've ever been with…at least, until Reggie."

"I don't know, man. Knowing that you've been with Reggie has really fucked with my head. It's made me question everything…everything I thought I knew about you…about us."

"What do you mean?"

"You told me so many times that you weren't interested in any other guys, that I was the only guy that you would ever be with. Now I know that's not true. You *are* into other guys. And then you came down so hard on me for fooling around with other dudes when—"

"I came down so hard on you because you never told me that you fooled around with other dudes. You never told me about Antonio. You'd been fucking this guy behind my back and then he's going around saying that he knows me and that he'd been in a threesome with me. How'd you expect me to react? I fucking trusted you, Kirby. You thought I was your only guy, but I thought you were my only guy, too, bro."

"You were—I mean, you are my only guy, Jake. Antonio never meant anything to me. He was my booty call. That's all it ever was. I don't mean to sound cold, but it's the truth. I was ready to drop him like a hat but I was never completely sure if you loved me the way I loved you, and I really didn't have anyone else who knew me—who knew about this side of me. I guess…in a way…Antonio helped me to come out to myself. Helped me to realize and accept that I liked guys more than girls. I turned to him when you weren't around or when you weren't available because you were with Amanda. It took me a long time to feel comfortable enough to admit to you how I truly felt about you, and then I finally told you. And then…."

Kirby started to become emotional. He turned to look away from Jake and stared out the passenger window for a moment. He sighed and regained his composure. "I was crushed when I realized that you didn't feel the same way about me, man. That what we shared wasn't truly the love I thought we mutually had for one another. I really thought you loved me, man. That you were in love with me. I felt so foolish and stupid. And then when you called things off with Amanda, I thought there would be a chance for us, but all this shit with Antonio came crashing down and you stopped talking to me. And then you wrote me off so easily after such a long friendship. Since middle school. Then, when you got with Reggie, a guy who happens to resemble me, physically speaking, it made me wonder if I ever meant anything to you or was I just helping you to live out a particular fantasy or fetish."

"Come on. Not at all—"

"But that's how it felt, Jake. You wrote me off and then found another black dude to be your fuck buddy, and all this time I thought, based on what you'd told me, your attraction was only for me."

"First of all, I admit that I am attracted to other guys. Have been since college actually, but I never felt attracted enough to act on it. I had you and that was enough for me. Besides, I was serious about my relationship with Amanda and was dead-set on marrying her. In my mind, you seemed determined to be with a girl too. Not Laren necessarily, but I'd assumed that you would've eventually found the right girl to be with and marry. I mean…over the course of the many years we've been friends, you've bedded a lot of chicks, man. So it was a surprise to me to hear you say that you were in love with me and wanted to be in a relationship with me…a gay, boyfriend-to-boyfriend kind of relationship. With that said, however, the idea that you were just some guy that I had been using to help me live out some sort of gay fantasy couldn't be further from the truth. Things might have started out that way when we were in high school, but over time, my feelings for you evolved too. I was jealous and upset to learn about your relationship with Antonio. And after we had our big blowup over him, I vowed to never speak to you again. I tried to force myself not to care about you anymore by shutting off all communication and contact with you, but it didn't work. I couldn't stop thinking about you. I thought about you all the time. I never lost my attraction to you or my feelings for you. I hooked up with Reggie as a way to suppress my desire to be with you. He was the closest thing I could find aesthetically to being with you. To satisfy my craving for what we had. But in the end it wasn't a very satisfying experience because what I had with you can't be replicated. The feelings, the emotions, they were real. We were making love, Kirby. It wasn't a fantasy. The love I felt for you was real. It still is."

Kirby turned to look into Jake's eyes softly. "Wow, I'm blown away right now, man. To hear those words coming out of your mouth. Wow. Just wow. I'm speechless."

Jake stared back into Kirby's eyes and reached over to place his right hand atop Kirby's knee. In that moment, Jake wanted to wrap himself in Kirby's embrace like a warm blanket—to be comforted, to feel the sensation of his best friend's love washing over him again.

Kirby placed his hand on top of Jake's, and then they interlocked their fingers together, tightly.

Jake wanted to lean in to kiss those lips. Those thick, full, moist, luscious lips of Kirby's. But he hesitated when a couple of guys, more than likely coming from the gym, walked by the front of the car. Jake could see a blurred image of them in his peripheral vision, and he could hear them talking. Being a little self-conscious, he sensed that they were staring, but he didn't know for sure because he kept his eyes locked on Kirby the whole time.

Kirby noticed the passersby, too, but he didn't break Jake's gaze. Almost in a show of defiance, Jake and Kirby both remained in the moment as they kept their eyes trained on each other and their fingers interlocked.

"You want to go over to my place?" Jake finally said.

"Yes," Kirby said simply and without hesitation.

CHAPTER
TWENTY-ONE

Jake pulled into the garage of his building after the short drive from the gym. He and Kirby walked over to the elevator to take it up to Jake's floor. The gravity of longing and desire pulling them together again was so intense that they couldn't resist the urge to physically connect with one another. Neither had the patience or inclination to wait until they made it inside Jake's apartment. The moment the elevator door closed behind them, they embraced immediately.

Jake wrapped his arms around Kirby's waist and held on to him tight. Then he lay his head on Kirby's shoulder and closed his eyes as he savored the feel of his body pressed against his friend's. The clean, fresh but distinctly masculine scent that permeated from Kirby's hard, muscular flesh filled Jake with a lustful urge.

When the elevator reached Jake's floor, Jake didn't want to let go as Kirby rubbed and caressed his back in a way that was loving but also sensual.

Just as the elevator door was about to close, they quickly broke their embrace and Kirby extended his arm to prevent the door from shutting all the way.

Jake unlocked the door to his apartment and they stepped inside. After closing the door, Kirby wrapped his arms around Jake's waist from behind and held on to him as he pressed his pelvis to Jake's bottom.

Jake could feel Kirby's hard-on, which immediately triggered his own. When Kirby began to kiss and gently nibble on the back of his right ear, it felt so tantalizingly good that Jake felt as though he was about to pass out from the rush of blood to his head.

"You don't know how much I've missed you," Kirby said as he moved his hands up Jake's torso to feel and caress his chest.

"I've missed you, too," Jake said as he placed his hands to Kirby's. Then he turned around to face him. When he did, his lips magnetically met Kirby's. Initially their kiss was eager yet tender and loving, but then Kirby pressed his tongue into Jake's mouth, which sent Jake over the edge. Jake moaned as he sucked on Kirby's tongue in a manner that clearly indicated how much he had hungered for his taste again. It was the ultimate pacifier—the next best thing to having Kirby's ten inches of manhood marinating in the wetness of his mouth.

"I need you, Kirby," Jake said breathlessly. "I need you so much right now."

"I'm yours," Kirby said before he offered his tongue to Jake again. Then he slid his hands down Jake's back to grab and squeeze his ass. Jake reacted by likewise slipping his hands around Kirby to grab and squeeze his taut, round, muscular ass.

They continued to kiss passionately, hungrily—feasting on each other with wet, openmouthed, tongue-swirling kisses. Their noses pressed together as they inhaled and exhaled onto each other audibly as if the oxygen in the room was wholly inadequate for the burst of heat and energy emanating from their bodies. Jake eventually moved his hands from Kirby's ass to lift up his shirt and rub and squeeze his pecs.

Kirby helped him out by pulling his shirt off completely, revealing nipples that were tight, erect, and eager to be tortured.

"Oooh, yeah," Jake slurred sensually, excited and aroused at the sight as he began to squeeze and twist them.

"Ahhh…fuck, yeah," Kirby said as he closed his eyes and tilted his head back at the sensation. It felt good and slightly painful at the same time, but he wanted more. "Bite me, man. Bite me," Kirby commanded.

Jake obliged happily as he knelt down slightly to circle each of Kirby's nipples with his tongue before tugging on each one with his teeth, causing

Kirby's body to shiver. Jake continued to suck and lick with vigor before he started to work his way down Kirby's torso, kissing and licking the crevices of his well-defined, sculptured abdominals. As he did so, Kirby's hard-on was pronounced and protruding against the soft polyester and elastane fabric of his gym tights.

Jake fell to his knees to press his face to the Black Mamba, to reacquaint himself with it again. When he did so, Kirby placed his left hand to the back of Jake's head to press his face to his stiffness harder. He then began to gyrate his hips to rub his hard-on up and down and all around Jake's face. Jake savored the taunting as he gripped Kirby's muscular thighs with each hand in eager anticipation of what would come next.

Jake couldn't take the taunting and teasing anymore. He yanked Kirby's workout tights down to reveal an untamed Black Mamba, primed and ready to assault an eager mouth. "Fuck...you're so beautiful," Jake said as he eyed Kirby's member with a salivating glance before extending his tongue to lick it from the base of the ten-inch shaft to the top of its very swollen head. He licked it again and again and then again, taking his time and savoring each lick more than the one before it. As Jake remained on his knees, he reached to pull down his own shorts and began to stroke himself as he went to town on Kirby with ferocious intensity and aim. Although Kirby was the one being serviced, Jake seemed to be having all the fun.

After Jake spent several minutes lubricating Kirby's tool with his wet and very hungry mouth, Kirby pulled Jake up to face him again. They kissed wildly and sloppily, feasting on one another with unrestrained abandon, soaking themselves in the wetness of the other's mouth. Kirby licked Jake's nose, cheeks, and jawline before he sucked on his chin. Jake responded in kind with equal fervor and zeal in his adoration. Jake could barely contain his excitement from the rush of adrenaline coursing through his body. Every nerve ending was on fire, experiencing sensory overload. He began to press his pelvis to Kirby's, humping him aggressively. Kirby humped back and grabbed Jake's ass tightly. Then he parted Jake's ass-cheeks to make his way toward the part of Jake's anatomy he thirsted for the most.

Jake jumped up to wrap his legs around Kirby's waist, animated and thoroughly aroused by the probing fingers that were spreading his hole and making it loose. "Ohhh, yeah. Fuck my hole, man," Jake cried. "Fuck me, fuck me. Oh God, yes, fuck me!"

Kirby grinned in reaction and then carried Jake into the bedroom. When they fell to the bed with Jake on his back and Kirby on top of him, Jake kept his legs wrapped around Kirby as Kirby continued to press his pelvis to Jake's in a fucking motion. As he did so, Kirby went from wet and wild kisses to softer, tender ones. "Are you ready for this? Do you really want me to fuck you?" Kirby stopped to ask.

"Yes, I do. I want to know what it feels like to have you inside me. I've thought about it, fantasized about it for so long. I want to experience it at least once."

"I've fantasized about it for a long time, too."

"You're the only guy I've ever wanted to experience this with."

Kirby grinned happily as he bent down to kiss Jake again.

Jake chuckled as he kissed him back, knowing how pleased Kirby must have felt about the arrival of this moment—the moment Jake and Kirby's flesh would become one.

Kirby pulled up to get a better view of Jake's body—lean and muscular, neatly groomed and clean, with smooth, even-toned, creamy skin with not a blemish or flaw in sight. He unwrapped Jake's legs from his waist, spread them apart, and pushed them back. When Kirby looked down and zeroed in on his target, he said, "You're so fucking beautiful," as if beholding Jake for the first time.

Jake grinned broadly and chuckled. "Okay, stud. Be gentle with me. Please don't break me in two."

Kirby laughed. "I won't. I'll take it nice and slow," he said before he pressed the head of his fully erect ten-inch tool to Jake's waiting hole.

Jake's heart raced in anticipation of what he was about to encounter. His lust for Kirby's manhood and desire to be topped by him outweighed whatever apprehension he felt in that moment.

"Yeaaah…nice and slow," Kirby said in a deep, sensual voice as he continued to tease and prep Jake's hole for expansion. "Then I'm going to fuck the shit out of you," Kirby said before busting out a laugh.

Jake rolled his eyes and chuckled along, but he knew that Kirby could and likely would fuck him 'til kingdom come all over that apartment. The thought both excited him and momentarily instilled a small degree of fear. "I think we're going to need some lube," Jake said as he pulled his legs back to his chest and turned to his side, away from Kirby, to hop off the bed.

"Don't worry, I'll lube you up real good when I stick my tongue up your sexy ass. I'm going to eat that shit out like a wet pussy."

Although Jake didn't have the words for a comeback, his body sufficiently communicated his reaction to Kirby's dirty talk. He had been rimmed by Kirby many times before, but the thought of that being followed up by actual intercourse this time made Jake's cock rise straight up at full attention.

"Are you nice and fresh for me?" Kirby said, dead serious about his intent.

Jake cracked a smile. "Yeah, I showered earlier, but wait, I'll be right back," he said before he went into the bathroom and shut the door.

A little more than a minute later, Jake emerged from the bathroom all giddy and excited. Seeing that Kirby was lying on his back, Jake hopped on the bed and straddled himself on all fours directly above Kirby with his ass pointed to Kirby's face. He knew Kirby would like it that way.

"Is that fresh enough for you, bro?" Jake said as he poked his ass out in an exaggerated way, revealing the sliver of his pinkish hole up close.

Kirby slapped and squeezed Jake's ass-cheeks with his hands as he gushed with satisfaction. "Yeaaah…."

When Kirby used his thumbs to stretch Jake's sphincter, Jake moaned in heat at the intrusion and gladly surrendered himself for further examination. To assist Kirby in his ass play, Jake lowered himself on top of Kirby and leaned on his elbows with his face directly above the Black Mamba.

On cue, Kirby got right to it, using the tip of his tongue to poke Jake's opening teasingly at first before he began to devour his buddy lasciviously—licking and sucking the rim before inserting his tongue inside, probing deeply.

The sensation of Kirby's penetrating tongue—wet, warm, and soft but also firm and slightly ticklish—drove Jake crazy. "Ahhh…fuck! Lick my ass, bro. That's it. Oh my God, that feels so fucking good," he said in aching pleasure.

Kirby happily obliged, probing deeper with his tongue, then pulling out to lick and suck on Jake balls. "Mmmm, you taste so fucking good," Kirby said, smacking his lips as he sucked and tugged on Jake's scrotum with his wet mouth.

"Mmmm," Jake moaned back as he sucked and tugged on the bulging head of Kirby's cock. "So do you," he said, coming up for air before stuffing his mouth again to resume his oral treatment. Jake closed his eyes, fully enjoying and exulting in the moment. *I love my life right now*, he thought to himself as he worked Kirby's tool and relished the feel of Kirby's tongue up his ass at the same time. That's how sex with Kirby always made him feel—on cloud nine. Making love to Kirby felt so good, so easy, so familiar, so natural, so comforting. It felt so right. And this time, there was no guilt associated with it since Jake was now single. He wasn't cheating on anyone like before, and breaking up with Amanda suddenly felt less painful considering that she might very well turn out to be the half-sister he never knew he had.

"Sit on my face," Kirby commanded, snapping Jake out of his daze.

Jake rose up and complied, positioning his ass directly over Kirby's face while stroking his own erection. Jake could feel his hole becoming more loose and relaxed. He loved the way it felt—cool and soaking wet from Kirby's saliva. He contracted his sphincter a few times, which drove Kirby mad, causing him to feast on Jake even more greedily.

Jake gasped. "Oh my God, you're so amazing. You do that so fucking good," he said before he leaned back down to return his mouth to the Black Mamba, still hard and throbbing.

Jake and Kirby were both so caught up in foreplay that it eventually turned into the main course as it consumed them for an extended period without interruption. There were just constant moans and gasps with the random expletive thrown in, among other exclamations, to express the delight, gratification, and sheer bliss each felt.

"You like the taste of that, don't you?" Jake said to Kirby tauntingly.

"Fuck, yeah. Can't get enough," Kirby said as he switched between sucking on Jake's hole and cock, both directly in his face for the taking.

Kirby had to stop what he was doing a few times to regain self-control and prevent an early orgasm. The combination of eating out his favorite boy, one of Kirby's favorite things to do sexually, while having said boy milk his tool at the same time had him sexually supercharged and on the brink.

Jake, on the other hand, was enjoying being in the driver's seat, making Kirby delirious. Recalling how Kirby had sucked him off to completion and swallowed when they were in Hawaii, Jake aimed to do the same when he sensed that Kirby might be approaching climax prematurely.

Increasingly unable to maintain control, Kirby bent his legs up and stretched them back out a few times as he gasped loudly in response to Jake's masterful manipulation of the Black Mamba. "Ahhh…shit…you son of a bitch," Kirby said stridently.

Jake stopped to laugh in response to Kirby's cry before quickly returning to tantalize him mercilessly with his hand and mouth, sucking and stroking with rhythmic precision.

"Fuck…you're going to make me come, dude," Kirby said, trying to pull himself away from Jake.

Jake, however, was persistent and wouldn't let the Black Mamba out of his grip. "I want to suck you off. I want to swallow your load so bad right now."

Kirby seemed surprised. "Yeah?"

"Let's come together, bro. You suck me off too," Jake said.

Kirby obliged as he and Jake turned on their sides to continue pleasuring one another in the sixty-nine. They sucked and moaned loudly like dogs in heat. "I love you, bro," Jake said with a sorrowful tone, feeling remorse for the extended separation and friction with his friend.

"I love you too, bro," Kirby said, sounding equally remorseful, as they continued to pleasure one another. Kirby couldn't hold back for much longer. With the eruption rising within and about to burst at the top, Kirby quickly hopped off the bed and stood to his feet. His body trembled and the muscles in his arms, chest, and abdominals contracted as he stroked himself rapidly.

Jake crawled over to the edge of the bed to position himself right in the line of sight of the impending deluge. He was thirsty for it.

"Oh, fuck!" Kirby yelled, breathing heavily.

Jake opened his mouth and held out his tongue in anticipation. Kirby stepped forward and then he came, spraying into Jake's mouth and partially on his face as well.

"Oh yeah," Jake slurred as he allowed the taste of Kirby's come to settle on his tongue for a few seconds before he swallowed it down. Then he took Kirby's tool, still oozing with cream, back into his mouth to finish the rest.

Kirby's knees buckled and his body went spastic as he fought to remain standing while Jake devoured him. When Jake had his way and finished him off, Kirby collapsed down to the bed and lay flat on his back. "Fuck, man. Oh my God. That was good," Kirby said in a daze.

Jake stepped away to the bathroom to quickly wipe his face and hands. Then he returned, still having the taste of his best buddy's come in his mouth. Drunk on lust, Jake's member was aching and throbbing, and he desperately wanted to shoot his load too. He lay on his back beside Kirby, pressing the side of his flesh to Kirby's, shoulder to shoulder. As Jake began to stroke himself, he placed his right leg atop Kirby's left leg. They turned their faces toward one another and kissed each other's lips tenderly in between Jake's gasps.

"Oh fuck…here I come," Jake announced as he stroked with increased vigor.

"Shoot it in my mouth, man; shoot it in my mouth," Kirby said urgently as he leaned up on his elbows.

Jake pulled himself up on his knees and straddled Kirby as he continued to stroke rapidly.

Kirby opened his mouth and flicked his tongue tauntingly a couple of times before holding it out steady.

As he stroked, Jake pushed his pelvis forward to center his aim right into Kirby's waiting mouth. Then he pushed forward a couple more times, feeling the impending explosion making its way out of him in slow, agonizing fashion. It was torture, but it felt amazing. Jake's body trembled as he pushed his pelvis forward one more time, at which point he shot his load perfectly into Kirby's mouth with the precision of a water gun hitting its target. Jake came with such force that he momentarily felt faint and a little dizzy.

Kirby swallowed with an audible gulp then licked his lips and swallowed again. "Mmmm, that was yummy," he said before poking his tongue out to show Jake that it was indeed all gone.

Jake smiled. "Attaboy," he said before leaning down to kiss Kirby, rolling the tip of his tongue to Kirby's. Then they tenderly gave each other a quick peck—once, twice, and then a third time, the sound of each kiss ricocheting from their lips.

"Lie on top of me," Kirby said.

Jake did so, spreading himself prostrate on top of Kirby—chest to chest, pelvis to pelvis, and with each of his legs bestriding Kirby's. Jake then wrapped his arms around Kirby's broad shoulders and leaned in so that his nose pressed up against the side of Kirby's face. Kirby immediately responded and wrapped his arms around Jake, rubbing his back and then intermittently squeezing their bodies more tightly together.

Jake absorbed the warmth and feel of his lean, ripped, muscular physique pressed to the hard, pumped, muscular flesh of his best friend and male lover. It felt comforting to be locked in Kirby's strong embrace again. It felt loving. It also felt erotic. And it turned him on. "Damn, you feel so good," Jake said with a sigh. Despite having just climaxed to the point of exhaustion, Jake's hard-on returned. He aided the swelling with a subtle but continuous thrust of his pelvis to Kirby's.

Jake allowed himself to get lost in the ecstasy of his feelings and emotions. It provided a much needed respite, albeit temporary, from the trouble he and his family faced. As he lay there, he contemplated how much Kirby loved him and wanted to be with him exclusively. This smart, funny, beautiful, fine-as-hell black Adonis that men and women alike ogled and wished they could have was Jake's for the taking. A sense of gratitude and appreciation fell over Jake—that Kirby was his longtime friend and, better yet, an option still if he chose to explore life with another man as an openly gay couple.

Jake and Kirby continued in silence for a few minutes, caressing, thrusting, and locking their bodies together. They kissed each other softly on the lips, then rolled the tips of their tongues together, stopping and repeating over and over.

Moments later, Kirby was ready to take things to the next level. He rolled Jake over on his back so that he was now on top of him in the missionary position. Jake instinctively opened his legs and wrapped them around Kirby's hard, muscular thighs.

"Are you ready for me to fuck you now?" Kirby said in a breathy voice.

Every nerve in Jake's body was bristling and fully charged. Mentally, he felt ready to submit himself to Kirby. He had imagined this moment and fantasized about it off and on for years. He'd even secretly done the deed on himself more than once using a dildo he'd mail-ordered and kept hidden away. Now the moment had arrived when Jake felt comfortable and free enough to bend his no-anal-sex rule. In this moment of personal turmoil, Jake had lost his resolve and threw all inhibition to the wind.

Jake was just about to respond to Kirby's question in the affirmative but was interrupted when his cell phone rang. "Let me see who this is," Jake said as he reached over to grab the phone from the nightstand. "It's Dad. I have to take this." Jake pushed Kirby back with his left arm in an innocuous way to indicate that he wanted to rise up.

"Hey, Dad," Jake said as he turned to place his feet to the floor and sat at the edge of the bed. Jake listened intently as Tom spoke on the other end of the line. He replied back minimally and by using only vague, nondescript terms. "Yeah…. Okay…. Okay…. That's fine…. That sounds fine…. All right…see you tomorrow. Bye."

The call took about five minutes. Tom did most of the talking. Meanwhile, Kirby had gotten up to check his own phone. He was texting someone back when Jake's call had ended.

Jake turned and lifted his feet back onto the bed. He then leaned his back against the headboard, stretched out, and crossed his legs comfortably as he waited for Kirby.

"I hate to be a killjoy, dude, but I need to go home, shower and change, and get back over to the studio. They're cutting shit out of the pilot, and I need to be there to make sure they don't mess shit up," Kirby said, sounding irritated as he dropped his phone to the bed and reached to put his gym clothes back on.

"Why are they cutting shit out?"

"The run time for the pilot is only supposed to be twenty to twenty-two minutes, but we have a little over thirty minutes of footage."

"But it's a thirty-minute show, isn't it?"

"Yeah, but you have to factor eight to ten minutes for commercials."

"Oh, right."

"I knew we were over and would have to cut some things out, but I don't agree with what they want to cut, so I'd best get my ass over there before it's too late."

Jake sat there quietly with mixed feelings as he watched Kirby get dressed and ramble on. Although the phone call with Tom had sapped some of his sexual urge and caused his hard-on to rapidly shrink, Jake still wanted to feel Kirby deep inside him. No, he wanted Kirby to pound him silly.

When Kirby finished getting dressed, he turned toward Jake to pick his phone up off the bed.

"What happened to the Black Mamba? He was so ready to strike with a vengeance a few moments ago," Jake teased as he slid his foot up between Kirby's legs to the groin.

Kirby chuckled and grinned from ear to ear as he pulled Jake's foot away and sat down on the edge of the bed beside him. "You've been granted a temporary reprieve. I guess this gives you a little more time to think about this life-altering decision you're making to be bred by the Black Mamba. Because you know what they say about the Black Mamba, don't you?"

Jake looked on keenly, anticipating the punchline.

"Once you go black, you never go back," Kirby said, busting out a laugh.

Jake laughed, too. "I knew you were going to say it. I knew that's what you'd say."

"That's right, bitch!" Kirby howled.

"But I'm already there. All I've ever had is black dick," Jake said, still laughing.

"Damn! You're right," Kirby stopped and said before continuing to laugh.

"Oh my God, I don't know what I'm going to do about you, Kirby," Jake said, becoming more serious in tone.

"What do you mean?"

Jake sighed and looked up at the ceiling as he contemplated how to express his feelings. "I'm not sure if I'll ever be able to separate myself from you like I'd been trying to do. I thought that if I just stopped talking to you and dated girls or tried to get back with Amanda, I'd get over you... get over my feelings for you. But being away from you these past few months and then being with you again now has made me realize that my attraction to you and the feelings I have for you are stronger than I've been willing to admit to myself. To be perfectly honest, I'm a little confused right now."

"Confused about what?"

"A lot of things, actually. So much is going on," Jake said, reticent to divulge details about the unfolding drama in his family's life.

"So where do we go from here?"

"I don't know."

Kirby sighed with an air of disappointment. "So the truth is that you love me but still don't want to be in a relationship with me."

"The truth is that I love you, Kirby, and I'm not sure what to do about it."

"Or maybe you're just afraid."

"Maybe I am."

Chapter Twenty-Two

Amanda and Lucy hunkered down for another long day at the small office they shared in Midtown Manhattan.

"Oh, yay! She's coming," Amanda said as she sat at her desk, poring through email.

"Who?" Lucy looked up and asked, curious.

"Lucia Visconti," Amanda said, exaggerating the fancy-sounding name.

"Oh, yeah, the *Glamour Girl* blogger. Cool. She's hot right now. Her blog has well over a million followers."

"I haven't met her before. Have you?"

"It's funny. I haven't. I've met most of the major fashion bloggers, but not her for some reason. She's sort of an enigma. You know she models, too, and has become kind of a celebrity in her own right. That must be why she's coming."

"For the celebrities?"

"Exactly. Our event's becoming the hot ticket, so of course she's going to come. As long as she stays away from Cass, we're cool. I hear she has a penchant for stealing boyfriends…at least in the modeling world."

Amanda smirked. "Well, you know the modeling world is a total swingers scene, so no surprise there."

"Oh, did I tell you the CEO of Delaney's is coming?"

"Really? I expected someone high-level but not that high. I still can't get over the fact that they've made such a large preorder with all these stipulations attached but aren't willing to pay for any of the production. They're one of the largest department stores in the country, for God's sake."

"Well, you know why?"

"Because we have trust funds," Amanda said sarcastically, rolling her eyes.

"Mom has a big account with them. Her line sells fairly well at their stores. I think they feel they're doing her a favor by allowing her daughter's bag line to be rolled out when we don't have a proven track record yet. And, yes, because our parents have money, they want us to pay for everything. That's the trade-off—they give us high-profile placement in their stores because we're linked to Alana Dupree, but we have to pay for it."

"I mean…I know it's a big deal to get into Delaney's as a new brand. I'm grateful and all for the exposure, but I'm concerned about being stuck with a bunch of inventory if most of the bags don't sell. I don't mean to talk this to death—it's a done deal—but this this whole all-or-nothing approach they're taking with us is just so impractical in my view."

"Look at the bright side. If our line does well at Delaney's and gets good traction, every other major luxury retailer will want a piece of the action. Our deal with them could be a big boon to business."

"Or a big bust. It's a risky strategy."

"Well, that's why there's such a thing as the markdown, if we come to that, and tax write-offs too."

"I guess," Amanda said in a conceding way, not wanting to belabor a point she'd already made several times in prior conversations. "Hey, speaking of tax write-offs, I was thinking that I could write off the apartment I'm going to lease as a business expense."

"Can you do that?"

"I don't know, but it's no different from expensing a hotel suite when I'm in town, right?"

"Sounds good to me, but I'm no tax accountant. So are you going to take the apartment you told me about across from the park?"

"I think so. I have to make a decision about it today because apparently somebody else wants it. I'm kind of on the fence about it all of a sudden, though."

"Why? You've been talking about getting a place here for over a year, when you and Jake were still together even. Just do it already."

Amanda hesitated for a moment, staring at Lucy and sizing up what her reaction might be to the recent news she'd received. A part of her wanted to keep it to herself. If she and Jake ended up speaking again, there could be advantages to staying quiet about it. She knew that her family and friends would strongly disapprove of her having any contact with him. She was curious nonetheless to see what Jake might attempt to do to win her back, even though she continued to believe reconciliation was out of the question. However, Amanda couldn't keep quiet. She had to tell someone.

"I've been meaning to tell you about this call I received from my mother while I was touring that apartment yesterday."

"About what?"

"About…Jake."

Lucy stared back at Amanda with a perplexed expression on her face.

"He wants to get back together with me, apparently."

"Shut the fuck up!" Lucy said, hopping out of her seat and walking over to stand in front of Amanda.

Amanda busted out laughing, covering her mouth with her hands.

Lucy was beside herself. "You have got to be fucking kidding me right now. Are you serious?"

Amanda laughed uncontrollably for a few moments before regaining her composure and ability to speak clearly. "I knew that's how you'd react. You're so funny."

"This is so out of left field."

"I know. He called and told my mom this, of all people."

"What? That's so crazy. Why? Oh my God. What a loser."

Amanda rolled her eyes and shook her head. Lucy's outrage was contagious and suddenly made her feel a little less sympathetic and more outraged too. "I know. It's stupid."

"Why would he call Camilla? Why couldn't he have just called you directly?"

"I have no idea. And then he said something weird about doing what my parents wanted him to do when he broke up with me."

"Huh? What's that supposed to mean?"

"God only knows. My mother was completely baffled. She thought he might've been high or something. She said he wasn't making any sense or was speaking incoherently or something. I don't know."

"Jake needs to pull his head out of his ass and start paying attention. You're with Adam now. Hellooo!"

"Well, that's the other thing. She thinks he's just jealous of me and Adam being together. Now he realizes how good things were, how good we had it, and wants it all back."

Lucy smirked and rolled her eyes. "Please. He was cheating on you."

"That's why I don't understand why he feels misled."

"Misled? Misled about what? He was the one doing the misleading the whole time—being a closet case, sleeping with his best friend, and God knows who else. I don't believe for a second that Kirby was the only one. I know you do, but that's bullshit. I'm sorry."

Amanda looked at Lucy, a little annoyed. She believed that Kirby was the only one. With the passage of time, the more she'd thought about it, the more plausible it seemed to her. "You know, Jake and Kirby had been extremely close from the very start. Jake introduced me to Kirby around the same time he introduced me to his parents, right after we'd started dating. We were both home in LA for Christmas break our junior year at Stanford. I recall him telling me that he wanted to introduce me to the most important people in his life. He was so serious and deep about it. The only people he introduced me to were his family on Christmas Eve and Kirby a couple days later. That was it. We met Kirby for drinks, and I remember Jake and Kirby hugged each other and kind of held on. I had seen guys who were friends embrace before, so it didn't shock me or anything, but I recall that when they did it there was, like…this affection…this bond between them. At the time I just thought it was really sweet that two guys felt so comfortable showing affection like that in public and then, after Jake introduced us, Kirby said to Jake, "So this is who I get to share you with?"

Lucy balked and shook her head, incredulous. "And what did Jake say back?"

"I don't recall Jake saying anything, really. He just kind of laughed it off. Anyway, I thought, okay, so this is Jake's best friend since prep school. Jake had many friends from prep school, but this is the only one he wanted me to meet. In fact, it was a while, months later, before I met any others. So I'm like, okay, he and Kirby are obviously very close, and I figured we'd spend a lot of time together. That's what I took the, quote, 'sharing' to mean. Needless to say, I see Kirby's comment in a completely different light now."

"Because they were sucking each other off the whole time," Lucy smarted off under her breath and rolled her eyes.

Amanda tried to ignore her and continued on. "The whole time we dated they always showed affection toward another—hugging and touching—but in a playful way. I just thought they were acting like typical bros and being silly half the time."

"So what's your point? It's okay that he cheated on you? That he lied to you? Deceived you? Were you guys even using protection?"

Amanda huffed and gave Lucy the eye.

"I'm sorry but, oh my God, he could've infected you with an STD or something."

"Lucy," Amanda said in exasperation.

"Mandi, I'm serious. I'm not trying to be cute or funny or anything. I know you think he was only with Kirby while you two were together, but what if he wasn't? And then, how many guys and girls had Kirby been with while he swapping come with Jake? I mean, Kirby was with Antonio too, and we all know Antonio is a total whore."

"Lucy, Jake never gave me an STD, okay? I've never had an STD. Never. And yes, I did get tested after Jake told me everything. Okay? Satisfied?"

"You did? Okay, good. You never told me that."

"It's all moot at this point. All I'm trying to say is that I feel that it's not so far-fetched to believe that the only guy Jake's ever been with is Kirby. Knowing him and knowing how he was with me, and just knowing about his relationship with Kirby and their long history together, it seems that, at least for Jake, it's possible. I can't speak for Kirby, but for Jake, I can see how maybe he could've developed these feelings for Kirby, especially after they'd started experimenting in prep school, with the situation kind of evolving from there into a friends-with-benefits sort of thing. It's not that unheard-of. We know and have heard of plenty of guys, especially in our industry, who've had these sorts of relationships or flings, particularly with married men."

"True, but I'm still not sure I get your point."

"I'm just acknowledging the fact that Jake is bi and apparently had sexual identity issues that I didn't recognize the whole time we were together. That's all."

"So what are you going to do if he calls you?"

"I don't know."

"What do you mean, you don't know? It's great that you seem so sympathetic and willing to forgive him for what he did, but at this point, why give him the time of day? You have a great life, and you're with Adam now. He loves you to death. I mean, seriously, the guy worships the ground you walk on. Why go backward?"

"I'm not saying that I'd get back with Jake, but if he wants to talk to me, I'd be willing to listen. He was my fiancé, for goodness' sake. We dated for six years. I don't hate him anymore. I've gotten over that. I feel more pity for him now than hate. He seems so lost and desperate, calling my mom like that out of the blue. That was just so random. It kind of makes me sad."

CHAPTER
TWENTY-THREE

"Hey, Jake!" Mike said as he popped into Jake's office.

"Good morning," Jake said stoically.

"So I hear you're joining me and your dad for a drink later today."

"Yes, I am."

"So you're going to help us recruit players for the Justice Leo Parillo Golf Tournament?"

"I guess," Jake answered vaguely. That's what Mike thought the meeting was about, but when Tom had called Jake the day before while he was with Kirby, he told him that they would use the meeting as an opportunity to confront Mike about his involvement in the scheme to stop Jake from marrying Amanda.

"It's all for a good cause. As you know, Justice Parillo is an emeritus member of the firm and has mediated a lot of cases for us since his retirement from the bench. So it's good for us to have a presence at the tournament. Tom and I have been co-chairs of the fundraising committee for the last eight or ten years or so."

"Well, I'll be there. I actually know a couple of guys who received the Leo Parillo Scholarship while I was in law school. Hopefully those dudes are giving back. In fact, I should hop on the phone and call them right now to see if they're purchasing tickets to play in the tourney too."

"Now you're talking. Good man. Want to join the fundraising committee?" Mike asked with a grin.

"Uh…I think I'll pass," Jake said with a forced smile.

"All right. Well, think about it. We could use some new blood. Anyway, I've got to run off to a meeting, but I'll see you later. By the way, thanks for taking on that SEC investigation matter. That's a good one for you. If we can get the situation resolved fast and avoid a court action or administrative proceeding, the client should be happy."

"Oh…hey, Mike!" Jake called as Mike had already stepped out of his office.

Mike reappeared seconds later. "Yeah?"

"I forgot to mention, I heard you guys had a conference call with Rick Climent on Monday about drawing up plans for an ESOP at one of his companies."

"Yes, we did," Mike said in a matter-of-fact way.

Jake struggled for the right choice of words as he looked at Mike. Mike looked back at him, slightly puzzled.

After a brief stare-down, Jake capitulated. "I just thought…. It's nothing. I'm sorry. Never mind."

"If you're wondering why I didn't include you on the call, I thought it would be obvious. I can't risk our business relationship with Rick by getting you involved in his deals. You have a personal conflict with him. Especially given what you told me about your intention to get in touch with Amanda, which you know he's emphatically against. I have no control over what you do in your personal life, but when it comes to business, I have to do what's in the best interest of the firm and our client. Our relationship with Rick might already be in jeopardy as it is. So moving forward, we have to do our best to keep our business relationship with the Climent family as separate as possible from your personal relationship with them. That means from now on, you won't be working on any client matters pertaining to Climent Partners or the Climent family anymore."

"I completely understand. I know how important that relationship is to the firm and to you personally, and I don't want to get in the way any more than I already have. Besides, there's plenty of work for me to do with other clients."

"Good. I'm glad we're on the same page. Is there anything else?" Mike said as he took a quick look at his watch.

"Has Rick spoken to you about me lately?"

"No. Why?"

"Well, you should know that I've attempted to contact him a couple times to inform him of my decision to reach out to Amanda."

Mike locked his jaw tight, and his mood became tense. "In light of what we've just talked about, do you really feel that's necessary?"

"I do, because I didn't want him to be caught by surprise and hear after the fact that I was communicating with Amanda again. Plus, I didn't know if you'd spoken with him or not about my change of heart about everything."

"I did speak to him about that, and he does know."

"Okay. I didn't know that. I guess that explains why he's not taking my calls."

"I had to tell him, Jake. I would've been derelict in my duty as his lawyer had I not made him aware that you no longer planned to abide by the agreement you'd made with him, even though it was more of a meeting of the minds than an actual written agreement."

"I understand. I just wish I'd known. I ended up calling and speaking to Camilla instead Monday evening."

"Why'd you call her?"

"Because Rick wasn't taking my calls, and I wanted to make sure they knew what I was planning to do beforehand out of respect. I didn't expect them to approve or anything, but I thought they should know nevertheless. It was interesting. When I spoke to Camilla, she didn't seem to know what I was talking about in terms of the agreement. She didn't even acknowledge that I'd broken up with Amanda because that's what she and Rick wanted me to do."

Mike frowned. "That's odd."

"I guess it's all just part of the façade," Jake said, glaring at Mike.

"What façade?"

"Mike, don't you think it's at all strange that Amanda is dating again and is in a very public relationship with a well-known celebrity-slash-producer? You didn't seem terribly surprised the last time I brought this up with you."

"Well, like I told you before, Rick said that Amanda wasn't having psychotic episodes like before, but that they would take whatever steps necessary to intervene if her symptoms returned. You know, maybe she had a lot of anxiety around marriage in general and about marrying you in particular. Perhaps that's what triggered the psychotic episodes in the first place, and this alternate personality, Maggie, was like a coping mechanism or an inner voice, kind of like a devil's advocate—"

"Mike, do you really know for a fact that Amanda was having psychotic episodes and was suffering from split personality or from some form of schizophrenia?"

"All I know is what Rick communicated to me."

"So you never spoke to her doctors?"

"No."

"And Rick never showed you any medical records?"

"No. I took Rick at his word. What reason would I have not to?"

"Interesting," Jake said, his tone dripping with skepticism.

"What? Do you think Rick was lying?"

"Yes, I do," Jake said flatly, not mincing words.

Mike stared at Jake for a moment with a startled expression on his face. "Look, I don't know where you're going with this, but if you intend on challenging Rick and Camilla on the validity of their statements about their own daughter's health and making some sort of hay out of all of this, then we have a problem on our hands that will need to be addressed. We do a lot of business with Climent Partners. They're too big and important a client to have a junior associate at our firm engaging in this level of personal acrimony with its chairman and principal shareholder. In fact, it wouldn't even be tolerated under normal circumstances. If you weren't Jake Doyle, you'd be out the door. By calling Rick and his wife, you're being nothing more than a nuisance, Jake. Now you're making accusations about their credibility? This is getting to be a bit much. You are no longer Amanda's fiancé. Therefore, you really shouldn't be contacting Rick and Camilla anymore. In fact, you should only be communicating with them through me, frankly. They hired me to communicate with you on their behalf. Remember?"

"Then maybe I need to get my own lawyer involved."

Mike turned red. He held out the palms of his hands to show his dismay as he spoke. "Jake, what are you doing?"

"Did you know that Amanda was pregnant?"

"No. Where'd you hear that?"

Jake smirked. "Oh…just a rumor that was flying around, I guess."

Mike glared at Jake, his anger obvious. "I'm late and need to run to this meeting, but we need to talk further. This is getting out of hand, and I don't appreciate your attitude right now."

"Well, you'll see me tonight, so I look forward to continuing the conversation then."

Mike didn't answer back as he turned away from Jake and stormed out of his office.

***

Later that afternoon, Jake headed out of the office for a late lunch, feeling anxious and stressed. He was more concerned and fretful about the call he was expecting to receive from Tom with the paternity results than he was about the terse conversation he'd had with Mike that morning.

Jake walked a couple of long blocks from his office building and arrived at his favorite downtown LA sandwich shop. He decided to order the same thing he always did, the turkey ciabatta. In between bites, he busied himself with his smartphone, checking emails and then perusing Internet sites like CNN and ESPN to get the latest news, anything to help take his mind off the impending news that Rick Climent might be his biological father. Jake was still very doubtful, but his mind raced with thoughts about what might happen next if it were true. How would such news be broken to Amanda and by whom? Distracted, Jake closed the ESPN page and pulled up Amanda's Facebook page to see her latest posts. He and Amanda had never unfriended one another, so her posts routinely appeared in his news feed and he usually read them. Amanda had become quite active on social media now that she was a budding designer building a brand and taking advantage of her growing celebrity as the It girl of the moment. Almost every day, she posted photos, links to articles with features or cover stories about her or about her and Lucy together, and tidbits about the upcoming launch of Novel. Jake was amazed at how quickly her page had evolved from an ordinary personal page with photos of family and friends at random social get-togethers, birthday parties, and weekend getaways to a page that was now much more professional and sophisticated in tone and appearance. Plus, she now had a lot more followers, and the number seemed to be growing by the day.

"Two hundred fifty thousand followers? Damn!" Jake said aloud to himself in astonishment.

Jake clicked to read one of the articles Amanda or her PR people, he surmised, had recently posted. It was about Novel with a particular focus on the fine handcrafted Italian leather that was being used for the product. As he read the article, Jake recalled the time he'd traveled to Italy with Amanda and Lucy more than a year and a half before on their first fact-finding trip in search of an atelier to make their bags. The trip had been a mix of business, fun, and lots of romance as it had taken place shortly after he'd proposed to Amanda.

After reading the article, Jake clicked on Amanda's photo album. He had looked through it many times before, but this time there was something that struck him and drew his attention. Before Amanda's page had blown up and developed a following, many of the photos she'd posted were of her and Jake, spanning several years from the time they were in college together at Stanford. Jake scrolled and scrolled, looking for those photos. He kept scrolling as far back as he could until it became abundantly evident that every single photo of him had been removed. "She deleted every single one?" Jake asked himself quietly. It made him sad, and his eyes watered. The fact that Amanda had left the pictures up for so long after their breakup was heartwarming. And when he had begun to contemplate getting back together with her, the photos offered a small glimmer of hope that the door might still be open for him. *Oh well, if you're my sister, things are definitely over between us. You might even have to share some of your money with me.* "That'll be a doozy," Jake said aloud to himself as he got up from his table to leave.

When he'd made it back to the office, Jake wondered why he hadn't yet heard from Tom with the paternity results. The day was growing late, so he decided to text him.

What's the status? Jake simply wrote.

Less than a minute later Tom replied back. *Still waiting to hear. They said before the end of the business day.*

Jake took a deep breath and patiently waited. For the remainder of the afternoon, he sat at his desk and buried himself in his work, drafting responses on behalf of his client to a set of questions sent from the Securities and Exchange Commission. Jake had become so engrossed in what he was doing that when he looked and noticed the time in the bottom right corner of his computer screen, two hours had passed and it was now five o'clock on the dot. It had been a productive couple of hours, and the work was stress-relieving. However, upon the seeing clock, Jake's angst immediately returned. He still hadn't heard from Tom, and they were set to meet in an hour with Mike in what he anticipated would be a most cantankerous confrontation. Jake wanted some time to digest the paternity news and to get in the right state of mind before the meeting took place, but the clock was ticking and time was running out.

Jake sighed hard as he rose from his desk and walked out of his office to the bathroom to take a leak. As he stood at the urinal, his heart began to pump faster and his mind raced with worst-case scenarios. *If Rick's my father I still won't demand anything. I don't want his money. But then, why not take my fair share of the family fortune if I turn out to be a Climent? Amanda will hate my guts for sure. Watch, I'll get blamed somehow for this whole mess if I don't keep quiet about it. Mom and Dad will probably divorce. Harry is going to shit on himself when he hears about all of this. My relationship with Mike won't survive this. I'm going to get fired. I should just leave anyway. I'm sick of this place already, and Mike's a crooked piece of shit—little did I know.*

When Jake got back to his desk and sat down, he looked at the clock again and saw that it was now a quarter past five. The meeting with Mike was at six. Growing impatient, Jake picked up his cell phone to call Tom. However, just as he did so, a call was coming through. The caller ID read *Dad*. "Thank God," Jake said, relieved. The moment of truth had finally arrived.

Jake was trembling. His heart was beating so hard and fast it felt as though it would pop right out of his chest. He paused, took a deep breath, and closed his eyes for two seconds. Then he answered the call.

"Hi, Dad."

CHAPTER TWENTY-FOUR

Jake sighed hard and slumped back in his chair after speaking with Tom. He rubbed his face with his hands and sat there quietly for a moment. He needed to decompress and gather his thoughts before he headed across the street to The California Club, where he and Tom were about to meet with Mike.

They had agreed during their call that Tom would take the lead in the discussion. Jake felt too worked up and angry and needed to gain control of his emotions. Besides, Tom wanted to take charge of the situation and confront his longtime friend and peer, man-to-man. Jake had told Tom about the testy exchange he'd had with Mike earlier that morning and said that he feared he was about to lose his job. Tom pledged to help Jake find a new job if things came to that and assured him that it wouldn't be a problem. After all, Tom was the executive vice president and general counsel of one of the largest global construction companies in the world. Any number of law firms would gladly hire anyone he recommended to them, especially someone who shared his last name.

Jake stepped out of his office and discreetly made his way down the hall opposite Mike's corner suite. He didn't want to run into him, let alone walk over to the meeting together with him. When he saw that the coast was clear, Jake hopped on the elevator and headed down to the lobby of the building. Then he made his way outside for the short walk across the street to The California Club. Just as Jake started to ascend the short set of stairs leading to the entrance of the stately members' only establishment, he saw Tom walking toward him. Tom's office was only a couple of blocks away.

Tom sported a broad smile as he approached Jake. Jake smiled back at him.

"See…I told you. How could you possibly be anybody else's son?" Tom said, clearly happy.

"I never really believed it. But I'm relieved to know officially that I'm your son and not Rick's."

"Come on. You're the spitting image of me," Tom said, wrapping his left arm around Jake's shoulder as they walked inside the building.

"You think? People always say Harry looks more like you."

"Nah…what do they know?"

"Well, needless to say, I don't look anything like Rick Climent or like anyone in that family. They all have dark features. Dark hair, dark eyes—"

"That's what I kept telling your mother, but she thought you, at least in appearance, had taken more after her in your DNA makeup. Anyway, regardless, it's resolved. You're not a Climent. You're a Doyle."

Jake followed Tom as they walked over to a corner table in the bar and took a seat.

"So I assume Mom knows the results?"

"Yeah, I spoke to her first."

"She must be feeling a little stupid right now."

Tom grimaced and looked away, his irritation with his wife still apparent.

Jake shook his head in disgust. "All of this—the lies, the cover-up, the multimillion dollar payoff offers—all for nothing. All Mom had to do, from the moment I first introduced Amanda to the two of you, was fess up about everything. We could've taken a DNA test way back then and gotten this over and done with. Amanda and her parents wouldn't have needed to know. We'd be married right now and possibly with a baby on the way. This whole fucking fiasco and the stress of it all is probably what caused her to miscarry. I can't fucking believe this, Dad. I'm so angry. And Amanda's with this other guy now and apparently they're already talking about getting married. It's not fair." Jake spoke sharply as his eyes watered and glistened with rage and disbelief.

"Jake, I don't know what to say other than I'm sorry. Sorry this happened to you. Had I known, I would've done exactly what you just said—taken the test to confirm paternity right away. And you're absolutely right, especially given that it turned out to be a false alarm—the Climents would've never known anything, and Mike wouldn't have been involved. However, that being said, the fact that he knowingly participated in this effort to deceive you does not sit well with me at all. I'm having a hard time getting my head around that—the lack of integrity and common decency, the lack of loyalty. Mike's one of my best friends. At least, that's what I thought. I can't believe he didn't come to me and tell me like a real friend's supposed to do."

"I guess he was lured by Rick's big fat pocketbook. I wonder how much he got paid to peddle this story about Amanda's phony sickness. Oh, did I tell you? When I spoke to him this morning, he admitted that he hadn't seen any medical records, nor had he spoken to any doctor who might've been treating Amanda. He said he just took Rick at his word."

Tom scoffed, rolling his eyes and shaking his head in disbelief, and then suddenly he noticed Mike walking across the room toward them. "Here he comes," Tom said through a forced smile as he rose to his feet to greet him.

"Hey, Tom," Mike said, extending his hand with a ready smile. "Sorry I'm a little late. Got held up on a call by this wannabe politician."

"Oh, yeah?" Tom said as he shook Mike's hand.

Jake remained in his seat, barely making eye contact with Mike.

"Hey, Jake," Mike said in obligatory acknowledgment before pulling out a chair to take a seat at the antique dark wood card table.

"Hey, Mike," Jake said unenthusiastically.

Jake was now in the middle with Tom to his left and Mike to his right. He sat and watched with a degree of chagrin as Tom and Mike began to engage in polite conversation as if everything was okeydokey.

"So who's the wannabe politician?" Tom asked.

"This guy I went to law school with. We weren't close but we've kept in touch over the years. He practiced in Fresno for quite a while before he became the top lobbyist for the California Agricultural Association. Now he runs this huge pomegranate farm in the Central Valley north of Bakersfield, making millions selling juice. He's in exclusive partnerships with two of the biggest juice-making companies in the country because his pomegranates are supposedly the best. And there's such a high demand in the industry around using pomegranates for all kinds of juice cocktails and concoctions because of the health benefits. They help to reduce heart disease and different types of cancers and such."

"How'd he get into farming?"

"The old-fashioned way—he married the wife of his former client. Of course, that was after he'd left his first wife."

"Oh, yeah?" Tom said, seeming amused and intrigued by the story.

"Apparently they were all friends, and the owner of the farm, who was my friend's client at some point, died of throat cancer a few years back. He hooked up with the widow not too long afterward and the rest is history. They didn't have children so she was left with everything. Now the farm and the business are all his and hers. Not a bad way to come into a lot of money, huh?"

"Now he wants to run for office?"

"Yeah, so anyway, he wants to run against Dianne Feinstein for her senate seat next year."

Tom raised his brow and snickered. "Good luck with that."

"I know, exactly. She's held that seat for almost twenty years and I don't think she's going anywhere anytime soon."

Right at that moment, a waiter appeared at the table and interrupted. "How about a drink, gentlemen?"

"I'll have a Scotch," Tom said immediately.

"Me too," Mike said.

"On the rocks?"

"Yes, please," Tom said.

"For me as well," Mike said. "Thanks."

The waiter then looked at Jake.

"I'll just have water," he said, feeling hot and nearly sweating. Jake wanted to get down to business. Enough with the pleasantries. However, to his annoyance, Tom and Mike continued to banter on about the wannabe politician like the old friends they'd long been. Jake looked over at his dad with a cutting glare, growing increasingly irritated and anxious, but he knew that was Tom's way—ever the courtly gentleman. Even when Jake got into trouble as a teenage boy, Tom would always ease his way into reprimanding or disciplining him with small talk about something completely unrelated. But Jake always knew that the other shoe would eventually drop. So he sat and waited for his dad to do that here.

The waiter returned to the table in short order and placed a drink in front of each man. Mike lifted his glass. "Well, gentlemen, here's to wishing my law school classmate comes to his senses and saves himself the money and embarrassment of trying to unseat an unbeatable incumbent for US Senate next year."

"I'll drink to that," Tom said, clinking his glass with Mike's.

Jake raised his glass to tap with theirs half-heartedly but kept quiet.

Mike finally took notice of Jake's stillness and attempted to bring him into the conversation. "Glad you're working on Jake about joining our fundraising committee. We need to increase our ranks. I'm afraid our numbers are beginning to thin. We need fresh blood," Mike said, reaching over to grab Jake by the shoulder good-naturedly.

Jake looked down without attempting to feign amusement or interest.

Tom looked over at him with an expression that indicated he knew how awkward and uncomfortable his son must feel.

Mike continued to talk. "Jake and I had a little disagreement this morning, and I can tell he's a little upset with me, but I'm sure we'll work everything out. Won't we, Jake?" Mike said, still holding Jake by the shoulder.

"I don't know about that," Jake said as he flipped his shoulder just enough to prompt Mike to remove his hand. Jake had had enough. No more dancing around the issue. "I'm actually here to continue our conversation from this morning, Mike, not to talk about fundraising or the golf tournament."

Mike pulled away from Jake, stunned. He looked over at Tom to register his reaction to what he considered to be intemperate behavior on Jake's part, but Tom stared back at him, stone-faced.

Taken aback, Mike looked at Jake again and then back at Tom. Mike acted as if he was expecting Tom to tell Jake to cool it, but Tom continued to stare at him coldly. "What? Am I being tag-teamed? What's this about?"

"It's about the role you played in telling this falsehood about Amanda being sick in order to get me to break up with her."

Mike turned red as he looked over at Tom and then back at Jake. "What falsehood?"

"Don't act like you don't know what I'm talking about, Mike. You fucking lied. You lied!" Jake said in a raised voice and pointing his finger at Mike for emphasis.

At that point, Tom stepped in to cool things down. He reached over and squeezed Jake on the arm. "Okay, okay. Settle down, and let's keep our voices down," he said calmly.

Mike was incredulous. "What's wrong with you? I didn't lie to you."

Jake snickered and shook his head mockingly.

"Mike, we know," Tom said.

"Know what?"

"We know the truth. Jamie's admitted everything—the affair with Rick, keeping it covered up for all of these years. We took a paternity test, and Jake's my son, not Rick's."

Mike looked at Tom with befuddlement. "I have no idea what you're talking about."

"Come on, man, cut the bullshit," Tom sneered, becoming impatient.

"Tom, I swear on my life. I don't know what you're talking about. You're telling me Jamie had an affair with Rick Climent?"

Tom looked at Mike sideways. "So you don't know that? What did Rick tell you when he hired you to get Jake to break up with Amanda?"

"I'm sorry…one moment, please," Mike struggled to say as he choked and then coughed hard a few times. He seemed caught off guard and a bit overwhelmed. He took a sip of his Scotch to help clear his throat before attempting to speak again. "Everything Rick told me is what I told Jake. That Amanda had and apparently still has dissociative identity disorder and that she was a danger to herself and potentially to others, specifically to you, leading up to your wedding," Mike said, turning to Jake. "He asked me to help explain that to you, and that's what I did. Rick felt if he'd told you this himself, you might not have believed him."

"Of course I wouldn't've believed him," Jake said. "I believed you. I took your word for it because I've known you since I was, like, five years old. You're like family. I never would've believed that you of all people would lie to me. I trusted you…like an uncle."

"Jake, I didn't lie to you. All I told you is what I knew."

"But Mike, you know it's all a lie. Don't you? Rick made the whole thing up because he thought Jake might be his son."

"So you're telling me Jamie had an affair with Rick at some point and they thought Jake might be his son and not yours?"

"Yes!" Tom and Jake both said in unison.

Mike turned white as he chuckled uncomfortably. "I'm sorry, but this is news to me. I swear to God, I knew nothing about this. When did all of this come to light?"

"Mike, Jamie had been keeping this secret all to herself for years. The affair with Rick occurred a long time ago. I guess a little more than a year into our marriage. It only lasted for about a month, she claims, but all this time she believed there was a strong possibility that Jake might be a by-product of the affair. At least, that's what she believed up until now."

"You said Jamie had kept this to herself for a number of years. So at some point she told Rick?"

"Yes, but she didn't tell him until about a couple of months before the wedding. She panicked after having waited for so long to tell the truth, and with the wedding being around the corner, she finally fessed up, but instead of coming clean and telling me and Jake, she went to Rick, and they decided to devise a plan to break Jake and Amanda up without revealing anything about the affair. They wanted to keep that a secret, obviously."

The astonishment on Mike's face said it all, but he articulated what he was feeling nevertheless. "This is fucking insane."

"Jamie left everything up to Rick. He told her that he'd handle everything. She didn't know what he'd done to convince Jake to call off the wedding. All she knew is that whatever he did or said had worked. Now we know a big part of the reason why—because you were involved. It was clever of Rick to enlist you to do his dirty work."

"So when did you find out about all of this…about the affair and everything?"

"Well, there's one other person Jamie spoke to."

"Who?"

"Our minister."

"He's the one who told me," Jake said. "Remember when you advised me to seek counseling or professional help after I'd become upset about seeing Amanda with this guy Adam Weinstock? Well, I decided to go see him. He thought I knew about the affair and the whole paternity issue, but I didn't, and he ended up telling me by accident."

"When was this?" Mike asked.

"Toward the end of last month."

"I'm speechless right now. I don't know what to say."

"So Rick told you Amanda had a mental disorder and you didn't substantiate it by reviewing any medical records or consulting with her physician?" Tom asked.

"Tom, you know I can't have access to her medical records. She's an adult. I'd need her consent."

"But you didn't think you needed her consent to go around telling people, namely her fiancé, that she had a mental illness? That's a pretty scandalous thing to say about someone without any hard evidence. Plus, she's not under the legal guardianship of her parents, is she? One would reasonably assume that if Amanda was as sick as Rick claimed and posed a serious risk to her own well-being, Rick and Camilla would've petitioned a court for full if not limited legal guardianship at a minimum."

"I did ask him about that. He said that since her alter ego appeared sporadically depending on the life event and not on a daily basis, he didn't feel guardianship was necessary at the moment. She could still function for the most part. He said they were keeping the option open but didn't feel the need to put her through the stress of a court hearing, especially when she was in denial about her condition."

Jake and Tom both shook their heads and chuckled derisively. "He didn't want to pursue a hearing because there's no basis to his claims. He would've been laughed right out of court," Jake said.

Mike seemed humiliated and embarrassed. "Look, I guess Rick had me fooled, I'm sorry to admit. I took him at his word. I was trying to help out a friend and a longtime client who appeared to be genuinely in need of my help."

"Looks more to me like you were trying to keep a lucrative business relationship intact at the expense of a twenty-plus-year relationship with me and my family," Tom said.

"Tom, come on. That's not the case at all."

"But what about Jake? Where was your concern for him in all of this?"

"I did my best make sure Jake would get taken care of and would be made whole to the greatest degree possible. In fact, I told Rick that I wouldn't even take the matter on unless he made Jake a minimum offer that I felt was acceptable in light of the circumstances."

"The five million?"

"Right. In fact, Rick had offered to pay more. You know that," Mike said, turning to Jake.

"It's not about the money. It never was. I was just trying to do what was best for Amanda based on what you and Rick told me."

"I still don't understand why you didn't come to me. You could've gotten me involved," Tom told Mike. "I would've dug deeper. That's for damn sure. I would've demanded medical records, some sort of written proof. Fuck this shit about Amanda being an adult and all. If she'd been sick with this ailment for as long as Rick claimed, since she was a small child, then they would have something in writing about it—a written diagnosis, prescriptions, treatment plans, something."

"Tom, if I could've spoken to you and gotten you involved, I would have, but Rick was adamant about keeping everything quiet. That's why he wanted Jake to sign a confidentiality agreement and offered to pay him millions of dollars."

"Well, for obvious reasons. The whole thing was nefarious. That son of a bitch should be criminally prosecuted. At a minimum, we have enough to bring a civil case for fraud."

Mike looked at Tom forebodingly. "Do you really want to go there? What about Jamie? She could be viewed as a coconspirator."

Tom glared at Mike, clearly agitated. "So what did you get out of this? What did Rick offer you?"

"I didn't get anything. Not a single dime. Rick offered to pay me a fee, but I declined."

"I see. As long as he and his companies continue to give you their business—"

"God damn it, Tom, don't try to impugn my character. Come on. You know me better than that. My motivation in all of this was to help Jake. I acknowledge that I might not have gone about it in the best way. I should've done more due diligence—seeking medical records and asking to speak with their family doctor—but at the end of the day, Jake has to take some responsibility for his role in this, too. We didn't hold a gun to his head. He walked away willingly." Mike turned to look at Jake. "It was your decision and your decision alone whether to break up with Amanda. When you think about it, Rick was basically at your mercy. You held all of the cards. You, too, could've pressed for more information, demanded to see medical records, requested to speak to a doctor, but you didn't. I know you had faith in my integrity and you trusted me, but Amanda was your fiancée, for Christ's sake. You could've put up more of a fight."

Jake sighed and sat back in his chair and listened. What could he say? Mike had a point. "You're right. I could've done more, but I didn't,"

Jake conceded before pausing for a moment to think back. "From the moment I uttered those words to Amanda…when I broke up with her… that I wasn't in love with her anymore, and that I couldn't marry her, I knew what I was doing was wrong."

"Then why'd you do it?" Tom asked.

Jake couldn't come up with an answer.

CHAPTER TWENTY-FIVE

The next day, Jake arrived to work early and immediately buried himself in the details of the case he was working on involving the SEC investigation of his client. Taking the lead in handling such an important case with a new client to the firm helped him to focus on his work with a renewed sense of energy and dedication. He remained confined to his office from the time he'd arrived at seven thirty that morning until well past noon.

Jake's assistant, Patti, pushed the partially closed door open and poked her head through. "Peekaboo!"

Jake stopped what he was doing, looked up at her, and smiled. "Come on in," he said, waving his arm.

"Your door's been pulled closed for so long, I thought maybe you'd left without me noticing," Patti said as she stepped toward the front of Jake's desk.

"Oh, I was just trying to keep from being distracted. How are you?"

"I'm fine. How are you? You've seemed so on edge this week. Has this new case got you in a tizzy?"

Jake chuckled. "No. I'm excited about this case, actually."

"Well, and I know you had a family matter to deal with earlier this week. I hope everything's okay."

"Thanks. Things are a little better," Jake said, keeping it vague.

"I hope nobody's sick or anything. That's always so stressful, dealing with a sick parent. When my mother was battling breast cancer before she passed away—this was before you started working here—I had to take so much time off to care for her with the chemotherapy treatments and all, and then she got sick from that and had to be admitted to the hospital because she had such a violent reaction to it. It made her condition worse."

Jake sensed that Patti was fishing, but he tried to be sympathetic. "Fortunately, nobody's sick. Just some unexpected family drama. So sorry to hear about your mom, though. I didn't know."

"Oh, thanks. She's been gone now for more than eight years. Anyway, did you have lunch?"

"No, I've been glued to my desk all day."

"Jake, you haven't even gone to lunch yet? What time is it?" Patti said as she lifted her arm to look at her watch. "Two thirty! It's two thirty, Jake. Aren't you hungry?"

"I am, actually."

"Jake, get out of here and go get you something to eat already."

"I know, I know. I'll go shortly."

"No. Right now, Jake. Come on," she said, motioning with her hand for Jake to rise from his seat. "Let's go, sweetie. I'm going to play your mama now. I'll play your assistant again when you get back. Let's go."

Amused at Patti's insistence, Jake laughed. "Oh, all right. I'll go. I could use a little walk, anyway. My legs feel a bit cramped," he said as he stood to his feet and walked around from behind his desk, wobbly.

Jake went downstairs to the food court in the basement of his building and bought a Chinese chicken salad along with a bottle of water. He then rode back up the escalator to sit and eat outside in the warm sun. Although it was midwinter, it was a cozy seventy-two degrees in LA. Jake put on his sunglasses and took a seat at a table without an umbrella in the massive courtyard that graced the front of his office tower complex.

Jake devoured his salad quickly, barely looking up to notice what was going on around him. He was hungrier than he'd realized, not stopping to take a drink of his water until he'd finished eating first. He took a long gulp of his water, nearly finishing it before setting the bottle back down on the table. He stretched out and crossed his legs, leaned back in his chair with his hands folded behind his head, and soaked in the warm, hypnotic feel of the sun splashing across his face. *This feels so good,* Jake thought as he closed his eyes and slowly drifted off to a light sleep—just enough to lose a degree of consciousness while still having marginal sensory awareness of the sound of moving traffic in the street and the faint voices of passersby. Jake heard himself as he began to snore. He popped his head up and opened his eyes briefly. He adjusted himself in his seat and folded his arms across his chest before he closed his eyes again and drifted off back to wonderland.

He probably would've ended up there longer than he'd planned had he not been awakened by the ring of his cell phone. Jake's eyes popped open at the sound. He picked up his phone off the table and saw a number appear across his caller ID that he didn't recognize. The area code read 212. *Who could be calling me from New York?*

"Hello, this is Jake."

"Hello, Jake. I guess you've been expecting my call."

"Who is this?" Jake asked, not recognizing the male voice at first.

"It's Rick. Rick Climent."

Stunned into silence, Jake didn't answer back. He actually wasn't expecting a call from Rick, certainly not at that moment.

"I'm sorry that I haven't gotten back to you. I've been traveling, but anyway, I think we need to talk."

"I know, Rick. I know everything. And in case you haven't heard yet, we took a paternity test, and I'm not your son."

There was silence on the other end of the line for a moment before Rick decided to speak again. "Listen, I'll be back in LA tomorrow. Would you be available to meet with me? I'd be happy to meet you wherever you'd like. Just name a time and place that works for you."

"Meet about what? I have nothing to say to you."

"I want to make a deal with you…to see if we could come to some sort of compromise."

"Compromise? What is there to compromise? Unless you have some magical powers enabling you to turn back time to August of last year when Amanda and I were about to walk down the aisle and get married, I don't see the point."

"Jake, there's a lot at stake."

"A lot at stake for whom? I've already lost in this whole situation. My ex-fiancée is now with another dude. My family's broken up or close to it. I mean…the bomb has already gone off."

"Jake, I don't expect you to have any sympathy for me, but let's be fair here. Your mother sprang this whole damn thing on me at the last minute. Right before your wedding. I had no idea she had believed all these years that you might be my son. She begged me to help her keep the whole thing a secret. And obviously, I didn't want my daughter marrying a guy she might be related to—"

"But you should've had the balls to own up to what you did. There's no excuse. None. We could've taken a paternity test back then, before the wedding. It could've been done in a low-key way. Nobody would've known. And, look, the test results proved that I'm not your son anyway. So everything would've worked out fine. You and Mom could've kept your dirty little secret to yourselves to some degree, and Amanda and I could've moved on with our lives. But you were so fucking selfish, you and my mom both. You guys really fucked up. Big time!"

"In hindsight, persuading Jamie to let us do a paternity test would've been the right thing to do, but—"

"But you had to go and make up this bullshit story instead. What do you think Amanda would have to say about that? And by the way, has your wife heard about all of this? Because as you probably know by now, I spoke to her earlier this week and she didn't seem to have a clue."

"Jake, I will give you what you want. Name your price. You know I'm good for it. I can help you write your ticket…to do whatever you want."

"So you want to pay for my silence, like before?"

"Yes. Let's just make this whole thing go away. You continue to stay away from Amanda and keep everything that's happened—the story I told you about Amanda's health, the affair I had with your mother, the paternity test—all to yourself in exchange for the offer of a lifetime… complete and total financial freedom."

"But why should I protect you?"

"Because if you care anything about your long-term financial security—"

"We've got money, Rick," Jake said testily.

"That's fair. Your family has modest wealth. Tom has done very well for himself climbing the corporate ladder, and he no doubt stands to inherit a moderate sum from his parents when the time comes. But if he stopped working today, I suspect that it would alter your family's lifestyle and future prospects for significant, uninterrupted wealth accumulation. You see, you and your dad have careers. You still have to work in order to make your wealth grow. You come from a family of distinguished lawyers and you've continued in that the tradition. There's nothing wrong with that. That's the path you've chosen and it's an honorable one. But the difference between my wealth and your family's is that you and your dad are either employed by multibillion-dollar companies or you represent them as counsel. I buy, sell, and own billion-dollar companies all day long. I have people on my payroll who make what your father makes and much more. I can see to it that you never have to work again a day in your life, Jake. You'd be free to pursue whatever dreams or aspirations you might have. Or you could be sitting pretty traveling the world, playing the best golf courses, and surfing the most beautiful beaches all day long. Whatever suits your fancy."

Jake rolled his eyes at Rick's pretention. Although he knew Rick's assertions about the Doyle family's wealth were true to an extent, Jake wasn't about to validate the comments, so he remained silent.

"You don't have to make a decision right now, Jake. Just think about it. I know you've been through a lot, and I'm partially to blame for that. I want to repay you somehow. Honestly, I do. Think about the possibilities before making a rash decision driven by irrational emotion and whatever disdain you must feel for me."

Jake sighed in agitation as he digested Rick's words. On the one hand, he wanted to tell Rick to go fuck himself, but on the other hand, his offer sounded enticing and extremely generous. It was as if the lottery jackpot was being handed to him freely without having to buy a single ticket. Hanging up on Rick would've seemed too ungracious, too hostile. Nevertheless, Jake kept his response curt and to the point. "Rick, if I'm interested in talking with you further about your offer, I'll let you know. In the meantime, don't feel the need to call me again. I'll call you. Good-bye," he said and then promptly clicked the off button to end the call.

Chapter
Twenty-Six

Amanda walked into her office, arriving a little later than usual. She'd had an appointment with her leasing agent first thing that morning.

"How'd it go? Is it official?" Lucy asked.

"It's official. I'm a New York City resident again," Amanda said, holding up the key to her new apartment.

Lucy let out a shrill of happy delight and clapped her hands. She rose from her seat to hug her friend. "That's so awesome. I'm so happy for you. We get to be neighbors."

"I know. I'm really excited about it. It's a great apartment. Can't wait to show it to you. You're going to love it."

"I can't wait to see it. I want help you decorate. We should go furniture shopping this weekend."

"Absolutely. I'd love to. I want to at least go and pick out a bed and sofa and maybe a dining table along with some dishes—you know, basic stuff like that so that I'm not sleeping and eating on the floor."

"No, exactly. I have some ideas of places we can go in SoHo. Have you heard of New York Designs? They have the most fabulous furniture."

"Yeah, but they're kind of pricey, aren't they? I don't want to spend a ton of money. I just want to find some nice pieces at a decent price. I don't plan on spending the kind of money I spent on my condo in LA."

"They're expensive, but they have good bargains sometimes, too. They mark stuff down all the time. We can at least go and have a look."

"Okay. Perfect. Let's plan for tomorrow," Amanda said as she picked up her phone to enter the date in her calendar.

Lucy reached for her phone too. Let's see, tomorrow's Saturday. What are you thinking, late morning, early afternoon?

"How about late morning, around ten thirty or eleven? We can go and see my place, have brunch afterward, and then go looking for furniture, if that works for you. I don't want to hog your day or anything."

"Oh, please. I have nothing else planned. Eleven sounds great. I'll meet you at your hotel," Lucy said.

"Yayyy," Amanda sang before taking a seat at her desk and turning her attention to a very full plate of work. The launch party for Novel was in less than two weeks and there was so much left to do. A project Amanda had been working on was helping to line up sponsors to donate items for the gift bags that would be handed out at the event. Initially it had been like herding cats getting other brands to give their stuff away at somebody else's product launch. However, after Amanda's high-profile appearances with Adam during the film awards season combined with the press she and Lucy had been receiving leading up to their event, the tide had turned. Their event was now the hot ticket in the New York fashion scene and sponsors were lining up to be part of the party; even ones that had not been approached were trying to buy their way into the event. Later that day, Amanda received a phone call with some exciting news from the public relations firm they'd hired to coordinate their launch event.

"Oh my God, guess what?" Amanda turned to Lucy and said.

"Who was that?"

"It was Nicole. You know those two girls from Korea who started that new skin care line, White Silk?"

"Yeah?"

"They want to donate three different samples of their products for our gift bag: their hand lotion, their facial wash, their Morning Glory moisturizer."

"Really?"

"But wait—there's more. On top of that, they're offering to pay a third of our costs for the launch party."

"What? No way."

"I know. Can you believe that? Their PR people think it would be a good for them to align their brand with American brands that target a similar demographic. They feel that the women who can afford to buy a moderate- to high-priced bag like ours are the kind of women who would buy their products, and apparently they too have entered into some sort of deal with Delaney's to introduce their products to the American market. Plus Nicole said that they like that we have similar stories. You know, how they're two young entrepreneurial women like we are. Did you know they left med school here in the States against their families' wishes to develop their line?"

"Yeah, I think I read that somewhere. They do have an interesting story."

"This could be great for us because their product is already doing pretty well in South Korea. Having an association with them could provide us with exposure to that market."

"Well, not in the short run because of our exclusive with Delaney's. They don't have stores or do much business outside the United States."

"But there are lots of Koreans who live here in the States. There's a huge Korean population in LA, for example. They have a lot of money, or at least some of them do, and they like to spend money on Western brands. White Silk would basically be like an endorsement of our brand to that market."

"Wow, this all sounds great, especially the offer to help cover the direct costs of the event. Nobody else is doing that."

"There's one caveat, though. They want an exclusive."

Lucy looked at Amanda forebodingly. "As in—"

"No other skin care lines or fragrances can be a sponsor of our event or contribute product for the gift bags."

"But what about my mom's new skin care line? She's already agreed to provide product at the event."

Amanda slapped her hand to her forehead. "Oh shit. That's right. I forgot."

"Would they be willing to share the spotlight with just one other skin care product? She's only doing a fragrance sample, I believe."

"No, I don't think so, because they also have a fragrance. Nicole said they were firm about wanting an exclusive deal and really weren't open to negotiation about it."

"So you didn't tell Nicole that Alana Dupree skin care had already committed to the event?"

Amanda felt bad about her mistake and spoke with a pained expression on her face. "I'm so sorry. I totally forgot to tell her…otherwise she probably wouldn't have even entertained their offer in the first place. What do you think we should do?"

"Oh, Amanda. Don't worry about it. My mom is a team player. If you think this is a good opportunity for us then she'll back out. It'll be fine." Lucy sounded half assuring and half annoyed at the same time, which made Amanda hesitant.

"Well, what do you think? Do you agree that it's a good opportunity? In many respects this will do more for us in terms of giving us an entree to a whole new market. I mean, I think people at the party would enjoy receiving a free sample of Alana's fragrance, but from a marketing standpoint it won't do much for us."

"Well…no…of course. The gift bag sponsors are promoting themselves and their own products, mostly. They don't go into these kinds of events thinking that they are going to provide exposure for us. We're giving them exposure in exchange for agreeing to provide some swag to make our party more fabulous. Listen, just do whatever you think is best. You've been handling lining up sponsors for the event with Nicole. I trust your decision. My mom doesn't need this event to promote her fragrance, but if you want her to pull out, don't ask me to speak to her about it. You should do it."

"I know Alana was only doing this as a favor to us. But I don't want her to be mad. Do you think she'll be upset?"

"No."

"Then why do you want me to speak to her and not you?"

"Because you are in charge of the launch event, Amanda. That's what we agreed to since I was busy trying to get buyers for our line before we inked the deal with Delaney's while you were off traveling and attending premiers with Adam. Now put on your big girl panties and make a decision."

Amanda snickered and rolled her eyes. "Okay, I'm going to call Nicole back to see if we can get them to do it while keeping Alana on board."

Amanda picked up the phone to dial Nicole back, but just as she did so a voice came across the line. It was the receptionist.

"Amanda?"

"Yes."

"You have a flower delivery here waiting for you."

"For me?" Amanda asked, surprised.

"Yeah. The delivery guy is standing right here. I told him that he could leave them here with me, but he says that you have to sign for them personally."

"Oh…okay. I'll be right out."

Amanda hung the phone up and rose to her feet. "Someone's sent me flowers."

Lucy looked up at her. "Who?"

"I don't know, but I have to sign for them personally, apparently."

"Oh God. I wonder if they're from Jake."

"Maybe, but Jake was never a flowers kind of guy. I'd be surprised if they were from him."

"I bet they are."

Amanda walked out of the office and down the corridor to the reception desk near the elevator. As she got closer, she could hear a male voice say something to the receptionist. The voice sounded familiar, but Amanda immediately dismissed the person she thought of, knowing that he was nowhere near Manhattan.

Amanda turned the corner and saw the receptionist sitting at her desk and the man holding the flowers with his back to her, looking at some photographs on the wall.It was wintertime in New York, and Amanda noticed the man's casual but dapper attire. He was wearing a dark pair of designer jeans, a wool sports coat, a turtleneck accented by a scarf around the collar, and a knitted beanie. Even through his layers, Amanda could tell that the tall man had a striking physique, and she admired his good taste in fashion. *How odd*, she thought, for a delivery man to be dressed so smartly and debonairly.

"Sir, here she is," the receptionist said to the man after Amanda had approached them.

The man turned around with a big smile across his face.

Amanda nearly fainted when she realized who it was.

CHAPTER TWENTY-SEVEN

"Surprise, surprise," the man said.

"Adam! Oh my God. What are you doing here?" Amanda said, slapping her hands to her cheeks. She was so overwhelmed and taken by surprise that she began to tear up.

"Aren't you happy to see me?" Adam said as he stepped toward her with the large vase of flowers in hand.

Amanda waved her hands in front of her face, not because she was hot but because she was overwhelmed. Then she wiped the corner of her eyes with her fingertips to dot away the tears. "Of course I am. Wait, how did you get here? I just spoke to you this morning, and you sent me a text like an hour ago telling me that you were on your way to meet someone very special."

"That's right, and here I am. I was on my way to meet you."

"Oh my God," Amanda said again as she stomped her foot and started to laugh, covering her face with her hands and shaking her head in disbelief.

"Awww, that's so sweet," the receptionist said with the biggest smile across her face ever.

"I thought you were on your way to meet someone related to your film project," Amanda said, visibly flummoxed. Then she turned to the receptionist to relay the exchange she'd had with Adam just an hour before via text. "He was like, 'I'm headed to an important meeting right now; I'm on my way to meet someone very special; I'll tell you about it later; I'm running behind.' And I'm like, 'Okay…have a good meeting. Good luck.'"

Adam handed the vase of flowers to Amanda.

"These are sooo beautiful. Thank you so much," Amanda said before Adam planted a big one on her lips, muffling the sound of her voice on the last word she uttered.

Amanda was so smitten by Adam's unexpected appearance and warm kiss that her knees nearly buckled. She leaned into him, placing her head to the top of his chest to keep from falling over. Adam immediately wrapped his left arm around her and held her tight against his body as he rubbed and caressed her back and then kissed the crown of her head. The warmth of his body, the feel of his clothes, and the fresh, clean manliness of his scent made Amanda's heart flutter.

"I've missed you," Amanda said, looking up at him.

"I've missed you, too," he replied, and then kissed her lips again. They turned to walk toward her office arm in arm, continuing to kiss each other softly and repeatedly.

"Look at who my delivery man turned out to be," Amanda said as she and Adam walked through the office door.

"Oh my God," Lucy screeched, lifting her hands to cover her mouth.

"Hey, Lucy," Adam said cheerfully.

"It was you? You were the guy delivering the flowers?"

Adam grinned broadly.

"Yep, he was the one, not who you thought," Amanda said as she placed her beautiful bouquet on top of her desk.

"How sweet are you? What a nice surprise," Lucy said as she stood up and walked over to give Adam a hug.

"Isn't he hottest-looking delivery man ever?" Amanda said as Lucy and Adam embraced. "He had his back to me when I first walked into the reception area, and I was like, damn, this guy has a hot ass."

They all busted out laughing.

"I'm surprised you didn't recognize me until I turned around," Adam said.

"You know, I heard your voice when I was walking down the hall and I thought, that sounds like Adam. But then I was like, he's in Toronto. He just texted me on his way to a meeting, so that can't be him."

"That's too funny. So your meeting's actually here in New York?" Lucy asked Adam, still not catching on.

"The meeting's with me. He was pulling my leg," Amanda replied.

"I just came to surprise my girl and to spend the weekend with her. I have no other business here," Adam said as he stepped over to Amanda, wrapped his arms around her from behind, and held her tight. Amanda could barely contain her glee as she melted in his embrace and kicked up her heel.

Lucy reacted emotionally to Adam's act of chivalry. She began to tear up just like Amanda had at first, but she felt a little envious too. "See? Why doesn't Cass surprise me like that?"

***

Adam and Amanda headed out shortly thereafter like two giddy teenagers with no place to go.

"What do you want to do?"

"I don't know. What do you want to do?" Adam replied coyly.

Amanda was already wet, imagining herself underneath Adam after having not seen him for a while, but she didn't want to be so forward. "Where are your bags?" she asked, changing the subject.

"I just brought my backpack. I dropped it off at my place already," Adam said, referring to his apartment and second home in New York, which he kept fully supplied with toiletries and clothes. "Where are you staying? Your usual place?"

"Yep. The Gramercy Park."

"You want to hang out with me at my place for the weekend?"

"Uhhh…sure, I'd love to," Amanda said, looking at Adam as they walked side by side. He looked back at her and then leaned over to rub the tip of his nose to hers, which caused Amanda to giggle and glance away.

"Did you really need to think about it? Gee whiz."

Amanda laughed at herself, embarrassed. "Well—⊠

"Well, what? Are you trying to play hard to get all of a sudden?"

"No. I just don't want to crowd your space or anything," she said bashfully.

Adam took her by the hand as they continued to walk. "You wouldn't be crowding my space, especially if I asked you to be there with me. I tell you all the time that you are more than welcome to use my apartment whenever you're in New York instead of spending six to seven hundred a night at the Gramercy Park Hotel."

"I know, but I've got a new place now."

"Even though you could've moved into my place, but I won't bring that up again."

Amanda looked away and rolled her eyes. "Anyway, I'm so excited to show it to you."

"And she changes the subject," he said sarcastically. "So where is this place?"

"I told you. In the East Village on Tenth Street. It's a great neighborhood. I love it."

"That is a great neighborhood," Adam agreed.

"Hey! Lucy and I were planning to go furniture shopping tomorrow."

"Great! I'll go with you."

Amanda and Adam continued to walk and talk hand and hand until they made it to the Gramercy Park Hotel, one of New York's most fashionable and popular hotels with the A-list celebrity crowd. It was happy hour by the time they'd arrived, so they decided to drop by the hotel's Rose Bar for a drink.

After they stepped inside the hotel lobby, Adam removed his beanie. Amanda took notice of his hair.

"Your hair's longer and curlier, too. That's why I don't think I recognized you before. Plus, you had your cap on."

"Yeah, I haven't had a haircut since I left LA."

"It looks good though. I like it," she said, reaching to touch his hair before wrapping her arms around him as they walked into the bar.

They sat cozily next each other on a sofa, sipping cocktails. Adam could barely keep his hands off Amanda as she tried to carry on a conversation with him about the state of his film project in Canada, the first he was directing himself. Slightly turned toward one another, Adam had his right arm around Amanda's waist, gripping her hip with his right hand. Then he raised his left hand up as if wanting her to give him a high five. Amanda responded by raising and touching her open hand to his while talking at the same time.

"So what's it been like directing Tobias Velasquez?" Amanda asked, referring to the film's lead actor.

Adam seemed more interested in foreplay than talking. He stared at Amanda seductively with his piercing, deep blue eyes, and with their hands still suspended in the air, he interlocked his fingers with hers, gripping her hand tightly. Then he licked his lips and moved in to kiss her with his mouth partly open.

Amanda was turned on by the sight of Adam's pink, succulent lips, which were framed by the stubble of a beard that looked as if it hadn't been shaved in a few days. She could feel the warmth of his breath on her mouth as he moved in closer to her and could practically taste the bourbon on his tongue from the whiskey sour he was drinking. The heat was rising in her chest. She wanted to kiss him. In fact, she wanted to jump him right there on that sofa, but she pulled back and acted unaffected, like a girl with self-control. She unlocked her hand from his and put it to his mouth to stop him. "Adam…aren't you going to answer my question? I'm curious to know about Tobias. He's such an amazing actor."

Adam smirked as he pulled Amanda's hand away from his mouth and held it down on his thigh, near his crotch. "An amazing pain in the ass. It's torture. He's too busy trying to tell me how to do my job instead of just acting and following direction. But I kind of knew what I was in getting myself into, so I really shouldn't complain."

"Then why did you choose to work with him?"

"Oh…you know me. I have a penchant for wanting to work with actors who are fucking…high-maintenance, narcissistic egomaniacs. I'm a masochist. What can I say?"

Before Amanda could manage a comeback, Adam quickly returned to foreplay, raising Amanda's hand back to his mouth. He closed his eyes as he kissed her palm softly. Then he inhaled it adoringly. "Mmmm, you smell so good," he moaned. Then he licked her palm. "And you taste so good," he said before attempting to suck her middle finger.

"Adam!" Amanda said, snatching her hand away and giggling. "There are people watching. Oh my God."

"Nobody's watching us," he said, looking around before turning his gaze back to her. "Who's watching us?"

"I'm trying to carry on a conversation with you—"

"And I'm trying to seduce you, but I don't know. It seems like I've lost my touch, lost my swagger, because you're acting all uptight and distant."

Amanda huffed. "No I'm not. How am I being distant?"

"When we were walking over here, you had to think about whether you wanted to stay with me at my place this weekend—"

"I really wasn't thinking that hard, Adam—"

"And look at you now, acting all tight and so civilized. This is how you were when we first met. I'm surprised we're not humping like wild animals by now."

Amanda laughed out loud and then covered her mouth to muffle the sound.

Adam grinned. "You know, like we were in Paris and Madrid. Remember that?" Adam said in a teasing, seductive tone. He still had his right arm wrapped around her waist with his right hand cupping her hip while using his left hand to rub and squeeze her knee as he talked.

Growing hotter and wetter, Amanda giggled, recalling the memory of her and Adam together during their travel from city to city for the world premiere of his last film, leading up to the Oscars. "Oh yes, I remember."

Adam piled on, raising his left hand to her chin to pinch and hold it gently. "Don't you want me, baby? I've missed you so much," he said before leaning in to kiss her lips softly.

Amanda didn't resist as Adam kissed them again and again, causing her to fall under his spell slowly but surely.

"You are so beautiful. You know that? You look so amazing right now. I love this blouse on you," Adam said as he tugged on her collar and gazed into her eyes. "I just want to rip it open and taste you...lick and suck on your tits," he said before leaning in to kiss her again.

Amanda closed her eyes, savoring the feel of his lips to hers. Then she opened them again and just stared at Adam, mesmerized, as he continued to taunt her seductively with his words and hands.

"Don't you want me to make you feel good, princess?" Adam asked as he reached back up to touch her neck. Then he ran his hand down to her open collar to gently touch the top of her chest before allowing his hand to fall to her lap, grazing her breast on the way down.

Reflexively, Amanda pushed her chest out in response. It was as if her body had instinctively taken over and invited Adam to grope and feel her up even more. At the same time, Amanda's nipples felt hard and prickly against the fabric of her blouse, which she wore sans a bra. Her breasts were screaming for attention—aching to be touched, squeezed, licked, and sucked.

Adam took notice of Amanda's swooning gaze, the flushness of her neck and upper chest, the provocation in her raised chest and taut nipples poking against her blouse, her silent submission. He knew that it was time—time to take charge. "Let's go to your room," he said assertively, rising up from the sofa and taking Amanda by the hand to lead her away.

CHAPTER TWENTY-EIGHT

The moment they'd stepped into the elevator, it was game on. Using one hand, Adam went straight for Amanda's crotch, practically lifting her off her feet and slamming her back against the elevator wall. He used his other hand to feel and caress her left breast as he slid his tongue deep into her mouth to kiss her voraciously. Amanda moaned in pleasure, enjoying being manhandled. Adam's aggressiveness turned her on and drove her crazy. She slapped her hands to his face when their mouths and tongues locked, kissing him back wildly. As he squeezed and rubbed her kitty aggressively, she lifted one of her legs to enhance the friction. She placed it back down and lifted it up again. It was like an involuntary impulse. The sensation was so intense and it felt so good; she could barely control herself. "Adam, oh Adam…oh, oh, oh my God," she said breathlessly.

Adam stopped his torture momentarily, wrapped his arms around her waist, and then reached down with both hands to feel her ass, slipping his fingers into the crack of her pants. He pressed her body tightly against his, pelvis to pelvis, so that she could feel the hardness of his cock.

"You feel that? You feel Big Papa?" Adam said, holding his pelvis to hers and rotating them forward, backward, and side to side.

Amanda's kitty was throbbing and soaking wet. "Yeah," she said, biting her lower lip before reaching down with her right hand to feel and squeeze Adam's bulge.

"Big Papa's in need of some serious attention," he said, and then the elevator doors opened.

When they stepped out of the elevator, Amanda pulled Adam by the crotch. Adam liked that, exaggerating his pelvis as he walked with her pulling him forward. "That's it. Take Big Papa by the reins, girl," he said, laughing and grinning before Amanda let go to search for her room key in her purse.

They made it inside Amanda's suite and closed the door behind them. "Nice room," Adam said as he and she both set their coats aside.

"And you're a nice surprise," Amanda said, then jumped on Adam, wrapping her legs around his waist and her arms around his neck.

He carried her to the bed as they kissed passionately and loudly. "Mmmm…mmmm," Adam moaned repeatedly with their mouths locked together.

Amanda ran her hands through Adam's hair, loving its length and fullness. She loved the prickly feel of his unshaven face brushing against her soft skin. She loved the faint scent of the men's face wash and moisturizer he used from Kiehl's. She loved the taste of bourbon on his tongue with a hint of mint flavor from the Trident gum he'd been chewing before they'd ordered their drinks. And those sexy, slim-fit jeans that cupped his ass so perfectly. The whole package was the perfect aphrodisiac.

Adam placed Amanda down onto the bed and lay on top of her. He reached down with his right hand, returning to massage her kitty through her pants while he smothered her with kisses on her lips, cheeks, and neck. Amanda was enraptured as she shrieked with pleasure at Adam's touch. She turned her face to the side as Adam nibbled on her cheek and jaw. Then he went for her right ear, kissing and licking it hungrily, causing Amanda to go into minor convulsions. It felt so good, so intense, and so erotic, but it tickled. Amanda couldn't take it anymore and she squealed. She did so at such a high pitch that it shook Adam to attention.

"What?" he said with alarm in his voice.

"It tickles," she said, laughing.

"It tickles?"

"Yeah. It feels good but it tickles too."

Adam grinned. "It tickles, huh?" He licked the tip of her nose teasingly. "Awww, you're ticklish, baby?"

Amanda giggled. "Shut up!"

He licked the tip of her nose once more. "Huh? Are you ticklish?" Adam said in a babying way, and then he held out his tongue as if inviting Amanda to kiss it back with her own. When she attempted to do so, he pulled his tongue back into his mouth, then pushed it out, and then pulled it in again, making her chase for it. They both laughed before Adam pushed his tongue out once more, this time allowing Amanda's to collide with his before their tangling tongues evolved into yet another deep, passionate kiss.

Adam broke their kiss gradually with stops and starts, moaning along the way in his deep, sensual, baritone voice. "Mmmm," he uttered repeatedly with one openmouthed, tongue-probing kiss after another. "I've got a lot more tickling to do to you," he said, groping Amanda's crotch aggressively. "You want to know what a real tickle feels like? Huh?"

Throbbing to the max and wet as a seal, Amanda could barely speak. All she could do was let out breathless moans and shrieks. She spread her legs in surrender, inviting Adam to torture her more.

"You want me to tickle you down there with my tongue?" Adam asked in reply to her nonverbal cue. "Huh? You want to know what it feels like?"

"Oh yes, yes," Amanda said in a heavy whisper.

Adam grinned devilishly. "I think you already know what it feels like," he said as he began to rip her pants open eagerly. "Nobody loves your pussy juicy more than me. And, boy, am I thirsty. Really, really, really thirsty."

Adam was in such a hurry to get his mouth down on the good stuff that he ripped a couple of buttons off Amanda's dark-colored wool pants in the process. He pulled them off and threw them to the floor. He then buried his face in her crotch, inhaling her scent at first and then licking the silky and now wet fabric of her Victoria's Secret panties. As he did so, he growled like a hungry dog staking out its territory and warding off any competitors for its coveted meal.

He pulled the lining of her panties to the side, just enough to reveal the loose, succulent lips of her beaver. He sucked and tugged on those lips long and hard. "Oh, baby…I missed you so much," he groaned in between sucks. He then pulled the lining away even more to get a view of her clit before licking and sucking on it deliriously. As he did so, he began to finger-fuck her too, intermittently removing his fingers to suck on them. "Mmmm…you taste so fucking good, babe," he said approvingly before reinserting two fingers to tantalize her more. He repeated the act over and over again, biting her clit while finger-fucking her at the same time, then stopping to insert his fingers into his mouth to suck. Adam was in Heaven.

He eventually removed her panties completely and ravaged her to no end as Amanda shrieked and cried out his name repeatedly. She ran her hands through his hair and held his head down to encourage his onslaught. She pleaded for him not to stop.

After eating her out and loosening her up more than sufficiently, Adam stood up and stripped naked. Amanda too removed her blouse, the last piece of clothing she had on.

When Amanda saw Adam's thick dong, erect and pointing directly at her, she grinned with excitement and anticipation. "There he is. Hi, Big Papa," she said all cutesy, waving her fingers at it. She then grabbed hold of it with her right hand and began to stroke it.

"Oh yeah…that's it…work Big Papa, girl," Adam said before he turned to fall back on the bed so Amanda could butter him up. Amanda knelt down on the floor in between his legs and began to stroke and suck him vigorously. Gagging frequently but undeterred, she handled him like a champion headmaster.

After a few minutes, Adam reached to pull Amanda up onto the bed with him so that they could get into the sixty-nine positon with her on top.

This made Amanda go wild. She pushed out and jiggled her hips provocatively as Adam ravaged her with gusto yet again. Amanda loved giving head this way—on top of her guy with her ass in his face as he ate her out. "Oh yeah…is it good? Does it taste good, baby?" she teased sultrily.

"Ohhh yeah, it sure does," Adam stopped and said with a laugh, loving that his girl was now in a slutty state of mind.

Before long, after tossing the salad a little, Adam was ready for the main course. He had Amanda bend down on her knees so that he could take her from behind, doggy style. A man of stamina, Adam was relentless. He banged her hard and fast, smacking her on the ass frequently as he shouted expletives to express his satisfaction.

Amanda loved it. She slapped her hands to the bed and yelled Adam's name repeatedly, begging him to keep it up. When her loud moans and cries turned into screams, she pulled a pillow over to bury her face in to muffle the sound.

After a while, Adam was hot and sweaty and teetering on the brink. "I'm gonna come, I'm gonna come," he said as he pounded her rapidly with vigor. "Oh God…come with me, babe. Oh fuck, baby…."

"Me too. Oh baby…oh baby…yeah…yeah," she moaned.

"Oh fuck!" Adam shouted one last time before he pressed his thick rod into her deep and held it there as he shot his load.

Exhausted and spent, Adam collapsed down on top of Amanda while still inside her. There they lay prostrate on the bed, locked together. "I love you," Adam said.

"I love you too," Amanda said back without hesitation or thought.

Adam kissed her on the cheek and then buried his face in the back of her head as he wrapped his arms around her tightly. Amanda closed her eyes and smiled to herself as she snuggled underneath him. In that moment, she couldn't have felt happier to be with Adam, the workaholic who'd left his beloved film project behind in Canada just to pay her a surprise visit. Jake couldn't have been further from her mind.

CHAPTER
TWENTY-NINE

Lucy had arrived at Amanda's hotel the next morning for their furniture shopping date.

I'm downstairs in the lobby, Lucy texted.

Okay, coming down, Amanda replied.

Amanda hurriedly put on her coat, grabbed her bag, and headed out the door. She texted Adam as she walked toward the elevator.

Lucy's here. Are you nearby?

In a cab. Will be there in less than 5.

Amanda stepped off the elevator andwalked into the lobby. When she spotted Lucy she gave her a big smile. "Heyyy!"

"Hey, girl. Look at you. You're glowing. Adam must've licked and sucked on your cherry pop until it melted away."

Amanda shrilled in shock at first and then laughed. "You know it," she said before she lifted her hands to high-ten Lucy. Lucy lifted and slapped her hands to Amanda's, and then they held on as they pulled them down while continuing to laugh like giddy teenage girls.

"So where is he?"

"He's on his way. He'll be here in a minute."

"I thought you said he stayed here with you last night."

"He did, but he went home to change clothes."

"So what'd you guys do last night? Did you go out?"

"No. We came straight here after we left the office yesterday. We had a drink downstairs at the Rose Bar, and then we went upstairs to my room and stayed in the whole night. Adam was really tired and didn't want to go out, so we ordered room service and watched movies. It was fun."

Lucy smirked. "Watched movies? Right. I bet he rode you like a cowboy all night long, or did you act like a cowgirl and do most of the riding? I know you like being on top sometimes."

Amanda slapped Lucy on the arm playfully and smirked. "Oh, hush," she said before spilling the tea. "He rode me before we started watching movies and then again in the middle of the night, like at two a.m. And then I rode him this morning in the shower. There's this nice little ledge to sit on in there. It's the perfect setup for the girl-on-top scenario, and you know I worked it," Amanda deadpanned with a sultry expression on her face.

"I'm sure you did, you slut!" Lucy said hysterically, looking Amanda up and down. Then they busted out laughing again, enjoying acting silly.

"How happy are you to see him? I can't believe he showed up like that just to surprise you."

"I know. It's so sweet."

"Luckily you were around this weekend."

"Well, he knew I'd be here. We talk on the phone every day. Oh my God, you know what he told me last night?"

"What?"

"I was having this craving for junk food. I wanted, like, chicken nuggets and fries—"

"Chicken nuggets?"

"I know, gross, but I was craving them for some reason, and a cheese-burger. Adam wanted sushi and so we got that too."

"Wait, you ate all of that?"

"Yes, but anyway, listen. So he says, 'Are you not telling me something?' and then looks down at my stomach—"

"He thinks you're pregnant?"

"I don't know if he really thought that, but that's what he insinuated because my appetite was so crazy. So I told him no, of course not. I'm like, please, I'm not interested in having your baby, and then he got kind of defensive about it and was like, 'You know I'd be a good baby daddy.'"

Lucy smirked.

"And I said, 'Yes, you would be.' And then he says, I'll be your baby daddy eventually, someday.'"

Lucy smirked again and covered her mouth.

"And he was all cocky about it. You know, not in a rude kind of way but more like in a self-confident sort of way. And I was like, 'Oh yeah?' And then, get this, he goes, 'Yeah, but you're going to marry me first.'"

Lucy gasped and then started to giggle.

"Like he was literally telling me that I was going to marry him as if it were a foregone conclusion."

Lucy suddenly widened her eyes to convey alert. "Oops, speaking of the devil," she said as Adam walked through the hotel doors.

Amanda, whose back was turned to the hotel entrance, immediately froze and stopped talking.

Lucy called out to him as he approached. "Hey there, Prince Charming."

Adam smiled at Lucy as he walked up on Amanda from behind and placed his hands on her shoulders, squeezing them lightly.

"Good morning," he said, looking at Lucy, smiling broadly, with a twinkle in his deep blue eyes.

Simultaneously, Amanda placed her right hand on top of the hand Adam had on her left shoulder. She then turned around to look at him. "Hi," she said all cutesy.

"Hi," Adam said back cutesy before stealing a quick kiss. "So where are we going shopping?" he asked.

"New York Designs," Lucy said excitedly.

"Perfect choice. I've bought stuff from there."

"You guys, they're so expensive," Amanda said. "I really don't want to spend that much on furnishing this apartment. I want it to be nice but simple. Nothing super fancy."

Adam brushed her off with a wave of his hand. "Ahhh, don't worry about it. Let's go."

They all hopped in a cab and headed over to view Amanda's new apartment first. Adam and Lucy both approved.

"This is perfect for you, and I love the view of the park," Lucy said as she stared out the front windows.

"Not bad," Adam said as he looked around the space, intrigued. "You know, I almost bought a place in this neighborhood before I opted for Chelsea. So what are you paying?"

"Four thousand. There was another unit that was three hundred less on the top floor, but it doesn't have a washer and dryer in unit. I would've had to use a shared laundry facility downstairs in the basement."

"Gross," Lucy said with a smirk.

"Do you even do your own laundry?" Adam questioned with a tint of sarcasm and humor in his tone.

Amanda balked but didn't answer him.

"Doesn't your maid back in LA do your laundry? What's her name…" Adam asked, snapping his fingers "…Lupe?"

Amanda still didn't answer back. She just looked at him bashfully with a grin.

Adam piled on. "You won't be doing any fucking laundry. In fact, have you ever done your own laundry?"

Lucy busted out laughing. "He has a point there."

"Yes, I have," Amanda finally said in her defense.

"When?"

"Adam, I washed my own clothes all through college and I still do now."

"So Lupe never washes your clothes?"

"Yes, but I do too… sometimes," she said with a giggle and a degree of capitulation.

"Oh, sometimes," he said with an eye roll. "See…I'm right. Lupe does your laundry…at least most of it. I know it and you know it. That's why you're laughing. You should've gone for the cheaper unit and saved yourself a little money."

Amanda continued to giggle bashfully but with slight annoyance. "Oh, whatever, Adam."

They eventually made their way over to the furniture store. Upon arriving, Amanda went gaga, engrossing herself in the wide selection of top-of-the-line modern and contemporary furnishings.

"Wow, everything's so posh and beautifully crafted," Amanda said as she perused the floor with Adam and Lucy at her side. Then she spotted something she really liked. "Look at that sofa," she said before making a beeline over to it. It was a stylish, modern, blond-colored sofa with tufted upholstery.

***

Amanda plopped herself down on it. "Oh my God, it's so soft," she said as she rubbed her hand across the surface of the smooth fabric.

Lucy sat down next to her. "Oooh, so comfortable. This would look great in your apartment, under the windows overlooking the park."

Adam took a peek at the tag and read aloud, "Made with the finest Italian leather."

Amanda was shocked. "This is leather? I've never sat on a leather sofa this soft. It doesn't even feel like leather. Come…sit down…feel it," she said to Adam, slapping her hand down on the cushion beside her.

Adam sat down next to her. "Nice. This almost feels like the kind of leather you would wear."

"I was thinking the same thing," Lucy said. "The fabric feels similar to the fabric on this leather jacket I have from my mom's collection. It's so soft and comfortable, I could sleep in it."

"Well, I could definitely fall asleep on this sofa. In fact, I feel like taking a nap right now," Amanda said, leaning back, folding her arms, and closing her eyes. "Doesn't this feel amazing, Adam? Can't you picture us snuggling up together and watching movies?" She placed her right hand on Adam's thigh and squeezed it as she spoke.

"Yeah," Adam said boyishly as he too leaned back against the sofa's frame and then wrapped his arms around Amanda, pulling her close. Then he whispered to her, "I can imagine us doing more on this couch than watching movies," he said before poking his tongue out to lick her ear.

Amanda shrieked at the tickling sensation, "Adam!" she said as she popped up and tried to break free from his embrace, but he wouldn't let go. He kept holding on as he attempted to lick her ear again, but Amanda looked away, toward Lucy, to prevent him from doing so. "Lucy, help!" Amanda said as she tried to pull loose from Adam's arm lock.

Lucy just giggled at them. "Okay, you guys need to settle down. This is not your hotel room."

Their playfulness caught the attention of one of store's design consultants who had walked over to them. "Are we having fun over here?" the woman asked.

Adam let Amanda go before he answered back with a quick wit. "We sure are. Want to join in?"

"No we're not," Amanda said as she straightened her clothes. "Ignore him. Despite the way it looks, we actually did come here to buy furniture."

Lucy chimed in. "He's her boyfriend and he flew into town yesterday to surprise her and to spend the weekend. As you can see, he can't keep his hands off her. I'm sure you know how it is."

"Actually, I don't, but I wish I did. Must be nice, especially when your boyfriend is an Oscar-nominated filmmaker." The woman glanced at Adam flatteringly.

"Oh...so you know who I am?"

"Of course I do. I love your films, Mr. Weinstock. You're a genius."

Adam grinned bashfully. "Well, other people are usually involved. Luckily I have access to great screenwriters who write great material, and for some reason, really good directors are crazy enough to work for me."

"You are so modest," the woman said admiringly.

Amanda and Lucy looked at each other and smirked. However, the design consultant was unfazed as she continued to shower Adam with praise.

"Well, you obviously have an eye for great material and know how to pull the right people together to make good films. That's why they keep getting nominated for Oscars and Golden Globes. You should've won the Oscar for best film, by the way. *The King's Speech* was good, but enough with all the films about the Brits and the royal family already."

Adam grinned broadly, nodding his head seemingly in agreement without actually voicing it. "Thank you, thank you very much. You're very kind. So what can I do for you?"

"No…what can I do for you? You're looking for new furniture, right?"

"Oh yes, right. Silly me," Adam said, shaking his head at himself.

Amanda raised her hand up timidly. "I am."

"Yeah, she is," Adam said. "She just got a new apartment and needs furniture."

"Oh…well, we have a great variety of selections here for you to choose from," the woman said, turning her attention to Amanda.

"I can see. The furniture here is really beautiful. I love this sofa. How much is it?"

"That sofa is ten thousand," the woman said flatly.

Amanda tried to contain her shock. "Well, that's more than I thought—"

However, before she could finish her thought, Adam cut her off. "We'll take it."

Amanda turned and looked at him, flabbergasted. "It's too expensive, Adam," she said in a lowered voice.

"Too expensive for whom? Don't worry about it. I've got it."

"Adam, no," Amanda said in disbelief, not expecting anyone other than herself to buy furniture for her new place. It's not that she didn't have the money. She could buy everything in the store if she wanted, but that was beside the point. People with trust funds had budgets too, and Amanda was diligent about sticking to hers.

Adam ignored her and addressed the consultant instead. "She doesn't realize that buying furniture for her new place was part of my surprise in coming here this weekend."

Amanda looked at him sideways with skepticism written on her face. "Adam, you didn't even know I was planning to go furniture shopping this weekend until you got here."

"Then my timing was perfect."

Amanda was completely taken aback. "Are you serious? You really don't have to do this, Adam."

"But I want to," he insisted.

Finally Lucy intervened to help her friend out. Turning to the design consultant, she shrugged her shoulders and smiled. "Welp, now that we've sorted out who's paying, I guess we should tell you a little about the apartment. It's amazing."

"Where is it?"

"In the East Village," Lucy answered, getting the conversation started about the apartment's size and layout along with her thoughts on colors that might work best in the unit. Adam followed Lucy's lead and chimed in with his own thoughts.

Soon thereafter, Amanda stopped resisting and gave in, reasserting herself as the principal customer and decision maker in the matter. They ended up spending the rest of the morning and half the afternoon at the store, exploring the various options the design consultant presented to them. Most of the items ultimately selected were in the store and just needed to be delivered, while a couple of other things needed to be ordered and shipped over from Italy, where most of the furnishings came from. When all was said and done, Adam had spent more than fifty thousand dollars to ensure that his princess had a home away from home in the Big Apple with furnishings equal to or better in quality than those of most five-star hotel suites.

CHAPTER THIRTY

Amanda, Adam, and Lucy decided to have a late lunch after they'd left the furniture store and popped into a few other stores along the way. They landed at a café in Union Square.

Right after they were led to their table, Lucy said, "I really have to pee."

"Me too. Watch our things, babe," Amanda said to Adam as she placed a couple of shopping bags down on her seat. Lucy did the same.

Adam, who was busily texting on his phone, looked up and gave her a quick glance. "Yeah, okay, sure," he said, seeming distracted.

Lucy walked into one stall and Amanda walked into the other right next to her. "My, you sure did hit the jackpot today," Lucy said as she relieved herself.

"I can't believe he did all that. To be honest, I'm not sure how I feel about it."

"Feel happy, for Christ's sake. Seriously, how many girls do you know have boyfriends, not husbands but boyfriends, who'd buy them fifty thousand dollars' worth of furniture on a whim? Cass wouldn't even do that."

"Don't get me wrong. I do appreciate it."

Amanda and Lucy both flushed their toilets and walked out of their stalls right about at the same time. They stepped toward the vanity to wash their hands and to check themselves out in the mirror. "I don't know," Amanda continued. "I guess I'm just not used to having a guy buy me nice things, at least not on that kind of level."

Lucy grumbled, "You got so accustomed to getting nothing from Jake and his tight ass. Adam's got money. Real money. Dropping fifty grand is nothing to him."

"It just feels a little awkward. It's not as if I needed him to do that."

"Of course you didn't need him to buy you furniture. That's not the point. The guy's in love with you. That's like his way of showing it, of proving it to you. You're his girl. He wants to make you happy."

"I know. I just feel a little guilty."

"Why? Adam loves you, Mandi. I mean, really loves you. There's nothing wrong with that. If he wants to spoil you and buy you nice things, let him. You should feel happy. Happy to have a guy who thinks that much of you, who cares for you, who's crazy about you, who comes here and surprises you out of the blue and does something so nice and generous for you. Why feel guilty? I could understand if you didn't love him back and didn't want to be with him and intended to dump him, but that's not the case. Is it? You do love him, I hope, by now, don't you?"

"Yes…I do," Amanda conceded reluctantly.

"Then stop holding back. You've got a great guy."

Adam was still texting when Amanda and Lucy returned to join him at their table. Feeling a sudden sense of gratitude after Lucy's pep talk, Amanda sat down and leaned over to kiss Adam on the cheek.

Adam mumbled in response as he completed his text without looking at her.

"You're still texting? Who are you texting?" Amanda asked, leaning over to take a peek at his phone.

Adam quickly finished up and put the phone down on the table. "This guy Manny, one of my assistant directors. Just puttin' out fires back on set."

"Everything okay?"

"Yeah, everything's fine. Just your run-of-the-mill bullshit. Tobias is a pain in the ass."

"Tobias? Who's Tobias?" Lucy asked.

"Tobias Velasquez," Amanda said.

"He's the playing the lead in the film I'm directing right now."

"Oh yeah. Great actor," Lucy said as she picked up her menu to peruse.

Amanda wrapped her arm around Adam's shoulder and leaned in to kiss him on the cheek again.

"Mmmm," Adam moaned as he turned his head to face her. They kissed on the lips, and then kissed again, and again. "You're being awfully affectionate all of a sudden. I like it."

Amanda wiggled her eyebrows up and down playfully and massaged the back of his head, gliding her fingers through his hair. She then initiated another round of sweet kisses on the lips. "Thank you for surprising me this weekend and for purchasing my furniture. You really didn't have to do that. It was very generous of you and completely unexpected."

"Well, get used to it," Adam said flatly.

Lucy pulled her menu down, grinning. Amanda grinned back at her.

"You've been upgraded," Adam said. "You're with a guy that knows how to treat you right."

"That's basically what I said," Lucy exclaimed. "Those are my sentiments exactly. You did a very nice thing, Adam."

"It's just…I've never had a guy do something that nice and generous for me," Amanda said.

Lucy shook her head in annoyance. "That's because she spent six years with that…." She stopped herself before uttering the less-than-flattering term she was about to use in reference to Jake. "I still can't believe that loser had the nerve to call your mom—⊠

Amanda waved her arm at Lucy. "Shush," she said with a look of alarm on her face.

"Who are we talking about?" Adam asked.

Amanda glanced at Lucy sideways in annoyance. She hadn't told Adam about Jake's outreach to her mother and hadn't planned to, at least for the time being.

Adam saw that neither of them was being very forthcoming. "Let me guess. Is it Jake we're talking about?"

Amanda and Lucy eyed one another before looking down in silence, which made Adam's guess very obviously correct.

"What did he do? He called Camilla?"

Feeling compelled to respond, Amanda sighed before trying to brush things aside. "He called my mom earlier this week. It's pointless and stupid."

"Why'd he call?"

Amanda and Lucy eyed each other again.

"Why are you being so reluctant to tell me?"

"I'm not. It's just that it doesn't matter."

"What doesn't matter?"

"He was just asking about me."

"And?"

Lucy smirked and shook her head as if she knew this wasn't about to go down well.

"What does he want? Is he trying to get back with you? Is that what you're trying not to tell me?"

"It doesn't matter," Amanda said. "I'm not getting back with him. You have nothing to worry about."

Growing impatient and visibly agitated, Adam snickered and grimaced.

"See, that's why I didn't want to tell you. Because I didn't want you to get all worked up and upset over nothing."

"Have you spoken to him?"

"No, I haven't."

"So he called your mom to tell her, what? That he wants to get back with you?"

"Bingo," Lucy said without looking up from the menu.

Amanda gave Lucy the death stare, but Lucy didn't look back at her.

"So he wants to get back with you, huh?"

"Something along those lines, and he feels like my parents somehow misled him and contributed to our breakup in some way."

Adam was incredulous. "Misled him?"

"I know. It's stupid."

"Can you believe that?" Lucy finally said, seeming to feel more comfortable jumping into the conversation now that the cat was fully out of the bag.

Adam removed the linen napkin from his lap and threw it down on the table in disgust. "This guy is a fucking piece of work. Seriously…the dude is mental."

"Riiight?" Lucy agreed.

"Anyway, as I said, I haven't spoken to Jake. He hasn't called me. I'm not taking him back. End of story," Amanda said as she picked up her menu in an attempt to turn everyone's attention to ordering food.

"But what if he does call you?"

Not able to think of a quick comeback, Amanda continued to study the menu in a preoccupied way. But Adam was insistent.

"Would you talk to him?"

Right at that moment they were interrupted by their waitress, to Amanda's relief.

"Hellooo, I'm Zoé. How are you guys doing today?"

With the tension at the table palpable, Lucy said, "Hi," with her best fake smile.

"Fine," Adam said stoically as he picked up the menu he had yet to peruse.

"Good. How are you?" Amanda said graciously and smiled.

"I'm doing great. Thanks for asking. So are you ready to order?"

"I think," Lucy said as she continued to look at the menu, clearly not ready to decide. Adam didn't answer as he too continued to look at the menu with a furrowed brow.

"I think we might need a little more time. We've been sitting here chatting," Amanda answered.

"Okay. No problem. Take your time," Zoé said before stepping away.

Adam didn't miss a beat. He glanced over at Amanda. "So…are you going to answer my question?"

Amanda wanted to put the kibosh on this topic, fast. Feeling cornered, she put up a little fuss as a way to push back. "Honey, I don't want to ruin this weekend and the wonderful surprise of having you here by talking about Jake. I'm already annoyed about the whole thing. Now you're annoyed and upset too, which is making me feel even worse. I really don't want to talk about him. Everything's over between us. Okay? Can we just order food and enjoy each other's company like we've been doing…please?" Amanda became emotional as she spoke. She thought she was being clever at first, but her conflicted feelings about Jake and the trauma caused by their breakup and her miscarriage just surfaced naturally, unexpectedly. It took her to a dark place. That's not where she was trying to go, but her heart took her there anyway.

Seeing that Amanda was near tears, Adam caved. "Well, I didn't bring him up," he said defensively, feeling bad.

"Neither did I," Amanda retorted as she eyeballed Lucy.

Adam reached over to rub her on the arm and tried to console her. "I'm sorry, princess. I didn't mean to upset you."

CHAPTER THIRTY-ONE

Jake had arrived at The Hudson in West Hollywood to meet Kirby. After not having seen Jake since their steamy reconciliation earlier in the week, Kirby had suggested that they meet for drinks and dinner Saturday night.

I'm here, Jake texted as he walked toward the restaurant.

Me too. I'm inside, Kirby wrote back.

Jake stepped through the door, and there Kirby stood, waiting for him.

"Hey, bro," Kirby said with a big smile, pearly whites on full display.

"Hey, brother," Jake said back as they did the slap-grab handshake and pulled in for a hug.

"What's up, man? Metallica!" Kirby said, noticing the throwback T-shirt Jake was wearing with the rock band's name written across it. "Man…that's from back in the day…way back. I forgot that you were once into heavy metal, especially during prep school. You still listen to that stuff?"

"Not really. Not as much as I used to. My tastes in music have evolved, but I've got a few metal songs on my playlist still. You know, the classics. It's like a guilty pleasure I engage in once in a while—blasting my speakers to the max, singing along to those tunes. It can be a good stress reliever."

"Just the two of you?" the hostess interrupted before escorting Jake and Kirby to their table. Jake followed behind her and Kirby behind him. Kirby was happy as a clam to be back with his best buddy and looked forward to picking up where he and Jake had left off the last time they'd seen one another.

Jake was wearing jeans along with his Metallica T-shirt. The combination proved flattering to his lean, taut, muscular physique, and Kirby liked it. Jake looked sexy, youthful, and strong. "That shirt looks good on you. Your arms and chest are popping, bro," Kirby said as he pinched Jake's biceps and then patted him on the chest to feel his swollen pecs.

Jake, slightly embarrassed, chuckled at Kirby's flirtatiousness as they sat down.

The hostess chuckled along as well but was more modest in her admiration as she checked Jake out too. "Nice T-shirt," she said with a grin, giving Jake the once-over before placing the menus down on the table before them.

"Thanks. Please excuse his inappropriate behavior, groping me like that in front of you. You pervert," Jake said to Kirby as he picked up his menu and swiped it at him.

"Oh, you know you like it, boo," Kirby said back in a girlish tone as he reached over to touch Jake on the arm affectionately while puckering his lips.

Jake played along, pulling his arm back and then slapping Kirby on the hand, "Oh, stop," he said with a girlish inflection of his own.

"Now boy, you know how much I love you," Kirby said, waving and bending his wrist in an effeminate way.

The hostess laughed and blushed at the melodrama the two were putting on in front of her. Jake and Kirby were back to their old ways, engaging in gay-like banter to psyche out and confuse strangers about their sexuality, something they'd done since their youth and still got a kick out of doing from time to time.

"I can tell you guys must know each other really well. You remind me of my brother and his crazy friends. They like to act silly and fool around like you guys do."

"Really? Does your brother like to play catcher or pitcher?" Kirby asked with a straight face.

Jake's eyes popped open wide and he grinned broadly in shock.

"What'd you say?" the hostess asked.

"Oh, never mind," Kirby said, laughing. Jake was on the verge of laughing too but held it in as best he could.

"No, I didn't understand you," she said, trying to get him to repeat his question.

"It's okay. Never mind," Kirby said, now barely able to contain his tickle.

Jake busted out laughing too, bending over the table and covering his face with his hands. He didn't want to make the hostess uncomfortable, but he couldn't help it.

"Enjoy your dinner, guys," she finally said, stepping away with an expression on her face that read that she now found their behavior juvenile and annoying. However, it was unclear whether she understood the euphemism about catchers being bottoms and pitchers being tops in gay sex lingo.

Jake and Kirby continued to laugh for a moment until Jake managed to get ahold of himself. "Dude…you're so bad. I can't believe you asked her that. Did you see her face when she walked away?"

"You think she understood what I meant?"

"I don't know. I couldn't tell. Maybe not…at least, I hope not," Jake said before they both started to laugh again.

It was as if the imbroglio in which the two had been engaged had never happened. A friendship that had seemed doomed forever now appeared uninterrupted. A few minutes later, after settling down and savoring their reunion, food and beers were ordered.

"Cheers, bro," Jake said, holding up his beer mug.

Kirby held up his mug too. "Brothers for life?"

"Brothers for life," Jake said in agreement, and then they clinked their mugs together and took a sip of their beers.

"So are you guys done editing your pilot?"

"Just about. Still working on it, but we're almost done."

"I'm sorry—remind me. This is a comedy where an orthodox Jewish man marries a black woman, right?"

"Right. It's called *Blended Family*. The Jewish guy is widowed with two young sons, and he starts dating a single black woman with two sons of her own. They eventually marry and become like a modern-day *Brady Brunch*, but everybody they know is shocked that they end up together, including the kids, at first. So in addition to the kids, the show deals with how other family members and their respective friends react to their relationship and how they work through their cultural differences and the prejudice they encounter as a new family."

"It sounds interesting, and it must be really funny too, no doubt."

"Yeah. It's been fun. I think people are going to like it."

"So were you able to persuade them to keep in the scenes they were talking about cutting out?"

"Yes…well, mostly. It wasn't about cutting scenes out, per se. It was more about editing and cutting scenes down to fit the format of a network show where you have to factor time for commercials. So for example, there's this one scene where the kids meet for the first time and they start talking about the kind of music they're into. The black kids mention hip-hop and rap artists that we all know, and then the Jewish kids mention some Jewish rapper from Israel that nobody's ever heard of. So they start to play one of the Jewish rapper's songs on YouTube so that the black kids can hear it, and the Jewish kids start rapping along and bopping around like this is the coolest, most dope shit ever, and the black kids are like, what the fuck is this?"

Jake started to laugh. "That's so funny."

Kirby laughed too. "It was fucking hilarious, but we had to cut it down."

"Oh no. Really? You cut the whole thing?"

"No, no, we still have the scene, but there are some other scenes that are more important to the storyline, so we had to cut that one down a bit."

"Okay, good. I want to see that."

"So anyway, I'm feeling good about the way the final cut is turning out. I'm just keeping my fingers crossed and hoping that the powers that be like it and that the show gets picked for a full first season."

"I'm sure it will. It sounds very original and funny. That's what they want, right?"

"I hope so."

"I'm so happy for you, bro. I can't wait to see it."

"Thanks, man. So what about you? What's going on in your world?"

"Dude...this has been one of the most stressful weeks ever."

"Really?" Kirby said in surprise, having no clue of the turmoil in which Jake had been embroiled over the previous few days.

"You have no idea," Jake said as he shook his head in continued disbelief at the situation.

"What's going on?"

"It's all family-related stuff."

"Is everything all right?"

"Not entirely, but we'll get through it and put it behind us at some point."

Kirby was curious and wanted to know more. Jake typically told him everything—that had been the pattern of their relationship—but he could see that Jake was holding back for some reason. Although tempted to probe, Kirby decided not to. He just tried to be empathetic. "My family was always the one that had a little bit of drama going on from time to time. Remember when I thought my parents were going to get a divorce my freshman year of college?"

"Yeah, I do."

"That was a crazy time," Kirby said contemplatively, followed by a sip of his beer.

Jake took a sip of his beer too. "I'm kind of going through something similar," he admitted.

Kirby looked at Jake for a moment, feeling surprised at such news, but he remained circumspect. "Interesting. You know, to me, your family has always been the perfect picture of wholesomeness: white picket fence, apple pie, baseball, and all of that, the model all-American family."

Jake smirked and took another sip of his beer. "I guess we're just really good at being posers and hiding our secrets well."

Kirby chuckled. "Every family's got issues of some sort or another, I guess."

"That's for sure."

"So how's Harry?" Kirby asked, launching them into extended conversation and gossip about family and friends.

As the evening progressed, Kirby and Jake continued to catch up after their relatively long hiatus from one another. The whole time, Kirby was looking for an opportunity to put the moves on Jake. His goal was for the two of them to end the night back at his place butt naked in his bed. Kirby sensed that Jake was holding back, however. The fire they'd experienced a few days before after running into each other at the gym and reconciling wasn't there for some reason. Kirby concluded that whatever was going on in Jake's family life was more than likely the culprit. Nevertheless, Kirby wasn't ready to throw in the towel.

"Where do you want to go?" Kirby asked.

"I don't know. I'm not really in a clubbing mood, and plus, two guys and no girls won't get us far."

Kirby snickered. "Connections, man. I've got connections. Not to worry. Look at us, man. When have we ever had a problem gettin' into a club? You can't have a club full of only girls, anyway. Girls want eye candy too. That's us."

"Well, eye candy is all I'm going to be," Jake said.

"Me too. I'm not looking to pick up girls or anything like that. You know, just a place to chill and have a few drinks. But I want to be around a hot crowd with some good people watching."

"Well, you pick the place. Whatever you decide is fine with me. You sound like you know where you want to go."

"How about The Abbey?" Kirby said with a grin.

"The Abbey?" Jake repeated, surprised. "So you're going to gay clubs now?"

"No. Not really, but I wanted to see what your reaction would be. Have you been there before?"

"No. Have you?"

"I've been there once. It's actually a pretty cool spot. Even though it's a gay club, I was surprised to see so many girls there. Like, really hot-looking, straight girls."

I've heard that. Actually, Amanda likes going there. She hangs out there with her friend Charlie sometimes."

"So…you want to go?"

Jake snickered at the thought. "Are you being serious? You really want to go there?"

"What…are you afraid of being around gay people?"

"No. I'm just a little surprised that you'd want to go there. So are you, like, open about being into guys now?"

"No. Not really, but I guess I've become a little more open-minded about trying new places different from what I normally would've gravitated toward in the past. Oooh, I have another idea."

"What?"

"There's this other club that I've gone to a couple times now in Hollywood that has a mixed crowed. And when I say mixed, I mean gay, straight, bi, pan—"

"Pan?"

"Pansexual. They don't give a fuck what you are or what type of equipment you have. They like it all…"

Jake snickered as he sipped more of his beer.

"…trannies, transgender, gay, straight, bi, they're into everything."

"So what's this place called?"

"The Naked Bunny."

"The Naked Bunny?"

"Yeah. It's a spoof off the Playboy Bunny theme. All of the waiters, most of whom are guys, wear these black Playboy-Bunny-like uniforms, except in the back their asses are exposed. Most all of them have pretty decent bodies so they can get away with that, but anyway, some wear their uniforms with fishnet stockings and platform high heels—"

"The guys do?"

"Yeah, man. It's crazy. It's all part of the theme. Some of the waiters have this androgynous look, like buff, worked-out bodies but then they're wearing like full makeup and walking around in heels, and then you have other guys who look like Chippendale dancers. And the female waiters do the same thing. Some look so androgynous that I really can't tell what they are."

"Who goes to this place? It sounds like a total freak show."

"All kinds of people, man. You've got celebrities up in there, industry people, models. It's your typical Hollywood crowd but it has a very avant-garde, edgy feel to it. They're all about pushing the envelope there."

"Like a more contemporary version of that club in New York," Jake said as he snapped his fingers, trying to recall the name. "You know, the one that was really big in the '70s and '80s and that they made a movie about…Studio 54!"

"Exactly. I was just about to say it. I knew that's the one you were thinking of. I swear, the last time I went to this club, there was like an orgy happening on the dance floor."

"Nooo…come on."

"I'm serious, man. Pretty close to it. People weren't completely naked but almost. You had this whole group of people feeling each other up, groping each other, right there in plain view. Guys on girls, girls on guys, girls on girls, guys on guys—all dry humping and kissing each other. I was like, damn!"

"They didn't care who was watching?"

"Nope, not at all. It was dark but you could still see what they were up to."

"What were other people in the club doing while this was going on?"

"Nothing. People were completely unaffected by it. It was like you either join in or sit back and be a voyeur and watch. I've got to take you to this place, dude. You've got to expand your horizons a little," Kirby said with a chuckle, patting Jake on the shoulder.

"Well, I must admit, I am a little curious. I'd definitely prefer it over The Abbey, that's for sure. Nothing against gay clubs, but I really don't want to run into any of Amanda's friends and get the rumors flying all over again."

"Yeah, this place doesn't bill itself as a gay club. There are a lot straight people who go there. Everybody goes there, really. It meets the definition of mixed crowd perfectly. Nobody's trying to figure out if you're gay, straight, bi, or whatever. It's just a wild, decadent club with no boundaries. You're free to be whoever you want to be there. No judgment."

"I'm just wearing a T-shirt and jeans. Should I go home and change?"

Kirby smirked as he eyeballed Jake up and down. "Jake, you make that T-shirt look good, like it's the hottest piece of clothing ever. You know, that's one thing I've always liked about you," Kirby said as he chuckled in a teasing way.

"What?" Jake asked with a dumbfounded expression on his face.

"You can be so humble and unassuming at times. It's very charming. Stay that way."

"Why? Because I think I should change clothes?"

"No. Because you seem to have no idea how sexy you are at times. You could be wearing a pair of raggedy overalls and people would think they were the hottest thing ever just because you were wearing them."

Jake grinned from ear to ear.

Kirby grinned too. His charm offensive appeared to be working. In his mind, his night with Jake was just getting started.

CHAPTER THIRTY-TWO

"Fuck, look at this line," Jake said when he and Kirby arrived outside the club.

"I know the promoter, or at least, I've met him."

"How'd you meet him?"

"Because a buddy of mine—a guy in the industry, you don't know him—is the one who first brought me here, and he knows the promoter. They're friends, and he introduced me to him."

"So are you on a list or something to get us in? Because I really don't plan on waiting around in this line."

"Don't worry about it. Just follow me," Kirby said as he walked straight to the head of the line and greeted one of the bouncers, a bald-headed, hulking black dude in a dark suit. He had the build of an NFL linebacker and must've weighted at least two hundred fifty pounds.

Kirby shook the bouncer's hand and bumped shoulders with him followed by a pat on the back. "Hey, man…."

After the initial greeting, Jake couldn't hear what else Kirby told the man, but whatever he said, it worked. The man unhooked the velvet rope and let them through. No questions asked.

Kirby led the way as they walked down a long dark hall with just enough dim lighting along the baseboards to make their way to the club's main room without tripping over themselves. The pulsating sound of electronic dance music could be heard louder and louder as they drew closer to the point of entry. They passed through a set of thick floor-to-ceiling curtains to enter the space, which was dark but dramatic, with electric candelabras everywhere. It was like walking into a secret lair for vampires. The intermittent flash of strobe lights revealed a room that was packed, alive, and full of revelry. The music pumped hard and the dance floor was lit. There were scantily clad male and female go-go dancers on risers above the dance floor. They were gyrating and pumping their bodies provocatively, drawing attention to themselves while guiding the crowd to follow their lead through the chorus of sound.

Kirby got caught up in the energy of the scene the minute he walked in. He started grooving to the music, swaying his body and snapping his fingers to the beat. "Isn't this cool?"

"Wow," is all Jake could muster. He couldn't believe his eyes—the debauchery and indulgence of it all. Just as Kirby had told him, there were people on the dance floor, including some bare-chested men and women wearing skimpy halter or bikini tops, dancing tight and close, touching, feeling, and holding on to each other. Some people seemed delirious like they were high on ecstasy while others seemed like they were having an out-of-body spiritual experience like in a Pentecostal church. They all seemed lost in the moment, lost in jubilation. They seemed free. Jake couldn't take his eyes off the go-go dancers, especially the male dancers and their buff bodies. They looked so sensual and erotic as they danced and tantalized the crowd with seeming obliviousness. One man in particular caught Jake's eye. He was very muscular and his skin glistened with oil like that of a bodybuilder in competition. In addition to a pair of black leather biker boots, all the male dancer was wearing was a G-string with suspenders that strung up from his crotch, over his shoulders and down his back, where they converged at the crack of his butt. The guy had the most monstrous, muscular ass Jake had ever seen. Jake's mouth fell open when the dancer swirled around to display it, holding onto the rail of the riser he was dancing on, taunting and teasing with every dance move. Then he turned back around. "Holy fuck," Jake said to himself when he noticed how hung the dude appeared to be. The strobe lights flashing and flickering made the size of the guy's endowment all the more apparent.

The dancer started to pump his pelvis while running his hands up and down his chest and abdomen seductively. Jake was mesmerized. He just stood still and watched the dancer's body as his own body began to react. He could feel an erection coming on as his tool began to twitch and fight for room to stretch underneath his underwear and tight jeans. It became so uncomfortable that he reached down to make an adjustment. He had a head-on view as the dancer kept pumping his pelvis with the beat of the music. Jake's mouth watered at the sight of the stud. It was one of the most erotic things he'd ever seen—a big, muscular guy in a G-string dancing around in front of a crowd so confidently, so seductively, effeminately even, while still dripping with so much testosterone and rugged masculinity. Jake kept his eyes glued on the guy's crotch until suddenly he realized that he too was being watched—by said dancer. The dancer caught Jake's gaze. He then stretched his arm out and pointed to Jake and with his index finger and motioned for Jake to come hither, over to him. Startled and a little embarrassed, Jake immediately looked away.

Jake glanced over at Kirby and could see that he was on the verge of joining the crowd on the dance floor. The music with its fast, up-tempo beat, emotional melody, and rhythmic crescendos was beckoning and casting a spell on his friend, but Jake didn't want to dance, at least not yet. He grabbed Kirby by the arm to get his attention and then leaned over to speak in his ear. "Where's the bar? Let's go get a drink."

"The bar?" Kirby said back over the loud music.

"Yeah. Let's go get a drink," Jake said, raising his voice so that Kirby could hear him better.

"I'm ready to dance, man. This music is on point right now. Whattaya think of this crowd?"

"It's just like you said it would be, but I didn't expect the go-go dancers."

"Isn't that hot? I love it. Check out that guy up there with the big ass. He's workin' it, isn't he?"

"I noticed him," Jake said with a smirk. Increasingly feeling the need for a drink to loosen up a bit, Jake looked around the room and finally spotted the bar. It had been hidden behind a crush of people that was beginning to break up a little. Jake took charge and pulled Kirby by the shirt. "I found the bar. Let's go."

Kirby pulled loose from Jake's grip. "Dude, I swear, you always want a drink. You just had three beers, man."

"Well, it's time for another one. This place is weirding me out. I need something a little harder to get me in the right mood."

Jake led the way, and Kirby followed behind him. "What are you having? It's on me," Jake said after they'd reached the bar.

"I don't know what I want."

"How about tequila?"

Kirby didn't seem too keen as he continued to hem and haw.

"Come on, let's do a few tequila shots, nice and straight."

"Man, I don't need that right now."

"But it loosens you up, makes you relaxed."

"I'm already relaxed. You're the one who's all uptight and needs to relax. I'm good, man…really. You go ahead and have however many shots it takes."

"Wait, you're going to let me drink by myself, bro? You're not going to have a shot with me, not even one?" Jake said with feigned incredulity.

Seeing that Kirby wasn't budging, Jake said, "All right, fine!" before turning to the bartender, who asked for his order.

"I'll take three tequila shots," Jake said as he opened his wallet and pulled out a wad of bills.

Kirby rolled his eyes. "Okay, I'll have a shot."

"A shot? That's it?"

"A shot," Kirby said firmly. "But only because I feel pity for you and don't want you drink alone."

"Oh, gee, thanks," Jake said before calling out to the bartender, "Can you add one more shot to that order, please?"

"Plus, you're so damn cute and irresistible when you pout. I can't help it."

Jake grinned. "You're so easy to guilt-trip."

The bartender placed the four shots on the bar in front of them. "Forty bucks," he said.

Jake handed him two twenties and a ten. "You can keep the change."

"Salud," Kirby said before he quickly downed his single shot while Jake looked on. Kirby opened his mouth wide and poked out his tongue afterward. "Ahhh," he exclaimed as he widened his eyes and shook his head slightly as if trying to shake off the burn in his throat. "Damn, that's some potent shit."

Jake snickered. "Want another one, bro? Here," Jake said teasingly as he attempted to hand Kirby one of his three shots.

"No, thanks. I'm good. I've never really liked doing shots, to be honest. Besides, any tequila expert will tell you that it's supposed to be sipped and savored like a good whiskey, not gulped like its fucking water or something."

"That's unless you're trying to get drunk quickly, in which case downing it is the better approach."

"Well then, get to it, bro. What are you waiting for? Although you're such a fish, I don't think three will be enough for you."

"Hey, don't push me or you'll be carrying me out of here over your shoulder."

"That's all right. Come on now…" Kirby said, taking the shot out of Jake's hand "… bottoms up." Kirby lifted the glass to serve it up to Jake.

Jake titled his head back and stuck out his tongue, waving it around tauntingly, and doing a little jiggle with his body, acting silly.

Kirby laughed and stepped toward him. "You ready, man?"

"Uh-huh," Jake uttered with his mouth wide open and head titled back.

"Here we go," Kirby said before putting the rim of the glass to Jake's bottom lip and then lifting it swiftly to pour into his mouth.

It came rushing down fast and quick. Jake began to gag and cough, stepping back and bending over.

"You all right, man?" Kirby said as he reached to pat Jake on the back.

Jake gathered himself and stood up straight. "Yeah…I'm fine," he said with a grimace, wiping his face as some of the tequila had fallen out of his mouth. "You poured it down too fast. I'm not a fuckin' drain, dude. Jeez."

Kirby laughed and then picked up another tequila shot. "Are you ready for the next one?"

"I'll do it myself," Jake said, taking the glass of tequila from Kirby. He then downed the second and third shots in short order.

A busty redhead approached them soon after. It wasn't clear if she died her hair or not, but the color was beautifully bright and uniform throughout and perfectly coiffed. She had kind of a throwback Farrah Fawcett vibe going on. Her skin was pale with light freckles, and she was a bit fleshy, but she wore it well. Her confidence was apparent, and she looked sexy as hell in her platform high heels, skinny, form fitting, rhinestone-covered designer jeans, and sequin mesh halter top that left little to the imagination. It stopped Kirby in midsentence.

"Damn," he said, looking her up and down as she stepped toward him.

"Hey," she said cheerfully, patting Kirby on the arm. "I remember you. Oh my gosh, your name is on the tip of my tongue. Wait, don't tell me. It's Tobey, right?"

Kirby started to laugh. Jake grinned as he looked on, distracted by the sight of her big breasts. He could hardly keep his eyes off them.

"Close. It's Kirby."

"Oh shit," she said, slapping her hand to her forehead. "I'm so sorry."

"That's okay. Don't worry about it."

"I'm so embarrassed. I always forget names."

"Oh, no worries. Come here," Kirby said, extending his arms to hug her. She stepped into his arms and Kirby held her tight and close. He made eye contact with Jake as he did so and winked.

Jake lifted his brow and grinned as he checked out the woman from behind.

"You're looking good, girl," Kirby said to her after they broke their embrace.

"So do you, and who's this hottie you're with over here, serving shots to?"

"Oh, you saw that?"

"I sure did," she answered all cutesy.

"This is my best friend, Jake."

"Hi! Katrina," she said, extending her hand to Jake.

"Nice to meet you," Jake said, shaking her hand.

"Yeah, that's right, Katrina," Kirby said.

"See, you didn't remember my name either."

Kirby chuckled, appearing slightly embarrassed. "I know. I'm just as bad about remembering names."

"So where's your other friend you were here with last time? I remember he's the one who introduced you to The Naked Bunny."

"I don't know if he'll be here tonight. I believe he's on location shooting a music video with JLo. You're right, though—he was my chaperone, but I'm good now. I've been sufficiently initiated, and I'm hooked on this place. I'm chaperoning him now," Kirby said with a nod of the head at Jake.

Katrina turned to Jake. "Oh, so this is your first time?"

"Yep, my first time."

"Love that shirt by the way. I love Metallica," she said, surveying Jake up and down.

"He thought he looked too underdressed," Kirby said.

Katrina giggled. "Oh no, you and that shirt go well together," she said while patting Jake on the chest. "Oooh…so firm," she said, lingering in her touch.

Jake grinned, enjoying the attention.

"Hey, hey, take it easy. Break him in nice and slow. He's still a cubby bear. All this gratuitous groping and touching going on around here was freaking him out just a few minutes ago."

"No it wasn't," Jake said defensively.

"Yes it was. Dude, don't lie. That's why he needed those tequila shots," Kirby said with a chuckle.

"Don't listen to him," Jake said.

"A newbie, huh? I like that. We should take him out on the dance floor. Get you all nice and sweaty and make you lose that shirt," Katrina said as she ran her index finger down Jake's shirt from his pecs to his navel.

"Now you're talkin'," Kirby agreed.

Jake grinned bashfully and tried to change the subject. "So anyway, what do you do?"

"I'm a performer. I sing. I act. I dance. I model. I'm a girl of many trades."

Although her response was typical for a girl one met at such a club in Hollywood, Jake acted genuinely interested and put on the charm. "Oh yeah? I love meeting a real showgirl. What have you done?"

"Oh, different things. I've been in a lot of music videos. When hip-hop artists want a white girl with big boobs and a big ass in their music videos, they call me."

Jake and Kirby both chuckled. "Yeah, I can see that. You definitely meet the criteria," Kirby wisecracked.

"Oh, hush," she said, waving him off playfully. "Plus, I'm a pretty good dancer. What can I say? I've got the right look and the right moves. That's why they want me. Anyways, what do you do?" she asked Jake.

"I'm a lawyer."

"Oooh…a lawyer. You don't see many lawyers coming through here, certainly none that look like you."

"What's that supposed to mean?" Jake said with a grin.

"Nothing bad, but I thought you were going to say you're a model or something. You just have that pretty boy look down pat with those blue eyes and the blond hair, and those muscles. Oh my God. You're so damn pretty. I feel so inadequate standing next you. Jesus!"

Jake blushed and looked down.

Kirby busted out a laugh. "Ain't he pretty? I tell him that all the time but he hates it."

"You too. You're both gorgeous. Do you guys have girlfriends?"

Kirby answered quickly, "Nope."

"No," Jake said in a more demure way.

"Or are you guys gay?"

Her forwardness threw Jake off. He made eye contact with Kirby, feeling a little startled at the question. Then they both grinned.

"If I had to guess, I'd say you guys are gay. Maybe bi."

"Why do you say that?" Kirby asked, incredulous.

"My gaydar is pretty accurate about ninety percent of the time. Plus, I'm a good reader of energy, and you two have great energy. There's like this chemistry, this magnetism between the two of you. You're very drawn to each other. You complement each other in many ways."

Jake was quietly astounded at this unexpected read. It made him uncomfortable. He knew that what she was saying was true, but the accuracy of it combined with the fact that the observation was coming from a complete stranger who didn't know him from Adam stunned him into silence. He turned to the bar, looking for a crutch to help him keep it together. However, he'd forgotten that he'd drunk all of the tequila shots already.

Kirby, on the other hand, who'd always taken pride in maintaining his straight appearance and keeping his gayness undetectable, challenged her assertion. "What do you mean, complement each other? Just because we're good-looking, have nice bodies, and work out, that makes us gay?"

"No. I don't mean that. I'm not talking about your bodies or your physical appearance, necessarily. There's a comfort there between you. There's trust. The way you two were fooling around when you were pouring that shot into his mouth. I know you were being playful and acting like bros or whatever, but it was also very tender the way you patted him on the back. Although it may be unintended, your affection for one another is more noticeable than you might realize."

Kirby grinned and then conceded in a jocular way, "Yeah...I admit, I do love the guy, most of the time."

Jake grinned but remained silent, not wanting to prolong this line of conversation.

"Well, neither of you are denying that you're gay, so that must be the case."

"Nah, nah, nah, let's not jump to conclusions, now," Kirby said.

"What? So are you bi? It's okay. I'm bi. I take a dip in the lady pond once in a while. In fact, my last relationship was with a woman. We dated for three months."

Kirby lit up. "Really? Now that's hot. Hey, I have no issues with gay dating whatsoever."

"Have you ever tried it? Dating a guy?"

At this point Jake was twitching, squirming, and becoming flushed in the face.

Kirby hesitated at first. Then he spilled the tea. "Yes…I have."

Katrina stomped her foot and poked Kirby in the tummy with her finger as if penetrating him with a dagger. "I knew it! I knew it!"

"But I've dated girls, lots of girls. I was even in a five-year relationship with a girl until last year."

"Oh yeah? But you like boys too, huh?"

Kirby smiled broadly, licked his top teeth, and laughed, looking caught red-handed.

"And I bet you're a top too? I can tell," she said conspiratorially before laughing at Kirby. His sheepish demeanor was a dead giveaway.

Katrina then turned to Jake. "And what about you? Gay? Bi?"

Jake was stumped for words momentarily as he struggled to come up with an answer. "I plead the Fifth," Jake finally said with a nervous giggle.

"Why? Who cares? Why would you need to plead the Fifth? If you like guys then you like guys. Who gives a shit?"

"I had a girlfriend too. We were engaged and almost got married."

"Really? When?"

"We broke up last August, right before our wedding."

"Why'd you break up?"

"It's a long story."

"So you're dating guys now?"

"No."

"Have you been with a guy before?"

Jake hesitated with his tongue in cheek, reluctant to answer the question. He then looked at Kirby.

Kirby stared back at him and started to grin. "Why are you looking at me, man?"

Jake started grinning too, and then he and Kirby both busted out laughing.

"What's so funny? Why are you guys laughing? Just admit it, dude. Jeez. Nobody cares. Is he gay? Just tell me," she said to Kirby.

"I'll let him answer," Kirby said through his chuckles.

"Come on. I know you like guys. Admit it already. I bet you guys are fuck buddies. Aren't you? You're the top…" she said, pointing at Kirby "…and you're the bottom," she said, pointing at Jake.

Jake and Kirby both continued to laugh, admitting to nothing about their relationship.

CHAPTER THIRTY-THREE

Kirby could see that Jake was trying hard to laugh off Katrina's assertions without having to acknowledge the truth about his homosexual tendencies. Kirby wanted to tell Katrina that her gaydar was on point and that, indeed, he and Jake had long been sexual playmates, even though they'd never done the deed fully as a top and bottom. It even felt good to Kirby to admit to someone he didn't know well that he had been with guys before and liked it. In that moment, at that club, in that environment, he suddenly felt relieved of the pressure to front as a straight man, of having to prove and defend his masculinity. He was surrounded by people who were either ambiguous about their sexuality or completely open about swinging one way or both ways, like Katrina. It felt liberating. However, Kirby could tell that Jake wasn't feeling it, and he sensed Jake's discomfort with the conversation. To prevent having the night end badly with Jake getting pissed off and wanting to leave, Kirby abruptly changed the subject. "Hey, you like to dance?"

"Of course I like to dance. I'm a dancer. That's what I do," Katrina said.

"Wanna dance? The dj tonight has got this place turned up." Kirby said as he started to sway to the beat of the music.

"Sure. I'd love to."

"Jake, come join us. He's a pretty good dancer," Kirby said to Katrina.

"Really?" Katrina looked Jake up and down with curiosity.

"I taught him everything he knows."

"Yeah, right," Jake said with an eye roll.

"A hot white boy who can dance too? You're making me wet. I'm gonna have to ditch the lady pond tonight."

Jake grinned as he put up his hands up in an attempt to decline the invitation to join them, but Katrina continued before he could get a word out.

"Well, he didn't admit to being gay, so I guess there's still hope for me. And you're bi, like me, so maybe I'll get lucky tonight and end up in the middle of you two. I love a ménage à trois." Katrina wiggled and brushed her shoulder up against Kirby's side while licking her lips sensually.

"Damn, girl, you're freaky," Kirby said with a chuckle and big smile.

"I think I'll pass. You guys go ahead. I'll watch from the sidelines," Jake said.

"Man, come on," Kirby pleaded with a small degree of agitation in his tone.

"Yeah, man. If you want pussy tonight, the best place to get it is on the dance floor. That's where the action is. All the hot girls and boys dance here," Katrina said.

"I'm not trying—"

"Dude, shut up and come on. Have some fun. You love to dance. Why are you holding back? That's why you drank those shots. To loosen up, right? Do you need more?"

"Come on, hot stuff. Don't be a fly on the wall," Katrina said as she grabbed Jake by the hand and pulled him forward.

"All right, all right. Jesus," Jake said, succumbing to the pressure.

"That's my boy," Kirby said with a big smile, stepping over to squeeze Jake on the shoulder, followed up by a quick bear hug. He then led the way to the dance floor.

Jake walked reluctantly as Katrina pulled him along.

They reached the dance floor and blended with the thick crowd, dancing tightly together. Katrina was in the middle, facing Kirby, and Jake was behind her. Katrina danced playfully and provocatively. She bent over a bit and pushed her butt out, inviting Jake to dry hump her, spank her, or whatever he had in mind. Jake looked at Kirby with a grin on his face. Then they both chuckled. "Go ahead. Hit it, bro. Hit it," Kirby said, encouraging Jake.

Jake took the bait. He placed one hand on her back, pressed his pelvis to her rear lightly, and incorporated a humping motion into his dance groove. Katrina pushed herself back into him more as if wanting to feel him closer. When she did so, Jake reciprocated and held her by the waist with both hands. Their bodies then moved together in a slow, sensual motion as she pushed out and Jake pushed in.

Kirby's eyes popped wide open at this sudden turn of events. A few moments before, Jake was clearly uncomfortable, reluctant to dance and acting reserved. Now he was really getting into it. Kirby thought it was kind of hysterical. He laughed aloud and clapped his hands. "That's my boy. Get it, Jake. Get it."

Jake laughed too. He appeared to be having a good time now.

"You like that, huh?" Kirby shouted, motioning down with his eyes at Katrina's big ass.

Jake gave Kirby a look that read, *Eww.*

Kirby laughed.

"It's the shots. They're kicking in," Jake shouted with a grin.

Katrina appeared oblivious to this exchange as she worked it, having a hot guy on either side of her. As she continued to shimmy, she slowly rose back up, and then she turned around to face Jake as they danced. She placed her hands to his chest and stared into his eyes as if to cast a spell and seduce him.

Jake wasn't feeling it, but he instinctively placed his hands to her waist anyway and swayed back and forth with her. Apparently thinking that her seduction was working, Katrina began to rub her hands up and down Jake's chest, then up to his shoulders, and then down his shoulder blades in back and over to his ripped, muscular triceps. She stopped to squeeze them before moving her hands to his chest again. She must've thought that she was advancing her cause and making progress in her conquest because she stepped closer to him and then went in for a kiss. Jake immediately broke her gaze and looked away, trying to play it off as if he didn't know what she was attempting to do. Katrina's lips landed on his neck. She then rested her head on his shoulder and wrapped her arms around him, holding on tight.

Jake looked at Kirby and rolled his eyes. He then lifted his hands from Katrina's waist and raised them in an expression that read, *Help*, or least that's how Kirby interpreted it.

Kirby, who at first viewed Katrina as just playful and wild and looking to have a little fun, could see that she appeared to be quite smitten with Jake. In his mind, Katrina was mostly a prop to help pull Jake out of his shell and to get him to relax a little, especially in this environment. Now she was becoming a nuisance even to him, and he didn't like that she was feeling Jake up and trying to make a move on him. Kirby decided that he needed to intervene and set the record straight about who Jake really was to him. So he stepped behind Jake as Katrina continued to hold on to him. Now Jake was in the middle. Kirby grabbed Jake from behind, wrapping his arms around his abdomen and pressing himself tightly against Jake in back. For a very brief moment, all three of them together swayed from side to side in synchronicity with the beat of the music, until Katrina lifted her head from Jake's shoulder and recognized that Jake was now in the middle with her and Kirby on either side of him.

Katrina let go of Jake and stepped back. She looked at Jake and then she looked at Kirby. Kirby stopped swaying and glared back at her. "This right here is mine, bitch," he said to her with his eyes.

Oh fuck, Jake thought to himself, not knowing what to do. He was rendered frozen and speechless in the grip of his male love. Kirby began to sway their bodies together again as Katrina watched. He lifted his hands under Jake's T-shirt and rubbed his abs. Then he reached higher to pinch Jake's nipples. Keeping his eyes locked with Katrina's, Kirby licked Jake's neck and continued to lick in one long stroke up the side of his face until he reached his ear. Kirby stopped there to punctuate his possession of Jake by licking and sucking on his ear in an over-the-top, demonstrative fashion.

Jake didn't want to see the reaction on Katrina's face. He felt a little embarrassed by Kirby's lascivious gesture, but he couldn't bring himself to break free from him. So he just closed his eyes and allowed himself to succumb to Kirby's touch, albeit with a smirk on his face.

"I knew it!" Katrina shouted. "I knew you two were fucking each other."

Kirby wasn't sure what to make of her reaction. She sounded offended—pissed off, even. She started to laugh at them. It seemed taunting. Kirby taunted back by piling on, reaching down to grab Jake by the crotch while keeping his other hand on Jake's torso.

Jake became emboldened too, placing his hands on top of Kirby's, the one holding his crotch and the one pressed to his chest. He started to move his body along with Kirby's in a more provocative, lewd way, throwing any remaining inhibition to the wind. He finally looked at Katrina and simply smiled.

She yelled something at them with a wicked grin on her face, and then she turned to walk way.

It was so loud on the dance floor with the music blaring that neither of them could make out what she'd said. But it didn't matter. They didn't care. They were into each other now, just as Kirby had hoped and wanted.

CHAPTER
THIRTY-FOUR

Jake and Kirby continued to dance together after Katrina had disappeared. As Jake grooved with Kirby alone, any remaining unease or self-consciousness about displaying his affection and sexual attraction openly for another man in that setting slowly melted away. He could see that he was in a safe place even with so many others around. People weren't paying attention to him and Kirby. They were caught up in the music, the joy, the exuberance, and the high energy that permeated the dance floor and filled the room. It felt like a celebration. Everyone seemed so happy and free. This made Jake feel a sense of freedom too.

Now facing each other, Kirby pulled Jake close by the waist and said into his ear, "You're so sexy when you dance. I love it."

Jake smiled. "You too."

Kirby smiled back and then pulled Jake even closer, moving his hands from Jake's waist to his ass, cupping his cheeks firmly. He stared into Jake's eyes as he pressed his pelvis to his so that their bodies touched and grooved together in unison.

Jake immediately reciprocated, grabbing hold of Kirby's ass. They moved their bodies together tightly, erotically, and taunted one another, grinning and staring each other down sensually. Their noses collided and they could feel the warmth of their tequila-tainted breaths as they exhaled onto each other. After their noses collided once more, Kirby kissed the tip of Jake's nose. The way he did it was tender and lingering. A chill shot through Jake's body. He could feel Kirby's love. Kirby then kissed Jake's lips softly. That led to another kiss and then another. By the fourth kiss, Kirby pressed his tongue into Jake's mouth, and Jake took it eagerly to suckle. What started out as a tender kiss quickly morphed into a full-blown make out right there on the dance floor.

I don't give a fuck who's watching us, Jake thought to himself while lip- and tongue-locked with Kirby. The music, the way they were dancing, the darkness of the room, the funky, free-wheeling, decadent crowd—it all made him feel raw with erotic desire and emotion. He wanted to strip naked and press his lean, rock-hard flesh to Kirby's right there for all to see. They didn't go that far, but both knew that it was time to leave.

They stepped outside the club to catch a cab. "My place or yours?" Kirby simply asked.

"I don't care. Either works," Jake said.

A cab pulled up to the curb fairly quickly. They hopped in and Kirby called out the address to his bungalow in the Hollywood Hills, which wasn't far from the location of the club. On the short ride up the hill, Jake and Kirby remained silent the whole time, but the sexual tension was palpable. Kirby pressed his knee to Jake's as they sat together in the back seat. Jake then reached to squeeze and hold on to Kirby's knee. Kirby reciprocated by touching and squeezing Jake's lower thigh.

After they were dropped off, they walked into Kirby's place. It was the first time Jake had been back there since he'd moved out nearly six months before. "Déjà vu," Jake said, looking around.

Kirby grinned as he threw his keys down on the coffee table.

"So you never got a new housemate?"

"Nope…" Kirby said as he turned to face Jake and then walked over toward him "…because I've been waiting for you to move back in."

They instantly kissed and embraced, picking up where they'd left off on the dance floor at The Naked Bunny. Although there was no music playing in the background, they rotated their bodies together, pelvis to pelvis, just like they'd done on the dance floor, rubbing and caressing each other as they embraced. They kissed with hunger and abandon, extending their tongues from their mouths, wrestling them together. Kirby reached down Jake's back to grab and rub his ass fervently. Jake had a hard-on immediately. He was desperate to press his skin against Kirby's. He lifted Kirby's shirt to feel his pecs. As always, they were muscular, hard, and bulging, and his nipples were taut and erect. Jake bent down slightly to lick and suck on them.

"Oh yeah, bite me," Kirby commanded and then closed his eyes as he absorbed the rough titillation. "Harder, man," Kirby exhorted, causing Jake to bite, suck, and tug with more vigor and urgency.

Kirby expressed his pleasure with Jake's skills. "Fuck yeah. Milk that shit, bro."

Jake stopped when Kirby lifted his shirt over his head to remove it completely. Kirby then flexed his pecs to taunt Jake, inviting him to resume his torture. Jake went crazy licking Kirby's pecs and sucking his nipples, covering them in his saliva. He couldn't get enough. He stopped to unbuckle Kirby's pants. Kirby, knowing what Jake was craving, did the rest, unbuttoning his pants and pulling them down and off along with his undies. The Black Mamba popped free, long, hard, and fully erect with its mushroom head big, bold, and shiny. Like in worshipping awe, Jake fell down on his knees, slapped his hands to Kirby's smooth, muscular thighs, and held on as he went to town—sucking on that mushroom head with the eagerness of a kid devouring a Tootsie Pop, eager to get to the yummy-tasting filling hidden in the middle.

Jake pulled back to stroke Kirby's tool with his hand. "I want to get you off and make you come in my mouth again. I've been thinking about it and craving it all week."

"Not so fast, man. You know we have unfinished business. We got interrupted last time, but I'm gonna fuck you tonight and come in your ass."

Without saying anything, Jake returned his mouth to Kirby's rod. He sucked rapidly, using his hand and mouth to stroke at the same time. He did his best to expedite Kirby's eventual climax, but Kirby seemed to be reserving his energy for the main event. So Kirby took charge, pumping Jake's face and causing him to gag and slobber all over The Black Mamba.

Jake took the abuse like a champ and didn't let up or give in. He liked it when things got a little messy. It tuned him on even more.

"Need a little air, bro?" Kirby asked after a few minutes of using Jake's mouth as if it were a personal sex toy.

Jake didn't answer as he caught his breath and wiped his wet mouth. Kirby reached down and lifted Jake up under his arms so that they stood face-to-face again. They kissed each other passionately once more with extended, wrestling tongues. As they did so, Kirby reached down to grab and feel Jake's hard on. Kirby then began to unbutton Jake's jeans. Jake took over from there to quickly undress himself. His body boiling all over from sex fire, Jake yanked off his pants and undies to reveal a cock hard and pointed straight up at attention. It throbbed and ached so that the slit was already wet and lined with pre-cum. Kirby got down on his knees to return his friend's love and worship. He extended his thick pink tongue to lick the pre-cum first and then sucked long and hard on Jake's swollen mushroom head as if he was trying extract more, seeming to savor the pre-cum's salty taste. Jake's knees nearly buckled from the weight of so much excitement and pleasure. The sensation was so intense and it felt so damn good. He held on to Kirby's shaved head to balance himself. He then closed his eyes and began to slowly pump Kirby's face, losing himself in the oral massage of his manhood.

Soon thereafter the two landed on the sofa butt naked, Jake straddling Kirby's lap. With their mouths locked in a wet, openmouthed, passionate kiss, Kirby teased Jake's hole, poking and stretching it with his fingers. It drove Jake mad. With his arms around Kirby's neck, Jake pumped his pelvis against Kirby's abdomen in a fucking motion, feeling hot and beyond bothered. Jake wanted to feel Kirby inside him so bad. He was ready for it. "Fuck me, Kirby, fuck me. Rip me open, man." However, he became apprehensive when Kirby began to open his heart to him again about how he deeply felt.

With emotion in his voice, Kirby replied, "I love you, Jake. You're the only person I've ever truly been in love with. No one has held my heart the way you have, as long as you have. When I fuck you it's going to be all over for me, man. It's going to wreck me and make me crazy. There's so much pent-up emotion there. I hope you can handle it."

Jake stopped pumping his pelvis. "What do you mean?"

"I'll be ready to make you my wifey, man," Kirby said with a chuckle.

Jake chuckled too and blushed a little at Kirby's adoration. It made him feel warm inside.

"Are you ready to feel my love inside you, Jake? Because once I unleash it, it's going to be deep, real deep."

Jake laughed again. "Okay, but not too deep. It'll be my first time."

"I'm not just talking physically though," Kirby said, sounding more serious. "The last time I saw you, you told me that you loved me but that you didn't know what to do about it. I know what I want to do about it. I want to go deeper with you—a deeper level of emotion and connection, a deeper level of commitment. How about you? Have been thinking about what you want to do about our relationship?"

Jake sighed and looked down. "I don't know. I'm confused, Kirby."

"Confused about what? You want me, don't you?"

"I love you, Kirby. Likewise, I haven't held on to anyone as long as I've held on to you either. I walked away from Amanda and I tried to walk away from you too, but here I am. I do feel a connection. I know how deep our relationship is and that it goes beyond sex. Yes, the attraction is there—it has been for a long time—but more importantly, I trust you, more than anyone really."

"Then what's the problem?"

Jake sighed and then pulled himself off Kirby. He sat close beside him on the sofa with the sides of his arms and legs touching Kirby's. "We probably shouldn't go through with this tonight."

Kirby turned to look at Jake. Jake turned to look back at him and then quickly glanced away, seeing the disappointment and frustration in Kirby's face.

"I'm sorry, Kirby. I'm horny as fuck, but I don't want to hurt you any more than I already have. I love you. Honestly, I do. And even though I want you to fuck me, it doesn't feel right to me now, knowing how you feel and knowing the emotion behind it. I respect your feelings, and I don't want you to think that I'm doing this just for the experience of being fucked by a guy. If that were the case, I would've done it a long time ago. Heck, I could've done it with Reggie, but at the end of the day I couldn't go through with it because there was no connection there. I want to do it with you because I trust you, and I care about you. This whole exploration of feelings and emotions I can have for a guy is something I've only truly experienced with you, and I know that if you fucked me it would be taking things to the next level. It would be like the natural progression of a relationship that has evolved over a long period of time."

"Well, you certainly have evolved, because you've resisted going all the way for a very long time."

"I have evolved, and I want to try it, and I want to try it with you. But there's this deeper emotion, this…expectation of commitment that you're attaching to it, and I'm just not there yet. I'm not one hundred percent certain that I want us to be boyfriends…you know, a gay couple and all."

"What else is there? What could possibly be better than what we have—the connection, the chemistry, the friendship, the trust, the attraction, the love?"

"Well…I kind of had that with Amanda too," Jake said with apprehension, knowing that's not what Kirby would want to hear.

"I hope you're not still craning for Amanda, dude. I saw her not that long ago, and she's clearly moved on. Seriously…she's over it."

Jake furrowed his brow in surprise. "When'd you see her?"

"At the Elton John party on Oscar night. We randomly ran into each other there."

"Hmmm," Jake uttered before he paused for a few seconds. He was hesitant to ask about her but couldn't help himself. He needed to know more. "What did she say?"

"About?"

"About…you know…about this whole situation."

"You know, it's funny—when she first saw me, she hugged me."

Jake was incredulous. "She hugged you?"

"Yeah, but that was before she realized what she was doing and caught herself and pulled away from me like I had the plague. Then she tore into me."

"What she say?"

"Basically, she couldn't believe that I had cheated on Laren; asked me why I'd done it; told me that I was a bad person, that you're a bad person, that we're both cheats, yada yada yada. You know…the kind of things you'd expect her to say. Then Adam came up to us."

"He did?"

"Yeah. He was acting all smug and shit, like he was going to handle me or something. I was like, whatever, dude. Fuck him," Kirby said, shaking his head in annoyance at the memory.

"What happened?"

"Nothing. He was just being fake—congratulating me on my pilot, stuff like that. Amanda shooed him away. She told him to give us a moment."

"She did?" Jake said with a chuckle, feeling satisfied at what he perceived as a dis at Adam.

"Anyway, she thought you broke up with her because of me. I told her that wasn't the case and there were other reasons, but I didn't elaborate or say anything about the payment her father offered you to break up with her or anything about this personality disorder stuff."

"Good. Thanks for not bringing that up."

"Of course. I wasn't about to get into any of that. Anyway, she wanted to know if you and I were still together, you know, as friends or lovers or whatever, and I told her no. At the time we weren't, so that's what I said. Then she asked me if I was trying to get back with you. I said no, and then I asked her if she was trying to get back with you. And she got all pissy and was like, 'Does it look like I'm trying to get back with Jake?' And then she said she was with Adam now and that they're happy and whatever."

"Oh yeah?" Jake said, feeling a little sad. He was kind of hoping to hear otherwise. That perhaps she had feelings for him still and that the door might still be cracked open, even though he wasn't one hundred percent sure he was prepared to walk through it if it was.

"Yeah. She was being all testy and said that you and I could have each other as far as she was concerned. I don't know. Maybe she was just putting on an act. I kind of was too, because it was right after I'd found out about you and Reggie, and I was angry. Obviously I wasn't going to tell her how hurt I was and that I still had feelings for you. Maybe she was still hurt and angry too. Regardless, I'm pretty sure she's moved on, man."

Jake was smug. "Maybe, maybe not."

"What do you mean by that?"

"Just that she might've been putting on airs too. That's all. I don't think she's in love with Adam. He was her rebound before and he's just her rebound now."

"Why does it matter? Who gives a fuck? You act like you still want her or something."

Jake sat in silence and didn't answer back as Kirby's agitation grew.

"Jake, look, I don't know if I can to do this anymore. You're draining me, man. I'm nearly running on empty. I don't know what more to do or say to convince you—"

"You don't need to convince me of anything, Kirby. Okay? I already know how you feel. I love you and care for you too. And I've thought about us being together…in a serious relationship. I've thought about it a lot. I just need to you be patient with me. Give me a little more time and space. A lot of shit has gone down in my family recently and some things have come to light, including about Amanda, that I need to deal with."

"So you think you're going to get back with her or something?"

"That's not what I'm saying."

"Then what are you saying?" Kirby said in a raised voice, clearly irritated.

"My life feels like it's sitting stuck in this great big gray area. I just need a little more time, Kirby, to figure things out, to clear the fog and get my head straight. And to be honest, until I do, I don't think I can be available to you the way you want me to be. The way you deserve."

Kirby sat silent for a moment. He stared across the room, appearing dejected and sad.

"I'm sorry, Kirby," Jake said as he placed his hand on Kirby's thigh.

Kirby hopped up immediately as if he didn't want Jake's sympathy or affection. "Don't worry about it, bro. I understand," he said before letting out a big yawn, stretching his arms upward in the air. "I think I'm going to bed. I'm too tired to drive you home right now. You can have the sofa if you want to stay the night. I'll drive you home when we wake up or you can call a cab to take you now. It's up to you."

"No, the sofa's fine. I'm tired too. I'll sleep right here." Jake reached for the throw blanket sitting on the sofa's armrest and then pulled it over him as he lay down.

Kirby turned off the lights, stepped into his bedroom, and shut the door behind him without saying anything further.

***

Not able to sleep, Jake tossed and turned with Amanda on his mind. He had a major decision to make—whether or not to tell Amanda about the bold-faced lie her father had told about her. Although still undecided about what to do, he felt the urge to call her. As the early morning hours dragged on, Jake grew increasingly restless. He looked at his phone and saw that it was ten minutes past five. After three and a half hours of lying there mostly awake, Jake decided to get up. He wanted to go home but figured that Kirby was likely sound asleep still. He tiptoed over to Kirby's bedroom door to check. He placed his ear to the door at first but didn't hear anything. So he slowly twisted the doorknob to open it for a peek. Kirby's room was dark, but there was just enough early morning light coming through the window for Jake to see Kirby lying on his stomach with his head tucked beneath a pillow. He was also snoring faintly. Jake closed the door softly. He stepped into the bathroom to take a leak. When he finished, he called a cab to take him home.

CHAPTER THIRTY-FIVE

It was already past ten Sunday morning in New York when Amanda tossed herself awake. She and Adam had slept in late following a whirlwind Saturday. After furniture shopping and a late afternoon lunch, they'd gone to Adam's place in Chelsea. While in the hallway, they'd run into a couple who were neighbors and good friends of Adam's. Pleasantly surprised to see him and wanting to get to know his new girlfriend better, they'd invited the two over for an impromptu house party. So later that evening, Adam and Amanda had ended up hanging out with them along with another couple Adam knew relatively well. They stayed up into the wee hours listening to music, talking, laughing, eating, and drinking a lot of wine.

Amanda rose up in bed and placed her hands to her forehead. "My head is spinning. I think I'm having vertigo."

Snuggled beside her in a fetal positon, Adam sighed heavily. "You're probably a little hungover," he mumbled without opening his eyes.

"I drank way too much," Amanda said while still holding her forehead. She paused and sat still for a few seconds. "Okay. It stopped. I think I can get out of bed now without falling flat on my face."

As she stepped out of bed, Adam reached for her arm but missed. "Where are you going?"

"It's time to get up. It's almost ten thirty and your flight leaves in three hours. Don't you want to get a bite to eat before you go?"

"I'd rather have sex."

"But I'm hungry, Adam," she replied in a plaintive tone while grinning at the same time.

"Okay. We'll have sex first and then we'll go eat."

Amanda snickered and shook her head. "We've had sex like five times over the past two days. All you think about is sex, sex, and more sex."

"I can't help it. I'm stuck in fucking Canada for three months with mostly a bunch of scruffy dudes, including a high-maintenance, know-it-all blowhard of an actor who thinks it's his job to tell me what to do. And on top of that, it's frickin' cold up there and I go home every night alone without a warm body to snuggle up with. And you know how restless Big Papa down here can be when he's not gettin' the daily, especially when we're in a cold environment. He pokes his head straight up, sniffing around for flesh to bury himself in to keep cozy and warm. So, you know, I have to stroke him pretty often to keep him calm or else he'll go crazy." Adam threw back the covers and lifted himself up to reveal the growing thickness of his rod. "See, look at him. He needs attention again. You've spoiled him. Settle down, man. Settle down now," Adam said while looking at and petting his big penis tenderly.

Amanda giggled and grinned broadly. "Awww, poor Papa. Good morning, Big Papa," she said all cutesy and waving hello with her fingers.

"All I have are my memories of you to jerk him off to. It gets old after a while. I need to experience and feel the real thing as much as possible. You know, to create more memories to hold me and him over until the next time I see you."

"Oh, all right. I've got to pee, but I'll take care of Big Papa when I get back," Amanda said as she walked over to the bathroom. "Be right back, Big Papa," she said, still giggling before closing the door.

"Hurry back. And don't wipe yourself or anything. He wants it a little funky," Adam shouted.

Amanda busted out laughing as she sat on the toilet. "Oh my God. Shut up!"

Adam sat up in bed, stroking himself to keep Big Papa primed and ready for what was to come. Then suddenly he heard a ping on the phone, indicating that a text message had just been received. He leaned over to reach for his cell phone, which was sitting on the nightstand next to Amanda's. When he looked at it, there wasn't a new message, only old messages from the day before. "Hmmm." *It must be Amanda's phone,* he thought to himself as he set his phone back down and picked up hers. When he saw who the message was from, Adam's hard-on rapidly went limp.

Hi Mandi. I need to see you. There's something very important I need to speak with you about. Are you in LA or New York right now?

"Fuck," Adam said, gritting his teeth.

Right after that moment, Amanda opened the door and stepped out of the bathroom completely nude. Feeling sexy and sensual, she walked toward the bed slowly and seductively. As she did so, she lifted her long, dark hair and flipped it over to the side to accentuate her sultry gaze. Meanwhile, Adam glared at her, unable to conceal the rage on his face. Amanda was so caught up in the moment that she didn't register his ire at first. Finally she noticed the phone in his hand and the anger in his eyes that she initially mistook for playful, animal-like intensity. He often would growl like a dog when he ate her out, so that's what she thought she was in for. But no, he looked mad, really mad.

"What's the matter?"

Adam threw her phone toward her, down on the bed. "It looks like the other man in your life is making plans to see you after I leave."

"What? Is that my phone?" Amanda asked as she furrowed her brow and stepped over to the bed's edge to pick it up. She paused for a second to read the text and then she sighed. The text from Jake wasn't shocking as much as it was irritating, having come at the worst possible time. She'd suspected that he'd contact her eventually, but she didn't know when or how. In that moment, however, she felt more bothered by Adam's snooping.

"Jake *is not* the other man in my life. You know that. What were you doing with my phone?"

"I heard a phone ping, and I picked up yours by accident, thinking that it was mine," Adam said half-truthfully.

Amanda didn't believe him. "Why were you reading my messages, Adam?"

"I wasn't. I said that I picked up your phone accidently. Your phone pings just like mine does and they were sitting right next each other. I picked up the wrong phone and there was Jake's message. What'd you expect me to do, shut my eyes and act like I didn't see it?"

"Yes! That would've been the more discreet thing to do."

Adam sighed and slapped his hand down on the bed. "It was a short fucking message for Christ's sake. It only took a second to read."

"I don't care if it took half a second and was only composed of one word. Don't read my messages and then throw a fit about them."

"Oh, come on. Don't try to turn the tables on me. What's worse, me stumbling upon a message from your ex or you carrying on these secret side conversations with him and hiding it from me?"

"I am not having secret conversations with him, Adam. I haven't spoken to Jake in five months."

"Didn't he email you not too long ago?"

"Yes, he emailed me in January asking me not to tell people he's gay, but I didn't even email him back. I've honestly had no communication with him, at least not coming from me."

"Then why the fuck is he texting you? I don't get it, especially now that we're in this very public relationship. Does he not watch TV or follow social media?"

"He knows we're together."

"If you're not sending him feelers or back-channel messages or anything like that, why does he think you two have anything more to talk about?"

"I don't know, Adam. Unless I speak to him to find out—"

Adam cut her off. "Oh, so you are going to speak him after all? Because at lunch yesterday you acted like you weren't. You said that everything is over between you two and that there's no point and how annoyed you were that he contacted your mother."

"I said *unless* I speak to him. I didn't say *I will* speak to him. It's over between us, and I am annoyed that he called her."

"Okay. Then promise me right now that you won't speak with him."

"Adam," Amanda said plaintively.

"No. If you're serious about being done with him and, more important, if you are serious about building a future with me, then I need to hear you say it—that you won't have any further contact with him. Ever again!"

Amanda just stared at Adam, feeling cornered and uncomfortable with his demand. Tears began to well in her eyes. She wanted to reassure him that their relationship had turned a corner and that she was indeed his girl now, but deep down inside she wanted to hear from Jake. She wanted to hear what he had to say. She wanted to know what was so important for him to speak with her about. And she wanted to know why he felt her parents had had a role in their breakup, notwithstanding how ridiculous and outlandish that sounded to her.

"Promise me, Amanda."

Torn inside, Amanda continued to stand there frozen and mum.

Adam grew increasingly impatient and angry. "Why can't you say it? Huh? Say it!"

"Adam, you can't make me promise you that right now."

"Why not?"

"Because it's unfair. It's not fair for you to expect that from me."

"Unfair? And it's not unfair to me that you want to maintain a chummy relationship with a guy who's trying to win you back? Who wants to rip us apart and tear down everything we've been working together toward as a couple? We've gone public, Amanda. We're officially a couple now. Do you know what that means? Do you know how it will look if word gets out that you are secretly, let alone openly, having conversations with your ex? For Christ's sake, come on, what's wrong with you? The guy dumped you practically at the altar to be with another man, and he cheated on you the entire time you were together. How much more abuse are you willing to take from him?"

"I'm not talking about maintaining some sort of chummy relationship him, Adam. What's wrong with just hearing him out if he has something more he wants or needs to say to me?"

"What's wrong? I'll tell you what's wrong. You're weak and that guy has a hold on you unlike anything I ever seen before. He doesn't even have to work for it all that hard. You make it so easy for him. Whenever Jake calls, there you go running—"

"That's not true."

"Yes it is true, because it happened before. You abruptly left me and became engaged to him. Remember? You fell hook, line, and sinker for that phony. He was just using you to conceal who he really was."

"Things are different now, Adam. That wouldn't happen again."

"Oh Amanda, enough with this bullshit. I can't take it," Adam said as he lifted himself out of bed and stood. "I swear to God, if you speak to him or have anything to do with him, I'm gone. I'm not fucking doing this again." Adam stormed over to the bathroom and slammed the door shut.

Amanda plopped herself down on the bed and buried her face in her hands, completely distraught.

CHAPTER
THIRTY-SIX

After their tiff, things were so icy between Amanda and Adam that they ended up not creating any new memories to hold over Big Papa until they met again. Adam showered and got dressed. He then turned on his laptop and became engrossed with work. Seeing that he was preoccupied and no longer paying attention to her, Amanda eventually decided to leave. Adam told her how great it was to see her. Amanda told him likewise and thanked him again for the furniture shopping spree. They kissed each other on the lips and hugged in a cursory way and then she opened the front door to walk out.

"I'll call you later tonight after I get back," Adam said just before she closed the door behind her.

Don't bother, Amanda said in her mind. She was so upset that Adam had given her an ultimatum.

A few minutes later she was in a coffee shop to have a bite to eat while on the phone with Lucy.

"Who the hell does he think he is, telling me who I can and cannot talk to? He doesn't fucking own me. I'm not his possession."

"But you have to look at it from his perspective too. He has invested so much time and energy trying to convince you that he's the right guy for you, to show you how much he loves you and wants to be with you. And just when it looks like you're completely falling for him and ready to take your relationship to the next level, Jake comes swooping in out of nowhere. Adam's worried and upset because he doesn't want to lose you again like before."

"That's kind of what he said, but he could've communicated his feelings better instead of threatening me. He's turning this into a situation where it's like I have to choose between him and Jake, as if I've been dating them both at the same time or something. That's not what this is about. I've been with Adam basically since Jake and I broke up and only with Adam—nobody else. I'm not trying to get back with Jake, and I've done nothing to suggest otherwise. I haven't called him. I haven't texted him. Nothing. I even deleted all of my photos of him on my Facebook account."

"I know, Mandi. I know how hard you've tried to move on, but it looks like Jake hasn't gotten the message if he's still texting you."

"I can't fucking control what Jake does. It's not my fault that he's texting me and calling my mother." Amanda sighed in frustration.

"So what are you going to do?"

"I don't know. I want to hear what Jake has to say. I guess I'm mostly just curious."

"Okay, call him back. Hear him out first, and then tell him once and for all that it's over, that you're in a new relationship, that it's very serious, and that you think it's best that you have no further communication with one another going forward. Wish him the best and tell him to move on. Over and done with."

"Yeah, but Adam doesn't want me to speak to him at all."

"Adam's going to have to chill and allow you deal with this situation, because if you don't, Jake will continue to contact you."

"I know, exactly. I guess I could just try to ignore him."

"But that won't work because you just said that you're curious and that you want to speak to him and hear what he has to say."

"I do."

"Okay, so here's what you should do. Call Jake and hear him out, like I said. And then after you tell him that it's truly over between you two and that you no longer want to be with him and that you're in love with somebody else, send him an email making the same points and blind-copy

Adam. That way Adam can see that you actually told Jake to leave you the fuck alone and to get on with his life."

"Hmmm, I like that idea. That might work, actually."

"Do it. Do it now. If I were you, I wouldn't wait around. I'd get back to Jake right away. You know the saying—strike while the iron is hot, while this issue is fresh on everyone's mind—your mind, Adam's mind, Jake's mind. That way Adam will be able to see that you dealt with the situation immediately and tried to put it to rest."

Amanda sighed, feeling hesitant. "It's funny. Even though I'm curious to hear what Jake has to say, I don't actually feel like talking to him. Maybe I could get him to just email me."

Lucy balked. "That would probably be a long freakin' email and there'd be a lot of back-and-forth that could go on for days. You don't want to create that kind of paper trail, especially in this day and age. You're a celebrity now, and that shit could end up on the Internet. I think you should call him. Call him now."

"Okay, okay. I will. Jesus."

***

Jake waited anxiously for Amanda's reply. More than two hours had passed since he'd texted her after leaving Kirby's place and returning home. The more time passed, the more unlikely it seemed that Amanda would get back to him, he thought. A handful of conflicting thoughts raced through Jake's mind as he sat on his sofa to watch the slate of NFL games scheduled on TV that day. *It's just as well if she doesn't call me back. What she doesn't know won't hurt her. She's all tied up with Adam now anyway, so what's the point? Getting back with her would be nice, though, but what am I going to do about Kirby? I fucking love Kirby. I never get bored with that. All day long, man, all day long, but I don't want to marry a guy, do I? That would be too fucking much. No political career for me as a moderate to liberal Republican if I marry a guy. Being perceived as a liberal would be a big enough hurdle as it is. But this is California. Arnie got elected governor as a Republican and he's moderate to liberal in his views. But he's a fucking celebrity married to a Kennedy. I'll need a wife too to pull it off, especially to reach that level of office like governor or US senator. No gay Republican would make it past the primary. Maybe I should just take the money and run. I wonder how much I could get out of Rick. No, fuck that. I want to be with Amanda again. I miss that feeling of being in love with a chick. I miss being in love with her. I don't know if I could give up pussy completely anyway. I don't know if I could give up dick either, though.* "Shit! What the fuck am I thinking?" Jake said aloud to the room, rubbing his hands on his face, feeling distressed.

Distracted and not paying much attention to the game, Jake decided to go out for a run. A good run would help him settle down, help him relax, he thought. He quickly changed into a pair of running shorts and a tank top and slipped on a pair of running shoes. He grabbed his running watch and put it on his wrist as he walked toward the front door of his apartment. Right when he was about to step out, he heard his phone ping thrice in rapid succession—an indication that he'd received multiple text messages. His heart stopped.

He walked over to the sofa where he'd left the phone and picked it up. He thought there'd be three messages per the three pings but he saw only two messages, both from his friend Will. The first message was an inside joke about a mutual friend who consistently had a losing record betting on NFL games. Jake chuckled. The second message was that Will and his fiancée Kerry were organizing a get-together at their place later that afternoon and they wanted Jake to join them.

Sounds good. Heading out for a run now. Just tell me what time and I'm there, Jake typed in reply to the second message.

Jake was about the put the phone down when he suddenly noticed the third message. It was from a number that he didn't recognize with a New York City area code.

Hi Jake. I'm in New York. What's this about?

Jake felt pretty confident that he knew who the message was from, but he asked to make sure. *Is this Amanda?*

Yes. I got your text.

Oh, hey. I was wondering. Did you change your number?

This is my work phone. My other phone ran out of juice. At a coffee shop and don't have my charger with me. What's up?

For a moment there Jake was frazzled. He didn't know where to begin, typing, deleting, and retyping again several times. *It would be better if we talked in person*, he finally wrote.

I won't be back in LA for another couple of weeks.

Jake hesitated for a moment, and then he quickly thought up the perfect comeback even though the claim he was about to make wasn't true. *I'll be in New York this week on business anyway, so I can make time to see you.*

"What?" Amanda said aloud to herself, incredulous. She rapidly typed back on her phone with annoyance, *I really don't think that will be necessary and to be honest this is not a good time. I'm about to launch my handbag line in less than two weeks and I'm very busy right now.*

I understand but this is very important and I'll already be there. Okay if I just call you right now instead of texting?

Amanda huffed and rolled her eyes. *Fine*, she wrote. Five seconds later, Jake's call came through.

"Hello," she answered with exasperation in her voice.

"Hi. How are you?" Jake said, feeling a sense of awe hearing Amanda's voice again for the first time in months.

"I'm fine. How are you?" she asked perfunctorily.

"Oh…there's a lot that's gone on this past week. I assume you don't have a clue."

"A clue about what?"

"Well, that's what I need to talk with you about."

"What is this all about, Jake? Seriously, can we just talk about this now over the phone?

"No. I prefer to do it in person."

"Why? I already know that you called my mother."

"Well, your mother doesn't even know half the story. She doesn't know anything, as far as I can tell."

"What are you talking about, Jake?"

"I really think we should save this conversation for when I get to New York."

"Why? Look, if you think there's a chance of you and me getting back together, because that's what my mom told me you said to her, then you're wasting your time. I'm dating Adam again, as you probably very well know, and I'm happy with where things are. I'm happy with my life, and I really don't want to revisit the past with you. I mean, I'm willing to listen to whatever it is you have to say, but I just want to be clear about my intentions and feelings. You made your choice, Jake. You walked away. There's no turning back now."

"Yes, you're right. It was my choice, and I walked away, but your parents or your dad, at least, had a hand in my decision to do so, and you should be aware of that."

"Jake, what are you talking about? You were cheating, and you chose to be with Kirby."

"That's not why I broke up with you. I've told you that before. Cheating on you was wrong. I admit that. But despite what went on between me and Kirby, it was still my intention to marry you until your con artist of a father stepped in to keep that from happening."

"Con artist?"

"Amanda, you have no idea. When I tell you what your father told me about you—"

"About me?"

"Yes, about you. You're going to freak. Your dad's a con man. I'm telling you. It worked. I was duped and it's my fault for falling for it at the end of the day, but your dad and my mother orchestrated our breakup. Those two have history, you know, and they conspired together to break us up."

"Okay, you're talking crazy right now. I can't—"

"He even offered to pay me lots of money for my silence. I'm talking millions of dollars, Amanda. He wanted to set me up for life. He still does, in fact."

"I don't believe a word you're saying to me right now."

"I have proof."

"What proof?"

"I'll bring it and show it to you when I see you. Besides, I seriously doubt your dad would deny anything I'm telling you at this point. The cat's out of the bag, and too many people are involved and know what's going on. Your dad probably hopes we'll all keep silent. But I'm not letting him off the hook. My own mother's not off the hook, so why should he be?"

Amanda sighed hard, slowly relenting to a meeting. "When do you get to New York?"

"Ahhh…Tuesday…Tuesday morning," Jake blurted, not even having a plane ticket yet. He figured that he'd need an extra day to inform the office that he was taking unexpected personal time off to travel to New York and to rearrange his schedule as he had client meetings lined up for that week.

"Shit, I can't be seen with you," Amanda said, the stress in her voice evident.

"Why?"

"We were an item, Jake. Our breakup has been written about, remember? And I'm with Adam now, which means even more media scrutiny, a lot more. If you and I are seen together, the tabloids will go crazy, and it would put Adam and me in a very bad situation. I don't want to drag him into this. He's already paranoid enough as it is about you reaching out to me."

"He knows?"

"Yes, he saw your text message to me this morning, and trust me, he's not happy about it. I think we should keep this whole meeting a secret as best we can."

"And I'd suggest that you not tell anyone what I've told you thus far, not even your parents. Wait until after we've met and I show you what it is that I have to show you to prove to you that I'm not lying."

"Okay. Well, just call me when you get here and we'll figure something out about when and where to meet up."

CHAPTER THIRTY-SEVEN

After she and Jake hung up, Amanda downed what was left of her now cold soy latte and then headed out of the coffee shop to make her way back to her hotel. She couldn't believe her ears. They felt like they were buzzing, hearing the accusation about her dad offering to pay Jake off. Amanda was so beside herself that she was shaking and struggled to walk straight. She spoke softly to herself in disbelief. "This can't be true. Why on earth would my dad pay Jake not to marry me? This is insane. This is outrageous. This is unreal. I can't believe it."

Amanda couldn't bear to walk any further and decided to hail a cab. Intense jitters fueled by shock combined with wet, cold weather rapidly freezing her limbs made her feel as though she'd collapse to the ground at any moment. After she flagged a cab down and hopped in, she immediately dialed Lucy. Although Jake had implored her not to repeat what he'd told her to anyone, she couldn't help herself. She had to tell someone.

"Hey, what's up?" Lucy asked upon answering the phone.

"I just got off the phone with Jake."

"And?"

"He's coming to New York."

"When?"

"Tuesday. We're going to meet."

"You're going to meet with him?" Lucy sounded incredulous.

"I think I have to."

"Why?"

"Lucy, oh my God, you won't believe what he told me. I'm shaking right now."

"What did he say?"

Amanda sighed. "You can't tell anyone, Lucy. Promise me."

"Okay. I promise. Now tell me."

"I'm serious, Lucy. You can't say anything to anyone. Oh my God, Lucy, I can't believe it…," Amanda said as her voice trailed off and then broke.

"Oh my God, Mandi, you're scaring me. Are you okay?"

On the verge of a breakdown, Amanda took a moment to regain her composure. She remained silent and closed her eyes tightly to prevent any teardrops from falling. "Yeah, I'm okay…I'm okay," she said finally.

"Where are you?"

"In a cab headed home…back to the hotel, I mean. Sorry. I'm reeling right now. Calm down, Amanda…calm down. Breathe…breathe," Amanda said slowly to herself before she inhaled and exhaled softly.

"What did Jake say to you?"

"He said that the real reason why he broke up with me, notwithstanding the fact that he was cheating, is that my dad offered him a lot of money not to marry me."

"What? Get…the fuck…out. That's ridiculous."

"He said he has proof."

"What proof?"

"That's what he's going to show me when he gets here. He must have something in writing, I gather."

Lucy snickered dismissively. "Why would Rick do that? That makes absolutely no sense."

"I don't know. Jake said that my dad told him a story about me, and I guess apparently it was enough to persuade Jake to break things off with me. Jake said that he was duped and that he fell for it, whatever it was he was told, and that my dad then offered him money for his silence."

"You can't be serious. This is fucking crazy, Amanda. Do you believe this story?"

Amanda sighed. "I don't know. Wait, sorry," she said to Lucy as her cab pulled in front of her hotel to drop her off. Amanda paid the driver, stepped out of the car, and then continued her thought.

"I mean, I wouldn't completely put it past my dad to do something like that. I don't know why he'd do it, but if he had a good enough reason or a good enough reason to *him*, he'd probably do it. I actually think he keeps a mistress or two and might even have a love child he's secretly funding."

"Hmmm, you've told me that before, but that's to cover his own ass. To keep his affairs covered up. That doesn't explain why he'd pay Jake. It's not like he's having an affair with Jake, or would he? Does Rick secretly like boys?"

Amanda smirked dismissively. "I don't think so, Lucy."

"Well, I don't know. I'm just trying to make sense of this. Maybe Jake has something on him and blackmailed him or something."

"No. Jake said my dad told him something about *me,* to persuade him not to marry me, and then offered him money to keep silent about it."

"Oh my God. This is crazy. I can't believe this, Amanda. Are you going to call your dad to tell him about this?"

"No. Jake said I should wait until after we've met, and I agree. I want to hear what my dad allegedly told him first and see what Jake has to show me. I swear to God, Lucy, if this is true, if my parents, my dad, had a role in breaking us up and offered Jake money not to marry me, shit is going to blow straight through the roof."

"I'm in shock right now. I don't know what to do. What about Adam? Have you told him any of this?"

"No. Not right now. I want to keep my plans to meet with Jake a secret for now. I've already told him that we can't be seen together."

"That's for sure, but where are you guys going to meet?"

"I don't know yet, but Lucy, you have to promise me that you won't say anything to anyone about Jake coming to New York, about me meeting with him, about what he's told me about my dad offering to pay him off—not a word about any of this."

"Amanda, I promise not to say a word to anyone. I swear to God. I'm literally holding my hand to my heart right now."

CHAPTER THIRTY-EIGHT

Jake arrived in New York at eight thirty Tuesday morning after having taken a red-eye flight overnight from Los Angeles. He had made a reservation at a Midtown Manhattan hotel, but his room wasn't to be available for check-in until three that afternoon. On the cab ride over from the airport, he called to see if there was any way he could check in sooner, but the hotel couldn't guarantee it as it had been sold out the night before. They put him on standby and told him that they'd send him a text message if a room became available sooner as there'd likely be early checkouts.

Once he made it to Midtown, Jake had the cab driver drop him off at a diner on Forty-Fifth Street near Times Square. It wasn't far from his hotel. The diner was full, mostly with what appeared to be tourists, but luckily Jake found one booth left open toward the back and snagged it right away. After taking a quick look at the menu, Jake ordered coffee, a vegetable and egg white omelet, and wheat toast. While waiting for his food, he decided to text Amanda to let her know that he'd arrived.

Hi, Mandi. I'm in NY. When are you free to meet?

He didn't get a reply back right away. So he sat, waited, and repeatedly looked at his phone, anticipating her reply at any moment. However, more than ten minutes passed and still no reply. Eventually Jake's food arrived. He gulped it down, all while wondering about Amanda. *Did she change her mind? I wonder if she ended up calling Rick and telling him what I told her.*

Other than seeing Amanda, Jake had no other business in New York. Therefore, it would end up being a big waste of time if she'd changed her mind about seeing him. And she didn't necessarily have an obligation to tell him so, especially since he'd given her the impression that he was in town on business and not there just to see her. After finishing his breakfast and sitting there for nearly an hour without hearing from her, Jake became filled with doubt about the likelihood of them meeting. "I'm screwed," he said aloud to himself as he thought about what to do next.

He got up, paid his bill, and headed out toward Times Square with no place to go. Lugging his small suitcase along, he walked aimlessly, staring blankly at the hustle and bustle of the city that surrounded him. Just as he was about to turn the corner onto Broadway, he heard his phone ping. The text he'd been expecting had finally come through.

Hi Jake, I'm tied up in meetings all morning. Where are you staying?

Hi. At the Hilton in Times Square.

I have some time free this afternoon.

Okay. I can come to you if that makes it easier. Are you staying at your parents' apartment?

No. The Gramercy Park Hotel. It's closer to my office.

Does your hotel have a bar or lounge where we could meet?

I don't want to meet there. Paparazzi stalk the place. Can I come to your hotel room?

Jake did a mental double take. He wasn't expecting that. *Sure but don't have a room yet. Check-in's at 3 but on standby for sooner.*

After 3 is fine. Let's say 4?

Okay. Should definitely have a room by then.

I'll text you when I'm on my way.

CHAPTER THIRTY-NINE

Amanda stepped into the lobby of the Hilton Hotel five minutes past four in the afternoon. She was wearing sunglasses and a wool parka with the hood pulled over her head to keep from being noticed. She looked around and saw that the lobby was relatively quiet for such a large and typically busy hotel. Sensing that nobody was paying the least bit of attention to her, she saw a sign for the restrooms and walked in that direction. She pushed through the restroom door, walked up to the vanity, took off her shades, and pulled her hood back to have a look at herself. She immediately started to fuss with her hair and became particularly annoyed with a lone strand that seemed suspended in air by some magnetic field and that refused let go.

"Oh, who gives a crap? I'm not here to impress him," she said before pulling her phone out of her coat pocket to call Jake.

"Hi," Jake answered.

"Hi. I'm downstairs. I assume you need an access key to get up to your floor."

"Yeah, you do. I'll come down right now and get you. Are you in the lobby?"

"In the restroom. I'm about to come out now."

"Just go over and stand by the elevators. I'll be right there."

"Okay."

Amanda left her hood off but put her shades back on. Staring straight ahead, she observed the scene from the corner of her eyes as she walked cautiously across the lobby floor over to the elevator bank. Although she knew the Hilton was a more commonplace hotel that mostly hosted tourists and traditional business travelers and not high-profile celebrities, she felt a little apprehensive nevertheless. She was now being photographed alone at times, without Adam by her side. She had become an It girl of the moment after all of the attention she'd received following the Golden Globes and Oscars. Her Facebook follows had blown up, increasing by the day, and there was bounty to be had if fresh photos of her could be procured as frequently as possible. All of the attention and scrutiny were new to Amanda and made her anxious. She'd gone from being a rich heiress occasionally mentioned in the likes of *Town & Country* and the *New York Social Diary*, because of her parents and family name, to a full-fledged person of interest on her own, covered by *Vogue*, *People*, and *Us*, among other celebrity rags.

Amanda stood in front of the elevators and waited, feeling slightly anxious about seeing Jake. The center elevator doors opened and there he stood, beautiful as ever. She immediately noticed his blond hair—slick, wet, and perfectly combed with a part on the side like a Ralph Lauren model. His icy blue eyes were especially striking set against lightly suntanned skin, courtesy of the continuous shine and warmth of the California sun. And that body—the lean, muscular definition of which was unmistakably apparent through the lightweight, dark blue, long-sleeved crewneck sweater that hugged his torso.

"Hi," Jake said, greeting his former girl love with a warm smile.

"Hi," Amanda said back as she fought to maintain her composure, offering a more restrained half smile so as not to seem in any way happy or joyful about being in his presence.

Jake extended his arm to hold the elevator door open as Amanda stepped in. After the doors closed, they stood and faced each other for a couple of seconds in silence before Jake spoke again.

"How are you? It's been a while."

"I'm good, thanks. Everything's good. How about you?"

"Not bad. This is my first time in New York since—"

"You were here with me, probably."

"Yeah. When was that?"

"I think the Christmas before last or right before. We went to Alana's Christmas party."

"Yeah, that's right. I remember," Jake said as they stepped out of the elevator, having reached his floor. "Can't believe it's been that long. That was more than a year ago."

"Yep," Amanda said simply as she followed behind Jake to his room. She stared at his backside from head to toe, observing the man she had once made love to endlessly and thought she'd be married to and together with forever. Sadness and longing fell over her, but she quickly shook them off and broke her gaze, recalling that the same man in front of her had cheated on her and deceived her about who he really was for a very long time. She needed to hold on to that thought in order to stay strong and to remain as unemotional and detached as possible.

Jake unlocked the door with his key card and then held it open, allowing Amanda to step in first. "After you," he said.

"Thanks," she said as she walked in, observing the room. It was pretty basic with a queen-size bed, a desk and chair, and a larger armchair in the corner with a matching ottoman. Clean, orderly, and unfussy. Kind of like Jake, she thought. She stepped over to the window to check out his view. "Nice view of the Empire State Building," she said before turning around to find Jake standing there quietly watching her. He looked solemn, if a bit awestruck. Amanda sensed that he was taking her in—taking in the moment of being with her again, alone. It felt a little awkward for her too.

"Can I get you anything to drink? There's juice, soda, and water in the fridge," he said, opening the door of the credenza to show her where the small fridge was hidden.

"No. I'm fine. Thanks," Amanda said as she sat on the end of the bed. She sighed huffishly and then said, "So," to get the conversation started.

"So…I assume you want to get right down to what it is I have to talk with you about."

"I have somewhere else to be by five or shortly thereafter," she lied.

"Oh, okay. Well—"

"You said that you had something to show me, to prove that my dad offered you money not to marry me. And first…can I just say how ridiculous this all sounds?"

"I know it does," Jake said as he pulled out the desk chair, turned it around, and sat in it, facing her. He leaned forward, rested his arms on his legs, and clasped his hands together. Very small beads of sweat appeared at the top of his forehead.

Amanda knew he was nervous and couldn't wait to hear his story.

"Do you remember that I told you the real reason I broke up with you was that I was trying to protect you?"

"Yes, but I thought that meant that you were trying to keep me from finding out the truth about your relationship with Kirby and your attraction to guys."

Jake sighed and shook his ahead in frustration. "Amanda, I told you that's not the reason I broke up with you. Yes, I had been fooling around—"

"Having sex with," she interrupted.

"Yes, having sex with Kirby—"

"For a very long time," she interrupted again.

"And…that was wrong for me do while we were together. I admit that, okay? I'm sorry for what I did, for cheating on you and betraying your trust. Honestly, I am truly sorry. But as I told you over the phone, it's what your dad told me about you that prompted my decision to end our relationship."

Amanda furrowed her brow and looked at Jake skeptically. "What did he tell you?"

Jake took a deep breath and paused for a few seconds as he looked down at the floor.

Amanda's heart began to race with anticipation and anxiety. *What can it be?*

Jake then looked up at her with a grave expression on his face and began to speak. "Amanda, about two weeks before our wedding, I was told that you were not well."

"What do you mean, not well?"

"That you were ill."

Amanda winced. "What?"

"At first, Mike Wallace—you remember him?"

"Yeah. He's like your mentor and your boss, and a friend of your family's, I recall."

"Right. And you know he's your dad's attorney, or at least, one of them. I'm sure he has a few."

"Yeah…right," Amanda slowly recalled. "I think I remember him telling me that when you introduced us at your firm's Christmas party way back when."

"Well, so anyway, your dad had Mike come to me first to try to convince me to break up with you because you supposedly had a life-threatening illness—"

"What?" she said with an expression of shock and disbelief.

"—but he wouldn't tell me what the illness was at first. He said that only your parents and your doctors knew about the illness and that they needed to keep it a secret. They didn't want anyone to know. And so I said no. I refused to comply with their wishes. I told him that he needed to tell me what your illness was first. I wasn't going to just walk away from our relationship and not go through with our wedding based on some vague innuendo. I'm like, I'm her fucking fiancé and soon-to-be husband. If she has a life-threatening illness, I have a right to know what it is. It's my job to help her with whatever treatment she'll need. But he said that you were in denial about being sick and were refusing treatment."

"What?" Amanda said once more, aghast. "Oh my God, I can't believe this. When was this? When did this guy Mike come to you and tell you this?"

"It was right before I left for my bachelor party in Vegas. You had already left to come here to New York for a quick business trip."

"Okay, I remember," Amanda said, recalling that weekend to her memory—the weekend when Adam had showed up to Cass Bettencourt's birthday dinner at Koi, to her dismay, and their subsequent confrontation outside the restaurant before she'd left. It was also the weekend she had become sick, not yet knowing at the time that the sickness was due to her unplanned pregnancy.

"When you'd come back from New York, you weren't feeling well," Jake said, recalling that particular memory too.

"So why didn't you tell me about this conversation you'd had with Mike after you'd gotten back from Vegas?"

"I wanted to, but I felt uneasy about it. They said it would've made your condition worse if I'd confronted you about it."

Amanda was beside herself. "It would've made my condition worse? What condition did they claim I had? And why would they tell you this lie?"

"Well, that's what I'm getting to. So I ended up meeting with your dad on that Monday following my bachelor party in Vegas."

"Where did you meet him?"

"I met him after work with Mike at The California Club. Rick decided to meet with me personally, I guess, when Mike told him that I wouldn't go along with what he wanted me to do."

Amanda grew impatient. "Okay. So what did my dad tell you? What illness did he say I had?"

"Basically…Rick said that you had a serious mental illness."

Amanda's mouth fell open and her eyes teared up as she looked at Jake in complete bewilderment. She couldn't believe it.

Registering her hurt, Jake's eyes teared up too as he continued to speak. "He specifically said that you had multiple personality disorder, or—dissociative identity disorder, I guess, is the official term for it now."

"Oh my God," Amanda said before she began to cry, covering her face with her hands and shaking her head.

Jake pulled up closer to her in his seat to console her, reaching to gently hold her by the wrists. "Amanda," he said softly. But he let go when she stripped her hands from her face and looked at him with a pained and befuddled expression.

"My dad told you that I had multiple personalities?" she asked incredulously as the tears continued to stream down her face.

"Yes."

"Jake…how could you have believed something like that? Why didn't you come to me?"

"I know this sounds crazy, but he was very convincing. He said that you'd had the disorder since you were a child. He claimed that you had a twin sister named Maggie who died of some rare blood disease when she was three. He said you two were very close—"

"That's ridiculous. I never had a twin. Alex is my only sister…my only sibling."

"I know that now, but he said at first, when you were still a little girl, like around five or six, you would say that you were having conversations with Maggie, but then by the time you were nine or ten, the signs of you having a split personality started to appear. He said that you thought you were Maggie. It was as if the loss of your twin suddenly hit you later in childhood and the way you dealt with the grief or trauma of her passing was to pretend to be her, or you became her somehow in your mind."

As Jake spoke, Amanda got up to grab a tissue to wipe her face, and then she sat back down. She just stared at Jake in stunned silence and anger. She couldn't believe what she was hearing.

"This is what Rick claimed," Jake said, sounding defensive as he registered the shock and dismay on her face. "To be honest, when Rick first said that you had a mental illness, I thought he was going to say you had ongoing bouts with anorexia or something like that because, if you recall, that weekend after you got back from New York and I got back from Vegas, you told me you'd received treatment for that while you were in boarding school. So I brought that up. I told him that you had just told me about having anorexia back then and the reason having to do with that guy Raoul you were dating at the time, but your dad dismissed that notion out of hand."

Amanda furrowed her brow, incredulous. "He dismissed it out of hand?"

"Yeah. He said that wasn't the real reason."

Amanda huffed in agitation. "Then what was the real reason?"

"He said that anorexia was just a symptom of your split personality and that Maggie caused you or prompted you to stop eating and to starve yourself because she didn't want this guy Raoul to take you away from her. Rick said that Maggie felt jealous about your relationship with Raoul, so making you starve was her way of holding on to you or scaring him away, I guess."

"This is fucking crazy. Where on earth did he come up with this stuff?"

"I don't know, but your dad is a good liar, I must say."

"But how would he know this?"

"Know what?"

"That this Maggie was jealous of my relationship with Raoul and, as a result, made me starve myself to keep me away from him?"

"Because I guess Maggie, meaning you when you acted like Maggie, told him and Camilla. He claimed that you only behaved like you were Maggie around them and that it had been a closely guarded family secret until this Maggie reappeared in the months leading up to our wedding."

"Oh my God," Amanda said, slapping the palm of her hand to her forehead and sighing. "So she became jealous of you too? Is that what he told you?"

"Exactly. He said that you—or Maggie, rather—had threatened to kill Amanda because she was so distraught that I would take you away from her forever if we got married. They, meaning Rick and Mike, even suggested that you might come after me and try to harm me."

"Oh my God. I can't believe this. This is so insane," Amanda said as she began to cry again, burying her face in her hands.

Jake rose from his chair and sat close beside her on the edge of the bed. He wrapped his left arm around her to comfort her. "Amanda, I am so sorry. I feel like such a fool for letting this happen."

"But why?" she asked plaintively through her tears. "Why did he do this? And what does your mother have to do with this? You said that she was involved too somehow."

Jake took a deep breath and then sighed hard. "So you recall that our parents, Rick and my mom, dated each other during high school."

Amanda nodded. "Okay."

"So of course, after high school they went their separate ways, and Rick eventually met Camilla at Princeton and they got married. My mom met my dad at Stanford and they ended up getting married too. However, apparently, your dad and my mom reconnected somehow after they were married and had an affair."

Amanda snickered and shook her head. "Oh, how surprising," she said mockingly. She already believed that her father was a philanderer.

"But that's not the worst part of it," Jake continued. "After the affair, my mom became pregnant...with me."

Amanda pulled back to look at Jake with a puzzled expression on her face. "I hope you're not about to tell me what I think you're about to tell me."

"My mom thought that Rick, your dad, might be my father too."

Amanda's eyes popped open wide as she gasped in astonishment and slapped her hand to her mouth. However, Jake quickly assuaged her horror.

"But he's not. I have since taken a DNA test, and you and I are not siblings. It turned out to be a false alarm."

"Thank...God. You just scared the shit out of me."

Jake continued to explain to Amanda all of the events that led to his decision to break up with her and the events that followed, including the revelation and false alarm about his paternal origin. Amanda sat and listened in complete bewilderment as Jake told her of his mother Jamie's attempt to keep her affair and Jake's paternity a secret until the very end; how Jamie had enlisted Rick's help to stop the wedding; the role Reverend O'Mahoney had played in bringing the secret to light; that he'd gone to a clinic in Santa Monica with his father, Tom, to take a DNA test and subsequently learned that Tom was indeed his natural father; and of

Rick's attempt to pay Jake off with an even larger sum of money after the DNA test to keep Jake silent about Rick's grotesque act of deception and defamation of his own daughter.

When Jake was done with the full story, Amanda was livid. Her hurt and sorrow had been overtaken by rage and indignation.

"Show me the contract. I want to see it…right now."

Jake got up and went over to his briefcase to fetch the contract that had been initially drafted but that he'd never signed stipulating that he'd stay away from Amanda for good after breaking up with her and not going through with their wedding in exchange for money. He pulled the contract out of a folder and handed it to her.

Amanda sat silently and read it. She gasped when she saw the amount of money he'd been offered. "Five million dollars?" she looked up and said to Jake, incredulous.

"Yeah. And like I said, he'd been offering me more, especially after it had been confirmed that he wasn't my father after all. The lies and drama for nothing—he wanted to keep it a secret. And like I told you before, I'm not sure how much your mother even knows about this. She seemed clueless when I spoke to her last week."

"She *was* clueless, because she said you told her you had done what she and my dad wanted, but she didn't know what you were talking about. She said you sounded crazy. She even accused you of being on drugs."

Jake just chuckled and rolled his eyes.

Amanda continued to read the rest of the contract. When she finished it, she placed the contract down beside her on the bed and went for her phone. "This is a fucking outrage," she said, seething, and then she hit the dial button to call a number from her contact list.

"What are you doing?" Jake asked.

"I'm calling my dad."

Chapter Forty

Amanda was so infuriated, she was shaking. As the phone rang, she stood to her feet to try to gain better control of her nerves and speak forcefully and clearly. On the fourth ring, Rick picked up.

"Hey, Mandi. How are you, darling?"

"How am I? The way you'd expect a daughter to be after just learning that her own father told the biggest lie imaginable to get her boyfriend to dump her."

"What do you mean, sweetie?" Rick asked, trying to sound innocent and perplexed.

"Jake's standing right here with me, Dad. He's told me everything."

"I don't know what you're talking about, honey—"

"Enough! Don't lie to me," Amanda yelled. "I have the contract in my hand…where you offered to pay him five million dollars not to see or speak to me ever again. All to cover up your mistake…the affair you'd had with Jamie? Instead of coming forward and admitting the truth, you had to make me suffer? I had to pay for your mistake? You invent this outlandish story to cover your ass and then make me look like I'm the crazy person? How dare you! Are you out of your fucking mind?"

Rick tried to interject. "Honey, I'm—"

"Don't *honey* me. You lied. You told a big fucking lie. You told Jake that I had multiple personality disorder? How could you? What the fuck is wrong with you? I'm your daughter, for Christ's sake. How could you do this me?" Amanda said, breaking down and crying again.

Jake looked on, astounded, as Amanda screamed at the top of her lungs. He'd never seen her so enraged. It was so out of character for her and disconcerting to witness. He had to take a seat.

"Mandi, I was trying to protect you, protect us, protect our family."

"That's bullshit! You were trying to protect yourself. You only cared about yourself in this situation, not about me, or else you wouldn't have allowed me to pay the price for your mistake."

"That's not true. Maybe I didn't go about things in the best way, but I was trying to protect you, honey, and protect your inheritance—"

"Oh please. Don't try to make this about money and inheritance."

"Well, it's true. His mother, Jamie, kept this whole thing about Jake possibly being my son all to herself for years. I didn't know anything about it until she came to me two months before your wedding and dropped this bombshell on me out of nowhere. I never really believed it, to tell you the truth. Jake doesn't look anything like me, but I thought the best thing to do was to separate you from him and not risk anything."

"What are you talking about? Risk what?"

"Mandi, look, you don't know what Jake is capable of. He's no good, honey. Getting him out of your life turned out to be for the best anyway. He cheated on you…with a guy. Jake was never right for you to begin with. He's a sleaze, a total scumbag."

"Who are you to call someone a scumbag? Huh?"

There was silence for a few seconds on the other end of the line. Amanda could tell that must've felt like a dagger to her dad's heart to hear those words coming from her mouth.

Rick's voice trembled, seemingly with restrained anger, as he spoke. "I beg your pardon, young lady, but I'm your father. I'm might not be perfect in every way, but I damn sure have taken very good care of you and our family, and I deserve your respect, or least the benefit of the doubt that I was operating with your best interests at heart. Had Jake turned out to be my illegitimate son, he could've come after our money, your money. You and Alex might've had to split your inheritance with him."

"You are fucking pathetic. You know that? Listen to yourself. Do hear the shit coming out of your mouth right now? You are in no place to pass judgment on anyone. You cheated on your wife like I'm sure you've done the whole time you've been married. And when you were told that you might have a son as a result of your immoral behavior, instead of doing the responsible thing and confirming whether or not it was in fact true, you went and told this horrific lie about your own daughter to cover your own ass. And then you go and offer someone millions to buy their silence so that I would never find out about what you had done. You are evil and there is no justification for what you did. None! Do you realize what you did, Dad? Do you fully comprehend the pain and agony you caused? I was destroyed. You nearly ruined my life. And you were okay with that."

"Mandi, that's not true, not true at all."

"It is true. Not only did you rob me of my dignity in telling my fiancé and the love of my life that I was too dangerous and unfit to be his wife, or anyone else's wife, for that matter, but you also robbed me, you robbed us of our child," Amanda charged as she began to sob. "You did that. You, you did it," she screamed.

That was the first time Jake had heard her acknowledge in his presence that they had had a child. It broke his heart to hear her say those words, "you robbed us of our child." Jake placed his hands to his face and cried quietly to himself as Amanda continued to rage at her father.

"You are responsible for the loss of my baby. All the stress and pain of being dumped by my fiancé and trying to figure out, alone, by myself, what to do about an unplanned pregnancy, all of the pressure you and Mom put on me to get an abortion, deciding whether I should be a single mother, and then trying to find adoptive parents—you have no idea. You have no fucking idea. All of the stress and trauma of that situation is what caused me to lose my baby. That's what caused the miscarriage. Are you proud of yourself? Does that make you happy? Huh? That's what you wanted anyway, isn't it?"

"Amanda, I don't know what else to say—"

"How about, 'Amanda, I apologize. I made a very bad mistake and caused you harm and unbelievable pain and suffering, unjustly. Please forgive me. I'm deeply sorry for what I did.' But no, you can't say that because you aren't truly sorry. You are too self-centered and self-absorbed to have empathy, to have the decency or capacity to show true remorse. You are an evil, selfish, deceitful maniac, and I hate you. I hate you so much right now. There aren't enough words for me to express how much I loathe you."

"You don't mean that, Mandi. I know you're hurting, honey, and you're upset with me, and rightfully so. I'll fly to New York now so that we can talk this through. I want to make this right. I want to make this up to you."

"Make this up how? Are you kidding me? I don't want to see you. You disgust me. Being in your presence would completely freak me out. Stay away from me. Just stay away. I don't want to see you. I'm ashamed of you…ashamed that you're my father," Amanda screamed through sobs before she hit the end call button.

Jake immediately stood up. He too was crying. "Mandi, I'm so sorry. I'm so sorry," he repeated before embracing her.

Amanda, inconsolable, didn't resist. She leaned her head to Jake's shoulder, keeping her hands down at her sides at first.

Sensing that she was receptive to his overture, Jake held on to her more tightly, pressing her body to his.

Although feeling awkward, deep down Amanda wanted to be held by him. She eventually gave in and wrapped her arms around his waist. When she did so, Jake lightly stroked the back of her head. He then kissed the crown of her head and kept his lips planted there.

Jake's touch made Amanda feel warm inside. To be locked in the embrace of her former love felt familiar, natural, and comforting. But she also had mixed and conflicting emotions about standing there with him like that. She was with Adam now. Her mind told her to pull away, but she couldn't let Jake go.

CHAPTER FORTY-ONE

"We had a baby, Jake, but I miscarried," Amanda said as she cried on Jake's shoulder.

"I know. I'm so sorry. I would've been there if you'd told me. I would've been there for you. I would've done whatever you needed me to do, anything to make sure that you and our baby were healthy and safe."

"That was our dream. That's what we wanted, to have a family together of our own. And we were almost there. It almost happened. But then everything was snatched away from us. It's so cruel. I can't believe they did this to us."

"I know. You didn't deserve this. We didn't deserve this. I feel like you've been taken from me, Mandi. I wanted to be your husband. I swear to God, I did."

"Jake, don't tell me that. Don't tell me that right now," Amanda said through continued tears. "I can't take it."

Jake pulled back slightly so that he could look at her. He then held her face with his hands. "But it's true. I was in love with you. I swear. I still am."

Amanda looked up into his eyes and then quickly broke her gaze, feeling a little embarrassed. She wiped her face with her hands. "Oh my God, I'm a mess. I need more tissue," she said, sniffling.

Jake let go of her and stepped over to the nightstand next to the bed to grab the tissue box. He held it for her as she pulled out several tissues to blow her nose and wipe her face.

"I guess I should take a couple too," Jake said, chuckling at himself as he pulled out a couple of tissues and then wiped his face as well.

"Now you know the truth…" he said, "…the real reason why I broke up with you. At the time, I thought I was doing the right thing. I'd do anything for you, and I thought I was doing what I needed to do to protect you. I feel so stupid now for letting you go, but I didn't know what else to do at the time. I felt so much pressure. They made the situation seem so dire and full of urgency. But I never stopped loving you, Mandi. You've been in my heart ever since. I haven't been able to let go of you."

"I haven't been able to completely let go of you either," Amanda admitted. "I've tried. I've tried really hard but I miss what we had. That's not to say that I'm not disturbed about your relationship with Kirby, because I am. I'm still hurt that you cheated on me and deceived me over the course of our entire relationship. But despite what you did, I believe in my heart that there was a bond we shared and that our love for one another was real. I know because I felt it, Jake. I did. I really did," Amanda said, tearing up again.

"I felt it too. I promise you, it was real for me too."

Amanda sighed hard. "Oh my God, I'm so confused right now. What does this mean, Jake? What does this mean for us? What are we going to do?"

Jake stepped up to her and held her face once more. "It can mean whatever we want it to mean. We can do whatever we want."

Amanda stared into his eyes. "You're still in love me, Jake?"

"Yes, I am," he said, gently stroking her cheeks with his thumbs. "Are you still in love me?"

A single tear streamed down Amanda's face as she paused to look into his eyes. "I am," she conceded.

Jake leaned in to kiss her lips. He kissed her softly, and then kissed her softly again, and again, and again. Each kiss was more earnest, lingering, and adoring than the one before.

Amanda was tentative at first, but Jake's persistent, soft, gentle kisses overtook her, and she threw all caution, resistance, and resentment to the wind. She allowed herself to succumb to his touch and affection. She leaned her body fully into his, wrapped her arms around his neck, and kissed him back eagerly.

Sensing an emotional breakthrough and feeling the passion between them reemerge after lying dormant for so long, Jake pressed his tongue into her mouth. Amanda took it willingly. A chill rushed through her body when she did so, and it caused her to shiver with relish as she tasted him again, touched him again, and smelled him again. It was altogether so intoxicating, sensual, and comforting that it made her weak in the knees. She felt as though she would collapse into his arms at any moment. Overwhelmed with emotion and longing, she wanted more. "Make love to me, Jake. I need you. I want to feel you inside me again. I've missed you so much," she cried.

"I've missed you too," he said before he pushed her chin up to kiss and lick it hungrily. Her fine, delicate jawline, her soft, supple skin, and her feminine, aromatic scent turned him on and made him long for her too. He wanted to bathe himself in her wetness once more. Jake walked Amanda back toward the bed until they both fell down onto it. When they landed, Jake cupped Amanda in his embrace, using his left arm, with her body partially underneath his. He touched and stroked her face with his right hand, then resumed smothering her with passionate, openmouthed, tongue-tussling kisses while intermittently sucking and licking her chin, jawline, and neck. On the brink, he was feeling it for his girl again as their passionate kisses intensified. The urge to strip and press his naked flesh to hers again was overwhelming. While still cupping her with his left arm, he reached down with his right hand to unbutton her pants. He wanted to slip his hand in to feel and massage her sex, to make her wet, to make her feel good, to daze her with sensual pleasure and bliss as he had done so often in the past. But then he stopped himself, leaving his hand on the first button for a few seconds, contemplating his actions. He then removed his hand from the button as they continued to kiss. Jake's body wanted to seize on Amanda's invitation, but his heart and head told him not to.

"What's wrong?" Amanda asked, sensing the sudden turndown in heat between them. She was more than willing and ready to submit her body to his manipulation and didn't understand why he wasn't proceeding.

"Nothing. I just want to hold you in my arms. I want to savor this moment. I don't want to rush." Jake played it off as best he could, and it appeared to work. As they lay there together in silence, taking a break from their rapturous make out moment, Amanda eventually turned over on her side, allowing Jake to spoon her from behind. He held on to her tight and thought about the moment.

He wanted to make love to her but knew that she was upset, emotional, and vulnerable. It wouldn't be fair to her, he thought, if he wasn't truly ready for the aftermath—her expectations, needs, and desires going forward. As he held her in his arms, he questioned his intentions. Was he truly prepared to commit himself and win the battle for her heart again? Was this truly about love, or was it about his ego and taking back what he felt had been stolen from him? Was it about settling a score with Rick? Was it about showing Adam that he owned Amanda's heart always and forever and could have her despite Adam's very best efforts to sway and woo her? Deep down Jake knew that it was a combination of all of the above. He loved her and could still see himself being happily married to her, but his ego was all wrapped up in it too. On top of that and perhaps most of all, he had just been with Kirby, and two-timing was no longer an option. Jake had made a personal vow to never do that again. And since he wasn't prepared to promise even to himself that the nature of his relationship with Kirby would end from that moment henceforth, Jake concluded that having sex with Amanda was out of the question, at least for now.

CHAPTER FORTY-TWO

Amanda eventually fell asleep, cuddled in Jake's arms. She awoke a little more than an hour later when Jake attempted to reposition himself. He had closed his eyes but hadn't fallen asleep. The whole time he just kept watch over Amanda until his left arm felt stiff and numb under her body weight. He tried to move it discreetly without waking her, but it didn't work.

Amanda rose up, slightly dazed. She placed her hands to her forehead and then wiped her eyes. How long was I asleep?

"For about an hour or a little more. It's almost six o'clock," Jake said as he sat up beside her.

"I can't believe I passed out like that…for over an hour," Amanda said, surprised.

"You probably needed it…to help you relax and calm down."

Amanda's mood had shifted somewhat after waking up. She no longer felt needy, wanting Jake to make love to her, but instead felt growing bewilderment and disbelief. She had questions for him.

"I don't know what to do, Jake. I can't believe this happened. I can't believe my own father did this to me. I don't know if I can ever face him again. What an incredibly shitty thing to do. It's just so unbelievable. I mean, how could anyone even believe the story he told? Multiple personality disorder? I don't even know what that looks like. It's something you only read about or maybe see in a movie or something. Anyone who's known me for any length of time should've been skeptical of such a ridiculous story. Considering how long we'd been together, I honestly can't believe you fell for that. And I can't believe that you didn't come to me."

"I wanted to. I should have. I allowed myself to get played," Jake said, shaking his head in disappointment at himself.

"But why? Why didn't you challenge him?"

"I was skeptical initially, and told him that it couldn't be possible and that I saw no sign of you having an alter ego or anything like that, but he was so insistent and grave and serious."

Amanda snickered and shook her head in an almost ridiculing way.

Jake became defensive. "He's your dad, Mandi. Who am I to contradict him or challenge him about something like that? You really expected me to say, 'Rick, you're lying. You don't know what you're talking about.' I mean, if anyone other than your parent came and told me the story, I wouldn't have believed it, but it *was* your parent. It was your father. And then he got Mike involved, which was very clever. I trusted Mike like I trusted my own father, and with the two of them telling me this together, I had no reason whatsoever to believe that they would make up such a story."

Amanda sighed and then began to cry again as she spoke. "I don't know. You were put in an unfair situation. I recognize that. I just wish you would've fought more—fought more for me, fought more for our relationship. It just seems like you acted so quickly. I mean, you could've just refused to go along with what they wanted you to do. You could've kept what they told you to yourself and been like, fuck it, I'm going to marry her anyway."

"I thought about doing that—"

"Then why didn't you?" Amanda asked with agitation in her voice.

Jake sighed and tried to search for the right answer, but he was having a hard time coming up with one.

"It just makes me feel like you didn't truly love me enough. That it wasn't worth it for you to dig a little deeper before you decided to end everything. But then again, you had this thing going with Kirby the whole time we were together, so I guess you never truly had real love for me as much as I've tried to convince myself that you did."

"Amanda, I did love you. I still love you. Having a sexual relationship with Kirby while I was with you was wrong. But I had made a choice, and my choice was to be with you, to be married to you, to be your husband. I acted on impulse, and it was self-indulgent and very selfish of me to be with you and Kirby at the same time. I can't apologize enough for what I did. I know that saying I'm sorry will never be enough. But before we were supposed to get married, I told Kirby that it was over and that we couldn't be sexual with one another anymore. In fact, we'd gotten into a big confrontation over it. Of course, I should've told him that a long time before, but he knew that I was trying to break things off with him and that I wanted to be committed to you and spend the rest of my life with you."

"But what would've happened? What would've happened had you married me? Would your relationship with Kirby have been any different? Would it have changed?"

"Yes. It would have. I wanted it to change."

"You wanted it to change. The question is would it have really changed?"

Jake didn't knee-jerk answer her back again. He remained silent and looked down blankly at the bed.

"You can't even answer the question," Amanda said accusatorily.

"Amanda, I had every intention of being faithful to you—"

"Well, I'm glad that was your intention, Jake, but given your track record prior to breaking up with me, I'm not convinced that you would've succeeded."

Jake shook his head, rubbed his face with his hands, and sighed. She had a point. What could he say?

"You said earlier that you're still in love with me, and you told my mom that you wanted me back. But where do things stand now between you and Kirby? Are you still no longer friends with him?"

Jake sighed and looked away for a second before answering her. "We actually reconnected recently and have become friends again," Jake said as if admitting guilt to something.

Amanda stared at Jake intently. She could read from his body language that he was covering up something and not being fully forthcoming. She nearly blurted, "Are you sleeping with him again?" but didn't. The answer was written all over his face, and she didn't want him to lie to her again, nor did she want him to acknowledge what she'd already suspected. At that moment, Amanda knew that she and Jake were through and would never be lovers or mates again. She felt anger. "How could you come here and say you're in love with me and still be fucking Kirby?" she wanted to scream at him but didn't. It didn't matter. This was where Jake was and had been stuck for a long time—caught in the middle of a love triangle of his own making. Only he could understand and sort out the how and why of it all, she quietly conceded to herself. This wasn't her battle to fight. It was his.

Amanda continued to stare at Jake, who appeared despondent, not meeting her gaze. As they sat there in silence for a few moments, Amanda sensed that there was shame, embarrassment, even self-loathing in Jake about his feelings for Kirby. It was as if he was deliberately suppressing his happiness about their rekindled relationship in order to prove that he still had desire to be with her. In that instant, her anger at Jake turned to sadness for him. She felt this need to help him, to switch out the hat of scorned ex-girlfriend with that of simply friend.

"Jake," Amanda said to summon to his attention.

He looked up at her with sadness in his eyes.

"I have a question to ask you, and I want you to be completely honest with me. I want you to tell me the truth. Okay?"

"Okay," he said softly.

"You said that you're in love with me...but are you also in love with Kirby?"

Jake stared blankly and didn't answer her at first.

"Jake, please tell me the truth. Be honest with me. Be honest with yourself."

Jake remained silent for a moment more, and then he sighed, and without looking at Amanda, he spoke. "Yes, I am."

"So tell me…right now…at this moment…who are you more in love with, me or Kirby?"

"I love you both the same. It's so hard," Jake bemoaned as he covered his face with his hands.

"You can't have us both, Jake. You can't do that anymore. You have to choose."

"I know…I know that I can't have you both. But I told you, though…I had chosen you, to marry you."

"That was back then, last summer. I'm talking about right now. Who do you feel more connected to? Who are you more drawn to emotionally? Who are you more attracted to? Who do you want to make love to more than anyone else? Who makes your soul sing? Him or me?"

Jake evaded the question. "I…I just want to be married and have a family. That's what I want, and I want that with you like I did before."

"But you can't have that with me…not when you're equally in love with someone else. No matter how much you love me, Jake, I don't think being with me and marrying me would be enough to help you overcome your feelings for Kirby. You can't use me like that. You can't use me to try to suppress your attraction to Kirby or to men in general. That wouldn't be fair."

"I know it wouldn't," Jake admitted.

"Then stop forcing yourself to feel like you need to be with me or with any girl, for that matter, if what you really want right now is to be with Kirby. Do you know if Kirby is in love with you too?"

"Yes, I do know. He is in love me. He came out to me and told me that last summer, right before we were supposed to get married. That's why he broke up with Laren. And after everything we've been through these past few months, he still wants to be with me."

"Have you thought about being with him in a real, committed relationship?"

"I've told him in the past that if I was ever going to be in an openly gay relationship, it would only be with him," Jake said with a chuckle, feeling lighthearted at the thought.

"Then what's holding you back?"

"It's just not how I saw myself…you know, being with another guy. I mean…I have nothing against being gay—"

"But, Jake, you are gay. Don't you see?"

"But I've never thought of myself as being fully gay because I'm still attracted to girls too. I had even been dating this chick back at work up until pretty recently."

"Okay, fine. You're bi. At the end of the day, the label—gay, bi—is irrelevant. It doesn't matter. What matters is that you're in love with another guy. That love is real and it's mutually felt. Embrace it. Explore it. You and Kirby have known each other for so long. Your love and affection for one another has never died. It just seems to keep growing stronger and stronger. And…." Amanda paused for a moment, becoming overtaken suddenly with emotion. She began to cry as she continued to speak. "And even though a part of me wishes that we had the same intensity of feeling for one another, I realize that we don't anymore. I've been holding on to you in my heart, hoping against hope that we could find our way back to each other, but I realize now, more than ever, that I have to let you go. Let you be free to be who you truly are. Free to be who you want to be. Free to be yourself without the pressure of trying to meet the expectations of others. I feel like you need to hear this from me."

Jake broke down too. "Oh, Amanda. I'm so sorry for everything I've done. I feel so bad and guilty. I feel that everything you've been through, all of the pain you've experienced, it's all my fault. I was such a coward, breaking up with you, and then I caused you to lose our baby. I cheated on you with Kirby and hid from you these feelings I've had about my sexuality. I've put you through so much, and I just want to make it up to you. I want to make it right. I want to make you happy. You deserve to be happy and so much more."

"But so do you, Jake. I don't need you to make me happy. That's my job. And don't blame yourself for everything that's happened. You were put in a very bad positon. Although I wish you had reacted differently, we more than likely would've been forced at some point down the road to confront this issue about Kirby anyway. I am confident of that. But you deserve to be happy too and to live in your truth. You shouldn't be afraid to explore your feelings for Kirby in a more open and honest way if he's who you truly want to be with right now. Even though you're not willing to admit it, I know that you're more attracted to Kirby and have a stronger emotional attachment to him. And that's okay. It really is. Embrace it, and stop running from it. Stop running from Kirby."

Jake sat quietly for a few moments, wiping his tears away, and allowing Amanda's words to sink in. "I love you, Amanda," he finally said. "I will always love you, no matter what." Jake reached over in a tentative way to hug Amanda, touching her back lightly at first with his left hand.

Amanda immediately reached over with both arms to embrace him back, assuredly, wrapping her arms tightly around his torso and then pressing the side of her forehead to his. At that point, Jake held on to her more tightly too with both his arms.

"I will always love you too, Jake. I want you to be happy," she said, and then they held on to one another for a few moments.

Amanda lifted her head from Jake's, kissed him on the nose, and then let go of him. "Thank you for coming to see me on your trip to New York. I know you must be really busy, so I guess I should get going."

"Well…the truth about that is, I only came here to see you. I'm not here on a business trip."

"Oh," Amanda said with a chuckle. "I feel like I know everything there is to know now."

"I kind of feel like I shouldn't have come. That I shouldn't have told you about what our parents did."

"Why?"

"Because part of my intention was to try to win you back in the process—you know, over time—but you've helped me to accept that the door on our relationship is closing or has already closed and that I should move on. Now you have all of this drama with your dad to deal with."

"Jake, I'm glad you told me the truth. I needed to know. And thank you for not taking advantage of the situation in my moment of weakness when I bared my heart and asked you to make love to me." Amanda slapped her hands to her face and shook her head at herself, feeling embarrassed.

"When you woke up, I was kind of scared that you'd ask me again."

Amanda removed her hands from her face and glanced at Jake, curious. "Why? You can't get it up for me anymore?"

Jake chuckled and grinned broadly. "No, no…that's not it at all. I just wasn't ready to go there yet. You know, with me and Kirby still being an open question and—"

"I get it. No need to explain. Go back home and get your man already, Jake. Jesus!" Amanda said sassily as she hopped off the bed.

Jake just smiled at her.

CHAPTER FORTY-THREE

"I am through with Jake, Myla, and I mean it this time."

"Oh my God, Kirby. Every time you call me it's a different story. Last week you were head over heels in love with the boy again and now you're saying you're through? Here we go again. What's it going to be, boo? Make up your mind."

"I've made up my mind. It's over…for real this time."

"What happened? You said you two had kissed and made up last week."

"Yeah, well, that was before he told me last Saturday or early Sunday, actually, that we shouldn't continue to have sex anymore, for the time being, because I want and expect too much and he doesn't want to hurt me. And mind you, that was while we were in the middle of doing the nasty on that same night."

"So you mean you guys finally went all the way?"

"Hell, no. He's still acting all skittish and shit because I told him how I felt about him as we were in the middle of doing it, and then he tells me we should wait because I'm too serious and he doesn't want to hurt me and shit since he's not ready to commit to being in a relationship. He says he needs more time to think about it."

"Think about what?"

"Everything, I guess. This dude tells me he loves me and can't get rid of me and trusts me more than anyone in his life but then tells me that we shouldn't continue to do anything sexual until he figures out what he wants. He needs more time and space to figure shit out."

"Oh please. This guy is such a drama queen. If he loves you and you love him, what else does he want?"

"I have no fucking idea. This fool is still craning for his ex-girlfriend Amanda. He thinks he can convince her to take his wishy-washy ass back or something."

"How do you know that?"

"This guy went to New York to see her."

"What? Oh my God. This is getting ridiculous."

"He's there right now. I texted him this morning, you know, just to check in, trying to keep the flame burning, and he tells me he's in New York because he needed to meet with her about something."

"Meet with her about what?"

"I don't know. When I last saw him, he said something had gone down recently that involved her and their families but he didn't elaborate. I mean, there is some pretty heavy shit that's taken place involving her family and their breakup that I know about, but I honestly don't know why he'd want to revisit any of that at this point. It's water under the bridge. Amanda doesn't want him anymore."

"Isn't she dating that big celebrity producer you worked for way back when?"

"Exactly!"

"They make a better-looking couple anyway."

"Thank you! Jake's hella jealous though. He can't stand them being together."

"Why should he even care?"

"Because he's confused and lost. I swear, I don't know why I'm still putting up with this shit and waiting for this boy to come around."

"This is bullshit. He's making out with you and telling you that he loves you and can't live without you and then flies to New York to see his ex? Jake is such a tease. It's like he takes you to the brink and then pulls back when it gets too uncomfortable for him, and then he accuses you of being too serious and wanting too much from him? What does he expect? You're human, for God's sake. Not a damn robot without any feelings or emotions. You're not a toy or some doll that he can manipulate and just turn on and turn off at will for his pleasure. Like I've told you before, Kirby, and I know you don't like me telling you this, but I think you're Jake's crutch. You make it possible for him to live out his gay romance fantasy without having to make a commitment. Meanwhile you're sittin' at home crying while he's out looking for the next girl he can con into marrying him, or maybe he'll convince Amanda to take him back. Who knows? Regardless, you're being played, Kirby, and it's high time for you to put a stop to it once and for all."

"I am going to put a stop to it as soon as he gets back. I can guarantee it. I've had enough."

***

The next day, following his phone conversation with Myla, Kirby received a text from Jake.

At JFK waiting to board my flight. I need to see you as soon as I get back to LA. I have something really important to tell you.

"I bet you do," Kirby said to himself cynically, thinking that Jake had likely succeeded in convincing Amanda to take him back. Jake wanted to meet to tell him that it was over between them and that he'd made a commitment once again to be with Amanda and not him. But this time, Kirby was determined to not let Jake have the last word.

I have something to tell you too, Kirby texted back.

Oh yeah? Did your pilot get picked up? Jake wrote back, guessing.

No. It's not about that.

Okay. Now I'm really curious. Don't know if I can wait.

I prefer to tell you in person.

My flight's supposed to land at LAX at 1 pm so I'll be free the rest of the day. Not planning to go back into the office until tomorrow.

Kirby didn't reply back immediately. He stopped to think about where he wanted to confront Jake. At first he thought of a bar or restaurant, but both ideas seemed too convivial for the occasion. He didn't want to have a drink, meal, or good laugh with Jake. He wanted to tell him off and slam the metaphorical door in his face. However, before Kirby could make up his mind, Jake quickly sent him another text with a suggestion of his own.

Want to come over to my place?

Kirby hesitated at first, but saying no would've seemed weird, he thought, since going over to Jake's place and vice versa would otherwise be the normal and routine thing to do. To avoid creating unnecessary drama and suspense, Kirby decided to accept the invitation.

What time?

Whenever is good for you.

Have an appointment at 4. I can come afterward around 6.

Perfect. See you then.

CHAPTER FORTY-FOUR

As Kirby drove to Jake's apartment, he rehearsed what he wanted to say to him over and over again in his head. Kirby was pumped and all riled up at first. He wanted to feed off that energy to assail Jake for continuing to toy with him and his emotions. He felt used, manipulated, even abused. Like Myla had said, Jake had taken him to the brink yet again, then pulled back. It was cruel to continue stringing him along like that, offering false hope. And to add insult to injury, Jake had flown all the way to New York to see Amanda. Kirby was convinced that they were getting back together, and Jake's purpose in wanting to meet with him was to tell him so. Even if Jake were to suggest that he and Kirby remain friends, Kirby knew that wouldn't be possible, at least not for him. He was too in love with Jake and they had too much history of being more than simply friends—all of the expressions of love, the passion, the intimacy, the unguarded emotions, the intense closeness. They had been lovers as much as they had been friends. Both went hand in hand. There could be no other way of being, no other path for them. A purely platonic relationship would not work. Kirby had come to accept this. He had lost and Jake's demons—self-loathing and fear of being outwardly gay—had won.

As Kirby drew closer to Jake's place, the thought of ending their relationship for good made him sad. When he parked and stepped out of his car, Kirby didn't know what he'd say now. He'd already forgotten what he'd rehearsed on the way over when he was feeling more agitated and riled up. He was filled with sadness now, and he didn't know how his words would come out. All he knew was that he needed to be firm. His relationship with Jake absolutely had to come to an end. It was time for him to move on with his life.

Jake opened the front door and greeted Kirby with a broad smile. "Hi." He looked as handsome and tempting as always, barefoot and wearing a pair of white shorts and a long-sleeve gray T-shirt that revealed the outline of his lean, muscular frame through the light cotton fabric.

"Hey," Kirby said, taking notice of Jake from head to toe without lingering. He walked right past him and sat down on the sofa. "So how was New York?"

"Eye-opening. I feel like I got the clarity that I needed on some things," Jake said as he too sat down on the sofa on the other end from Kirby.

Kirby wanted to get right down to business. He didn't want this to be a long and drawn-out conversation. It was best to keep it short and to the point as much as possible. He wasn't even interested in hearing what he thought Jake had to tell him about a presumed reunion with Amanda. He just wanted to get off his chest what he had to say. "I feel like I've gotten clarity on some things too."

"Clarity about what?"

"About us,"

"Okay," Jake said, gazing at Kirby, a little stumped. He'd been looking forward to hearing what Kirby had to tell him, but he'd assumed that it might be related to some new professional or personal endeavor.

"I might as well get right down to it," Kirby said before pausing for a second. His heart was beating fast. He rubbed his face with his right hand and took a deep breath before continuing to speak. "The clarity for me is that I've put my heart on the line for you. I've told you how I feel. I'm in love you with, Jake. I told you that way back in August. And many times before that I told you that I loved you. Even though, in the past, I was telling you that as a friend or in the heat of the moment when we were being physical, it was always a deeper, emotional kind of love I felt for you. The kind of love you can only have for someone you feel romantically inclined about. Despite all of the tumult and separation we've experienced these past few months, I'm still in love with you…more than I've ever been. When we reconnected last week, I had so much hope that things between us would get back on track and then, even better, you shocked me when you said that you were in love with me. You finally said it. I was like, oh my God, he finally admitted it. We're finally getting somewhere. Maybe we'll end up together after all, like I'd been hoping for. But then you pulled back again, talking about how we shouldn't continue to be sexual with another until you figure out what you really want because you don't want to hurt me or disappoint me again. Well, I'm already hurt, Jake. I'm already disappointed, and I can't do this anymore. My love alone is not enough to keep this relationship going. It seems like the more I pour my heart out to you and tell you how I feel, the more you resist and push me away. I can't take it anymore, Jake. We both need to have our hearts in this or the relationship won't work. And we can't just be friends. We've never been that way. I know you're attracted to me, and maybe you are in love with me, but the clarity for me is what you've shown and proven to me. And what you've shown and proven is that your heart is not in this. You may feel love for me, but you aren't willing to give your heart to me fully and completely and likely never will. I realize that now. I've come to accept it.…"

"I am now," Jake said calmly. However, Kirby talked over him, not hearing him.

Kirby tried his best not to cry but couldn't help it. A single tear streamed down his face as he continued to talk rapidly. It almost became an incoherent, emotional ramble.

"Kirby!" Jake said as he reached over to grab and squeeze Kirby's left arm, which was resting along the top of the sofa's backrest.

Kirby abruptly stopped talking. He could see that Jake was still and his piercing blue eyes were locked on him. Jake's stare and touch sent a shiver through Kirby's body, a shiver of love and desire that he was trying hard to suppress. "What?" Kirby asked weakly.

"Did you hear me? I said that I am now. I'm ready to give my heart to you…completely."

"Don't play with me, Jake. Don't play with me, man. You always do this." Kirby pulled his arm away and then folded both his arms across his chest.

"I'm not playing, Kirby," Jake said, trying to convince him by moving up closer to him and grabbing his arms to convey the sincerity of his intentions. But Kirby wasn't having it.

"No…no…no," Kirby said, closing his eyes and shaking his head sternly. "No, Jake. Don't do this. Don't do this. You always do this. Stop playing, man," Kirby said as he unfolded his arms curtly so Jake's hands would fall off.

"Kirby, I love you too, and I want to be with you too," Jake said, pleading emotionally. "This is what I wanted to tell you."

"Jake, you always say you love me, and then you run away."

"I'm not running away anymore. The clarity for me is that I realize I can't be without you. That there's nobody that I'm more attracted to, closer to, more emotionally connected to; nobody that I'm more in love with than you; nobody that makes my soul sing more than you. I know it may sound corny, but it's true. All this time, I've been afraid to accept my love for you because I've had this picture in my mind about what my life was supposed to look like. I've had these ideas about how my life should unfold in order to meet certain standards and expectations, to reach certain goals professionally, and to be accepted into certain circles, and to be liked by certain people. Having a wife and kids was like part of the natural order of things. They were part of this package I was putting together to represent who I was to the world, to control and dictate how the world should view me. This is what I was raised to think I had to do. You know my family. I mean…they're not that stuffy. They're good people, but they've lived a certain way for a long time and have a certain mindset about how things should be done, and they pass that mindset down from one generation to the next. You have to go to the right prep school, get into the right college and join the right fraternity, go to the right law school, become a partner at the right law firm, get into the right country club, marry a girl from a good family, and so on. But I don't fucking care about all that anymore,

Kirby. I want you. Please…take me. I'll give myself to you completely, the way you want. I love the way you make me feel. I love the way you love me. There's nothing like it. There's nothing that makes me feel so wanted, so desired, so lifted. I've been running away because it scared me at first. I was afraid that it would take me off my path, this mission I was on to control how my life should be and look. But I don't care about all that anymore. I've thought about what it would be like to have a life with you as a couple in a committed relationship. I've thought about it a lot, and I'm ready to pursue it, to explore that with you. Although I must admit, this will all be new for me, and I can't say that I'll be the perfect partner for you, but I want to try. I want to give us a real chance to express this love we have for one another openly and honestly. Please, Kirby, take me," Jake said, reaching to touch Kirby again.

Kirby was taken aback and speechless at this outpouring. It wasn't anything close to what he'd expected to hear and he wasn't quite sure how to respond. Despite the emotion and earnestness with which Jake spoke, Kirby was still a little skeptical. "So why did you go to New York to see Amanda?"

"There was some information I needed to share with her."

"Did you tell her that her father offered to pay you off so that you wouldn't marry her?"

"Yes, I did."

"Holy shit! You did? What did she say? Does she really have that mystery illness you refused to tell me about?"

"I really don't want to get into all of the details about that right now, but there's no illness. It was all a hoax. The bottom line is, I love Amanda, okay? I care about her a ton, and a part of me wanted to get back with her, but I think that was mostly out of guilt for walking away from her the way I did. I wanted to make things up to her and make her happy, but she helped me to realize that I needed to focus on my own happiness. She basically got me to admit that between the two of you, I love you more."

Tears welled in Kirby's eyes at Jake's confirmation of that truth.

"She also thinks that had we married, I more than likely would've continued to be unfaithful to her no matter how hard I tried and that I would've been trotting off to hook up with you still."

Kirby grinned slyly. "Now, she's right about that."

Jake laughed. "You're like my addiction, dude. I can't give you up, and Amanda knows it. I guess it took her telling me that to get it through my thick head. She convinced me to stop fighting the feelings I have for you. She's on your side."

"That's my girl," Kirby said with a broad grin while rubbing his chin. "I always liked her."

"Or do you just really like her now?" Jake said with a chuckle and roll of the eyes.

"No, no, man. Come on now. You know I've always liked Amanda, but yes, I like her even more right now. She helped you to see the light. I'm completely amazed right now. I've been begging you to be with me while you've been chasing Amanda the whole time, and then she tells you to be with me and that does the trick. Wow. And that's saying a lot for her to have told you that, because that girl was head over heels in love with you. If you had jumped off a cliff she'd be following right behind you, as far I'm concerned. I wouldn't even do that," Kirby said with a laugh. "I mean, I love you and all, but I'm not crazy. Not crazy in love like Beyoncé," he said in reference to her well-known track.

"Oh yeah? You're not crazy in love with me yet?" Jake said with a grin on his face. He then got up to straddle Kirby's lap.

Receptive to Jake's attempt at physical contact and connection, Kirby repositioned his posture so that Jake could straddle him more comfortably. Jake then sat on Kirby's lap facing him with his knees bent all the way down on either side of Kirby's hips and thighs, and with his groin pressed against Kirby's. Jake rubbed and held Kirby's neck affectionately, looked into his eyes, and asked him again, "You're not crazy in love?"

Kirby's body tingled with a warm sensation and his eyes glazed over at Jake's touch and massage of his neck. It felt so good to have the one he so loved stroke and pet him. Kirby just grinned as he stared back into

Jake's eyes, allowing him to work his seductive magic.

"So what will I have to do to make you fall crazy in love me?" Jake asked as he wiggled his buttocks lightly against Kirby's lap.

Kirby seemingly missed Jake's cue and tease. "I don't know," he said in a daze from Jake's touch and massage.

"Well, I'm ready to be crazy in love with you," Jake said, and then he leaned in to kiss Kirby's full, succulent lips in a way that was ardent and sensual yet tender and loving at the same time.

Kirby closed his eyes and moaned deeply, craving another taste of Jake's sweet lips.

"I think I know what it will take to make you fall crazy in love with me."

Kirby opened his eyes, "Oh yeah?"

"Yeah," Jake said, as he rubbed the tip of his nose to Kirby's, and then kissed his lips again. "Remember what you said when we were last together?"

"What did I say?" Kirby asked with a bit of a slur, slowly falling under Jake's spell and appearing slightly drunk on love.

"You said, 'When I fuck you it's going to be all over for me. It's going to wreck me and make me crazy.' Remember that?"

Kirby smiled broadly and chuckled. "Oh yeah. I did say that, huh?"

Jake grinned and chuckled too. "Yeah, you did," he said, and then he went in for another kiss that was more passionate and aggressive this time, inserting his tongue into Kirby's mouth. Kirby kissed him back hard. He sucked on Jake's tongue like a pacifier, wrapped his arms around him tightly, and held him close, chest to chest. Within seconds the heat between them was fully on, and their kiss became wild, sloppy, and wet as they feasted on one another with intense hunger and abandon.

Jake began to pump his pelvis in a steady fucking motion. "Touch me, Kirby. Touch my ass. Don't you still want it? It's yours, man. Take it. Take it," he said breathlessly before retuning his mouth to Kirby's.

Kirby didn't hesitate in his response to Jake's invitation. He slipped his hands up under Jake's shorts to grab and squeeze his butt-cheeks aggressively. Then he went straight for his hole, spreading it wide and inserting his right middle finger.

Kirby's finger fuck drew Jake to the edge. "Oh fuck, yeah. Fuck me, man. Oh yeah…fuck me, fuck me, fuck me. Fuck me now, Kirby. I'm yours. Own that shit, man."

"You know I will," Kirby said firmly before resuming their kiss. He then rose up from the sofa to stand on his feet with Jake still holding on to him—his arms wrapped around Kirby's neck and legs wrapped tightly around his waist. As they kissed, Kirby slowly carried Jake to the bedroom to initiate his ultimate conquest, at last.

CHAPTER FORTY-FIVE

Once they entered the bedroom, Kirby set Jake down. They both quickly stripped naked, revealing erections standing upright at full attention. Jake placed his hands to Kirby's muscular pecs to feel and squeeze. They were hard and solid as always. Kirby returned his hands to Jake's ass, grabbing and squeezing each cheek lasciviously. Kirby then inserted his thick pink tongue into Jake's mouth. Jake took it eagerly and sucked on it hard. As they stood there and kissed, they swung their hips from side to side so that their cocks collided together. After a few moments, Jake reached down with his hands to hold and stroke them at the same time.

Kirby was so aroused and thirsty for Jake's hole that the Black Mamba was throbbing and already oozing with a light but steady stream of pre-cum.

"Fuck yeah," Jake said when he saw the pre-cum and realized that he'd gotten some of it on his hand. He then lifted his hand to his mouth to lick it off. He did so by extending his tongue from his mouth demonstratively to lick the palm of his hand while moaning his delight at the taste of Kirby's sex juice.

"Does it taste good?" Kirby asked with a grin.

"Sure does," Jake said before reaching down and using his index finger to swipe the tip of Kirby's bulging cock head for more. He inserted his index finger into his mouth and sucked on it long and hard as he stared into Kirby's eyes. Jake pulled his finger out of his mouth and said to Kirby, "Want a taste?" He then reached down with his finger to swipe Kirby's cock head again before lifting the finger to Kirby's mouth. Kirby took it willingly, sucking on Jake's finger. He then got carried away and started sucking on multiple fingers all at once and then licking Jake's open palm like a lap dog obsessed with its owner's scent. Jake chuckled at Kirby's zealousness. Kirby smiled and chuckled at himself too. The two then kissed once again, extending their tongues from their mouths, pressing and rolling the tips of their tongues together, and then they devoured each other in a full, soaking wet, openmouthed kiss. They couldn't get enough of each other.

Jake eventually knelt down before the throbbing Black Mamba. A single stream of pre-cum rolled all the way down the long, thick shaft, its creamy color striking against Kirby's smooth chocolate skin. Jake extended his tongue to lick the shaft clean, starting at Kirby's balls and making his way all the way up to the budging cock head in one sweep. He swallowed and then repeated the sweep from the base of the shaft to the head. He then took Kirby's full cock into his mouth and milked it greedily.

After standing there for a little while and allowing Jake to have his way with his manhood, Kirby decided that it was time to take control of the situation and began to pump Jake's face.

To accommodate the force of Kirby's thrust, Jake simply opened his mouth as wide as he comfortably could and surrendered himself to Kirby's use and pleasure.

"That's it. Take that shit," Kirby said as he pumped his rod in and out of Jake's mouth. Intermittently he pulled out and slapped his wet ten-inch monster across Jake's face and poked his nostrils with it before shoving it back into his mouth. The warm wetness of Jake's hungry mouth felt amazing. Jake had so much stamina. No girl could ever handle such a relentless, deep-throated face fuck the way Jake could, and Kirby loved that about him. Kirby's libido was on overdrive. He felt as if he could stand there and go on for days, but he and the Black Mamba were eager to get to the main course.

Kirby pulled out of Jake's mouth and then reached to lift him up so that they faced each other again. They momentarily resumed their wet and sloppy openmouthed kiss, taking turns to suck on the other's tongue. "I love the taste of my dick on your mouth," Kirby stopped to say before returning to suckle Jake's tongue some more. As he sucked, Kirby walked Jake backward toward the bed and then pushed him down onto it.

When Jake fell back on the bed, he instinctively pulled his legs back and spread them wide to provide an unobstructed view of what he knew Kirby wanted to see. "It's nice and ready for you. I made sure I was squeaky clean for you, just the way you like, in case we decided to make this happen."

"That's my boy. Thanks for planning ahead," Kirby said with a grin as he beheld the beautiful man that lay before him. Those lean, muscular legs with a contrasting tan line at the pelvis and buttocks, topped off with a hole that was light pink, succulent, and tempting. Kirby salivated as the very sight of it always gave him the biggest adrenaline rush. However, this time more than ever before. Not wasting any time, Kirby pulled Jake by the legs closer to the edge of the bed. He then knelt down, pushed and held Jake's legs back, and got busy. He went down on Jake's asshole and pigged out like there was no tomorrow.

Jake smiled broadly, feeling happy that things were going the way he'd hoped while relishing the attention his most private body part was receiving. "Fuck yeah," Jake said with a big grin. "You like that man pussy, don't you?"

"There's nothing better," Kirby said as he feverishly licked, sucked, and probed. After going at it for several minutes, sufficiently lubricating Jake, Kirby rose up and then lay on top of him. "You taste so fucking good," he said before resuming kissing Jake. "You like the taste of your pussy?" Kirby said as they extended and wrestled their tongues together.

"Yeah," Jake said, reveling in the moment. So turned on was he by Kirby's dirty talk that he wrapped his legs around him tightly and ran his hands over his shaved head as they kissed with fierce passion.

Kirby began to pump his pelvis to Jake's in a rigid fucking motion with their hard cocks rubbing against each other. The sensation of it caused Jake to become overwhelmed with intense feeling and desire for his friend.

"Oh my God, Kirby. I love you so much. Please fuck me. I've been waiting for this for so long. I can't take it anymore, bro. I want to feel you inside me," Jake said with emotion in his voice.

"I love you too, Jake. I can't take it anymore either. Trust me."

Kirby then rose up, sat back slightly, lifted Jake's legs, and spread them apart. While Jake held each leg back, Kirby began to press the head of his cock to Jake's hole, inserting it slowly but not all the way to loosen him up.

"Oh fuck," Jake said, wincing in reaction to the penetration. Although Kirby was not yet fully in, the pressure was intense nevertheless, and it burned a little too. "Wait, wait," Jake said, pressing his hand to Kirby's thigh to hold him off and to relieve the initial pain.

"Are you all right?"

"Yeah, I'm fine. I just need a moment," Jake said before taking a deep breath and exhaling hard.

"Have you got some lube?"

"Yeah, that should help," Jake said as he got up and went to the bathroom to retrieve it, along with a towel. When he returned, he set the towel down on the bed, handed the lube to Kirby, and then got back into position on the bed with his legs raised and pulled back.

Kirby squeezed some gel in his hand and stroked his cock with it first. He then squeezed some more on his fingers and lubed up Jake's hole, inside and out. Kirby wiped his hands with the towel, and then he once again slowly inserted his thick ten-inch rod inside Jake's slippery, wet hole. This time Kirby continued to penetrate Jake slowly until he made it all the way in. As he did so, Jake squinted and gritted his teeth. "Aaaaaaah...fuck!" Jake yelled before starting to hyperventilate a little.

"Just take a deep breath and relax, man," Kirby said, stopping for a second but not pulling out. "That's virgin ass, man. You've never been worked out before, and you're all tight and locked up right now. Try to relax your muscle and don't squeeze it. Just let me in and don't resist. It'll feel better when you begin to loosen up a bit."

"Okay," Jake said, still wincing. "Just take it slow, bro. Please!"

Kirby slowly pushed deeper and deeper with the tip of his cock pressed against the softness of Jake's internal flesh. He held himself there for a few short seconds to allow Jake's body to adjust to the intrusion.

Jake was lightly panting and sweating on the forehead a little. "Oh my God," he said with a gasp.

"You okay?"

"Yeah, just take it slow. Take it slow, bro."

Kirby slowly pumped his pelvis back and forth without pulling all the way out.

At first, Jake continued to wince and gasp with a few expletives said in between. However, the more Kirby pumped, the less painful the penetration eventually became as Jake could feel his canal expanding to accommodate Kirby's girth and length.

Kirby started pumping faster when Jake began to appear less agitated and more relaxed. "Yeah, that's it. Take it," he said to Jake.

"Oh fuck, Kirby," Jake said breathlessly, this time not so much in pain but more in awe and wonder at having this hot, muscular black Adonis fucking him. His body started to become more acclimated to the feel of Kirby's thick rod pumping his hole with rapid force. The harder and deeper Kirby fucked, the more limp and numb to pain his hole became, and Jake liked it. He started to get really into it, reaching down with his hands to hold his ass-cheeks apart to enhance the thrill and sensation of having Kirby deep inside him.

"You like that? Huh?" Kirby said as he fucked.

"Oh fuck yeah. You look so fucking hot fucking me," Jake said, placing the soles of his feet flat against Kirby's chest to feel his muscles. They seemed more pronounced during the sex act.

With Jake seemingly more relaxed and less bothered by pain, Kirby switched up his rhythm a little, pulling his thick rod in and all the way out, in and out, several times.

Jake shrieked and gasped at the pressure of the repeated exit and reentry. It felt a little painful but it felt good too, and he couldn't get enough. He wanted more. "Oh fuck yeah. Fuck my ass. That's it, make me your bitch. Fuck that pussy," he encouraged.

The declaration was enough to drive Kirby mad, and he started to pound Jake's ass with relentless fervor. He commanded Jake to turn over and get on all fours so that he could fuck him from behind, doggy style. Jake obliged and even aided in his own ravishing by pushing himself backward as Kirby pushed forward, going in deep and hard at a steady, unyielding pace. Jake took the pounding like a champ. He was in it to win it, aiming to please his man. Kirby was amazed at his endurance, especially with it being his first time.

Kirby had Jake lie prostrate on his stomach with his legs stretched out. He then got on top of him so that their bodies were tight together, legs outstretched and intertwined, and feet touching. The position allowed for maximum body contact and stimulation. Kirby then used his hip and gluteal muscles to press and drill into Jake as deep as he could. It felt so amazing to have his bareback rod buried deep inside his male love's warm flesh. He moaned and expressed his delight repeatedly with breathy expletives. "Oh fuck. You feel so fucking good. You're so fucking amazing. I love you so much."

"I love you too," Jake said back.

On the brink of climax, Kirby started to pump faster. "Oh my God, I love you so much, Jake," he said again with emotion in his voice.

"I love you too, Kirby," Jake repeated with equal emotion and sincerity.

Kirby had Jake to turn over again on his back so that he could face him when they came. He held Jake's legs back, reinserted his rod, and then lay on top of him, chest to chest. Jake immediately wrapped his legs around Kirby's waist and his arms around his back.

Kirby held Jake's head in the palms of his hands as he fucked him rapidly. "Oh God, I'm going to come, dude. Oh my God, Jake," he said breathily.

"Oh fuck, you're going to make me come too," Jake said, looking deep into Kirby's eyes as his face hovered over his at close range.

"Here it comes," Kirby said, lifting himself up slightly to pull out. He was intending to stroke himself to completion and shoot his load onto Jake's chest or perhaps into his mouth as he'd previously done.

"No! Come inside me, bro. Breed me. I love you, and I want you, every piece of you."

With that plea, Kirby stayed in and fucked Jake uncontrollably.

With their chests and abs pressed together, Jake involuntarily came first, his seed shooting out in between them. He was momentarily rendered paralyzed in motion and in speech. All he could do was let out an exhalation. So overwhelmed was he with ecstasy and a deep sense of love for his friend, a single tear streamed down his face.

Kirby began to moan and shriek loudly as he fucked with ferocious vigor, causing the bed's headboard to crash against the wall with each thrust. Kirby gave one final, deep thrust into Jake's flesh and held it there. Then sweet release came and overflowed as Kirby filled Jake with love from his loins.

His conquest now complete, Kirby wrapped his arms around Jake and held him tightly, possessively. Jake held on tightly back. Kirby could feel Jake's heartbeat and Jake could feel his. They kissed each other's lips softly, again and again and again. As they did so, they touched and rubbed the tips of their noses together and stared into each other's eyes. Their kisses were lingering and full of mutual adoration. They couldn't stop.

Finally Kirby started to chuckle and grinned broadly.

"What?" Jake asked, smiling back at him.

"That was fun."

"Yeah it was. I could get used to this."

"Okay, I'm officially putting you on notice," Kirby said. "Now I'm crazy in love with you and will never let you go. Ever!"

CHAPTER FORTY-SIX

Sixteen months later, Jake and Kirby were still kissing and making love, settling into their new life together as an openly gay couple. Shortly after they'd consummated their relationship and committed themselves to being a real couple, they began living together again at the bungalow in the Hollywood Hills they'd previously shared. Kirby, of course, was delighted to have Jake back, this time not as his housemate and best friend with occasional benefits but as his boyfriend and partner.

They had kept the nature of their relationship under wraps and close to the vest the first six months. Kirby had told Myla but nobody else. Jake assumed Amanda knew, but they did not see or speak to each other again after their rendezvous in New York. Jake and Kirby allowed the rest of their family and friends to think that they were still simply best friends who'd decided to live together again after patching up their differences. They were both initially apprehensive about letting people in on their little secret right away. Kirby's career in television was just starting to take off, and he feared that if it came to light that he was gay, it would've been a distraction, taking attention away from his talent as a screenwriter. Jake, on the other hand, wanted to be sure that he wouldn't vacillate or grow weary of being with another man before coming out as gay. Reimagining his life in a nontraditional, nonconformist way, without a wife and kids and all that represented, took some mental retooling. However, with the passage of time, their fears and apprehension subsided.

Kirby's pilot had gotten picked up by the GTV network, and with the first season premiering to critical and audience acclaim, he was well on his way to realizing his dream as an acclaimed Hollywood writer and producer. He loved Jake beyond measure and began to care less about what others might think with his career now more secure. Likewise, Jake's love for Kirby and level of comfort being with him in a committed relationship grew stronger too. He even began to contemplate the prospect of marrying Kirby and having biracial kids with him some day. Kirby was not only keen about the idea but enthusiastic about it. The guy who'd once felt a sense of shame about his gayness and thought that he would've needed to remain in the closet somewhat, even if he and Jake had ended up together, no longer had that point of view. Kirby was a changed man, and by the time their six-month anniversary had rolled around, he was the one to suggest that he and Jake start coming out to their families and friends. When they did so, they were most surprised at how unsurprised others were to learn of their romance. There were a few metaphorical gasps, but most of their friends expressed support and love. Two friends they'd grown up and attended prep school with even claimed to have known all along.

In the sixteen months since she'd last seen Jake, Amanda too was eventually able to move on with her life, but the road had been rocky. While she had assumed that Jake and Kirby were together, Amanda initially didn't inquire or seek to know anything about their status. There was enough happening for her to worry about in her own life. Namely, her mother, Camilla, decided to leave Rick after learning of his grotesque deception and false claim about his own daughter. It was the final straw that broke the camel's back on their marriage. In the months that followed, their split was fodder for the tabloids. However, the Climents and Doyles were unified in fierce determination to keep the whole scandal a closely guarded secret. Neither side wanted the story to leak out. As a result, the most common and bandied-about claim about the cause of the Climents' breakup was that Rick had long been a serial adulterer and had kept mistresses for years. In fact, the tabloids had been successful in tracking down two of his former mistresses and had exposed their lavish lifestyle, compliments of the Climent fortune. The whole episode had thrown the Climent family into crisis mode, and there were many dark days.

Nonetheless, in the midst of the tumult, Amanda was able to successfully launch the Novel handbag line with her best pal and partner, Lucy, at her side. They'd received the support of celebrities and high-powered industry insiders alike thanks to their many connections. And their high-profile boyfriends played no small part in driving press coverage of their launch event. The heartthrob producer Adam and heartthrob actor Cass were both more than happy to leverage their notoriety and fame on their girlfriends' behalf.

After the product launch, Amanda's work became the therapy she desperately needed to help combat the stress and drama swirling around in her personal life. In addition to her parents' messy, well-publicized breakup, she still had the loss of her relationship with Jake to deal with in the months following their ill-fated meeting. Although she was happy to have helped Jake embrace his true self and desire, it stung nevertheless to have the man to whom she'd once been engaged admit to being more in love with and attracted to someone else. She needed time to heal and recover from that. So she'd decided to live mostly in New York to focus her energy on building her business. Getting married and having a family became less of a priority. She'd even broken off communication with any remaining mutual friends she and Jake shared to avoid hearing any tidbits of information about his life. However, now that more than a year had passed and a degree of normalcy had returned to her life, Amanda had grown less emotionally attached and instead more curious about Jake. She decided to email him out of the blue one day. Their exchange was brief, but they agreed to see each other in LA during one of her upcoming visits. At her suggestion, the three of them—she, Jake, and Kirby—would all meet for lunch. A date was set.

Jake and Kirby had arrived at the restaurant first. They both looked as handsome and dapper as ever and like the happy couple they now were. Although not exactly matching, they each had on Ralph Lauren shorts and shirts. Jake had completed his ensemble with a pair of Sperrys sans socks and Kirby a casual pair of leather loafers sans socks. They had a reservation, so they decided to be seated as they waited for Amanda to arrive.

"Are you nervous?" Kirby asked.

"No," Jake answered quickly and then amended his statement after a brief pause. "Maybe a little."

"I can't believe how long it's been since we've seen her…in person, that is. Obviously we've seen and read about her and her family over the last year. Man, she's been through a lot. Her parents, her breakup with Adam—"

"I know but let's not bring any of that stuff up. I don't want the conversation to turn sour."

"Oh no, of course not. I don't want things to get uncomfortable either. This already feels awkward enough. It's amazing that she even wants to see us."

"I know. I was a little surprised too when she emailed me. We've had absolutely no contact with one another whatsoever since we met in New York. And that was what…a year…year and half ago? I mean…the meeting ended on somewhat of a positive note, but you know, I'd just dropped a bomb on her about her father's evil-doing and then another bomb by admitting that I wanted to be with you more than her. So to be honest, I really didn't expect to hear from her again."

"Well, now you will because here she comes," Kirby said, noticing Amanda walking over toward them.

"Hey fellas," Amanda said with a broad smile across her face. It was summertime and Amanda looked tan, svelte, and relaxed with very light makeup and her dark hair straight and long with a part down the middle.

Kirby and Jake immediately stood to greet her. "Heyyy," they both sang in unison, returning her smile.

"Ohhh, it's so nice to see you guys," Amanda said as she reached to hug Jake and then Kirby. Each embrace was lingering and tight, the affection, familiarity, and history between them apparent.

"You two look great, and, oh my God, so happy too," she said.

Both men beamed and looked at each other with wide grins on their faces.

"You look amazing too," Jake said to her.

"I am so happy that you two are still together."

Jake smiled and said, "So are we."

"When Jake said in his email that you two were now officially boyfriends, I nearly cried. Well…I actually did cry…a little. I was so happy and insisted that he bring you along. I wanted to see you," she said, looking at Kirby.

"Thanks. I wanted to see you too, and I must say, I agree with Jake. You look stunning."

"You really do," Jake underscored.

"Aww, thanks. So guys are sweet."

They continued to engage in initial pleasantries for a while—swapping gossip about old friends, talking about Kirby's new TV show, which Amanda had steadfastly watched and loved, and hearing about Jake's new job. No longer comfortable working with Mike Wallace, Jake had left his law firm job and had become an in-house attorney at the tech startup company his fraternity brother, Lyle Spiegelman, had founded. Likewise, Amanda shared about the progress of her Novel bag line.

After settling into each other's company with ease, they eventually ordered wine. With a few sips of chardonnay, they all let their guard down, and the mood became even more relaxed, which allowed for a more open and revealing conversation.

"So are you living in New York now?" Jake asked.

"Yes, I am. I still have my condo here at Sierra Towers, but after we launched Novel, I decided to live and work mostly in New York. It's been good for me. I needed to get out of LA and have a little change of scenery, if you know what I mean."

"Yeah, I understand," Jake said demurely, indeed knowing what she meant.

"I'm sure you've heard that my parents are getting divorced."

"Yeah, I did hear," Jake said. "I thought it already happened, actually."

"Well, you know how these things can get dragged out. They're still in the midst of settlement negotiations. There was no prenuptial agreement, and my mother can be pretty demanding—" at which point Jake chuckled "—but I think they're close to reaching an agreement."

"Since California is a no-fault divorce state, wouldn't she automatically just get fifty percent?" Kirby asked.

"Well, that's been a big point of contention. They've had to figure out what that fifty percent is exactly. My family's finances are pretty convoluted and complex with money tied up in various trusts, and then there are inheritance issues too, so it's not so cut-and-dry. Needless to say, regardless, my mother will come out of the situation sitting pretty. Nobody will be crying for her. Trust me."

"I'm sure the lawyers will be sitting pretty too," Jake nearly said but bit his tongue. "So how is Camilla?"

"She's fine. She lives in New York too, now. This whole experience has humbled her. It's amazing what public humiliation can do for a person. She's much more relaxed and compassionate now. She's even more fun to be around. We've become pretty good friends. We've never been closer, actually."

"That's great," Jake said with a smile.

"You might also know that I am newly single."

"Yeah, I heard a little bit," Jake said sheepishly, not wanting to admit that he'd read the tabloid headlines about her recent breakup with Adam.

"I'm so surprised. I was convinced that you and Adam would get married," Kirby blurted.

Amanda took it in stride and spoke frankly. "I just couldn't see myself having kids with Adam. He's a very neurotic person who places a lot of pressure on himself to be successful, to be the best. It's an admirable quality, but it causes a lot of stress and anxiety, which leads to a lot self-medicating and other unhealthy behavior. I couldn't deal with it anymore. I felt like I was becoming his babysitter. And plus, he became really demanding about getting married. He was like, 'If you don't marry me now I'm gonna walk,' and I said, 'Have a nice walk,' and that was the end of that."

Jake and Kirby both snickered.

"Please don't repeat any of this," Amanda said, leery of having anything she said leaked to the press.

"Oh, of course," Jake said.

"Anyway, enough about me. I want to hear about you two. Are you guys out? Do people know?"

"Yeah. Everybody knows. It's been almost a year now since we told everybody," Jake answered.

"Who's everybody?"

"All of our friends we grew up with from Harvard-Westlake. Our Stanford friends. I'm surprised you haven't heard anything."

"Oh, I've sort of been out of the loop," Amanda said with a dismissive chuckle at herself. "What about your parents? And speaking of parents, how are they? Are they still together?"

"They're fine, and still hanging in there," Jake said, not wanting to seem boastful about his parents sticking together in light of the demise of the Climents' marriage.

"Good for them. Tom and Jamie always seemed to have stronger, more old-school values about marriage. I'm not surprised to see them sticking it out."

"Yeah. They're troopers," Jake said.

"And how did they react to you coming out?"

Jake shrugged his shoulders, nonchalant. "They're fine with it. At least, that's how they've been to my face. But to be honest, if I told my parents I was dating an orangutan, they'd probably go along with it." Amanda and Kirby both chuckled at this. "They've bent over backward to show Kirby and me love. They've been nothing but supportive the whole time."

"Guilt will do that every time," Kirby chimed in with a wicked grin.

"They just want me to be happy," Jake added to clarify what he believed their true intention to be.

"How about your parents, Kirby?" Amanda asked.

"You know, it's funny. Dad took the news better than Mom did. He was like, okay, whatever, as long as you're happy and live responsibly, yada yada, but Mom cried. She was pretty much in shock and disbelief. You know, I think she always imagined me with a wife and kids, and I think she'd been hoping against hope that Laren and me would get back together. That's because she didn't know anything about me dating guys. It was big news to her. But now that it's been almost a year since we told them, she's come around. She's already asking me about when Jake and I plan on having kids." Kirby looked over at Jake. "She loves the surrogacy idea, by the way."

"You told her?" Jake asked.

"Yeah, and she's down with it."

Amanda's face lit up. "Surrogate?"

"Yeah," Jake answered. "We want to eventually have kids and are thinking about working with an agency to find an anonymous donor for the eggs in addition to a surrogate to carry the fertilized eggs to term. We want at least two, one fertilized with Kirby's sperm and one with mine. We're aiming for just one egg donor so that the kids can actually be linked biologically as siblings."

Amanda was overwhelmed by this news and her eyes welled with tears. "Oh my God…that's so amazing. I'm so happy for you. When do you plan on making this happen?" she asked as she dotted her eyes with her napkin.

Jake and Kirby looked over at each other. Then Jake turned back to her and answered. "We don't know yet, but in the near future. We're pretty excited about it."

"I'm excited too. This is so amazing. I want to help you make this happen."

When Amanda said that, Jake and Kirby looked at each other again with curiosity in their eyes. They were both thinking the same thing, but Jake verbalized it. He looked back at Amanda. "Would you be interested in donating the eggs?" he asked flippantly with a grin, but deep down he was serious.

Amanda stared at him, stumped for a moment. "Me?"

"Yeah, why not?"

"That's a great idea," Kirby chimed in enthusiastically. "You'd be awesome! This would be even better than finding an anonymous donor. You could even be involved in helping us raise the little munchkins if you wanted to."

"Oh my God," Amanda said, covering her mouth and contemplating the thought as she stared at them in silence. She was completely caught off guard at the suggestion that she could be the egg donor. "I don't know. I'd need to think about it," she finally said.

"Do it, do it," Kirby said, feeling excited at the prospect.

Jake was more calm and diplomatic, however. "Take all the time you need. It's not as if we plan on making this happen tomorrow, but we'd love to discuss it in more detail with you and work something out if you're seriously interested."

Amanda nodded. "Okay, I'll think about it." Then she smirked to herself. "You know, Jake, we always dreamed of having a family together. This would be a rather unusual if not extreme way to make that happen."

Jake chuckled. "I know, huh? But I think it would be kind of cool too."

"And you know these kids would be the most good-looking kids on the planet," Kirby chimed in to laugher all around.

"Oh my God, I can't believe we're discussing this right now. But I must admit, I am a little intrigued," Amanda said.

"Well, the media likes to call you the Platinum Princess," Kirby said. "But if we decide to create a family together, they'll have to come up with a name for three of us. What do you think it would be?" he asked them playfully.

"I don't know," Jake said, trying to think of something good.

Amanda was picking her brain but nothing came to mind right away.

"Oh…I've got it," Kirby said. "The Platinum Triangle. You know, in keeping with the Platinum Princess theme."

"Well, we're definitely a triangle. This relationship has been all about triangulation from the start," Jake said, poking fun at their history and laughing about it.

"Riiight?" Amanda winked and said, laughing along.

Kirby raised his wineglass. "Cheers to the future and never-ending posterity of The Platinum Triangle."

"Hear, hear, I'll drink to that," Jake said, raising his glass too.

"Cheers," Amanda said and smiled as she raised her glass as well.

They clinked their glasses, all giddy, and sipped their wine. Each seemed happy and hopeful about the idea of a reimagined relationship in which they'd still be together well into the future. It was a nice, warm, comforting thought, if not a passing fancy.

***

A little less than two years later, two boys were born hours apart on the same day: Alphonso Smith-Doyle and Julian Smith-Doyle. Two surrogates had been implanted with fertilized eggs at the same time so that the births could be as close to simultaneous as possible. Jake and Amanda had long agreed that if they had a son together he'd be named for her ancestor, the Spanish nobleman and Californio Alphonso Climent. They kept that agreement. The other boy, Julian, was named for Kirby's great-great grandfather, the man who'd founded the bank the Smith family still maintained a majority ownership of. Jake and Kirby had married prior to the birth of the boys and legally changed their last names to Smith-Doyle so that their sons could share that name too. Although it was ultimately decided that Jake and Kirby would raise Alphonso and Julian alone, Amanda used assets from her own inheritance to establish trust funds for each boy. Her involvement was welcomed, but it was unclear how much of a presence Amanda would choose to have in the boys' lives going forward. Their identities as Climents along with Amanda's name as their biological mother would remain sealed for the foreseeable future. Thus, a new secret was born. Jake, Kirby, and Amanda were now bound by a secret of their own making that would keep them linked together forever as The Platinum Triangle.

The End

THE PLATINUM SERIES

Book One
The Platinum Triangle

Book Two
The Platinum Rebound

Book Three
The Platinum Reunion

Keep in Touch

Thank you for reading The Platinum Reunion. I hope you enjoyed the story and will post a review to share your thoughts with other readers on Amazon, Barnes & Noble, Goodreads, or wherever else you post reviews about the books you read.

You can stay on top of the latest news about my projects and activities by:

1. Subscribing to my mail list at www.tvhartwell.com
2. Following me on Facebook at www.facebook.com/tvhartwell
3. Following me on Twitter at www.twitter.com/tvhartwell
4. Following me on Goodreads at www.goodreads.com/tvhartwell

I look forward to keeping in touch. Thank you for supporting my work and spreading the word about The Platinum Series.

Cheers,
T V Hartwell

www.ingramcontent.com/pod-product-compliance
Lightning Source LLC
Chambersburg PA
CBHW020244200626
46816CB00001BA/124